HEAVENLY PRAISE FOR GOOD OMENS

"FULL-BORE CONTEMPORARY LUNACY. A STEAMROLLER OF SILLINESS THAT MADE ME GIGGLE OUT LOUD."
—*San Diego Union-Tribune*

"Something like what would have happened if Thomas Pynchon, Tom Robbins, and Don DeLillo had collaborated on the screenplay of a remake of the Jack Benny film *The Horn Blows at Midnight* . . . It's a wow . . . It would make one hell of a movie. Or a heavenly one. Take your pick."
—*Washington Post Book World*

"It reads like the Book of Revelation as penned by Monty Python's Flying Circus."
—*Phoenix New Times*

"Terrifically entertaining."
—*Dayton Daily News*

"A direct descendant of *The Hitchhiker's Guide to the Galaxy*."
—*The New York Times*

"Outrageous . . . *Good Omens* shouldn't be pegged into a category. It should just be enjoyed . . . Read it for a riotous good laugh."
—*Orlando Sentinel*

DEVILISHLY GOOD REVIEWS FOR

Neil Gaiman

"A WRITER IMBUED WITH RICH STORYTELLING QUALITIES AND A BOUNDLESS IMAGINATION."
—*St. Louis Post-Dispatch*

"Gaiman is fast becoming one of the most important of modern writers."
—*Denver Rocky Mountain News*

"Gaiman is a trickster in the best sense of the word."
—*Houston Chronicle*

"He is a treasure house of story and we are lucky to have him."
—Stephen King

"When you take a free-fall plunge into a Neil Gaiman book, anything can happen and anything invariably does."
—*Entertainment Weekly*

AND

Terry Pratchett

"A MASTER OF LAUGH-OUT-LOUD FICTION."
—*Chicago Tribune*

"Terry Pratchett seems constitutionally unable to write a page without at least a twitch of the grin muscles . . . [But] the notions Pratchett plays with are nae so narrow or nae so silly as your ordinary British farce."
—*San Diego Union-Tribune*

"Pratchett is well able to combine the hilarious with the topical, acerbic and incisive."
—*Toronto Star*

"A top-notch satirist."
—*Denver Post*

"Terry Pratchett may still be pegged as a comic novelist, but . . . he's a lot more. In his range of invented characters, his adroit storytelling, and his clear-eyed acceptance of humankind's foibles, he reminds me of no one in English literature as much as Geoffrey Chaucer. No kidding."
—*Washington Post Book World*

ALSO BY TERRY PRATCHETT

The Carpet People • The Dark Side of the Sun
Strata • The Bromeliad Trilogy: Truckers
Diggers • Wings • Only You Can Save Mankind
Johnny and the Dead • Johnny and the Bomb
The Unadulterated Cat (with Gray Jolliffe)
The Amazing Maurice and His Educated Rodents
The Wee Free Men • A Hat Full of Sky
Wintersmith • I Shall Wear Midnight
The Shepherd's Crown

THE DISCWORLD SERIES

The Color of Magic • The Light Fantastic
Equal Rites • Mort • Sourcery
Wyrd Sisters • Pyramids • Guards! Guards!
Eric (with Josh Kirby) • Moving Pictures
Reaper Man • Witches Abroad • Small Gods
Lords and Ladies • Men at Arms • Soul Music
Feet of Clay • Interesting Times • Maskerade
Hogfather • Jingo • The Last Continent
Carpe Jugulum • The Fifth Elephant
The Truth • Thief of Time • Night Watch
Monstrous Regiment • Going Postal • Thud!
Where's My Cow? • Making Money
Unseen Academicals • Snuff • Raising Steam
The Last Hero (with Paul Kidby)
The Art of Discworld (with Paul Kidby)
Mort: A Discworld Big Comic (with Graham Higgins)
The Streets of Ankh-Morpork (with Stephen Briggs)
The Discworld Companion (with Stephen Briggs)
The Discworld Mapp (with Stephen Briggs)

ALSO BY NEIL GAIMAN

NOVELS

The Ocean at the End of the Lane
The Graveyard Book • Anansi Boys • Coraline
American Gods • Stardust • Neverwhere

NONFICTION

Make Good Art
The View from the Cheap Seats
Art Matters

COLLECTIONS

Trigger Warning • Fragile Things
Smoke and Mirrors

ILLUSTRATED STORIES

The Truth Is a Cave in the Black Mountains
illustrated by Eddie Campbell
The Sleeper and the Spindle
illustrated by Chris Riddell

FOR YOUNGER READERS

Fortunately, the Milk illustrated by Skottie Young
Hansel and Gretel illustrated by Lorenzo Mattotti
Instructions illustrated by Charles Vess
Odd and the Frost Giants
illustrated by Brett Helquist
Crazy Hair illustrated by Dave McKean
Blueberry Girl illustrated by Charles Vess
The Dangerous Alphabet illustrated by Gris Grimly
M Is for Magic illustrated by Teddy Kristiansen

GOOD OMENS

The NICE and ACCURATE Prophecies of Agnes Nutter, WITCH

Neil Gaiman & Terry Pratchett

wm
WILLIAM MORROW
An Imprint of HarperCollins*Publishers*

CAVEAT

Bringing about Armageddon can be dangerous. Do not attempt it in your own home.

A hardcover edition of this book was published in 1990 by Workman Publishing Company, Inc.; a trade paperback edition was published in 1992 by The Berkley Publishing Group; and a mass market edition in 1996 and a trade paperback edition in 2001 were published by Ace Books, a division of Penguin Putnam, Inc.

First William Morrow mass market printing: March 2019
First William Morrow premium printing: March 2019
First William Morrow paperback printing: August 2007
First HarperTorch mass market printing: December 2006
First William Morrow hardcover printing: March 2006

Print Edition ISBN: 978-0-06-085398-3
Digital Edition ISBN: 978-0-06-199112-7

22 23 BVGM 45

The authors would like to join the demon Crowley
in dedicating this book to the memory of

G. K. CHESTERTON

A man who knew what was going on.

Foreword

People say: What was it like writing *Good Omens*?

And we say: We were just a couple of guys, okay? We still are. It was a summer job. We had a great time doing it, we split the money in half, and we swore never to do it again. We didn't think it was important.

And, in a way, it still isn't. *Good Omens* was written by two people who at the time were not at all well known except by the people who already knew them. They weren't even certain it would sell. They certainly didn't know they were going to write the most repaired book in the world. (Believe us: We have signed a delightfully large number of paperbacks that have been dropped in the bath, gone a worrying brown color, got repaired with sticky tape and string, and, in one case, consisted entirely of loose pages in a plastic bag. On the other hand, there was the guy who'd had a special box made up of walnut and silver filigree, with the paperback nestling inside on black velvet. There were silver runes on the lid. We didn't ask.) Etiquette tip: It's okay, more or less, to ask an author to sign your arm, but not good manners to then nip around to the tattoo parlor next door and return half an hour later to show them the inflamed result.

We didn't know we'd do some signing tours that would be weird even by our generous standards, talking about humor in fifteen-second bursts in between newsflashes about the horrific hostage situation down at the local Burger King, being interviewed by an ill-prepared New York radio presenter who hadn't got the message that *Good Omens* was a work of what we in the trade call "fiction," and getting a stern pre-interview warning about swearing from the diminutive Director of Protocol of a public-service radio station "because you English use bad language all the time."

In fact, neither of us swear much, especially not on the radio, but for the next hour we found ourselves automatically speaking in very short, carefully scanned sentences, while avoiding each other's eyes.

And then there were the readers, Gawd bless them. We must have signed hundreds of thousands of copies for them by now. The books are often well read to the point of physical disintegration; if we run across a shiny new copy, it's usually because the owner's previous five have been stolen by friends, struck by lightning or eaten by giant termites in Sumatra. You have been warned. Oh, and we understand there's a copy in the Vatican library. It'd be nice to think so.

It's been fun. And it continues.

GOOD OMENS

IN THE BEGINNING

IT WAS A NICE DAY.

All the days had been nice. There had been rather more than seven of them so far, and rain hadn't been invented yet. But clouds massing east of Eden suggested that the first thunderstorm was on its way, and it was going to be a big one.

The angel of the Eastern Gate put his wings over his head to shield himself from the first drops.

"I'm sorry," he said politely. "What was it you were saying?"

"I *said*, that one went down like a lead balloon," said the serpent.

"Oh. Yes," said the angel, whose name was Aziraphale.

"I think it was a bit of an overreaction, to be honest," said the serpent. "I mean, first offense and everything. I can't see what's so bad about knowing the difference between good and evil, anyway."

"It must *be* bad," reasoned Aziraphale, in the slightly concerned tones of one who can't see it either, and is worrying about it, "otherwise *you* wouldn't have been involved."

"They just said, Get up there and make some trouble," said the serpent, whose name was Crawly, although he was thinking of changing it now. Crawly, he'd decided, was not *him.*

"Yes, but you're a demon. I'm not sure if it's actually possible for you to do good," said Aziraphale. "It's down to your basic, you know, nature. Nothing personal, you understand."

"You've got to admit it's a bit of a pantomime, though," said Crawly. "I mean, pointing out the Tree and saying 'Don't Touch' in big letters. Not very subtle, is it? I mean, why not put it on top of a high mountain or a long way off? Makes you wonder what He's really planning."

"Best not to speculate, really," said Aziraphale. "You can't second-guess ineffability, I always say. There's Right, and there's Wrong. If you do Wrong when you're told to do Right, you deserve to be punished. Er."

They sat in embarrassed silence, watching the raindrops bruise the first flowers.

Eventually Crawly said, "Didn't you have a flaming sword?"

"Er," said the angel. A guilty expression passed across his face, and then came back and camped there.

"You did, didn't you?" said Crawly. "It flamed like anything."

"Er, well—"

"It looked very impressive, I thought."

"Yes, but, well—"

"Lost it, have you?"

"Oh no! No, not exactly lost, more—"

"Well?"

Aziraphale looked wretched. "If you must know," he said, a trifle testily, "I gave it away."

Crawly stared up at him.

"Well, I had to," said the angel, rubbing his hands distractedly. "They looked so cold, poor things, and she's expecting *already*, and what with the *vicious* animals out there and the storm coming up I thought, well, where's the harm, so I just said, look, if you come back there's going to be an almighty row, but you might be needing this sword, so here it is, don't bother to thank me, just do everyone a big favor and don't let the sun go down on you here."

He gave Crawly a worried grin.

"That was the best course, wasn't it?"

"I'm not sure it's actually possible for you to do evil," said Crawly sarcastically. Aziraphale didn't notice the tone.

"Oh, I do hope so," he said. "I really do hope so. It's been worrying me all afternoon."

They watched the rain for a while.

"Funny thing is," said Crawly, "*I* keep wondering whether the apple thing wasn't the right thing to do, as well. A demon can get into real trouble, doing the right thing." He nudged the angel. "Funny if we both got it wrong, eh? Funny if I did the good thing and you did the bad one, eh?"

"Not really," said Aziraphale.

Crawly looked at the rain.

"No," he said, sobering up. "I suppose not."

Slate-black curtains tumbled over Eden. Thunder growled among the hills. The animals, freshly named, cowered from the storm.

Far away, in the dripping woods, something bright and fiery flickered among the trees.

It was going to be a dark and stormy night.

GOOD OMENS

A Narrative of Certain Events occurring in the last eleven years of human history, in strict accordance as shall be shewn with:

The Nice and Accurate Prophecies of Agnes Nutter

Compiled and edited, with Footnotes of an Educational Nature and Precepts for the Wise, by Neil Gaiman and Terry Pratchett.

DRAMATIS PERSONAE

Supernatural Beings

God (God)

Metatron
(The Voice of God)

Aziraphale
(An Angel, and part-time rare book dealer)

Satan
(A Fallen Angel; the Adversary)

Beelzebub
(A Likewise Fallen Angel and Prince of Hell)

Hastur
(A Fallen Angel and Duke of Hell)

Ligur
(Likewise a Fallen Angel and Duke of Hell)

Crowley
(An Angel who did not so much Fall as Saunter Vaguely Downwards)

Apocalyptic Horsepersons

DEATH (Death)

War (War)

Famine (Famine)

Pollution (Pollution)

Humans

Thou-Shalt-Not-Commit-Adultery Pulsifer
(A Witchfinder)

Agnes Nutter
(A Prophetess)

Newton Pulsifer
(Wages Clerk and Witchfinder Private)

Anathema Device
(Practical Occultist and Professional Descendant)

Shadwell
(Witchfinder Sergeant)

Madame Tracy
(Painted Jezebel [mornings only,
Thursdays by arrangement] and Medium)

Sister Mary Loquacious
(A Satanic Nun of the Chattering Order
of St. Beryl)

Mr. Young
(A Father)

Mr. Tyler
(A Chairman of a Residents' Association)

A Delivery Man

Them

ADAM
(An Antichrist)

Pepper
(A Girl)

Wensleydale
(A Boy)

Brian
(A Boy)

Full Chorus of Tibetans, Aliens, Americans, Atlanteans and other rare and strange Creatures of the Last Days.

And:

Dog
(Satanical hellhound and cat-worrier)

ELEVEN YEARS AGO

CURRENT THEORIES on the creation of the Universe state that, if it was created at all and didn't just start, as it were, unofficially, it came into being between ten and twenty thousand million years ago. By the same token the earth itself is generally supposed to be about four and a half thousand million years old.

These dates are incorrect.

Medieval Jewish scholars put the date of the Creation at 3760 B.C. Greek Orthodox theologians put Creation as far back as 5508 B.C.

These suggestions are also incorrect.

Archbishop James Ussher (1580–1656) published *Annales Veteris et Novi Testamenti* in 1654, which suggested that the Heaven and the Earth were created in 4004 B.C. One of his aides took the calculation further, and was able to announce triumphantly that the Earth was created on Sunday the 21st of October, 4004 B.C., at exactly 9:00 A.M., because God liked to get work done early in the morning while he was feeling fresh.

This too was incorrect. By almost a quarter of an hour.

The whole business with the fossilized dinosaur

skeletons was a joke the paleontologists haven't seen yet.

This proves two things:

Firstly, that God moves in extremely mysterious, not to say, circuitous ways. God does not play dice with the universe; He plays an ineffable game of His own devising, which might be compared, from the perspective of any of the other players,* to being involved in an obscure and complex version of poker in a pitch-dark room, with blank cards, for infinite stakes, with a Dealer who won't tell you the rules, and who *smiles all the time*.

Secondly, the Earth's a Libra.

The astrological prediction for Libra in the "Your Stars Today" column of the *Tadfield Advertiser*, on the day this history begins, read as follows:

> ♎ LIBRA. September 24–October 23.
> **You may be feeling run down and always in the same old daily round. Home and family matters are highlighted and are hanging fire. Avoid unnecessary risks. A friend is important to you. Shelve major decisions until the way ahead seems clear. You may be vulnerable to a stomach upset today, so avoid salads. Help could come from an unexpected quarter.**

This was perfectly correct on every count except for the bit about the salads.

IT WASN'T A DARK AND STORMY NIGHT.

It should have been, but that's the weather for

* i.e., everybody

you. For every mad scientist who's had a convenient thunderstorm just on the night his Great Work is finished and lying on the slab, there have been dozens who've sat around aimlessly under the peaceful stars while Igor clocks up the overtime.

But don't let the fog (with rain later, temperatures dropping to around forty-five degrees) give anyone a false sense of security. Just because it's a mild night doesn't mean that dark forces aren't abroad. They're abroad all the time. They're *everywhere*.

They always are. That's the whole point.

Two of them lurked in the ruined graveyard. Two shadowy figures, one hunched and squat, the other lean and menacing, both of them Olympic-grade lurkers. If Bruce Springsteen had ever recorded "Born to Lurk," these two would have been on the album cover. They had been lurking in the fog for an hour now, but they had been pacing themselves and could lurk for the rest of the night if necessary, with still enough sullen menace left for a final burst of lurking around dawn.

Finally, after another twenty minutes, one of them said: "Bugger this for a lark. He should of been here *hours* ago."

The speaker's name was Hastur. He was a Duke of Hell.

MANY PHENOMENA—wars, plagues, sudden audits—have been advanced as evidence for the hidden hand of Satan in the affairs of Man, but whenever students of demonology get together the M25 London orbital motorway is generally agreed to be among the top contenders for Exhibit A.

Where they go wrong, of course, is in assuming that the wretched road is evil simply because of the incredible carnage and frustration it engenders every day.

In fact, very few people on the face of the planet know that the very shape of the M25 forms the sigil *odegra* in the language of the Black Priesthood of Ancient Mu, and means "Hail the Great Beast, Devourer of Worlds." The thousands of motorists who daily fume their way around its serpentine lengths have the same effect as water on a prayer wheel, grinding out an endless fog of low-grade evil to pollute the metaphysical atmosphere for scores of miles around.

It was one of Crowley's better achievements. It had taken *years* to achieve, and had involved three computer hacks, two break-ins, one minor bribery and, on one wet night when all else had failed, two hours in a squelchy field shifting the marker pegs a few but occultly incredibly significant meters. When Crowley had watched the first thirty-mile-long tailback he'd experienced the lovely warm feeling of a bad job well done.

It had earned him a commendation.

Crowley was currently doing 110 mph somewhere east of Slough. Nothing about him looked particularly demonic, at least by classical standards. No horns, no wings. Admittedly he was listening to a *Best of Queen* tape, but no conclusions should be drawn from this because all tapes left in a car for more than about a fortnight metamorphose into *Best of Queen* albums. No particularly demonic thoughts were going through his head. In fact, he was currently wondering vaguely who Moey and Chandon were.

Crowley had dark hair and good cheekbones and he was wearing snakeskin shoes, or at least presumably he was wearing shoes, and he could do really weird things with his tongue. And, whenever he forgot himself, he had a tendency to hiss.

He also didn't blink much.

The car he was driving was a 1926 black Bentley, one owner from new, and that owner had been Crowley. He'd looked after it.

The reason he was late was that he was enjoying the twentieth century immensely. It was much better than the seventeenth, and a *lot* better than the fourteenth. One of the nice things about Time, Crowley always said, was that it was steadily taking him further away from the fourteenth century, the most bloody boring hundred years on God's, excuse his French, Earth. The twentieth century was anything but boring. In fact, a flashing blue light in his rearview mirror had been telling Crowley, for the last fifty seconds, that he was being followed by two men who would like to make it even more interesting for him.

He glanced at his watch, which was designed for the kind of rich deep-sea diver who likes to know what the time is in twenty-one world capitals while he's down there.*

* It was custom-made for Crowley. Getting just one chip custom-made is incredibly expensive but he could afford it. *This* watch gave the time in twenty world capitals and in a capital city in Another Place, where it was always one time, and that was Too Late.

The Bentley thundered up the exit ramp, took the corner on two wheels, and plunged down a leafy road. The blue light followed.

Crowley sighed, took one hand from the wheel, and, half turning, made a complicated gesture over his shoulder.

The flashing light dimmed into the distance as the police car rolled to a halt, much to the amazement of its occupants. But it would be nothing to the amazement they'd experience when they opened the hood and found out what the engine had turned into.

IN THE GRAVEYARD, Hastur, the tall demon, passed a dogend back to Ligur, the shorter one and the more accomplished lurker.

"I can see a light," he said. "Here he comes now, the flash bastard."

"What's that he's drivin'?" said Ligur.

"It's a car. A horseless carriage," explained Hastur. "I expect they didn't have them last time you was here. Not for what you might call general use."

"They had a man at the front with a red flag," said Ligur.

"They've come on a bit since then, I reckon."

"What's this Crowley like?" said Ligur.

Hastur spat. "He's been up here too long," he said. "Right from the Start. Gone native, if you ask me. Drives a car with a telephone in it."

Ligur pondered this. Like most demons, he had a very limited grasp of technology, and so he was just about to say something like, I bet it needs a lot of wire, when the Bentley rolled to a halt at the cemetery gate.

"And he wears sunglasses," sneered Hastur, "even when he dunt need to." He raised his voice. "All hail Satan," he said.

"All hail Satan," Ligur echoed.

"Hi," said Crowley, giving them a little wave. "Sorry I'm late, but you know how it is on the A40 at Denham, and then I tried to cut up toward Chorleywood and then—"

"*Now* we art all here," said Hastur meaningfully, "we must recount the Deeds of the Day."

"Yeah. Deeds," said Crowley, with the slightly guilty look of one who is attending church for the first time in years and has forgotten which bits you stand up for.

Hastur cleared his throat.

"I have tempted a priest," he said. "As he walked down the street and saw the pretty girls in the sun, I put Doubt into his mind. He would have been a saint, but within a decade we shall have him."

"Nice one," said Crowley, helpfully.

"I have corrupted a politician," said Ligur. "I let him think a tiny bribe would not hurt. Within a year we shall have him."

They both looked expectantly at Crowley, who gave them a big smile.

"You'll like this," he said.

His smile became even wider and more conspiratorial.

"I tied up *every* portable telephone system in

Central London for forty-five minutes at lunchtime," he said.

There was silence, except for the distant swishing of cars.

"Yes?" said Hastur. "And then what?"

"Look, it wasn't easy," said Crowley.

"That's *all*?" said Ligur.

"Look, people—"

"And exactly what has that done to secure souls for our master?" said Hastur.

Crowley pulled himself together.

What could he tell them? That twenty thousand people got bloody furious? That you could hear the arteries clanging shut all across the city? And that then they went back and took it out on their secretaries or traffic wardens or whatever, and *they* took it out on other people? In all kinds of vindictive little ways which, and here was the good bit, *they thought up themselves*. For the rest of the day. The pass-along effects were incalculable. Thousands and thousands of souls all got a faint patina of tarnish, and you hardly had to lift a finger.

But you couldn't tell that to demons like Hastur and Ligur. Fourteenth-century minds, the lot of them. Spending years picking away at one soul. Admittedly it was *craftsmanship*, but you had to think differently these days. Not big, but wide. With five billion people in the world you couldn't pick the buggers off one by one any more; you had to spread your effort. But demons like Ligur and Hastur wouldn't understand. They'd never have thought up Welsh-language television, for example. Or VAT. Or Manchester.

He'd been particularly pleased with Manchester.

"The Powers that Be seem to be satisfied," he said. "Times are changing. So what's up?"

Hastur reached down behind a tombstone.

"This is," he said.

Crowley stared at the basket.

"Oh," he said. "No."

"Yes," said Hastur, grinning.

"Already?"

"Yes."

"And, er, it's up to me to—?"

"*Yes.*" Hastur was enjoying this.

"Why me?" said Crowley desperately. "You know me, Hastur, this isn't, you know, my scene . . ."

"Oh, it is, it is," said Hastur. "Your scene. Your starring role. Take it. Times are changing."

"Yeah," said Ligur, grinning. "They're coming to an end, for a start."

"Why *me*?"

"You are obviously highly favored," said Hastur maliciously. "I imagine Ligur here would give his right arm for a chance like this."

"That's right," said Ligur. Someone's right arm, anyway, he thought. There were plenty of right arms around; no sense in wasting a good one.

Hastur produced a clipboard from the grubby recesses of his mackintosh.

"Sign. Here," he said, leaving a terrible pause between the words.

Crowley fumbled vaguely in an inside pocket and produced a pen. It was sleek and matte black. It looked as though it could exceed the speed limit.

"'S'nice pen," said Ligur.

"It can write under water," Crowley muttered.

"Whatever will they think of next?" mused Ligur.

"Whatever it is, they'd better think of it quickly," said Hastur. "*No*. Not A. J. Crowley. Your *real* name."

Crowley nodded mournfully, and drew a complex, wiggly sigil on the paper. It glowed redly in the gloom, just for a moment, and then faded.

"What am I supposed to *do* with it?" he said.

"You will receive instructions." Hastur scowled. "Why so worried, Crowley? The moment we have been working for all these centuries is at hand!"

"Yeah. Right," said Crowley. He did not look, now, like the lithe figure that had sprung so lithely from the Bentley a few minutes ago. He had a hunted expression.

"Our moment of eternal triumph awaits!"

"Eternal. Yeah," said Crowley.

"And you will be a tool of that glorious destiny!"

"Tool. Yeah," muttered Crowley. He picked up the basket as if it might explode. Which, in a manner of speaking, it would shortly do.

"Er. Okay," he said. "I'll, er, be off then. Shall I? Get it over with. Not that I *want* to get it over with," he added hurriedly, aware of the things that could happen if Hastur turned in an unfavorable report. "But you know me. Keen."

The senior demons did not speak.

"So I'll be popping along," Crowley babbled. "See you guys ar—see you. Er. Great. Fine. *Ciao*."

As the Bentley skidded off into the darkness Ligur said, "Wossat mean?"

"It's Italian," said Hastur. "I think it means 'food.' "

"Funny thing to say, then." Ligur stared at the retreating taillights. "You trust him?" he said.

"No," said Hastur.

"Right," said Ligur. It'd be a funny old world, he reflected, if demons went round trusting one another.

CROWLEY, SOMEWHERE west of Amersham, hurtled through the night, snatched a tape at random and tried to wrestle it out of its brittle plastic box while staying on the road. The glare of a headlight proclaimed it to be Vivaldi's *Four Seasons.* Soothing music, that's what he needed.

He rammed it into the Blaupunkt.

"Ohshitohshit*ohshit.* Why now? Why me?" he muttered, as the familiar strains of Queen washed over him.

And suddenly, Freddie Mercury was speaking to him.

BECAUSE YOU'VE EARNED IT, CROWLEY.

Crowley blessed under his breath. Using electronics as a means of communication had been his idea and Below had, for once, taken it up and, as usual, got it dead wrong. He'd hoped they could be persuaded to subscribe to Cellnet, but instead they just cut in to whatever it happened to be that he was listening to at the time and twisted it.

Crowley gulped.

"Thank you very much, lord," he said.

WE HAVE GREAT FAITH IN YOU, CROWLEY.

"Thank you, lord."

THIS IS IMPORTANT, CROWLEY.

"I know, I know."

THIS IS THE BIG ONE, CROWLEY.

"Leave it to me, lord."

THAT IS WHAT WE ARE DOING, CROWLEY. AND IF IT GOES WRONG, THEN THOSE INVOLVED WILL SUFFER GREATLY. EVEN YOU, CROWLEY. ESPECIALLY YOU.

"Understood, lord."

HERE ARE YOUR INSTRUCTIONS, CROWLEY.

And suddenly he knew. He hated that. They could just as easily have told him, they didn't suddenly have to drop chilly knowledge straight into his brain. He had to drive to a certain hospital.

"I'll be there in five minutes, lord, no problem."

GOOD. I see a little silhouetto of a man scaramouche scaramouche will you do the fandango . . .

Crowley thumped the wheel. Everything had been going so well, he'd had it really under his thumb these few centuries. That's how it goes, you think you're on top of the world, and suddenly they spring Armageddon on you. The Great War, the Last Battle. Heaven versus Hell, three rounds, one Fall, no submission. And that'd be that. No more world. That's what the end of the world *meant*. No more world. Just endless Heaven or, depending who won, endless Hell. Crowley didn't know which was worse.

Well, *Hell* was worse, of course, by definition. But Crowley remembered what Heaven was like, and it had quite a few things in common with Hell. You couldn't get a decent drink in either of them, for a start. And the boredom you got in Heaven was almost as bad as the excitement you got in Hell.

But there was no getting out of it. You couldn't be a demon and have free will.

. . . I will not let you go (let him go) . . .

Well, at least it wouldn't be this year. He'd have time to do things. Unload long-term stocks, for a start.

He wondered what would happen if he just stopped the car here, on this dark and damp and empty road, and took the basket and swung it round and round and let go and . . .

Something dreadful, that's what.

He'd been an angel once. He hadn't meant to Fall. He'd just hung around with the wrong people.

The Bentley plunged on through the darkness, its fuel gauge pointing to zero. It had pointed to zero for more than sixty years now. It wasn't all bad, being a demon. You didn't have to buy petrol, for one thing. The only time Crowley had bought petrol was once in 1967, to get the free James Bond bullet-hole-in-the-windscreen transfers, which he rather fancied at the time.

On the back seat the thing in the basket began to cry; the air-raid siren wail of the newly born. High. Wordless. And *old.*

IT WAS QUITE A NICE HOSPITAL, thought Mr. Young. It would have been quiet, too, if it wasn't for the nuns.

He quite liked nuns. Not that he was a, you know, left-footer or anything like that. No, when it came to avoiding going to church, the church he stolidly avoided going to was St. Cecil and All Angels, no-nonsense C. of E., and he wouldn't have dreamed of avoiding going to any other. All the others had the wrong smell—floor polish for the Low, somewhat suspicious incense for the High. Deep in the leather armchair of his soul, Mr. Young knew that God got embarrassed at that sort of thing.

But he liked seeing nuns around, in the same way that he liked seeing the Salvation Army. It made you feel that it was all *all right*, that people somewhere were keeping the world on its axis.

This was his first experience of the Chattering Order of Saint Beryl, however.* Deirdre had run

* Saint Beryl Articulatus of Cracow, reputed to have been martyred in the middle of the fifth century. According to legend, Beryl was a young woman who was betrothed against her will to a pagan, Prince Casimir. On their wedding night she prayed to the Lord to intercede, vaguely expecting a miraculous beard to appear, and she had in fact already laid in a small ivory-handled razor, suitable for ladies, against this very eventuality; instead the Lord granted Beryl the miraculous ability to chatter continually about whatever was on her mind, however inconsequential, without pause for breath or food.

According to one version of the legend, Beryl was strangled by Prince Casimir three weeks after the wedding, with their marriage still unconsummated. She died a virgin and a martyr, chattering to the end.

across them while being involved in one of her causes, possibly the one involving lots of unpleasant South Americans fighting other unpleasant South Americans and the priests egging them on instead of getting on with proper priestly concerns, like organizing the church cleaning rota.

The point was, nuns should be quiet. They were the right shape for it, like those pointy things you got in those chambers Mr. Young was vaguely aware your hi-fi got tested in. They shouldn't be, well, chattering all the time.

He filled his pipe with tobacco—well, they called it tobacco, it wasn't what he thought of as tobacco, it wasn't the tobacco you used to get—and wondered reflectively what would happen if you asked a nun where the Gents was. Probably the Pope sent you a sharp note or something. He shifted his position awkwardly, and glanced at his watch.

One thing, though: At least the nuns had put their foot down about him being present at the birth. Deirdre had been all for it. She'd been *reading* things again. One kid already and suddenly she's declaring that this confinement was going to be the most joyous and sharing experience two human beings could have. That's what came of letting her

---

According to another version of the legend, Casimir bought himself a set of earplugs, and she died in bed, with him, at the age of sixty-two.

The Chattering Order of Saint Beryl is under a vow to emulate Saint Beryl at all times, except on Tuesday afternoons, for half an hour, when the nuns are permitted to shut up, and, if they wish, to play table tennis.

order her own newspapers. Mr. Young distrusted papers whose inner pages had names like "Lifestyle" or "Options."

Well, he hadn't got anything against joyous sharing experiences. Joyous sharing experiences were fine by him. The world probably needed more joyous sharing experiences. But he had made it abundantly clear that this was one joyous sharing experience Deirdre could have by herself.

And the nuns had agreed. They saw no reason for the father to be involved in the proceedings. When you thought about it, Mr. Young mused, they probably saw no reason why the father should be involved *anywhere*.

He finished thumbing the so-called tobacco into the pipe and glared at the little sign on the wall of the waiting room that said that, for his own comfort, he would not smoke. For his own comfort, he decided, he'd go and stand in the porch. If there was a discreet shrubbery for his own comfort out there, so much the better.

He wandered down the empty corridors and found a doorway that led out onto a rain-swept courtyard full of righteous dustbins.

He shivered, and cupped his hands to light his pipe.

It happened to them at a certain age, wives. Twenty-five blameless years, then suddenly they were going off and doing these robotic exercises in pink socks with the feet cut out and they started blaming you for never having had to work for a living. It was hormones, or something.

A large black car skidded to a halt by the dustbins. A young man in dark glasses leaped out into the drizzle holding what looked like a carrycot and snaked toward the entrance.

Mr. Young took his pipe out of his mouth. "You've left your lights on," he said helpfully.

The man gave him the blank look of someone to whom lights are the least of his worries, and waved a hand vaguely toward the Bentley. The lights went out.

"That's handy," said Mr. Young. "Infra-red, is it?"

He was mildly surprised to see that the man did not appear to be wet. And that the carrycot appeared to be occupied.

"Has it started yet?" said the man.

Mr. Young felt vaguely proud to be so instantly recognizable as a parent.

"Yes," he said. "They made me go out," he added thankfully.

"Already? Any idea how long we've got?"

We, Mr. Young noted. Obviously a doctor with views about co-parenting.

"I think we were, er, getting on with it," said Mr. Young.

"What room is she in?" said the man hurriedly.

"We're in Room Three," said Mr. Young. He patted his pockets, and found the battered packet which, in accord with tradition, he had brought with him.

"Would we care to share a joyous cigar experience?" he said.

But the man had gone.

Mr. Young carefully replaced the packet and looked reflectively at his pipe. Always in a rush, these doctors. Working all the hours God sent.

THERE'S A TRICK they do with one pea and three cups which is very hard to follow, and something like it, for greater stakes than a handful of loose change, is about to take place.

The text will be slowed down to allow the sleight of hand to be followed.

Mrs. Deirdre Young is giving birth in Delivery Room Three. She is having a golden-haired male baby we will call Baby A.

The wife of the American Cultural Attaché, Mrs. Harriet Dowling, is giving birth in Delivery Room Four. She is having a golden-haired male baby we will call Baby B.

Sister Mary Loquacious has been a devout Satanist since birth. She went to Sabbat School as a child and won black stars for handwriting and liver. When she was told to join the Chattering Order she went obediently, having a natural talent in that direction and, in any case, knowing that she would be among friends. She would be quite bright, if she was ever put in a position to find out, but long ago found that being a scatterbrain, as she'd put it, gave you an easier journey through life. Currently she is being handed a golden-haired male baby we will call the Adversary, Destroyer of Kings, Angel of the Bottomless Pit, Great Beast that is called Dragon, Prince of This World, Father of Lies, Spawn of Satan, and Lord of Darkness.

Watch carefully. Round and round they go. . . .

"Is that him?" said Sister Mary, staring at the baby. "Only I'd expected funny eyes. Red, or green. Or teensy-weensy little hoofikins. Or a widdle tail." She turned him around as she spoke. No horns either. The Devil's child looked ominously normal.

"Yes, that's him," said Crowley.

"Fancy me holding the Antichrist," said Sister Mary. "And bathing the Antichrist. And counting his little toesy-wosies. . . ."

She was now addressing the child directly, lost in some world of her own. Crowley waved a hand in front of her wimple. "Hallo? Hallo? Sister Mary?"

"Sorry, sir. He is a little sweetheart, though. Does he look like his daddy? I bet he does. Does he look like his daddywaddykins . . ."

"No," said Crowley firmly. "And now I should get up to the delivery rooms, if I were you."

"Will he remember me when he grows up, do you think?" said Sister Mary wistfully, sidling slowly down the corridor.

"Pray that he doesn't," said Crowley, and fled.

Sister Mary headed through the nighttime hospital with the Adversary, Destroyer of Kings, Angel of the Bottomless Pit, Great Beast that is called Dragon, Prince of This World, Father of Lies, Spawn of Satan, and Lord of Darkness safely in her arms. She found a bassinet and laid him down in it.

He gurgled. She gave him a tickle.

A matronly head appeared around a door. It said, "Sister Mary, what are you doing here? Shouldn't you be on duty in Room Four?"

"Master Crowley said—"

"Just glide along, there's a good nun. Have you seen the husband anywhere? He's not in the waiting room."

"I've only seen Master Crowley, and he told me—"

"I'm sure he did," said Sister Grace Voluble firmly. "I suppose I'd better go and look for the wretched man. Come in and keep an eye on her, will you? She's a bit woozy but the baby's fine." Sister Grace paused. "Why are you winking? Is there something wrong with your eye?"

"You know!" Sister Mary hissed archly. "The babies. The exchange—"

"Of course, of course. In good time. But we can't have the father wandering around, can we?" said Sister Grace. "No telling what he might see. So just wait here and mind the baby, there's a dear."

She sailed off down the polished corridor. Sister Mary, wheeling her bassinet, entered the delivery room.

Mrs. Young was more than woozy. She was fast asleep, with the look of determined self-satisfaction of someone who knows that other people are going to have to do the running around for once. Baby A was asleep beside her, weighed and name-tagged. Sister Mary, who had been brought up to be helpful, removed the name-tag, copied it out, and attached the duplicate to the baby in her care.

The babies looked similar, both being small, blotchy, and looking sort of, though not really, like Winston Churchill.

Now, thought Sister Mary, I could do with a nice cup of tea.

Most of the members of the convent were old-fashioned Satanists, like their parents and grandparents before them. They'd been brought up to it and weren't, when you got right down to it, particularly evil. Human beings mostly aren't. They just get carried away by new ideas, like dressing up in jackboots and shooting people, or dressing up in white sheets and lynching people, or dressing up in tie-dye jeans and playing guitars at people. Offer people a new creed with a costume and their hearts and minds will follow. Anyway, being *brought up* as a Satanist tended to take the edge off it. It was something you did on Saturday nights. And the rest of the time you simply got on with life as best you could, just like everyone else. Besides, Sister Mary was a nurse and nurses, whatever their creed, are primarily nurses, which had a lot to do with wearing your watch upside down, keeping calm in emergencies, and dying for a cup of tea. She hoped someone would come soon; she'd done the important bit, now she wanted her tea.

It may help to understand human affairs to be clear that most of the great triumphs and tragedies of history are caused, not by people being fundamentally good or fundamentally bad, but by people being fundamentally people.

There was a knock at the door. She opened it.

"Has it happened yet?" asked Mr. Young. "I'm the father. The husband. Whatever. Both."

Sister Mary had expected the American Cultural Attaché to look like Blake Carrington or J. R. Ewing. Mr. Young didn't look like any American she'd ever seen on television, except possibly for the avuncular sheriff in the better class of murder mystery.* He was something of a disappointment. She didn't think much of his cardigan, either.

She swallowed her disappointment. "Oooh, yes," she said. "Congratulations. Your lady wife's asleep, poor pet."

Mr. Young looked over her shoulder. "Twins?" he said. He reached for his pipe. He stopped reaching for his pipe. He reached for it again. "*Twins?* No one said anything about twins."

"Oh, no!" said Sister Mary hurriedly. "*This* one's yours. The other one's . . . er . . . someone else's. Just looking after him till Sister Grace gets back. No," she reiterated, pointing to the Adversary, Destroyer of Kings, Angel of the Bottomless Pit, Great Beast that is called Dragon, Prince of This World, Father of Lies, Spawn of Satan, and Lord of Darkness, "this one's definitely yours. From the top of his head to the tips of his hoofywoofies—which he hasn't got," she added hastily.

Mr. Young peered down.

"Ah, yes," he said doubtfully. "He looks like my side of the family. All, er, present and correct, is he?"

"Oh, yes," said Sister Mary. "He's a very normal child," she added. "Very, very normal."

There was a pause. They stared at the sleeping baby.

"You don't have much of an accent," said Sister Mary. "Have you been over here long?"

* With a little old lady as the sleuth, and no car chases unless they're done very slowly.

"About ten years," said Mr. Young, mildly puzzled. "The job moved, you see, and I had to move with it."

"It must be a very exciting job, I've always thought," said Sister Mary. Mr. Young looked gratified. Not everyone appreciated the more stimulating aspects of cost accountancy.

"I expect it was very different where you were before," Sister Mary went on.

"I suppose so," said Mr. Young, who'd never really thought about it. Luton, as far as he could remember, was pretty much like Tadfield. The same sort of hedges between your house and the railway station. The same sort of people.

"Taller buildings, for one thing," said Sister Mary, desperately.

Mr. Young stared at her. The only one he could think of was the Alliance and Leicester offices.

"And I expect you go to a lot of garden parties," said the nun.

Ah. He was on firmer ground here. Deirdre was very keen on that sort of thing.

"Lots," he said, with feeling. "Deirdre makes jam for them, you know. And I normally have to help with the White Elephant."

This was an aspect of Buckingham Palace society that had never occurred to Sister Mary, although the pachyderm fitted right in.

"I expect they're the tribute," she said. "I read where these foreign potentates give her all sorts of things."

"I'm sorry?"

"I'm a big fan of the Royal Family, you know."

"Oh, so am I," said Mr. Young, leaping gratefully onto this new ice floe in the bewildering stream of consciousness. Yes, you knew where you were with the Royals. The proper ones, of course, who pulled their weight in the hand-waving and bridge-opening department. Not the ones who went to discos all night long and were sick all over the paparazzi.*

"That's nice," said Sister Mary. "I thought you people weren't too keen on them, what with revoluting and throwing all those tea-sets into the river."

She chattered on, encouraged by the Order's instruction that members should always say what was on their minds. Mr. Young was out of his depth, and too tired now to worry about it very much. The religious life probably made people a little odd. He wished Mrs. Young would wake up. Then one of the words in Sister Mary's wittering struck a hopeful chord in his mind.

"Would there be any possibility of me possibly being able to have a cup of tea, perhaps?" he ventured.

"Oh my," said Sister Mary, her hand flying to her mouth, "whatever am I thinking of?"

Mr. Young made no comment.

"I'll see to it right away," she said. "Are you sure you don't want coffee, though? There's one of those vendible machines on the next floor."

"Tea, please," said Mr. Young.

* It is possibly worth mentioning at this point that Mr. Young thought that paparazzi was a kind of Italian linoleum.

"My word, you really *have* gone native, haven't you," said Sister Mary gaily, as she bustled out.

Mr. Young, left alone with one sleeping wife and two sleeping babies, sagged onto a chair. Yes, it must be all that getting up early and kneeling and so on. Good people, of course, but not entirely compost mentis. He'd seen a Ken Russell film once. There had been nuns in it. There didn't seem to be any of *that* sort of thing going on, but no smoke without fire and so on. . . .

He sighed.

It was then that Baby A awoke, and settled down to a really good wail.

Mr. Young hadn't had to quiet a screaming baby for years. He'd never been much good at it to start with. He'd always respected Sir Winston Churchill, and patting small versions of him on the bottom had always seemed ungracious.

"Welcome to the world," he said wearily. "You get used to it after a while."

The baby shut its mouth and glared at him as if he were a recalcitrant general.

Sister Mary chose that moment to come in with the tea. Satanist or not, she'd also found a plate and arranged some iced biscuits on it. They were the sort you only ever get at the bottom of certain tea-time assortments. Mr. Young's was the same pink as a surgical appliance, and had a snowman picked out on it in white icing.

"I don't expect you normally have these," she said. "They're what you call cookies. We call them *bis-cuits*."

Mr. Young had just opened his mouth to explain

that, yes, so did he, and so did people even in Luton, when another nun rushed in, breathless.

She looked at Sister Mary, realized that Mr. Young had never seen the inside of a pentagram, and confined herself to pointing at Baby A and winking.

Sister Mary nodded and winked back.

The nun wheeled the baby out.

As methods of human communication go, a wink is quite versatile. You can say a lot with a wink. For example, the new nun's wink said:

Where the hell have you been? Baby B has been born, we're ready to make the switch, and here's you in the wrong room with the Adversary, Destroyer of Kings, Angel of the Bottomless Pit, Great Beast that is called Dragon, Prince of This World, Father of Lies, Spawn of Satan, and Lord of Darkness, drinking tea. Do you realize I've nearly been shot?

And, as far as she was concerned, Sister Mary's answering wink meant:

Here's the Adversary, Destroyer of Kings, Angel of the Bottomless Pit, Great Beast that is called Dragon, Prince of This World, Father of Lies, Spawn of Satan, and Lord of Darkness, and I can't talk now because there's this outsider here.

Whereas Sister Mary, on the other hand, had thought that the orderly's wink was more on the lines of:

Well done, Sister Mary—switched over the babies all by herself. Now indicate to me the superfluous child and I shall remove it and let you get on with your tea with his Royal Excellency the American Culture.

And therefore her own wink had meant:

There you go, dearie; that's Baby B, now take him

away and leave me to chat to his Excellency. I've always wanted to ask him why they have those tall buildings with all the mirrors on them.

The subtleties of all this were quite lost on Mr. Young, who was extremely embarrassed at all this clandestine affection and was thinking: That Mr. Russell, he knew what he was talking about, and no mistake.

Sister Mary's error might have been noticed by the other nun had not she herself been severely rattled by the Secret Service men in Mrs. Dowling's room, who kept looking at her with growing unease. This was because they had been trained to react in a certain way to people in long flowing robes and long flowing headdresses, and were currently suffering from a conflict of signals. Humans suffering from a conflict of signals aren't the best people to be holding guns, especially when they've just witnessed a natural childbirth, which definitely looked an un-American way of bringing new citizens into the world. Also, they'd heard that there were missals in the building.

Mrs. Young stirred.

"Have you picked a name for him yet?" said Sister Mary archly.

"Hmm?" said Mr. Young. "Oh. No, not really. If it was a girl it would have been Lucinda after my mother. Or Germaine. That was Deirdre's choice."

"Wormwood's a nice name," said the nun, remembering her classics. "Or Damien. Damien's very popular."

ANATHEMA DEVICE—her mother, who was not a great student of religious matters, happened to read the word one day and thought it was a lovely name for a girl—was eight and a half years old, and she was reading The Book, under the bedclothes, with a torch.

Other children learned to read on basic primers with colored pictures of apples, balls, cockroaches, and so forth. Not the Device family. Anathema had learned to read from The Book.

It didn't have any apples and balls in it. It did have a rather good eighteenth-century woodcut of Agnes Nutter being burned at the stake and looking rather cheerful about it.

The first word she could recognize was *nice*. Very few people at the age of eight and a half know that *nice* also means "scrupulously exact," but Anathema was one of them.

The second word was *accurate*.

The first sentence she had ever read out loud was:

"I tell ye thif, and I charge ye with my wordes. Four shalle ryde, and Four shalle alfo ryde, and Three sharl ryde the Skye as twixt, and Wonne shal ryde in flames; and theyr shall be no stopping themme: not fish, nor rayne, nor rode, neither Deville nor Angel. And ye shalle be theyr alfo, Anathema."

Anathema liked to read about herself.

(There were books which caring parents who read the right Sunday papers could purchase with their children's names printed in as the heroine or hero. This was meant to interest the child in the book. In Anathema's case, it wasn't only *her* in The Book—and it had been spot on so far—but her parents, and her grandparents, and everyone, back to the seventeenth century. She was too young and too self-centered at this point to attach any importance to the fact that there was no mention made of her children, or indeed, any events in her future further away than eleven years' time. When you're eight and a half, eleven years is a lifetime, and of course, if you believed The Book, it would be.)

She was a bright child, with a pale face, and black eyes and hair. As a rule she tended to make people feel uncomfortable, a family trait she had inherited, along with being more psychic than was good for her, from her great-great-great-great-great grandmother.

She was precocious, and self-possessed. The only thing about Anathema her teachers ever had the nerve to upbraid her for was her spelling, which was not so much appalling as 300 years too late.

THE NUNS TOOK BABY A and swapped it with Baby B under the noses of the Attaché's wife and the Secret Service men, by the cunning expedient of wheeling one baby away ("to be weighed, love, got to do that, it's the law") and wheeling another baby back, a little later.

The Cultural Attaché himself, Thaddeus J. Dowling, had been called back to Washington in a hurry a few days earlier, but he had been on the phone to Mrs. Dowling throughout the birth experience, helping her with her breathing.

It didn't help that he had been talking on the other line to his investment counselor. At one point he'd been forced to put her on hold for twenty minutes.

But that was okay.

Having a baby is the single most joyous co-experience that two human beings can share, and he wasn't going to miss a second of it.

He'd got one of the Secret Service men to videotape it for him.

EVIL IN GENERAL does not sleep, and therefore doesn't see why anyone else should. But Crowley liked sleep, it was one of the pleasures of the world. Especially after a heavy meal. He'd slept right through most of the nineteenth century, for example. Not because he needed to, simply because he enjoyed it.*

One of the pleasures of the world. Well, he'd better start really enjoying them now, while there was still time.

The Bentley roared through the night, heading east.

Of course, he was all in favor of Armageddon in *general* terms. If anyone had asked him why he'd been spending centuries tinkering in the affairs of mankind he'd have said, "Oh, in order to bring about Armageddon and the triumph of Hell." But it was one thing to work to bring it about, and quite another for it to actually happen.

Crowley had always known that he would be

* Although he did have to get up in 1832 to go to the lavatory.

around when the world ended, because he was immortal and wouldn't have any alternative. But he'd hoped it would be a long way off.

Because he rather liked people. It was a major failing in a demon.

Oh, he did his best to make their short lives miserable, because that was his job, but nothing he could think up was half as bad as the stuff they thought up themselves. They seemed to have a talent for it. It was built into the design, somehow. They were born into a world that was against them in a thousand little ways, and then devoted most of their energies to making it worse. Over the years Crowley had found it increasingly difficult to find anything demonic to do which showed up against the natural background of generalized nastiness. There had been times, over the past millennium, when he'd felt like sending a message back Below saying, Look, we may as well give up right now, we might as well shut down Dis and Pandemonium and everywhere and move up here, there's nothing we can do to them that they don't do themselves and they do things we've never even thought of, often involving electrodes. They've got what we lack. They've got *imagination*. And electricity, of course.

One of them had written it, hadn't he . . . "Hell is empty, and all the devils are here."

Crowley had got a commendation for the Spanish Inquisition. He *had* been in Spain then, mainly hanging around cantinas in the nicer parts, and hadn't even *known* about it until the commendation arrived. He'd gone to have a look, and had come back and got drunk for a week.

That Hieronymus Bosch. What a weirdo.

And just when you'd think they were more malignant than ever Hell could be, they could occasionally show more grace than Heaven ever dreamed of. Often the same individual was involved. It was this free-will thing, of course. It was a bugger.

Aziraphale had tried to explain it to him once. The whole point, he'd said—this was somewhere around 1020, when they'd first reached their little Arrangement—the whole point was that when a human was good or bad it was because they wanted to be. Whereas people like Crowley and, of course, himself, were set in their ways right from the start. People couldn't become truly holy, he said, unless they also had the opportunity to be definitively wicked.

Crowley had thought about this for some time and, around about 1023, had said, Hang on, that only works, right, if you start everyone off equal, okay? You can't start someone off in a muddy shack in the middle of a war zone and expect them to do as well as someone born in a castle.

Ah, Aziraphale had said, that's the good bit. The lower you start, the more opportunities you have.

Crowley had said, That's lunatic.

No, said Aziraphale, it's ineffable.

Aziraphale. The Enemy, of course. But an enemy for six thousand years now, which made him a sort of friend.

Crowley reached down and picked up the car phone.

Being a demon, of course, was supposed to mean

you had no free will. But you couldn't hang around humans for very long without learning a thing or two.

MR. YOUNG HAD NOT BEEN too keen on Damien, or Wormwood. Or any of Sister Mary Loquacious' other suggestions, which had covered half of Hell, and most of the Golden Years of Hollywood.

"Well," she said finally, a little hurt, "I don't think there's anything wrong with Errol. *Or* Cary. Very nice American names, both of them."

"I had fancied something more, well, traditional," explained Mr. Young. "We've always gone in for good simple names in our family."

Sister Mary beamed. "That's right. The old names are always the best, if you ask me."

"A decent English name, like people had in the Bible," said Mr. Young. "Matthew, Mark, Luke, or John," he said, speculatively. Sister Mary winced. "Only they've never struck me as very good Bible names, really," Mr. Young added. "They sound more like cowboys and footballers."

"Saul's nice," said Sister Mary, making the best of it.

"I don't want something *too* old-fashioned," said Mr. Young.

"Or Cain. Very modern sound, Cain, really," Sister Mary tried.

"Hmm." Mr. Young looked doubtful.

"Or there's always . . . well, there's always Adam," said Sister Mary. That should be safe enough, she thought.

"Adam?" said Mr. Young.

IT WOULD BE NICE to think that the Satanist Nuns had the surplus baby—Baby B—discreetly adopted. That he grew to be a normal, happy, laughing child, active and exuberant; and after that, grew further to become a normal, fairly contented adult.

And perhaps that's what happened.

Let your mind dwell on his junior school prize for spelling; his unremarkable although quite pleasant time at university; his job in the payroll department of the Tadfield and Norton Building Society; his lovely wife. Possibly you would like to imagine some children, and a hobby—restoring vintage motorcycles, perhaps, or breeding tropical fish.

You don't want to know what *could* have happened to Baby B.

We like your version better, anyway.

He probably wins prizes for his tropical fish.

IN A SMALL HOUSE in Dorking, Surrey, a light was on in a bedroom window.

Newton Pulsifer was twelve, and thin, and bespectacled, and he should have been in bed hours ago.

His mother, though, was convinced of her child's genius, and let him stay up past his bedtime to do his "experiments."

His current experiment was changing a plug on an ancient Bakelite radio his mother had given him to play with. He sat at what he proudly called his "work-top," a battered old table covered in curls of wire, batteries, little light bulbs, and a homemade crystal set that had never worked. He hadn't managed to get the Bakelite radio working yet either, but then again, he never seemed able to get that far.

Three slightly crooked model airplanes hung on cotton cords from his bedroom ceiling. Even a casual observer could have seen that they were made by someone who was both painstaking and very careful, and also no good at making model airplanes. He was hopelessly proud of all of them, even the Spitfire, where he'd made rather a mess of the wings.

He pushed his glasses back up the bridge of his nose, squinted down at the plug, and put down the screwdriver.

He had high hopes for it this time; he had followed all the instructions on plug-changing on page five of the *Boy's Own Book Of Practical Electronics, Including A Hundred and One Safe and Educational Things to Do With Electricity.* He had attached the correct color-coded wires to the correct pins; he'd checked that it was the right amperage fuse; he'd screwed it all back together. So far, no problems.

He plugged it in to the socket. Then he switched the socket on.

Every light in the house went out.

Newton beamed with pride. He was getting better. Last time he'd done it he'd blacked out the whole of Dorking, and a man from the Electric had come over and had a word with his mum.

He had a burning and totally unrequited passion for things electrical. They had a computer at school, and half a dozen studious children stayed on after school doing things with punched cards. When the teacher in charge of the computer had finally acceded to Newton's pleas to be allowed to join them, Newton had only ever got to feed one little card into the machine. It had chewed it up and choked fatally on it.

Newton was certain that the future was in computers, and when the future arrived he'd be ready, in the forefront of the new technology.

The future had its own ideas on this. It was all in The Book.

ADAM, THOUGHT MR. YOUNG. He tried saying it, to see how it sounded. "Adam." Hmm . . .

He stared down at the golden curls of the Adversary, Destroyer of Kings, Angel of the Bottomless Pit, Great Beast that is called Dragon, Prince of This World, Father of Lies, Spawn of Satan, and Lord of Darkness.

"You know," he concluded, after a while, "I think he actually looks like an Adam."

IT HAD NOT BEEN A DARK AND STORMY NIGHT.

The dark and stormy night occurred two days later, about four hours after both Mrs. Dowling and Mrs. Young and their respective babies had left the building. It was a particularly dark and stormy night, and just after midnight, as the storm reached its height, a bolt of lightning struck the Convent of the Chattering Order, setting fire to the roof of the vestry.

No one was badly hurt by the fire, but it went on for some hours, doing a fair amount of damage in the process.

The instigator of the fire lurked on a nearby hilltop and watched the blaze. He was tall, thin, and a Duke of Hell. It was the last thing that needed to be done before his return to the nether regions, and he had done it.

He could safely leave the rest to Crowley.

Hastur went home.

TECHNICALLY AZIRAPHALE was a Principality, but people made jokes about that these days.

On the whole, neither he nor Crowley would have chosen each other's company, but they were both men, or at least men-shaped creatures, of the world, and the Arrangement had worked to their advantage all this time. Besides, you grew accustomed to the only other face that had been around more or less consistently for six millennia.

The Arrangement was very simple, so simple in fact that it didn't really deserve the capital letter, which it had got for simply being in existence for so long. It was the sort of sensible arrangement that many isolated agents, working in awkward conditions a long way from their superiors, reach with their opposite number when they realize that they have more in common with their immediate opponents than their remote allies. It meant a tacit non-interference in certain of each other's activities. It made certain that while neither really won, also neither really lost, and both were able to demonstrate to their masters the great strides they were making against a cunning and well-informed adversary.

It meant that Crowley had been allowed to develop Manchester, while Aziraphale had a free hand in the whole of Shropshire. Crowley took Glasgow, Aziraphale had Edinburgh (neither claimed any responsibility for Milton Keynes,* but both reported it as a success).

And then, of course, it had seemed even natural that they should, as it were, hold the fort for one another whenever common sense dictated. Both were of angel stock, after all. If one was going to Hull for a quick temptation, it made sense to nip across the city and carry out a standard brief moment of divine ecstasy. It'd get done *anyway*, and being sensible about it gave everyone more free time and cut down on expenses.

Aziraphale felt the occasional pang of guilt about this, but centuries of association with humanity was having the same effect on him as it was on Crowley, except in the other direction.

Besides, the Authorities didn't seem to care much who did anything, so long as it got done.

Currently, what Aziraphale was doing was standing with Crowley by the duck pond in St. James' Park. They were feeding the ducks.

The ducks in St. James' Park are so used to being

* Note for Americans and other aliens: Milton Keynes is a new city approximately halfway between London and Birmingham. It was built to be modern, efficient, healthy, and, all in all, a pleasant place to live. Many Britons find this amusing.

fed bread by secret agents meeting clandestinely that they have developed their own Pavlovian reaction. Put a St. James' Park duck in a laboratory cage and show it a picture of two men—one usually wearing a coat with a fur collar, the other something somber with a scarf—and it'll look up expectantly. The Russian cultural attaché's black bread is particularly sought after by the more discerning duck, while the head of MI9's soggy Hovis with Marmite is relished by the connoisseurs.

Aziraphale tossed a crust to a scruffy-looking drake, which caught it and sank immediately.

The angel turned to Crowley.

"Really, my dear," he murmured.

"Sorry," said Crowley. "I was forgetting myself." The duck bobbed angrily to the surface.

"Of course, we knew something was going on," Aziraphale said. "But one somehow imagines this sort of thing happening in America. They go in for that sort of thing over there."

"It might yet do, at that," said Crowley gloomily. He gazed thoughtfully across the park to the Bentley, the back wheel of which was being industriously clamped.

"Oh, yes. The American diplomat," said the angel. "Rather *showy*, one feels. As if Armageddon was some sort of cinematographic show that you wish to sell in as many countries as possible."

"*Every* country," said Crowley. "The Earth and all the kingdoms thereof."

Aziraphale tossed the last scrap of bread at the ducks, who went off to pester the Bulgarian naval attaché and a furtive-looking man in a Cambridge tie, and carefully disposed of the paper bag in a wastepaper bin.

He turned and faced Crowley.

"We'll win, of course," he said.

"*You* don't want that," said the demon.

"Why not, pray?"

"*Listen*," said Crowley desperately, "how many musicians do you think your side have got, eh? First grade, I mean."

Aziraphale looked taken aback.

"Well, I should think—" he began.

"Two," said Crowley. "Elgar and Liszt. That's *all*. We've got the rest. Beethoven, Brahms, all the Bachs, Mozart, the lot. Can you imagine eternity with Elgar?"

Aziraphale shut his eyes. "All too easily," he groaned.

"That's it, then," said Crowley, with a gleam of triumph. He knew Aziraphale's weak spot all right. "No more compact discs. No more Albert Hall. No more Proms. No more Glyndbourne. Just celestial harmonies all day long."

"Ineffable," Aziraphale murmured.

"Like eggs without salt, you said. Which reminds me. No salt, no eggs. No gravlax with dill sauce. No fascinating little restaurants where they know you. No *Daily Telegraph* crossword. No small antique shops. No bookshops, either. No interesting old editions. No"—Crowley scraped the bottom of Aziraphale's barrel of interests—"Regency silver snuffboxes . . ."

"But after we win life will be better!" croaked the angel.

"But it won't be as interesting. Look, you *know* I'm right. You'd be as happy with a harp as I'd be with a pitchfork."

"You know we don't play harps."

"And we don't use pitchforks. I was being rhetorical."

They stared at one another.

Aziraphale spread his elegantly manicured hands.

"My people are more than happy for it to happen, you know. It's what it's all about, you see. The great final test. Flaming swords, the Four Horsemen, seas of blood, the whole tedious business." He shrugged.

"And then Game Over, Insert Coin?" said Crowley.

"Sometimes I find your methods of expression a little difficult to follow."

"I like the seas as they are. It doesn't have to happen. You don't have to test everything to destruction just to see if you made it right."

Aziraphale shrugged again.

"That's ineffable wisdom for you, I'm afraid." The angel shuddered, and pulled his coat around him. Gray clouds were piling up over the city.

"Let's go somewhere warm," he said.

"You're asking me?" said Crowley glumly.

They walked in somber silence for a while.

"It's not that I disagree with you," said the angel, as they plodded across the grass. "It's just that I'm not allowed to disobey. You know that."

"Me too," said Crowley.

Aziraphale gave him a sidelong glance. "Oh, come now," he said, "you're a demon, after all."

"Yeah. But my people are only in favor of disobedience in general terms. It's *specific* disobedience they come down on heavily."

"Such as disobedience to themselves?"

"You've got it. You'd be amazed. Or perhaps you wouldn't be. How long do you think we've got?" Crowley waved a hand at the Bentley, which unlocked its doors.

"The prophecies differ," said Aziraphale, sliding into the passenger seat. "Certainly until the end of the century, although we may expect certain phenomena before then. Most of the prophets of the past millennium were more concerned with scansion than accuracy."

Crowley pointed to the ignition key. It turned.

"What?" he said.

"You know," said the angel helpfully, "'And thee Worlde Unto An Ende Shall Come, in tumpty-tumpty-tumpty One.' Or Two, or Three, or whatever. There aren't many good rhymes for Six, so it's probably a good year to be in."

"And what sort of phenomena?"

"Two-headed calves, signs in the sky, geese flying backwards, showers of fish. That sort of thing. The presence of the Antichrist affects the natural operation of causality."

"Hmm."

Crowley put the Bentley in gear. Then he remembered something. He snapped his fingers.

The wheel clamps disappeared.

"Let's have lunch," he said. "I owe you one from, when was it . . ."

"Paris, 1793," said Aziraphale.

"Oh, yes. The Reign of Terror. Was that one of yours, or one of ours?"

"Wasn't it yours?"

"Can't recall. It was quite a good restaurant, though."

As they drove past an astonished traffic warden his notebook spontaneously combusted, to Crowley's amazement.

"I'm pretty certain I didn't mean to do that," he said.

Aziraphale blushed.

"That was me," he said. "I had always thought that *your* people invented them."

"Did you? *We* thought they were yours."

Crowley stared at the smoke in the rearview mirror.

"Come on," he said. "Let's do the Ritz."

Crowley had not bothered to book. In his world, table reservations were things that happened to other people.

AZIRAPHALE COLLECTED BOOKS. If he were totally honest with himself he would have to have admitted that his bookshop was simply somewhere to store them. He was not unusual in this. In order to maintain his cover as a typical second-hand bookseller, he used every means short of actual physical violence to prevent customers from making a purchase. Unpleasant damp smells, glowering looks, erratic opening hours—he was incredibly good at it.

He had been collecting for a long time, and, like all collectors, he specialized.

He had more than sixty books of predictions concerning developments in the last handful of centuries of the second millennium. He had a penchant for Wilde first editions. And he had a complete set of the Infamous Bibles, individually named from errors in typesetting.

These Bibles included the Unrighteous Bible, so called from a printer's error which caused it to proclaim, in I Corinthians, "Know ye not that the unrighteous shall inherit the Kingdom of God?"; and the Wicked Bible, printed by Barker and Lucas in 1632, in which the word *not* was omitted from the seventh commandment, making it "Thou shalt commit Adultery." There were the Discharge Bible, the Treacle Bible, the Standing Fishes Bible, the Charing Cross Bible and the rest. Aziraphale had them all. Even the very rarest, a Bible published in 1651 by the London publishing firm of Bilton and Scaggs.

It had been the first of their three great publishing disasters.

The book was commonly known as the Buggre Alle This Bible. The lengthy compositor's error, if such it may be called, occurs in the book of Ezekiel, chapter 48, verse five.

2. And bye the border of Dan, fromme the east side to the west side, a portion for Afher.

3. And bye the border of Afher, fromme the east side even untoe the west side, a portion for Naphtali.

4. And bye the border of Naphtali, from the east side untoe the west side, a portion for Manaffeh.

5. **Buggre Alle this for a Larke. I amme sick to mye Hart of typefettinge. Master Biltonn if no Gentelmann, and Master Scagges noe more than a tighte fisted Southwarke Knobbefticke. I telle you, onne a daye laike thif Ennywone with half an oz. of Sense shoulde bee oute in the Sunneshain, ane nott Stucke here alle the liuelong daie inn thif mowldey olde By-Our-Lady Workefhoppe. @ *"Æ@;!***
6. **And bye the border of Ephraim, from the east fide even untoe the west fide, a portion for Reuben.***

* The Buggre Alle This Bible was also noteworthy for having twenty-seven verses in the third chapter of Genesis, instead of the more usual twenty-four.

They followed verse 24, which in the King James version reads:

"So he drove out the man; and he placed at the east of the garden of Eden Cherubims, and a flaming sword which turned every way, to keep the way of the tree of life," and read:

> 25 And the Lord spake unto the Angel that guarded the eastern gate, *saying* Where is the flaming sword which was given unto thee?
>
> 26 And the Angel said, I had it here only a moment ago, I must have put *it* down some where, forget my own head next.
>
> 27 And the Lord did not ask him again.

It appears that these verses were inserted during the proof stage. In those days it was common practice for printers to hang proof sheets to the wooden beams outside their shops, for the edification of the populace and some free proofreading, and since the whole print run

Bilton and Scaggs's second great publishing disaster occurred in 1653. By a stroke of rare good fortune they had obtained one of the famed "Lost Quartos"—the three Shakespeare plays never reissued in Folio edition, and now totally lost to scholars and playgoers. Only their names have come down to us. This one was Shakespeare's earliest play, *The Comedie of Robin Hoode, or, The Forest of Sherwoode.**

Master Bilton had paid almost six guineas for the quarto, and believed he could make nearly twice that much back on the hardcover Folio alone.

Then he lost it.

Bilton and Scaggs's third great publishing disaster was never entirely comprehensible to either of them. Everywhere you looked, books of prophecy were selling like crazy. The English edition of Nostradamus' *Centuries* had just gone into its third printing, and five Nostradamuses, all claiming to be the only genuine one, were on triumphant signing tours. And Mother Shipton's *Collection of Prophecies* was sprinting out of the shops.

Each of the great London publishers—there were eight of them—had at least one Book of

---

was subsequently burned anyway, no one bothered to take up this matter with the nice Mr. A. Ziraphale, who ran the bookshop two doors along and was always so helpful with the translations, and whose handwriting was instantly recognizable.

* The other two are *The Trapping of the Mouse,* and *Golde Diggers of 1589.*

Prophecy on its list. Every single one of the books was wildly inaccurate, but their air of vague and generalized omnipotence made them immensely popular. They sold in the thousands, and in the tens of thousands.

"It is a licence to printe monney!" said Master Bilton to Master Scaggs.* **"The public are crying out for such rubbishe! We must straightway printe a booke of prophecie by some hagge!"**

The manuscript arrived at their door the next morning; the author's sense of timing, as always, was exact.

Although neither Master Bilton nor Master Scaggs realized it, the manuscript they had been sent was the sole prophetic work in all of human history to consist entirely of completely correct predictions concerning the following three hundred and forty-odd years, being a precise and accurate description of the events that would culminate in Armageddon. It was on the money in every single detail.

It was published by Bilton and Scaggs in September 1655, in good time for the Christmas trade,** and it was the first book printed in England to be remaindered.

It didn't sell.

* Who had already had a few thoughts in that direction, and spent the last years of his life in Newgate Prison when he eventually put them into practice.

** Another master stroke of publishing genius, because Oliver Cromwell's Puritan Parliament had made Christmas illegal in 1654.

Not even the copy in the tiny Lancashire shop with **"Localc Author"** on a piece of cardboard next to it.

The author of the book, one Agnes Nutter, was not surprised by this, but then, it would have taken an awful lot to surprise Agnes Nutter.

Anyway, she had not written it for the sales, or the royalties, or even for the fame. She had written it for the single gratis copy of the book that an author was entitled to.

No one knows what happened to the legions of unsold copies of her book. Certainly none remain in any museums or private collections. Even Aziraphale does not possess a copy, but would go weak at the knees at the thought of actually getting his exquisitely manicured hands on one.

In fact, only one copy of Agnes Nutter's prophecies remained in the entire world.

It was on a bookshelf about forty miles away from where Crowley and Aziraphale were enjoying a rather good lunch and, metaphorically, it had just begun to tick.

AND NOW IT WAS THREE O'CLOCK. The Antichrist had been on Earth for fifteen hours, and one angel and one demon had been drinking solidly for three of them.

They sat opposite one another in the back room of Aziraphale's dingy old bookshop in Soho.

Most bookshops in Soho have back rooms, and most of the back rooms are filled with rare, or at least very expensive, books. But Aziraphale's books didn't have illustrations. They had old brown covers and crackling pages. Occasionally, if he had no alternative, he'd sell one.

And, occasionally, serious men in dark suits would come calling and suggest, very politely, that perhaps he'd like to sell the shop itself so that it could be turned into the kind of retail outlet more suited to the area. Sometimes they'd offer cash, in large rolls of grubby fifty-pound notes. Or, sometimes, while they were talking, other men in dark glasses would wander around the shop shaking their heads and saying how inflammable paper was, and what a firetrap he had here.

And Aziraphale would nod and smile and say that he'd think about it. And then they'd go away. *And they'd never come back.*

Just because you're an angel doesn't mean you have to be a fool.

The table in front of the two of them was covered with bottles.

"The point is," said Crowley, "the point is. The point is." He tried to focus on Aziraphale.

"The point *is*," he said, and tried to think of a point.

"The point I'm trying to make," he said, brightening, "is the dolphins. That's my point."

"Kind of fish," said Aziraphale.

"Nononono," said Crowley, shaking a finger. " 'S mammal. Your actual mammal. Difference is—" Crowley waded through the swamp of his mind and tried to remember the difference. "Difference is, they—"

"Mate out of water?" volunteered Aziraphale.

Crowley's brow furrowed. "Don't think so. Pretty sure that's not it. Something about their young. Whatever." He pulled himself together. "The point is. The *point* is. Their brains."

He reached for a bottle.

"What about their brains?" said the angel.

"Big brains. That's my point. Size of. Size of. Size of damn big brains. And then there's the whales. Brain city, take it from me. Whole damn sea full of brains."

"Kraken," said Aziraphale, staring moodily into his glass.

Crowley gave him the long cool look of someone who has just had a girder dropped in front of his train of thought.

"Uh?"

"Great big bugger," said Aziraphale. "Sleepeth beneath the thunders of the upper deep. Under loads of huge and unnumbered polypol—polipo—bloody great seaweeds, you know. Supposed to rise to the surface right at the end, when the sea boils."

"Yeah?"

"Fact."

"There you are, then," said Crowley, sitting back. "Whole sea bubbling, poor old dolphins so much seafood gumbo, no one giving a damn. Same with gorillas. Whoops, they say, sky gone all red, stars crashing to ground, what they putting in the bananas these days? And then—"

"They make nests, you know, gorillas," said the angel, pouring another drink and managing to hit the glass on the third go.

"Nah."

"God's truth. Saw a film. Nests."

"That's birds," said Crowley.

"Nests," insisted Aziraphale.

Crowley decided not to argue the point.

"There you are then," he said. "All creatures great and smoke. I mean small. Great and small. Lot of them with brains. And then, bazamm."

"But *you're* part of it," said Aziraphale. "You tempt people. You're good at it."

Crowley thumped his glass on the table. "That's different. They don't have to say yes. That's the ineffable bit, right? Your side made it up. You've got to keep testing people. But not to destruction."

"All right. All right. I don't like it any more than you, but I told you. I can't disod—disoy—not do what I'm told. 'M a'nangel."

"There's no theaters in Heaven," said Crowley. "And very few films."

"Don't you try to tempt *me*," said Aziraphale wretchedly. "I know you, you old serpent."

"Just you think about it," said Crowley relentlessly. "You know what eternity is? You know what eternity is? I mean, d'you know what eternity is? There's this big mountain, see, a mile high, at the end of the universe, and once every thousand years there's this little bird—"

"What little bird?" said Aziraphale suspiciously.

"This little bird I'm talking about. And every thousand years—"

"The same bird every thousand years?"

Crowley hesitated. "Yeah," he said.

"Bloody ancient bird, then."

"Okay. And every thousand years this bird flies—"

"—limps—"

"—*flies* all the way to this mountain and sharpens its beak—"

"Hold *on*. You can't do that. Between here and the end of the universe there's loads of—" The angel waved a hand expansively, if a little unsteadily. "Loads of buggerall, dear boy."

"But it gets there anyway," Crowley persevered.

"How?"

"It doesn't matter!"

"It could use a spaceship," said the angel.

Crowley subsided a bit. "Yeah," he said. "If you like. Anyway, this bird—"

"Only it is the *end* of the universe we're talking about," said Aziraphale. "So it'd have to be one of those spaceships where your descendants are the ones who get out at the other end. You have to tell your descendants, you say, When you get to the Mountain, you've got to—" He hesitated. "What have they got to do?"

"Sharpen its beak on the mountain," said Crowley. "And then it flies back—"

"—in the spaceship—"

"And after a thousand years it goes and does it all again," said Crowley quickly.

There was a moment of drunken silence.

"Seems a lot of effort just to sharpen a beak," mused Aziraphale.

"Listen," said Crowley urgently, "the point is that when the bird has worn the mountain down to nothing, right, then—"

Aziraphale opened his mouth. Crowley just *knew* he was going to make some point about the relative hardness of birds' beaks and granite mountains, and plunged on quickly.

"—then *you still won't have finished watching The Sound of Music.*"

Aziraphale froze.

"And you'll *enjoy* it," Crowley said relentlessly. "You really will."

"My dear boy—"

"You won't have a choice."

"Listen—"

"Heaven has no taste."

"Now—"

"And not one single sushi restaurant."

A look of pain crossed the angel's suddenly very serious face.

"I can't cope with this while 'm drunk," he said. "I'm going to sober up."

"Me too."

They both winced as the alcohol left their bloodstreams, and sat up a bit more neatly. Aziraphale straightened his tie.

"I can't interfere with divine plans," he croaked.

Crowley looked speculatively into his glass, and then filled it again.

"What about diabolical ones?" he said.

"Pardon?"

"Well, it's got to be a diabolical plan, hasn't it? *We're* doing it. My side."

"Ah, but it's all part of the overall *divine* plan," said Aziraphale. "Your side can't do anything without it being part of the ineffable divine plan," he added, with a trace of smugness.

"You wish!"

"No, that's the—" Aziraphale snapped his fingers irritably. "The thing. What d'you call it in your colorful idiom? The line at the bottom."

"The bottom line."

"Yes. It's that."

"Well . . . if you're sure . . ." said Crowley.

"No doubt about it."

Crowley looked up slyly.

"Then you can't be certain, correct me if I'm wrong, you can't be certain that thwarting it isn't part of the divine plan too. I mean, you're supposed to thwart the wiles of the Evil One at every turn, aren't you?"

Aziraphale hesitated.

"There is that, yes."

"You see a wile, you thwart. Am I right?"

"Broadly, broadly. Actually I encourage humans to do the actual thwarting. Because of ineffability, you understand."

"Right. Right. So all you've got to do is thwart. Because if I know anything," said Crowley urgently, "it's that the birth is just the start. It's the upbringing that's important. It's the Influences. Otherwise the child will never learn to use its powers." He hesitated. "At least, not necessarily as intended."

"Certainly our side won't mind me thwarting you," said Aziraphale thoughtfully. "They won't mind that at all."

"Right. It'd be a real feather in your wing." Crowley gave the angel an encouraging smile.

"What will happen to the child if it doesn't get a Satanic upbringing, though?" said Aziraphale.

"Probably nothing. It'll never know."

"But genetics—"

"Don't tell me from genetics. What've they got to do with it?" said Crowley. "Look at Satan. Created as an angel, grows up to be the Great Adversary. Hey, if you're going to go on about genetics, you might as well say the kid will grow up to be an angel. After all, his father was really big in Heaven in the old days. Saying he'll grow up to be a demon just because his dad *became* one is like saying a mouse with its tail cut off will give birth to tailless mice. No. Upbringing is everything. Take it from me."

"And without unopposed Satanic influences—"

"Well, at worst Hell will have to start all over again. And the Earth gets at least another eleven years. That's got to be worth something, hasn't it?"

Now Aziraphale was looking thoughtful again.

"You're saying the child isn't evil of itself?" he said slowly.

"*Potentially* evil. Potentially good, too, I suppose. Just this huge powerful *potentiality*, waiting to be shaped," said Crowley. He shrugged. "Anyway, why're we talking about this *good* and *evil*? They're just names for sides. *We* know that."

"I suppose it's got to be worth a try," said the angel. Crowley nodded encouragingly.

"Agreed?" said the demon, holding out his hand.

The angel shook it, cautiously.

"It'll certainly be more interesting than saints," he said.

"And it'll be for the child's own good, in the long run," said Crowley. "We'll be godfathers, sort of. Overseeing his religious upbringing, you might say."

Aziraphale beamed.

"You know, I'd never have thought of that," he said. "*Godfathers*. Well, I'll be damned."

"It's not too bad," said Crowley, "when you get used to it."

SHE WAS KNOWN AS SCARLETT. At that time she was selling arms, although it was beginning to lose its savor. She never stuck at one job for very long. Three, four hundred years at the outside. You didn't want to get in a rut.

Her hair was true auburn, neither ginger nor brown, but a deep and burnished copper color, and it fell to her waist in tresses that men would kill for, and indeed often had. Her eyes were a startling orange. She looked twenty-five, and always had.

She had a dusty, brick-red truck full of assorted weaponry, and an almost unbelievable skill at getting it across any border in the world. She had been on her way to a small West African country, where a minor civil war was in progress, to make a delivery which would, with any luck, turn it into a major civil war. Unfortunately the truck had broken down, far beyond even her ability to repair it.

And she was very good with machinery these days.

She was in the middle of a city* at the time. The city in question was the capital of Kumbolaland, an African nation which had been at peace for the last

* Nominally a city. It was the size of an English county town, or, translated into American terms, a shopping mall.

three thousand years. For about thirty years it was Sir-Humphrey-Clarksonland, but since the country had absolutely no mineral wealth and the strategic importance of a banana, it was accelerated toward self-government with almost unseemly haste. Kumbolaland was poor, perhaps, and undoubtedly boring, but peaceful. Its various tribes, who got along with one another quite happily, had long since beaten their swords into ploughshares; a fight had broken out in the city square in 1952 between a drunken ox-drover and an equally drunken ox-thief. People were still talking about it.

Scarlett yawned in the heat. She fanned her head with her broad-brimmed hat, left the useless truck in the dusty street, and wandered into a bar.

She bought a can of beer, drained it, then grinned at the barman. "I got a truck needs repairing," she said. "Anyone around I can talk to?"

The barman grinned white and huge and expansively. He'd been impressed by the way she drank her beer. "Only Nathan, miss. But Nathan has gone back to Kaounda to see his father-in-law's farm."

Scarlett bought another beer. "So, this Nathan. Any idea when he'll be back?"

"Perhaps next week. Perhaps two weeks' time, dear lady. Ho, that Nathan, he is a scamp, no?"

He leaned forward.

"You traveling alone, miss?" he said.

"Yes."

"Could be dangerous. Some funny people on the roads these days. Bad men. Not *local* boys," he added quickly.

Scarlett raised a perfect eyebrow.

Despite the heat, he shivered.

"Thanks for the warning," Scarlett purred. Her voice sounded like something that lurks in the long grass, visible only by the twitching of its ears, until something young and tender wobbles by.

She tipped her hat to him, and strolled outside.

The hot African sun beat down on her; her truck sat in the street with a cargo of guns and ammunition and land mines. It wasn't going anywhere.

Scarlett stared at the truck.

A vulture was sitting on its roof. It had traveled three hundred miles with Scarlett so far. It was belching quietly.

She looked around the street: a couple of women chatted on a street corner; a bored market vendor sat in front of a heap of colored gourds, fanning the flies; a few children played lazily in the dust.

"What the hell," she said quietly. "I could do with a holiday anyway."

That was Wednesday.

By Friday the city was a no-go area.

By the following Tuesday the economy of Kumbolaland was shattered, twenty thousand people were dead (including the barman, shot by the rebels while storming the market barricades), almost a hundred thousand people were injured, all of Scarlett's assorted weapons had fulfilled the function for which they had been created, and the vulture had died of fatty degeneration.

Scarlett was already on the last train out of the country. It was time to move on, she felt. She'd been doing arms for too damn long. She wanted a change. Something with openings. She quite fancied herself as a newspaper journalist. A possibility. She fanned herself with her hat, and crossed her long legs in front of her.

Farther down the train a fight broke out. Scarlett grinned. People were always fighting, over her, and around her; it was rather sweet, really.

SABLE HAD BLACK HAIR, a trim black beard, and he had just decided to go corporate.

He did drinks with his accountant.

"How we doing, Frannie?" he asked her.

"Twelve million copies sold so far. Can you believe that?"

They were doing drinks in a restaurant called Top of the Sixes, on the top of 666 Fifth Avenue, New York. This was something that amused Sable ever so slightly. From the restaurant windows you could see the whole of New York; at night, the rest of New York could see the huge red 666s that adorned all four sides of the building. Of course, it was just another street number. If you started counting, you'd be bound to get to it eventually. But you had to smile.

Sable and his accountant had just come from a small, expensive, and particularly exclusive restaurant in Greenwich Village, where the cuisine was entirely *nouvelle:* a string bean, a pea, and a sliver of chicken breast, aesthetically arranged on a square china plate.

Sable had invented it the last time he'd been in Paris.

His accountant had polished her meat and two

veg off in under fifty seconds, and had spent the rest of the meal staring at the plate, the cutlery, and from time to time at her fellow diners, in a manner that suggested that she was wondering what they'd taste like, which was in fact the case. It had amused Sable enormously.

He toyed with his Perrier.

"Twelve million, huh? That's pretty good."

"That's *great.*"

"So we're going corporate. It's time to blow the big one, am I right? California, I think. I want factories, restaurants, the whole schmear. We'll keep the publishing arm, but it's time to diversify. Yeah?"

Frannie nodded. "Sounds good, Sable. We'll need—"

She was interrupted by a skeleton. A skeleton in a Dior dress, with tanned skin stretched almost to snapping point over the delicate bones of the skull. The skeleton had long blond hair and perfectly made-up lips: she looked like the person mothers around the world point to, muttering, "*That*'s what'll happen to you if you don't eat your greens"; she looked like a famine-relief poster with style.

She was New York's top fashion model, and she was holding a book. She said, "Uh, excuse me, Mr. Sable, I hope you don't mind me intruding, but, your book, it changed my life, I was wondering, would you mind signing it for me?" She stared imploringly at him with eyes deep-sunk in gloriously eyeshadowed sockets.

Sable nodded graciously, and took the book from her.

It was not surprising that she had recognized him,

for his dark gray eyes stared out from his photo on the foil-embossed cover. *Foodless Dieting: Slim Yourself Beautiful*, the book was called. *The Diet Book of the Century!*

"How do you spell your name?" he asked.

"Sherryl. Two Rs, one Y, one L."

"You remind me of an old, old friend," he told her, as he wrote swiftly and carefully on the title page. "There you go. Glad you liked it. Always good to meet a fan."

What he'd written was this:

Sherryl,

A measure of wheat for a penny, and three measures of barley for a penny, and see thou hurt not the oil and the wine.

Rev. 6:6.

Dr. Raven Sable.

"It's from the Bible," he told her.

She closed the book reverently and backed away from the table, thanking Sable, he didn't know how much this meant to her, he had changed her life, truly he had. . . .

He had never actually earned the medical degree he claimed, since there hadn't been any universities in those days, but Sable could see she was starving to death. He gave her a couple of months at the outside. *Foodless.* Handle your weight problem, terminally.

Frannie was stabbing at her laptop computer hungrily, planning the next phase in Sable's transformation of the eating habits of the Western World.

Sable had bought her the machine as a personal present. It was very, very expensive, very powerful, and ultra-slim. He liked slim things.

"There's a European outfit we can buy into for the initial toehold—Holdings (Holdings) Incorporated. That'll give us the Liechtenstein tax base. Now, if we channel funds out through the Caymans, into Luxembourg, and from there to Switzerland, we could pay for the factories in . . ."

But Sable was no longer listening. He was remembering the exclusive little restaurant. It had occurred to him that he had never seen so many rich people so hungry.

Sable grinned, the honest, open grin that goes with job satisfaction, perfect and pure. He was just killing time until the main event, but he was killing it in such exquisite ways. Time, and sometimes people.

SOMETIMES HE WAS called White, or Blanc, or Albus, or Chalky, or Weiss, or Snowy, or any one of a hundred other names. His skin was pale, his hair a faded blond, his eyes light gray. He was somewhere in his twenties at a casual glance, and a casual glance was all anyone ever gave him.

He was almost entirely unmemorable.

Unlike his two colleagues, he could never settle down in any one job for very long.

He had had all manner of interesting jobs in lots of interesting places.

(He had worked at the Chernobyl Power Station,

and at Windscale, and at Three Mile Island, always in minor jobs that weren't very important.)

He had been a minor but valued member of a number of scientific research establishments.

(He had helped to design the petrol engine, and plastics, and the ring-pull can.)

He could turn his hand to anything.

Nobody really noticed him. He was unobtrusive; his presence was cumulative. If you thought about it carefully, you could figure out he had to have been doing something, had to have been somewhere. Maybe he even spoke to you. But he was easy to forget, was Mr. White.

At this time he was working as deckhand on an oil tanker, heading toward Tokyo.

The captain was drunk in his cabin. The first mate was in the head. The second mate was in the galley. That was pretty much it for the crew: the ship was almost completely automated. There wasn't much a person could do.

However, if a person just happened to press the EMERGENCY CARGO RELEASE switch on the bridge, the automatic systems would take care of releasing huge quantities of black sludge into the sea, millions of tons of crude oil, with devastating effect on the birds, fish, vegetation, animals, and humans of the region. Of course, there were dozens of fail-safe interlocks and foolproof safety backups but, what the hell, there always were.

Afterwards, there was a huge amount of argument as to exactly whose fault it was. In the end it was left unresolved: the blame was apportioned equally. Neither the captain, the first mate, nor the second mate ever worked again.

For some reason nobody gave much of a thought to Seaman White, who was already halfway to Indonesia on a tramp steamer piled high with rusting metal barrels of a particularly toxic weedkiller.

AND THERE WAS ANOTHER. He was in the square in Kumbolaland. And he was in the restaurants. And he was in the fish, and in the air, and in the barrels of weedkiller. He was on the roads, and in houses, and in palaces, and in hovels.

There was nowhere that he was a stranger, and there was no getting away from him. He was doing what he did best, and what he was doing was what he was.

He was not waiting. He was working.

HARRIET DOWLING returned home with her baby, which, on the advice of Sister Faith Prolix, who was more persuasive than Sister Mary, and with the telephonic agreement of her husband, she had named Warlock.

The Cultural Attaché returned home a week later, and pronounced the baby the spit of his side of the family. He also had his secretary advertise in *The Lady* for a nanny.

Crowley had seen *Mary Poppins* on television one Christmas (indeed, behind the scenes, Crowley had had a hand in most television; although it was on the invention of the game show that he truly prided himself). He toyed with the idea of a hurricane as an effective and incredibly stylish way of disposing of the queue of nannies that would certainly form, or possibly stack up in a holding pattern, outside the Cultural Attaché's Regent's Park residence.

He contented himself with a wildcat tube strike, and when the day came, only one nanny turned up.

She wore a knit tweed suit and discreet pearl earrings. Something about her might have said *nanny*, but it said it in an undertone of the sort employed by British butlers in a certain type of American film. It also coughed discreetly and muttered that she could well be the sort of nanny who advertises unspecified but strangely explicit services in certain magazines.

Her flat shoes crunched up the gravel drive, and a gray dog padded silently by her side, white flecks of saliva dripping from its jaw. Its eyes glinted scarlet, and it glanced from side to side hungrily.

She reached the heavy wooden door, smiled to herself, a brief satisfied flicker, and rang the bell. It *donged* gloomily.

The door was opened by a butler, as they say, of the old school.*

"I am Nanny Ashtoreth," she told him. "And this," she continued, while the gray dog at her side eyed the butler carefully, working out, perhaps, where it would bury the bones, "is Rover."

She left the dog in the garden, and passed her

* A night school just off the Tottenham Court Road, run by an elderly actor who had played butlers and gentlemen's gentlemen in films and television and on the stage since the 1920s.

interview with flying colors, and Mrs. Dowling led the nanny to see her new charge.

She smiled unpleasantly. "What a delightful child," she said. "He'll be wanting a little tricycle soon."

By one of those coincidences, another new member of staff arrived the same afternoon. He was the gardener, and as it turned out he was amazingly good at his job. No one quite worked out why this should be the case, since he never seemed to pick up a shovel and made no effort to rid the garden of the sudden flocks of birds that filled it and settled all over him at every opportunity. He just sat in the shade while around him the residence gardens bloomed and bloomed.

Warlock used to come down to see him, when he was old enough to toddle and Nanny was doing whatever it was she did on her afternoons off.

"This here's Brother Slug," the gardener would tell him, "and this tiny little critter is Sister Potato Weevil. Remember, Warlock, as you walk your way through the highways and byways of life's rich and fulsome path, to have love and reverence for all living things."

"Nanny says that wivving fings is fit onwy to be gwound under my heels, Mr. Fwancis," said little Warlock, stroking Brother Slug, and then wiping his hand conscientiously on his Kermit the Frog overall.

"You don't listen to that woman," Francis would say. "You listen to me."

At night, Nanny Ashtoreth sang nursery rhymes to Warlock.

Oh, the grand old Duke of York
He had Ten Thousand Men
He Marched them Up To The Top of The Hill
And Crushed all the nations of the world and brought them under the rule of Satan our master.

and

This little piggy went to Hades
This little piggy stayed home
This little piggy ate raw and steaming human flesh
This little piggy violated virgins
And this little piggy clambered over a heap of dead bodies toget to the top.

"Bwuvver Fwancis the gardener says that I mus' selfwesswy pwactice virtue an' wuv to all wivving fings," said Warlock.

"You don't listen to that *man*, darling," the nanny would whisper, as she tucked him into his little bed. "You listen to me."

And so it went.

The Arrangement worked perfectly. A no-score win. Nanny Ashtoreth bought the child a little tricycle, but could never persuade him to ride it inside the house. And he was scared of Rover.

In the background Crowley and Aziraphale met on the tops of buses, and in art galleries, and at concerts, compared notes, and smiled.

When Warlock was six, his nanny left, taking Rover with her; the gardener handed in his resignation on the same day. Neither of them left with quite the same spring in their step with which they'd arrived.

Warlock now found himself being educated by two tutors.

Mr. Harrison taught him about Attila the Hun, Vlad Drakul, and the Darkness Intrinsicate in the Human Spirit.* He tried to teach Warlock how to make rabble-rousing political speeches to sway the hearts and minds of multitudes.

Mr. Cortese taught him about Florence Nightingale,** Abraham Lincoln, and the appreciation of art. He tried to teach him about free will, self-denial, and Doing unto Others as You Would Wish Them to Do to You.

They both read to the child extensively from the Book of Revelation.

Despite their best efforts Warlock showed a regrettable tendency to be good at maths. Neither of his tutors was entirely satisfied with his progress.

When Warlock was ten he liked baseball; he liked plastic toys that transformed into other plastic toys indistinguishable from the first set of plastic toys except to the trained eye; he liked his stamp collection; he liked banana-flavor bubble gum; he liked comics and cartoons and his B.M.X. bike.

Crowley was troubled.

They were in the cafeteria of the British Mu-

* He avoided mentioning that Attila was nice to his mother, or that Vlad Drakul was punctilious about saying his prayers every day.

** Except for the bits about syphilis.

seum, another refuge for all weary foot soldiers of the Cold War. At the table to their left two ramrod-straight Americans in suits were surreptitiously handing over a briefcase full of deniable dollars to a small dark woman in sunglasses; at the table on their right the deputy head of MI7 and the local KGB section officer argued over who got to keep the receipt for the tea and buns.

Crowley finally said what he had not even dared to think for the last decade.

"If you ask me," Crowley said to his counterpart, "he's too bloody *normal.*"

Aziraphale popped another deviled egg into his mouth, and washed it down with coffee. He dabbed his lips with a paper napkin.

"It's my good influence," he beamed. "Or rather, credit where credit's due, that of my little team."

Crowley shook his head. "I'm taking that into account. Look—by now he should be trying to warp the world around him to his own desires, shaping it in his own image, that kind of stuff. Well, not actually *trying*. He'll do it without even knowing it. Have you seen *any* evidence of that happening?"

"Well, no, but . . ."

"By now he should be a powerhouse of raw force. Is he?"

"Well, not as far as I've noticed, but . . ."

"He's too normal." Crowley drummed his fingers on the table. "I don't like it. There's something wrong. I just can't put my finger on it."

Aziraphale helped himself to Crowley's slice of angel cake. "Well, he's a growing boy. And, of course, there's been the heavenly influence in his life."

Crowley sighed. "I just hope he'll know how to cope with the hell-hound, that's all."

Aziraphale raised one eyebrow. "Hell-hound?"

"On his eleventh birthday. I received a message from Hell last night." The message had come during "The Golden Girls," one of Crowley's favorite television programs. Rose had taken ten minutes to deliver what could have been quite a brief communication, and by the time non-infernal service was restored Crowley had quite lost the thread of the plot. "They're sending him a hell-hound, to pad by his side and guard him from all harm. Biggest one they've got."

"Won't people remark on the sudden appearance of a huge black dog? His parents, for a start."

Crowley stood up suddenly, treading on the foot of a Bulgarian cultural attaché, who was talking animatedly to the Keeper of Her Majesty's Antiques. "Nobody's going to notice *anything* out of the ordinary. It's reality, angel. And young Warlock can do what he wants to *that*, whether he knows it or not."

"When does it turn up, then? This dog? Does it have a name?"

"I told you. On his eleventh birthday. At three o'clock in the afternoon. It'll sort of home in on him. He's supposed to name it himself. It's very important that he names it himself. It gives it its purpose. It'll be Killer, or Terror, or Stalks-by-Night, I expect."

"Are you going to be there?" asked the angel, nonchalantly.

"Wouldn't miss it for the worlds," said Crowley. "I do hope there's nothing *too* wrong with the child.

We'll see how he reacts to the dog, anyway. That should tell us something. I *hope* he'll send it back, or be frightened of it. If he *does* name it, we've lost. He'll have all his powers and Armageddon is just around the corner."

"I think," said Aziraphale, sipping his wine (which had just ceased to be a slightly vinegary Beaujolais, and had become a quite acceptable, but rather surprised, Château Lafite 1875), "I think I'll see you there."

WEDNESDAY

IT WAS A HOT, fume-filled August day in Central London.

Warlock's eleventh birthday was very well attended.

There were twenty small boys and seventeen small girls. There were a lot of men with identical blond crew cuts, dark blue suits, and shoulder holsters. There was a crew of caterers, who had arrived bearing jellies, cakes, and bowls of crisps. Their procession of vans was led by a vintage Bentley.

The Amazing Harvey and Wanda, Children's Parties a Specialty, had both been struck down by an unexpected tummy bug, but by a providential turn of fortune a replacement had turned up, practically out of the blue. A stage magician.

Everyone has his little hobby. Despite Crowley's urgent advice, Aziraphale was intending to turn his to good use.

Aziraphale was particularly proud of his magical skills. He had attended a class in the 1870s run by John Maskelyne, and had spent almost a year practicing sleight of hand, palming coins, and taking rabbits out of hats. He had got, he had felt at the time, quite good at it. The point was that although

Aziraphale was capable of doing things that could make the entire Magic Circle hand in their wands, he never applied what might be called his *intrinsic* powers to the practice of sleight-of-hand conjuring. Which was a major drawback. He was beginning to wish that he'd continued practicing.

Still, he mused, it was like riding a velocipede. You never forgot how. His magician's coat had been a little dusty, but it felt good once it was on. Even his old patter began to come back to him.

The children watched him in blank, disdainful incomprehension. Behind the buffet Crowley, in his white waiter's coat, cringed with contact embarrassment.

"Now then, young masters and mistresses, do you see my battered old top hat? What a shocking bad hat, as you young 'uns do say! And see, there's nothing in it. But bless my britches, who's this rum customer? Why, it's our furry friend, Harry the rabbit!"

"It was in your pocket," pointed out Warlock. The other children nodded agreement. What did he think they were? Kids?

Aziraphale remembered what Maskelyne had told him about dealing with hecklers. "Make a joke of it, you pudding-heads—and I do mean you, Mr. Fell" (the name Aziraphale had adopted at that time). "Make 'em laugh, and they'll forgive you anything!"

"Ho, so you've rumbled my *hat trick*," he chuckled. The children stared at him impassively.

"You're rubbish," said Warlock. "I wanted cartoons anyway."

"He's right, you know," agreed a small girl with a ponytail. "You *are* rubbish. And probably a faggot."

Aziraphale stared desperately at Crowley. As far as he was concerned young Warlock was obviously infernally tainted, and the sooner the Black Dog turned up and they could get away from this place, the better.

"Now, do any of you young 'uns have such a thing as a thrup-penny bit about your persons? No, young master? Then what's this I see behind your ear . . . ?"

"I got cartoons at *my* birthday," announced the little girl. "An I gotter transformer anna mylittle-pony anna decepticonattacker anna thundertank anna . . ."

Crowley groaned. Children's parties were obviously places where any angel with an ounce of common sense should fear to tread. Piping infant voices were raised in cynical merriment as Aziraphale dropped three linked metal rings.

Crowley looked away, and his gaze fell on a table heaped high with presents. From a tall plastic structure two beady little eyes stared back at him.

Crowley scrutinized them for a glint of red fire. You could never be certain when you were dealing with the bureaucrats of Hell. It was always possible that they had sent a gerbil instead of a dog.

No, it was a perfectly normal gerbil. It appeared to be living in an exciting construction of cylinders, spheres, and treadmills, such as the Spanish Inquisition would have devised if they'd had access to a plastics molding press.

He checked his watch. It had never occurred to

Crowley to change its battery, which had rotted away three years previously, but it still kept perfect time. It was two minutes to three.

Aziraphale was getting more and more flustered.

"Do any of the company here assembled possess such a thing about their persons as a pocket handkerchief? *No?*" In Victorian days it had been unheard of for people not to carry handkerchiefs, and the trick, which involved magically producing a dove who was even now pecking irritably at Aziraphale's wrist, could not proceed without one. The angel tried to attract Crowley's attention, failed, and, in desperation, pointed to one of the security guards, who shifted uneasily.

"You, my fine jack-sauce. Come here. Now, if you inspect your breast pocket, I *think* you might find a fine silk handkerchief."

"Nossir. 'Mafraidnotsir," said the guard, staring straight ahead.

Aziraphale winked desperately. "No, go on, dear boy, take a look, *please.*"

The guard reached a hand inside his inside pocket, looked surprised, and pulled out a handkerchief, duck-egg-blue silk, with lace edging. Aziraphale realized almost immediately that the lace had been a mistake, as it caught on the guard's holstered gun, and sent it spinning across the room to land heavily in a bowl of jelly.

The children applauded spasmodically. "Hey, not bad!" said the ponytailed girl.

Warlock had already run across the room, and grabbed the gun.

"Hands up, dogbreaths!" he shouted gleefully.

The security guards were in a quandary.

Some of them fumbled for their own weapons; others started edging their way toward, or away from, the boy. The other children started complaining that they wanted guns as well, and a few of the more forward ones started trying to tug them from the guards who had been thoughtless enough to take their weapons out.

Then someone threw some jelly at Warlock.

The boy squeaked, and pulled the trigger of the gun. It was a Magnum .32, CIA issue, gray, mean, heavy, capable of blowing a man away at thirty paces, and leaving nothing more than a red mist, a ghastly mess, and a certain amount of paperwork.

Aziraphale blinked.

A thin stream of water squirted from the nozzle and soaked Crowley, who had been looking out the window, trying to see if there was a huge black dog in the garden.

Aziraphale looked embarrassed.

Then a cream cake hit him in the face.

It was almost five past three.

With a gesture, Aziraphale turned the rest of the guns into water pistols as well, and walked out.

Crowley found him on the pavement outside, trying to extricate a rather squishy dove from the arm of his frock coat.

"It's late," said Aziraphale.

"I can see that," said Crowley. "Comes of sticking it up your sleeve." He reached out and pulled the limp bird from Aziraphale's coat, and breathed life back into it. The dove cooed appreciatively and flew off, a trifle warily.

"Not the bird," said the angel. "The dog. It's late."

Crowley shook his head, thoughtfully. "We'll see."

He opened the car door, flipped on the radio. *I-should-be-so-lucky-lucky-lucky-lucky-lucky, I-should-be-so-lucky-in- HELLO CROWLEY.*

"Hello. Um, who is this?"

DAGON, LORD OF THE FILES, MASTER OF MADNESS, UNDER-DUKE OF THE SEVENTH TORMENT. WHAT CAN I DO FOR YOU?

"The hell-hound. I'm just, uh, just checking that it got off okay."

RELEASED TEN MINUTES AGO. WHY? HASN'T IT ARRIVED? IS SOMETHING WRONG?

"Oh no. Nothing's wrong. Everything's fine. Oops, I can see it now. Good dog. *Nice* dog. Everything's terrific. You're doing a great job down there, people. Well, lovely talking to you, Dagon. Catch you soon, huh?"

He flipped off the radio.

They stared at each other. There was a loud bang from inside the house, and a window shattered. "Oh dear," muttered Aziraphale, not swearing with the practiced ease of one who has spent six thousand years not swearing, and who wasn't going to start now. "I must have missed one."

"No dog," said Crowley.

"No dog," said Aziraphale.

The demon sighed. "Get in the car," he said. "We've got to talk about this. Oh, and Aziraphale . . . ?"

"Yes."

"Clean off that blasted cream cake before you get in."

IT WAS A HOT, silent August day far from Central London. By the side of the Tadfield road the dust weighed down the hogweed. Bees buzzed in the hedges. The air had a leftover and reheated feel.

There was a sound like a thousand metal voices shouting "Hail!" cut off abruptly.

And there was a black dog in the road.

It had to be a dog. It was dog-shaped.

There are some dogs which, when you meet them, remind you that, despite thousands of years of man-made evolution, every dog is still only two meals away from being a wolf. These dogs advance deliberately, purposefully, the wilderness made flesh, their teeth yellow, their breath a-stink, while in the distance their owners twitter, "He's an old soppy really, just poke him if he's a nuisance," and in the green of their eyes the red campfires of the Pleistocene gleam and flicker. . . .

This dog would make even a dog like that slink nonchalantly behind the sofa and pretend to be extremely preoccupied with its rubber bone.

It was already growling, and the growl was a low, rumbling snarl of spring-coiled menace, the sort of growl that starts in the back of one throat and ends up in someone else's.

Saliva dripped from its jaws and sizzled on the tar.

It took a few steps forward, and sniffed the sullen air.

Its ears flicked up.

There were voices, a long way off. *A* voice. A boyish voice, but one it had been created to obey, could not *help* but obey. When that voice said "Follow," it would follow; when it said "Kill," it would kill. His master's voice.

It leapt the hedge and padded across the field beyond. A grazing bull eyed it for a moment, weighed its chances, then strolled hurriedly toward the opposite hedge.

The voices were coming from a copse of straggly trees. The black hound slunk closer, jaws streaming.

One of the other voices said: "He never will. You're always saying he will, and he never does. Catch your dad giving you a pet. An int'restin' pet, anyway. It'll prob'ly be stick insects. That's your dad's idea of int'restin'."

The hound gave the canine equivalent of a shrug, but immediately lost interest because now the Master, the Center of its Universe, spoke.

"It'll be a dog," it said.

"Huh. You don't *know* it's going to be a dog. No one's *said* it's going to be a dog. How d'you know it's goin' to be a dog if no one's *said*? Your dad'd be complaining about the food it eats the whole time."

"Privet." This third voice was rather more prim than the first two. The owner of a voice like that would be the sort of person who, before making a plastic model kit, would not only separate and count all the parts before commencing, as per the instructions, but also paint the bits that needed painting first and leave them to dry properly prior to construction. All that separated this voice from chartered accountancy was a matter of time.

"They don't eat privet, Wensley. You never saw a dog eatin' privet."

"Stick insects do, I mean. They're jolly interesting, actually. They eat each other when they're mating."

There was a thoughtful pause. The hound slunk closer, and realized that the voices were coming from a hole in the ground.

The trees in fact concealed an ancient chalk quarry, now half overgrown with thorn trees and vines. Ancient, but clearly not disused. Tracks crisscrossed it; smooth areas of slope indicated regular use by skateboards and Wall-of-Death, or at least Wall-of-Seriously-Grazed-Knee, cyclists. Old bits of dangerously frayed rope hung from some of the more accessible greenery. Here and there sheets of corrugated iron and old wooden boards were wedged in branches. A burnt-out, rusting Triumph Herald Estate was visible, half-submerged in a drift of nettles.

In one corner a tangle of wheels and corroded wire marked the site of the famous Lost Graveyard where the supermarket trolleys came to die.

If you were a child, it was paradise. The local adults called it The Pit.

The hound peered through a clump of nettles, and spotted four figures sitting in the center of the quarry on that indispensible prop to good secret dens everywhere, the common milk crate.

"They don't!"

"They do."

"Bet you they don't," said the first speaker. It had a certain timbre to it that identified it as young and female, and it was tinted with horrified fascination.

"They do, *actually*. I had six before we went on holiday and I forgot to change the privet and when I came back I had one big fat one."

"Nah. That's not stick insects, that's praying mantises. I saw on the television where this big female one ate this other one and it dint hardly take any notice."

There was another crowded pause.

"What're they prayin' about?" said his Master's voice.

"Dunno. Prayin' they don't have to get married, I s'pect."

The hound managed to get one huge eye against an empty knothole in the quarry's broken-down fence, and squinted downward.

"Anyway, it's like with bikes," said the first speaker authoritatively. "*I* thought I was going to get this bike with seven gears and one of them razorblade saddles and purple paint and everything, and they gave me this light blue one. With a basket. A *girl's* bike."

"Well. You're a girl," said one of the others.

"That's *sexism*, that is. Going around giving people girly presents just because they're a girl."

"*I'm* going to get a dog," said his Master's voice, firmly. His Master had his back to him; the hound couldn't quite make out his features.

"Oh, yeah, one of those great big Rottenweilers, yeah?" said the girl, with withering sarcasm.

"No, it's going to be the kind of dog you can have fun with," said his Master's voice. "Not a big dog—"

—the eye in the nettles vanished abruptly downwards—

"—but one of those dogs that's brilliantly intelligent and can go down rabbit holes and has one funny ear that always looks inside out. And a proper mongrel, too. A *pedigree* mongrel."

Unheard by those within, there was a tiny clap of thunder on the lip of the quarry. It might have been caused by the sudden rushing of air into the vacuum caused by a very large dog becoming, for example, a small dog.

The tiny popping noise that followed might have been caused by one ear turning itself inside out.

"And I'll call him . . ." said his Master's voice. "I'll call him . . ."

"Yes?" said the girl. "What're you goin' to call it?"

The hound waited. This was the moment. The Naming. This would give it its purpose, its function, its identity. Its eyes glowed a dull red, even though they were a lot closer to the ground, and it dribbled into the nettles.

"I'll call him Dog," said his Master, positively. "It saves a lot of trouble, a name like that."

The hell-hound paused. Deep in its diabolical canine brain it knew that something was wrong, but it was nothing if not obedient and its great sudden love of its Master overcame all misgivings. Who was it to say what size it should be, anyway?

It trotted down the slope to meet its destiny.

Strange, though. It had always wanted to jump

up at people but, now, it realized that against all expectation it wanted to wag its tail at the same time.

"YOU SAID IT WAS HIM!" moaned Aziraphale, abstractedly picking the final lump of cream cake from his lapel. He licked his fingers clean.

"It *was* him," said Crowley. "I mean, I should know, shouldn't I?"

"Then someone else must be interfering."

"There isn't anyone else! There's just us, right? Good and Evil. One side or the other."

He thumped the steering wheel.

"You'll be amazed at the kind of things they can do to you, down there," he said.

"I imagine they're very similar to the sort of things they can do to one up there," said Aziraphale.

"Come off it. Your lot get ineffable mercy," said Crowley sourly.

"Yes? Did you ever visit Gomorrah?"

"Sure," said the demon. "There was this great little tavern where you could get these terrific fermented date-palm cocktails with nutmeg and crushed lemongrass—"

"I meant afterwards."

"Oh."

Aziraphale said: "Something must have happened in the hospital."

"It couldn't have! It was full of our people!"

"Whose people?" said Aziraphale coldly.

"My people," corrected Crowley. "Well, not *my* people. Mmm, you know. Satanists."

He tried to say it dismissively. Apart from, of

course, the fact that the world was an amazing interesting place which they both wanted to enjoy for as long as possible, there were few things that the two of them agreed on, but they did see eye to eye about some of those people who, for one reason or another, were inclined to worship the Prince of Darkness. Crowley always found them embarrassing. You couldn't actually be rude to them, but you couldn't help feeling about them the same way that, say, a Vietnam veteran would feel about someone who wears combat gear to Neighborhood Watch meetings.

Besides, they were always so depressingly enthusiastic. Take all that stuff with the inverted crosses and pentagrams and cockerels. It mystified most demons. It wasn't the least bit necessary. All you needed to become a Satanist was an effort of will. You could be one all your life without ever knowing what a pentagram *was*, without ever seeing a dead cockerel other than as Chicken Marengo.

Besides, some of the old-style Satanists tended, in fact, to be quite nice people. They mouthed the words and went through the motions, just like the people they thought of as their opposite numbers, and then went home and lived lives of mild unassuming mediocrity for the rest of the week with never an unusually evil thought in their heads.

And as for the rest of it . . .

There were people who called themselves Satanists who made Crowley squirm. It wasn't just the things they did, it was the way they blamed it all on Hell. They'd come up with some stomach-churning idea that no demon could have thought of in a thousand years, some dark and mindless unpleasantness that only a fully functioning human brain could conceive, then shout "The Devil Made Me Do It" and get the sympathy of the court when the whole point was that the Devil hardly ever made anyone do anything. He didn't have to. That was what some humans found hard to understand. Hell wasn't a major reservoir of evil, any more than Heaven, in Crowley's opinion, was a fountain of goodness; they were just sides in the great cosmic chess game. Where you found the real McCoy, the real grace and the real heart-stopping evil, was right inside the human mind.

"Huh," said Aziraphale. "Satanists."

"I don't see how they could have messed it up," said Crowley. "I mean, two babies. It's not exactly taxing, is it . . . ?" He stopped. Through the mists of memory he pictured a small nun, who had struck him at the time as being remarkably loose-headed even for a Satanist. And there had been someone else. Crowley vaguely recalled a pipe, and a cardigan with the kind of zigzag pattern that went out of style in 1938. A man with "expectant father" written all over him.

There must have been a third baby.

He told Aziraphale.

"Not a lot to go on," said the angel.

"We know the child must be alive," said Crowley, "so—"

"How do we know?"

"If it had turned up Down There again, do you think I'd still be sitting here?"

"Good point."

"So all we've got to do is find it," said Crowley. "Go through the hospital records." The Bentley's engine coughed into life and the car leapt forward, forcing Aziraphale back into the seat.

"And then what?" he said.

"And then we find the child."

"And *then* what?" The angel shut his eyes as the car crabbed around a corner.

"Don't know."

"Good grief."

"I suppose—*get off the road you clown*—your people wouldn't consider—*and the scooter you rode in on!*—giving me asylum?"

"I was going to ask you the same thing—*Watch out for that pedestrian!*"

"It's on the street, it knows the risks it's taking!" said Crowley, easing the accelerating car between a parked car and a taxi and leaving a space which would have barely accepted even the best credit card.

"Watch the road! Watch the road! Where is this hospital, anyway?"

"Somewhere south of Oxford!"

Aziraphale grabbed the dashboard. "You can't do ninety miles an hour in Central London!"

Crowley peered at the dial. "Why not?" he said.

"You'll get us killed!" Aziraphale hesitated. "Inconveniently discorporated," he corrected, lamely, relaxing a little. "Anyway, you might kill other people."

Crowley shrugged. The angel had never really come to grips with the twentieth century, and didn't realize that it is perfectly possible to do ninety miles an hour down Oxford Street. You just arranged matters so that no one was in the way. And since everyone knew that it was impossible to do ninety miles an hour down Oxford Street, no one noticed.

At least cars were better than horses. The internal combustion engine had been a godse—a blessi—a windfall for Crowley. The only horses he could be seen riding on business, in the old days, were big black jobs with eyes like flame and hooves that struck sparks. That was *de rigueur* for a demon. Usually, Crowley fell off. He wasn't much good with animals.

Somewhere around Chiswick, Aziraphale scrabbled vaguely in the scree of tapes in the glove compartment.

"What's a Velvet Underground?" he said.

"You wouldn't like it," said Crowley.

"Oh," said the angel dismissively. "Be-bop."

"Do you know, Aziraphale, that probably if a million human beings were asked to describe modern music, they wouldn't use the term 'be-bop'?" said Crowley.

"Ah, this is more like it. Tchaikovsky," said Aziraphale, opening a case and slotting its cassette into the Blaupunkt.

"You won't enjoy it," sighed Crowley. "It's been in the car for more than a fortnight."

A heavy bass beat began to thump through the Bentley as they sped past Heathrow.

Aziraphale's brow furrowed.

"I don't recognize this," he said. "What is it?"

"It's Tchaikovsky's 'Another One Bites the Dust,' "

said Crowley, closing his eyes as they went through Slough.

To while away the time as they crossed the sleeping Chilterns, they also listened to William Byrd's "We Are the Champions" and Beethoven's "I Want To Break Free." Neither were as good as Vaughan Williams's "Fat Bottomed Girls."

IT IS SAID THAT THE DEVIL HAS ALL THE BEST TUNES.

This is broadly true. But Heaven has the best choreographers.

THE OXFORDSHIRE plain stretched out to the west, with a scattering of lights to mark the slumbering villages where honest yeomen were settling down to sleep after a long day's editorial direction, financial consulting, or software engineering.

Up here on the hill a few glowworms were lighting up.

The surveyor's theodolite is one of the more direful symbols of the twentieth century. Set up anywhere in open countryside, it says: there will come Road Widening, yea, and two-thousand-home estates in keeping with the Essential Character of the Village. Executive Developments will be manifest.

But not even the most conscientious surveyor surveys at midnight, and yet here the thing was, tripod legs deep in the turf. Not many theodolites have a hazel twig strapped to the top, either, or crystal pendulums hanging from them and Celtic runes carved into the legs.

The soft breeze flapped the cloak of the slim figure who was adjusting the knobs of the thing. It was quite a heavy cloak, sensibly waterproof, with a warm lining.

Most books on witchcraft will tell you that witches work naked. This is because most books on witchcraft are written by men.

The young woman's name was Anathema Device. She was not astonishingly beautiful. All her features, considered individually, were extremely pretty, but the entirety of her face gave the impression that it had been put together hurriedly from stock without reference to any plan. Probably the most suitable word is "attractive," although people who knew what it meant and could spell it might add "vivacious," although there is something very Fifties about "vivacious," so perhaps they wouldn't.

Young women should not go alone on dark nights, even in Oxfordshire. But any prowling maniac would have had more than his work cut out if he had accosted Anathema Device. She was a witch, after all. And precisely because she was a witch, and therefore sensible, she put little faith in protective amulets and spells; she saved it all for a foot-long bread knife which she kept in her belt.

She sighted through the glass and made another adjustment.

She muttered under her breath.

Surveyors often mutter under their breath. They mutter things like "Soon have a relief road through here faster than you can say Jack Robinson," or

"That's three point five meters, give or take a gnat's whisker."

This was an entirely different kind of muttering.

"Darksome night / And shining Moon," muttered Anathema, "East by South / By West by Southwest . . . West-southwest . . . got you . . ."

She picked up a folded Ordnance Survey map and held it in the torchlight. Then she produced a transparent ruler and a pencil and carefully drew a line across the map. It intersected another pencil line.

She smiled, not because anything was particularly amusing, but because a tricky job had been done well.

Then she collapsed the strange theodolite, strapped it onto the back of a sit-up-and-beg black bicycle leaning against the hedge, made sure The Book was in the basket, and wheeled everything out to the misty lane.

It was a very ancient bike, with a frame apparently made of drainpipes. It had been built long before the invention of the three-speed gear, and possibly only just after the invention of the wheel.

But it was nearly all downhill to the village. Hair streaming in the wind, cloak ballooning behind her like a sheet anchor, she let the two-wheeled juggernaut accelerate ponderously through the warm air. At least there wasn't any traffic at this time of night.

THE BENTLEY'S ENGINE went *pink*, *pink* as it cooled. Crowley's temper, on the other hand, was heating up.

"You said you saw it signposted," he said.

"Well, we flashed by so quickly. Anyway, I thought you'd been here before."

"Eleven years ago!"

Crowley hurled the map onto the back seat and started the engine again.

"Perhaps we should ask someone," said Aziraphale.

"Oh, yes," said Crowley. "We'll stop and ask the first person we see walking along a—a *track* in the middle of the night, shall we?"

He jerked the car into gear and roared out into the beech-hung lane.

"There's something odd about this area," said Aziraphale. "Can't you feel it?"

"What?"

"Slow down a moment."

The Bentley slowed again.

"Odd," muttered the angel, "I keep getting these flashes of, of . . ."

He raised his hands to his temples.

"What? What?" said Crowley.

Aziraphale stared at him.

"Love," he said. "Someone really *loves* this place."

"Pardon?"

"There seems to be this great sense of love. I can't put it any better than that. Especially not to *you*."

"Do you mean like—" Crowley began.

There was a whirr, a scream, and a clunk. The car stopped.

Aziraphale blinked, lowered his hands, and gingerly opened the door.

"You've hit someone," he said.

"No I haven't," said Crowley. "Someone's hit me."

They got out. Behind the Bentley a bicycle lay in the road, its front wheel bent into a creditable Möbius shape, its back wheel clicking ominously to a standstill.

"Let there be light," said Aziraphale. A pale blue glow filled the lane.

From the ditch beside them someone said, "How the hell did you do that?"

The light vanished.

"Do what?" said Aziraphale guiltily.

"Uh." Now the voice sounded muzzy. "I think I hit my head on something . . ."

Crowley glared at a long metallic streak on the Bentley's glossy paintwork and a dimple in the bumper. The dimple popped back into shape. The paint healed.

"Up you get, young lady," said the angel, hauling Anathema out of the bracken. "No bones broken." It was a statement, not a hope; there had been a minor fracture, but Aziraphale couldn't resist an opportunity to do good.

"You didn't have any lights," she began.

"Nor did you," said Crowley guiltily. "Fair's fair."

"Doing a spot of astronomy, were we?" said Aziraphale, setting the bike upright. Various things clattered out of its front basket. He pointed to the battered theodolite.

"No," said Anathema, "I mean, yes. And look what you've done to poor old Phaeton."

"I'm sorry?" said Aziraphale.

"My bicycle. It's bent all to—"

"Amazingly resilient, these old machines," said the angel brightly, handing it to her. The front wheel gleamed in the moonlight, as perfectly round as one of the Circles of Hell.

She stared at it.

"Well, since that's all sorted out," said Crowley, "perhaps it'd be best if we just all got on our, er. Er. You wouldn't happen to know the way to Lower Tadfield, would you?"

Anathema was still staring at her bicycle. She was almost certain that it hadn't had a little saddlebag with a puncture repair kit when she set out.

"It's just down the hill," she said. "This is *my* bike, isn't it?"

"Oh, certainly," said Aziraphale, wondering if he'd overdone things.

"Only I'm *sure* Phaeton never had a pump."

The angel looked guilty again.

"But there's a place for one," he said, helplessly. "Two little hooks."

"Just down the hill, you said?" said Crowley, nudging the angel.

"I think perhaps I must have knocked my head," said the girl.

"We'd offer to give you a lift, of course," said Crowley quickly, "but there's nowhere for the bike."

"Except the luggage rack," said Aziraphale.

"The Bentley hasn't— Oh. Huh."

The angel scrambled the spilled contents of the bike's basket into the back seat and helped the stunned girl in after them.

"One does not," he said to Crowley, "pass by on the other side."

"Your one might not. This one does. We have got

other things to do, you know." Crowley glared at the new luggage rack. It had tartan straps.

The bicycle lifted itself up and tied itself firmly in place. Then Crowley got in.

"Where do you live, my dear?" Aziraphale oozed.

"My bike didn't have lights, either. Well, it did, but they're the sort you put those double batteries in and they went moldy and I took them off," said Anathema. She glared at Crowley. "I have a bread knife, you know," she said. "Somewhere."

Aziraphale looked shocked at the implication.

"Madam, I assure you—"

Crowley switched on the lights. He didn't need them to see by, but they made the other humans on the road less nervous.

Then he put the car into gear and drove sedately down the hill. The road came out from under the trees and, after a few hundred yards, reached the outskirts of a middle-sized village.

It had a familiar feel to it. It had been eleven years, but this place definitely rang a distant bell.

"Is there a hospital around here?" he said. "Run by nuns?"

Anathema shrugged. "Don't think so," she said. "The only large place is Tadfield Manor. I don't know what goes on there."

"Divine planning," muttered Crowley under his breath.

"And gears," said Anathema. "My bike didn't have gears. I'm sure my bike didn't have gears."

Crowley leaned across to the angel.

"Oh lord, heal this bike," he whispered sarcastically.

"I'm sorry, I just got carried away," hissed Aziraphale.

"Tartan straps?"

"Tartan is stylish."

Crowley growled. On those occasions when the angel managed to get his mind into the twentieth century, it always gravitated to 1950.

"You can drop me off here," said Anathema, from the back seat.

"Our pleasure," beamed the angel. As soon as the car had stopped he had the back door open and was bowing like an aged retainer welcoming the young massa back to the old plantation.

Anathema gathered her things together and stepped out as haughtily as possible.

She was quite sure neither of the two men had gone around to the back of the car, but the bike was unstrapped and leaning against the gate.

There was definitely something very weird about them, she decided.

Aziraphale bowed again. "So glad to have been of assistance," he said.

"Thank you," said Anathema, icily.

"Can we get on?" said Crowley. "Goodnight, miss. Get *in*, angel."

Ah. Well, that explained it. She had been perfectly safe after all.

She watched the car disappear toward the center of the village, and wheeled the bike up the path to the cottage. She hadn't bothered to lock it. She was sure that Agnes would have mentioned it if she was going to be burgled, she was always very good at personal things like that.

She'd rented the cottage furnished, which meant that the actual furniture was the special sort you find in these circumstances and had probably been left out for the dustmen by the local War on Want shop. It didn't matter. She didn't expect to be here long.

If Agnes was right, she wouldn't be *anywhere* long. Nor would anyone else.

She spread her maps and things out on the ancient table under the kitchen's solitary light bulb.

What had she learned? Nothing much, she decided. Probably IT was at the north end of the village, but she'd suspected that anyway. If you got too close the signal swamped you; if you were too far away you couldn't get an accurate fix.

It was infuriating. The answer must be in The Book somewhere. The trouble was that in order to understand the Predictions you had to be able to think like a half-crazed, highly intelligent seventeenth-century witch with a mind like a crossword-puzzle dictionary. Other members of the family had said that Agnes made things obscure to conceal them from the understanding of outsiders; Anathema, who suspected she could occasionally think like Agnes, had privately decided that it was because Agnes was a bloody-minded old bitch with a mean sense of humor.

She'd not even—

She didn't have The Book.

Anathema stared in horror at the things on the table. The maps. The homemade divinatory theodolite. The Thermos that had contained hot Bovril. The torch.

The rectangle of empty air where the *Prophecies* should have been.

She'd lost it.

But that was ridiculous! One of the things Agnes was always very specific about was what happened to The Book.

She snatched up the torch and ran from the house.

"A FEELING LIKE, OH, like the opposite of the feeling you're having when you say things like 'this feels spooky,'" said Aziraphale. "That's what I mean."

"I never say things like 'this feels spooky,'" said Crowley. "I'm all for spooky."

"A *cherished* feel," said Aziraphale desperately.

"Nope. Can't sense a thing," said Crowley with forced jolliness. "You're just oversensitive."

"It's my *job*," said Aziraphale. "Angels can't be *over*sensitive."

"I expect people round here like living here and you're just picking it up."

"Never picked up anything like this in London," said Aziraphale.

"There you are, then. Proves my point," said Crowley. "And *this* is the place. I remember the stone lions on the gateposts."

The Bentley's headlights lit up the groves of overgrown rhododendrons that lined the drive. The tires crunched over gravel.

"It's a bit early in the morning to be calling on nuns," said Aziraphale doubtfully.

"Nonsense. Nuns are up and about at all hours," said Crowley. "It's probably Compline, unless that's a slimming aid."

"Oh, cheap, very cheap," said the angel. "There's really no need for that sort of thing."

"Don't get defensive. I told you, these were some of ours. Black nuns. We needed a hospital close to the air base, you see."

"You've lost me there."

"You don't think American diplomats' wives usually give birth in little religious hospitals in the middle of nowhere, do you? It all had to seem to happen naturally. There's an air base at Lower Tadfield, she went there for the opening, things started to happen, base hospital not ready, our man there said, 'There's a place just down the road,' and there we were. Rather good organization."

"Except for one or two minor details," said Aziraphale smugly.

"But it *nearly* worked," snapped Crowley, feeling he should stick up for the old firm.

"You see, evil always contains the seeds of its own destruction," said the angel. "It is ultimately negative, and therefore encompasses its downfall even at its moments of apparent triumph. No matter how grandiose, how well-planned, how apparently foolproof an evil plan, the inherent sinfulness will by definition rebound upon its instigators. No matter how apparently successful it may seem upon the way, at the end it will wreck itself. It will founder upon the rocks of iniquity and sink headfirst to vanish without trace into the seas of oblivion."

Crowley considered this. "Nah," he said, at last. "For my money, it was just average incompetence. Hey—"

He whistled under his breath.

The graveled forecourt in front of the manor was crowded with cars, and they weren't nun cars. The Bentley was if anything outclassed. A lot of the cars had GT or Turbo in their names and phone aerials on their roofs. They were nearly all less than a year old.

Crowley's hands itched. Aziraphale healed bicycles and broken bones; *he* longed to steal a few radios, let down some tires, that sort of thing. He resisted it.

"Well, well," he said. "In my day nuns were packed four to a Morris Traveller."

"This can't be right," said Aziraphale.

"Perhaps they've gone private?" said Crowley.

"Or you've got the wrong place."

"It's the right place, I tell you. Come on."

They got out of the car. Thirty seconds later someone shot both of them. With incredible accuracy.

IF THERE WAS ONE THING that Mary Hodges, formerly Loquacious, was good at, it was attempting to obey orders. She liked orders. They made the world a simpler place.

What she wasn't good at was change. She'd really liked the Chattering Order. She'd made friends for the first time. She'd had a room of her own for the first time. Of course, she knew that it was engaged in things which might, from certain viewpoints, be considered bad, but Mary Hodges had seen quite a lot of life in thirty years and had no illusions about what most of the human race had to do in order to make it from one week to the next. Besides, the food was good and you got to meet interesting people.

The Order, such as was left of it, had moved after the fire. After all, their sole purpose in existing had been fulfilled. They went their separate ways.

She hadn't gone. She'd rather liked the Manor and, she said, someone ought to stay and see it was properly repaired, because you couldn't trust workmen these days unless you were on top of them the whole time, in a manner of speaking. This meant breaking her vows, but Mother Superior said this was all right, nothing to worry about, breaking vows was perfectly okay in a black sisterhood, and it would all be the same in a hundred years' time or, rather, eleven years' time, so if it gave her any pleasure here were the deeds and an address to forward any mail unless it came in long brown envelopes with windows in the front.

Then something very strange had happened to her. Left alone in the rambling building, working from one of the few undamaged rooms, arguing with men with cigarette stubs behind their ears and plaster dust on their trousers and the kind of pocket calculator that comes up with a different answer if the sums involved are in used notes, she discovered something she never knew existed.

She'd discovered, under layers of silliness and eagerness to please, Mary Hodges.

She found it quite easy to interpret builders' estimates and do VAT calculations. She'd got some books from the library, and found finance to be both interesting and uncomplicated. She'd stopped reading the kind of women's magazine that talks about romance and knitting and started reading the kind of women's magazine that talks about orgasms, but apart from making a mental note to have one if ever the occasion presented itself she dismissed them as only romance and knitting in a new form. So she'd started reading the kind of magazine that talked about mergers.

After much thought, she'd bought a small home computer from an amused and condescending young dealer in Norton. After a crowded weekend, she took it back. Not, as he thought when she walked back into the shop, to have a plug put on it, but because it didn't have a 387 co-processor. That bit he understood—he was a dealer, after all, and could understand quite long words—but after that the conversation rapidly went downhill from his point of view. Mary Hodges produced yet more magazines. Most of them had the term "PC" somewhere in their title, and many of them had articles and reviews that she had circled carefully in red ink.

She read about New Women. She hadn't ever realized that she'd been an Old Woman, but after some thought she decided that titles like that were all one with the romance and the knitting and the orgasms, and the really important thing to be was yourself, just as hard as you could. She'd always been inclined to dress in black and white. All she needed to do was raise the hemlines, raise the heels, and leave off the wimple.

It was while leafing through a magazine one day that she learned that, around the country, there was an apparently insatiable demand for commodious buildings in spacious grounds run by people who understood the needs of the business community. The following day she went out and ordered some stationery in the name of the Tadfield Manor Conference and Management Training Center, reasoning that by the time it had been printed she'd know all that was necessary to know about running such places.

The ads went out the following week.

It had turned out to be an overwhelming success, because Mary Hodges realized early in her new career as Herself that management training didn't have to mean sitting people down in front of unreliable slide projectors. Firms expected far more than that these days.

She provided it.

CROWLEY SANK DOWN with his back against a statue. Aziraphale had already toppled backward into a rhododendron bush, a dark stain spreading across his coat.

Crowley felt dampness suffusing his own shirt.

This was ridiculous. The last thing he needed now was to be killed. It would require all sorts of explanations. They didn't hand out new bodies just like that; they always wanted to know what you'd done with the old one. It was like trying to get a new pen from a particularly bloody-minded stationery department.

He looked at his hand in disbelief.

Demons have to be able to see in the dark. And he could see that his hand was yellow. He was bleeding yellow.

Gingerly, he tasted a finger.

Then he crawled over to Aziraphale and checked the angel's shirt. If the stain on it was blood, something had gone very wrong with biology.

"Oo, that stung," moaned the fallen angel. "Got me right under the ribs."

"Yes, but do you normally bleed blue?" said Crowley.

Aziraphale's eyes opened. His right hand patted his chest. He sat up. He went through the same crude forensic self-examination as Crowley.

"Paint?" he said.

Crowley nodded.

"What're they playing at?" said Aziraphale.

"I don't know," said Crowley, "but I think it's called silly buggers." His tone suggested that he could play, too. And do it better.

It was a game. It was tremendous fun. Nigel Tompkins, Assistant Head (Purchasing), squirmed through the undergrowth, his mind aflame with some of the more memorable scenes of some of the better Clint Eastwood movies. And to think he'd believed that management training was going to be boring, too. . . .

There *had* been a lecture, but it had been about the paint guns and all the things you should never do with them, and Tompkins had looked at the fresh young faces of his rival trainees as, to a man, they resolved to do them all if there was half a chance of getting away with it. If people told you business was a jungle and then put a gun in your hand, then it was pretty obvious to Tompkins that they weren't expecting you to simply aim for the shirt; what it was all about was the corporate head hanging over your fireplace.

Anyway, it was rumored that someone over in United Consolidated had done his promotion prospects a considerable amount of good by the anonymous application of a high-speed earful of paint to an immediate superior, causing the latter to complain of little ringing noises in important meetings and eventually to be replaced on medical grounds.

And there were his fellow trainees—fellow sperms, to switch metaphors, all struggling forward in the knowledge that there could only ever be one Chairman of Industrial Holdings (Holdings) PLC, and that the job would probably go to the biggest prick.

Of course, some girl with a clipboard from Personnel had told them that the courses they were going on were just to establish leadership potential, group cooperation, initiative, and so on. The trainees had tried to avoid one another's faces.

It had worked quite well so far. The white-water canoeing had taken care of Johnstone (punctured eardrum) and the mountain climbing in Wales had done for Whittaker (groin strain).

Tompkins thumbed another paint pellet into the gun and muttered business mantras to himself. Do Unto Others Before They Do Unto You. Kill or Be Killed. Either Shit or Get Out of the Kitchen. Survival of the Fittest. Make My Day.

He crawled a little nearer to the figures by the statue. They didn't seem to have noticed him.

When the available cover ran out, he took a deep breath and leapt to his feet.

"Okay, douchebags, grab some sk—*ohnoooeeeeee . . .*"

Where one of the figures had been there was something *dreadful.* He blacked out.

Crowley restored himself to his favorite shape.

"I hate having to do that," he murmured. "I'm always afraid I'll forget how to change back. And it can ruin a good suit."

"I think the maggots were a bit over the top, myself," said Aziraphale, but without much rancor. Angels had certain moral standards to maintain and so, unlike Crowley, he preferred to buy his clothes rather than wish them into being from raw firmament. And the shirt had been quite expensive.

"I mean, just look at it," he said. "I'll never get the stain out."

"Miracle it away," said Crowley, scanning the undergrowth for any more management trainees.

"Yes, but *I'll* always know the stain was there. You know. Deep down, I mean," said the angel. He picked up the gun and turned it over in his hands. "I've never seen one of these before," he said.

There was a pinging noise, and the statue beside them lost an ear.

"Let's not hang around," said Crowley. "He wasn't alone."

"This is a very odd gun, you know. Very strange."

"I thought your side disapproved of guns," said Crowley. He took the gun from the angel's plump hand and sighted along the stubby barrel.

"Current thinking favors them," said Aziraphale. "They lend weight to moral argument. In the right hands, of course."

"Yeah?" Crowley snaked a hand over the metal. "That's all right, then. Come on."

He dropped the gun onto the recumbent form of Tompkins and marched away across the damp lawn.

The front door of the Manor was unlocked. The pair of them walked through unheeded. Some plump young men in army fatigues spattered with paint were drinking cocoa out of mugs in what had once been the sisters' refectory, and one or two of them gave them a cheery wave.

Something like a hotel reception desk now occupied one end of the hall. It had a quietly competent look. Aziraphale gazed at the board on an aluminum easel beside it.

In little plastic letters let into the black fabric of the board were the words: *August 20–21: United Holdings [Holdings] PLC Initiative Combat Course.*

Meanwhile Crowley had picked up a pamphlet from the desk. It showed glossy pictures of the Manor, with special references to its Jacuzzis and indoor heated swimming pool, and on the back was the sort of map that conference centers always have, which makes use of a careful mis-scaling to suggest that it is handy for every motorway exit in the nation while carefully leaving out the labyrinth of country lanes that in fact surrounds it for miles on every side.

"Wrong place?" said Aziraphale.

"No."

"Wrong time, then."

"Yes." Crowley leafed through the booklet, in the hope of any clue. Perhaps it was too much to hope that the Chattering Order would still be here. After all, they'd done their bit. He hissed softly. Probably they'd gone to darkest America or somewhere, to convert the Christians, but he read on anyway. Sometimes this sort of leaflet had a little historical bit, because the kind of companies that hired places like this for a weekend of Interactive Personnel Analysis or A Conference on the Strategic Marketing Dynamic liked to feel that they were strategically interacting in the very building—give or take a couple of complete rebuildings, a civil war, and two major fires—that some Elizabethan financier had endowed as a plague hospital.

Not that he was actually expecting a sentence like "until eleven years ago the Manor was used as a convent by an order of Satanic nuns who weren't in fact all that good at it, really," but you never knew.

A plump man wearing desert camouflage and holding a polystyrene cup of coffee wandered up to them.

"Who's winning?" he said chummily. "Young Evanson of Forward Planning caught me a right zinger on the elbow, you know."

"We're all going to lose," said Crowley absently.

There was a burst of firing from the grounds. Not the snap and zing of pellets, but the full-throated crackle of aerodynamically shaped bits of lead traveling extremely fast.

There was an answering stutter.

The redundant warriors stared one on another. A further burst took out a rather ugly Victorian stained glass window beside the door and stitched a row of holes in the plaster by Crowley's head.

Aziraphale grabbed his arm.

"What the hell is it?" he said.

Crowley smiled like a snake.

NIGEL TOMPKINS had come to with a mild headache and a vaguely empty space in his recent memory. He was not to know that the human brain, when faced with a sight too terrible to contemplate, is remarkably good at scabbing it over with forced forgetfulness, so he put it down to a pellet strike on the head.

He was vaguely aware that his gun was somewhat heavier, but in his mildly bemused state he did not realize why until some time after he'd pointed it at trainee manager Norman Wethered from Internal Audit and pulled the trigger.

"I DON'T SEE WHY YOU'RE so shocked," said Crowley. "He wanted a real gun. Every desire in his head was for a real gun."

"But you've turned him loose on all those unprotected people!" said Aziraphale.

"Oh, no," said Crowley. "Not exactly. Fair's fair."

THE CONTINGENT from Financial Planning were lying flat on their faces in what had once been the haha, although they weren't very amused.

"I always said you couldn't trust those people from Purchasing," said the Deputy Financial Manager. "The bastards."

A shot pinged off the wall above him.

He crawled hurriedly over to the little group clustered around the fallen Wethered.

"How does it look?" he said.

The assistant Head of Wages turned a haggard face toward him. "Pretty bad," he said. "The bullet went through nearly all of them. Access, Barclaycard, Diners—the lot."

"It was only the American Express Gold that stopped it," said Wethered.

They looked in mute horror at the spectacle of a credit card wallet with a bullet hole nearly all the way through it.

"Why'd they do it?" said a wages officer.

The Head of Internal Audit opened his mouth to say something reasonable, and didn't. Everyone had a point where they crack, and his had just been hit with a spoon. Twenty years in the job. He'd wanted to be a graphic designer but the careers master hadn't heard of that. Twenty years of double-checking Form BF18. Twenty years of cranking the bloody hand calculator, when even the people in Forward Planning had computers. And now for reasons unknown, but possibly to do with reorganization and a desire to do away with all the expense of early retirement, they were shooting at him with bullets.

The armies of paranoia marched behind his eyes.

He looked down at his own gun. Through the mists of rage and bewilderment he saw that it was bigger and blacker than it had been when it was issued to him. It felt heavier, too.

He aimed it at a bush nearby and watched a stream of bullets blow the bush into oblivion.

Oh. So that was their game. Well, *someone* had to win.

He looked at his men.

"Okay, guys," he said, "let's get the bastards!"

"THE WAY I SEE IT," said Crowley, "no one has to pull the trigger."

He gave Aziraphale a bright and brittle grin.

"Come on," he said. "Let's have a look around while everyone's busy."

BULLETS STREAKED ACROSS THE NIGHT.

Jonathan Parker, Purchasing Section, was wriggling through the bushes when one of them put an arm around his neck.

Nigel Tompkins spat a cluster of rhododendron leaves out of his mouth.

"Down there it's company law," he hissed, through mud-encrusted features, "but up here it's me . . ."

"THAT WAS A PRETTY LOW TRICK," said Aziraphale, as they strolled along the empty corridors.

"What'd I do? What'd I do?" said Crowley, pushing open doors at random.

"There are people out there shooting one another!"

"Well, that's just it, isn't it? They're doing it themselves. It's what they really want to do. I just assisted them. Think of it as a microcosm of the universe. Free will for everyone. Ineffable, right?"

Aziraphale glared.

"Oh, all right," said Crowley wretchedly. "No one's actually going to get killed. They're all going to have miraculous escapes. It wouldn't be any fun otherwise."

Aziraphale relaxed. "You know, Crowley," he said, beaming, "I've always said that, deep down inside, you're really quite a—"

"All right, all *right*," Crowley snapped. "Tell the whole blessed world, why don't you?"

AFTER A WHILE, loose alliances began to emerge. Most of the financial departments found they had interests in common, settled their differences, and ganged up on Forward Planning.

When the first police car arrived, sixteen bullets from a variety of directions had hit it in the radiator before it had got halfway up the drive. Two more took out its radio aerial, but they were too late, too late.

MARY HODGES WAS just putting down the phone when Crowley opened her office door.

"It must be terrorists," she snapped. "Or poachers." She peered at the pair of them. "You are the police, aren't you?" she said.

Crowley saw her eyes begin to widen.

Like all demons, he had a good memory for faces, even after eleven years, the loss of a wimple, and the addition of some rather severe makeup. He snapped his fingers. She settled back in her chair, her face becoming a blank and amiable mask.

"There was no need for that," said Aziraphale.

"Good"—Crowley glanced at his watch—"morning, ma'am," he said, in a sing-song voice. "We're just a couple of supernatural entities and we were just wondering if you might help us with the whereabouts of the notorious Son of Satan." He smiled coldly at the angel. "I'll wake her up again, shall I? And you can say it."

"Well. Since you put it like that . . ." said the angel slowly.

"Sometimes the old ways are best," said Crowley. He turned to the impassive woman.

"Were you a nun here eleven years ago?" he said.

"Yes," said Mary.

"There!" said Crowley to Aziraphale. "See? I knew I wasn't wrong."

"Luck of the devil," muttered the angel.

"Your name then was Sister Talkative. Or something."

"Loquacious," said Mary Hodges in a hollow voice.

"And do you recall an incident involving the switching of newborn babies?" said Crowley.

Mary Hodges hesitated. When she did speak, it

was as though memories that had been scabbed over were being disturbed for the first time in years.

"Yes," she said.

"Is there any possibility that the switch could have gone wrong in some way?"

"I do not know."

Crowley thought for a bit. "You must have had records," he said. "There are always records. Everyone has records these days." He glanced proudly at Aziraphale. "It was one of my better ideas."

"Oh, yes," said Mary Hodges.

"And where are they?" said Aziraphale sweetly.

"There was a fire just after the birth."

Crowley groaned and threw his hands in the air. "That was Hastur, probably," he said. "It's his style. Can you believe those guys? I bet he thought he was being really clever."

"Do you recall any details about the other child?" said Aziraphale.

"Yes."

"Please tell me."

"He had lovely little toesie-wosies."

"Oh."

"And he was very sweet," said Mary Hodges wistfully.

There was the sound of a siren outside, abruptly broken off as a bullet hit it. Aziraphale nudged Crowley.

"Get a move on," he said. "We're going to be knee-deep in police at any moment and I will of course be morally obliged to assist them in their enquiries." He thought for a moment. "Perhaps she can remember if there were any other women giving birth that night, and—"

There was the sound of running feet downstairs.

"Stop them," said Crowley. "We need more time!"

"Any more miracles and we'll really start getting noticed by Up There," said Aziraphale. "If you *really* want Gabriel or someone wondering why forty policemen have gone to sleep—"

"Okay," said Crowley. "That's it. That's it. It was worth a try. Let's get out of here."

"In thirty seconds you will wake up," said Aziraphale, to the entranced ex-nun. "And you will have had a lovely dream about whatever you like best, and—"

"Yes, yes, fine," sighed Crowley. "Now can we go?"

NO ONE NOTICED THEM leaving. The police were too busy herding in forty adrenaline-drunk, fighting-mad management trainees. Three police vans had gouged tracks in the lawn, and Aziraphale made Crowley back up for the first of the ambulances, but then the Bentley swished into the night. Behind them the summerhouse and gazebo were already ablaze.

"We've really left that poor woman in a dreadful situation," said the angel.

"You think?" said Crowley, trying to hit a hedgehog and missing. "Bookings will double, you mark my words. If she plays her cards right, sorts out the waivers, ties up all the legal bits. Initiative training with real guns? They'll form queues."

"Why are you always so cynical?"

"I said. Because it's my *job.*"

They drove in silence for a while. Then Aziraphale said, "You'd think he'd show up, wouldn't you? You'd think we could detect him in some way."

"He won't show up. Not to us. Protective camouflage. He won't even know it, but his powers will keep him hidden from prying occult forces."

"Occult forces?"

"You and me," explained Crowley.

"*I'm* not occult," said Aziraphale. "Angels aren't occult. We're ethereal."

"Whatever," snapped Crowley, too worried to argue.

"Is there some other way of locating him?"

Crowley shrugged. "Search me," he said. "How much experience do you think I've got in these matters? Armageddon only happens once, you know. They don't let you go around again until you get it right."

The angel stared out at the rushing hedgerows.

"It all seems so peaceful," he said. "How do you think *it* will happen?"

"Well, thermonuclear extinction has always been very popular. Although I must say the big boys are being quite polite to each other at the moment."

"Asteroid strike?" said Aziraphale. "Quite the fashion these days, I understand. Strike into the Indian Ocean, great big cloud of dust and vapor, goodbye all higher life forms."

"Wow," said Crowley, taking care to exceed the speed limit. Every little bit helped.

"Doesn't bear thinking about it, does it," said Aziraphale gloomily.

"All the higher life forms scythed away, just like that."

"Terrible."

"Nothing but dust and fundamentalists."

"That was nasty."

"Sorry. Couldn't resist it."

They stared at the road.

"Maybe some terrorist—?" Aziraphale began.

"Not one of ours," said Crowley.

"Or ours," said Aziraphale. "Although ours are freedom fighters, of course."

"I'll tell you what," said Crowley, scorching rubber on the Tadfield bypass. "Cards on the table time. I'll tell you ours if you tell me yours."

"All right. You first."

"Oh, no. You first."

"But you're a demon."

"Yes, but a demon of my word, I should hope."

Aziraphale named five political leaders. Crowley named six. Three names appeared on both lists.

"See?" said Crowley. "It's just like I've always said. They're cunning buggers, humans. You can't trust them an inch."

"But I don't think any of ours have any big plans afoot," said Aziraphale. "Just minor acts of ter—political protest," he corrected.

"Ah," said Crowley bitterly. "You mean none of this cheap, mass-produced murder? Just personal service, every bullet individually fired by skilled craftsmen?"

Aziraphale didn't rise to it. "What are we going to do now?"

"Try and get some sleep."

"You don't need sleep. *I* don't need sleep. Evil never sleeps, and Virtue is ever-vigilant."

"Evil in general, maybe. This specific part of it has got into the habit of getting its head down occasionally." He stared into the headlights. The time would come soon enough when sleep would be right out of the question. When those Below found out that he, personally, had lost the Antichrist, they'd probably dig out all those reports he'd done on the Spanish Inquisition and try them out on him, one at a time and then all together.

He rummaged in the glove compartment, fumbled a tape at random, and slotted it into the player. A little music would . . .

. . . *Bee-elzebub has a devil put aside for me, for me* . . .

"For me," murmured Crowley. His expression went blank for a moment. Then he gave a strangled scream and wrenched at the on-off knob.

"Of course, we might be able to get a human to find him," said Aziraphale thoughtfully.

"What?" said Crowley, distractedly.

"Humans are good at finding other humans. They've been doing it for thousands of years. And the child *is* human. As well as . . . you know. He would be hidden from us, but other humans might be able to . . . oh, sense him, perhaps. Or spot things we wouldn't think of."

"It wouldn't work. He's the Antichrist! He's got this . . . sort of automatic defense, hasn't he? Even if he *doesn't* know it. It won't even let people suspect him. Not yet. Not till it's ready. Suspicion will slide off him like, like . . . whatever it is water slides off of," he finished lamely.

"Got any better ideas? Got one *single* better idea?" said Aziraphale.

"No."

"Right, then. It could work. Don't tell me you haven't got any front organizations you could use. I know I have. We could see if they can pick up the trail."

"What could they do that we couldn't do?"

"Well, for a start, they wouldn't get people to shoot one another, they wouldn't hypnotize respectable women, they—"

"Okay. Okay. But it hasn't got a snowball's chance in Hell. Believe me, I know. But I can't think of anything better." Crowley turned onto the motorway and headed for London.

"I have a—a certain network of agents," said Aziraphale, after a while. "Spread across the country. A disciplined force. I could set them searching."

"I, er, have something similar," Crowley admitted. "You know how it is, you never know when they might come in handy . . ."

"We'd better alert them. Do you think they ought to work together?"

Crowley shook his head.

"I don't think that would be a good idea," he said. "They're not very sophisticated, politically speaking."

"Then we'll each contact our own people and see what they can manage."

"Got to be worth a try, I suppose," said Crowley.

"It's not as if I haven't got lots of other work to do, God knows."

His forehead creased for a moment, and then he slapped the steering wheel triumphantly.

"Ducks!" he shouted.

"What?"

"That's what water slides off!"

Aziraphale took a deep breath.

"Just drive the car, please," he said wearily.

They drove back through the dawn, while the cassette player played J. S. Bach's Mass in B Minor, vocals by F. Mercury.

Crowley liked the city in the early morning. Its population consisted almost entirely of people who had proper jobs to do and real reasons for being there, as opposed to the unnecessary millions who trailed in after 8 A.M., and the streets were more or less quiet. There were double yellow no-parking lines in the narrow road outside Aziraphale's bookshop, but they obediently rolled back on themselves when the Bentley pulled in to the curb.

"Well, okay," he said, as Aziraphale got his coat from the back seat. "We'll keep in touch. Okay?"

"What's this?" said Aziraphale, holding up a brown oblong.

Crowley squinted at it. "A book?" he said. "Not mine."

Aziraphale turned a few of the yellowed pages. Tiny bibliophilic bells rang in the back of his mind.

"It must have belonged to that young lady," he said slowly. "We ought to have got her address."

"Look, I'm in enough trouble as it is, I don't want it to get about that I go around returning people's property to them," said Crowley.

Aziraphale reached the title page. It was probably a good job Crowley couldn't see his expression.

"I suppose you could always send it to the post office there," said Crowley, "if you really feel you must. Address it to the mad woman with the bicycle. Never trust a woman who gives funny names to means of transport—"

"Yes, yes, certainly," said the angel. He fumbled for his keys, dropped them on the pavement, picked them up, dropped them again, and hurried to the shop door.

"We'll be in touch then, shall we?" Crowley called after him.

Aziraphale paused in the act of turning the key.

"What?" he said. "Oh. Oh. Yes. Fine. Jolly good." And he slammed the door.

"Right," mumbled Crowley, suddenly feeling very alone.

TORCHLIGHT FLICKERED IN THE LANES.

The trouble with trying to find a brown-covered book among brown leaves and brown water at the bottom of a ditch of brown earth in the brown, well, grayish light of dawn, was that you couldn't.

It wasn't there.

Anathema tried every method of search she could think of. There was the methodical quartering of the ground. There was the slapdash poking at the bracken by the roadside. There was the nonchalant sidling up to it and looking out of the side of her eye. She even tried the one which every romantic nerve in her body insisted should work, which consisted of theatrically giving up, sitting down, and letting her glance fall naturally on a patch of earth which, if she had been in any decent narrative, should have contained The Book.

It didn't.

Which meant, as she had feared all along, that it was probably in the back of a car belonging to two consenting cycle repairmen.

She could feel generations of Agnes Nutter's descendants laughing at her.

Even if those two were honest enough to want to return it, they'd hardly go to all the trouble of finding a cottage they'd barely seen in the dark.

The only hope was that they wouldn't know what it was they'd got.

AZIRAPHALE, LIKE MANY Soho merchants who specialized in hard-to-find books for the discerning connoisseur, had a back room, but what was in there was far more esoteric than anything normally found inside a shrink-wrapped bag for the Customer Who Knows What He Wants.

He was particularly proud of his books of prophecy.

First editions, usually.

And every one was signed.

He'd got Robert Nixon,* and Martha the Gypsy, and Ignatius Sybilla, and Old Ottwell Binns. Nostradamus had signed, "To myne olde friend Azerafel, with Beste wishes"; Mother Shipton had spilled drink on his copy; and in a climate-controlled cabinet in one corner was the original scroll in the shaky handwriting of St. John the Divine of Patmos, whose "Revelation" had been the all-time best seller. Aziraphale had found him a nice chap, if a bit too fond of odd mushrooms.

What the collection did *not* have was a copy of *The Nice and Accurate Prophecies of Agnes Nutter*, and Aziraphale walked into the room holding it as a keen philatelist might hold a Mauritius Blue that had just turned up on a postcard from his aunt.

He'd never even seen a copy before, but he'd heard about it. Everyone in the trade, which considering it was a highly specialized trade meant about a dozen people, had heard of it. Its existence was a sort of vacuum around which all sorts of strange stories had been orbiting for hundreds of years. Aziraphale realized he wasn't sure if you could orbit a vacuum, and didn't care; *The Nice and Accurate Prophecies* made the Hitler Diaries look like, well, a bunch of forgeries.

His hands hardly shook at all as he laid it down on a bench, pulled on a pair of surgical rubber gloves, and opened it reverentially. Aziraphale was an angel, but he also worshiped books.

* A sixteenth-century half-wit, not related to any U.S. president.

The title page said:

THE NIFE AND ACCURATE PROPHEFIES
OF AGNES NUTTER

In slightly smaller type:

Being a Certaine and Prefice Hiftory from the Prefent Day
Unto the Endinge of this World.

In slightly larger type:

Containing therein Many Diuerse Wonders and
precepts for the Wife

In a different type:

more complete than ever yet
before pvolifhed

In smaller type but in capitals:

CONCERNING THE STRANGE TIMES AHEADE

In slightly desperate italics:

And events of a Wonderful Nature

In larger type once more:

'Reminifent of Noftradamus at hif beft'—Ursula Shipton

The prophecies were numbered, and there were more than four thousand of them.

"Steady, steady," Aziraphale muttered to himself. He went into the little kitchenette and made himself some cocoa and took some deep breaths.

Then he came back and read a prophecy at random.

Forty minutes later, the cocoa was still untouched.

THE RED-HAIRED WOMAN in the corner of the hotel bar was the most successful war correspondent in the world. She now had a passport in the name of Carmine Zuigiber; and she went where the wars were.

Well. More or less.

Actually she went where the wars weren't. She'd already been where the wars were.

She was not well known, except where it counted. Get half a dozen war correspondents together in an airport bar, and the conversation will, like a compass orienting to North, swing around to Murchison of *The New York Times*, to Van Horne of *Newsweek*, to Anforth of I.T.N. News. The war correspondents' War Correspondents.

But when Murchison, and Van Horne, and Anforth ran into each other in a burnt-out tin shack in Beirut, or Afghanistan, or the Sudan, after they'd admired each other's scars and had downed a few, they would exchange awed anecdotes of "Red" Zuigiber, from the *National World Weekly*.

"That dumb rag," Murchison would say, "it doesn't goddamn know what it's goddamn got."

Actually the *National World Weekly* did know just what it had got: it had a War Correspondent. It just didn't know why, or what to do with one now it had her.

A typical *National World Weekly* would tell the world how Jesus' face was seen on a Big Mac bun bought by someone from Des Moines, with an artist's impression of the bun; how Elvis Presley was recently sighted working in a Burger Lord in Des Moines; how listening to Elvis records cured a Des Moines housewife's cancer; how the spate of werewolves infesting the Midwest are the offspring of noble pioneer women raped by Bigfoot; and that Elvis was taken by Space Aliens in 1976 because he was too good for this world.*

That was the *National World Weekly.* They sold four million copies a week, and they needed a War Correspondent like they needed an exclusive interview with the Secretary-General of the United Nations.**

So they paid Red Zuigiber a great deal of money to go and find wars, and ignored the bulging, badly typed envelopes she sent them occasionally from around the globe to justify her—generally fairly reasonable—expense claims.

They felt justified in this because, as they saw it, she really wasn't a very good war correspondent although she was undoubtedly the most attractive, which counted for a lot on the *National World*

* Remarkably, one of these stories is indeed true.

** The interview was done in 1983 and went as follows:

Q: You're the Secretary-General of the United Nations, then?

A: *Si.*

Q: Ever sighted Elvis?

Weekly. Her war reports were always about a bunch of guys shooting at each other, with no real understanding of the wider political ramifications, and, more importantly, no Human Interest.

Occasionally they would hand one of her stories over to a rewrite man to fix up. ("Jesus appeared to nine-year-old Manuel Gonzalez during a pitched battle on the Rio Concorsa, and told him to go home because his mother worried about him. 'I knew it was Jesus,' said the brave little child, 'because he looked like he did when his picture miraculously appeared on my sandwich box.' ")

Mostly the *National World Weekly* left her alone, and carefully filed her stories in the rubbish bin.

Murchison, and Van Horne, and Anforth didn't care about this. All they knew was that whenever a war broke out, Ms. Zuigiber was there first. Practically *before*.

"How does she do it?" they would ask each other incredulously. "How the hell does she do it?" And their eyes would meet, and silently say: if she was a car she'd be made by Ferrari, she's the kind of woman you'd expect to see as the beautiful consort to the corrupt generalissimo of a collapsing Third World country, and she hangs around with guys like us. We're the lucky guys, right?

Ms. Zuigiber just smiled and bought another round of drinks for everybody, on the *National World Weekly*. And watched the fights break out around her. And smiled.

She had been right. Journalism suited her.

Even so, everyone needs a holiday, and Red Zuigiber was on her first in eleven years.

She was on a small Mediterranean island which made its money from the tourist trade, and that in itself was odd. Red looked to be the kind of woman who, if she took a holiday on any island smaller than Australia, would be doing so because she was friends with the man who owned it. And had you told any islander a month before that war was coming, he would have laughed at you and tried to sell you a raffiawork wine holder or a picture of the bay done in seashells; that was then.

This was now.

Now a deep religio-political divide, concerning which of four small mainland countries they weren't actually a part of, had split the country into three factions, destroyed the statue of Santa Maria in the town square, and done for the tourist trade.

Red Zuigiber sat in the bar of the Hotel de Palomar del Sol, drinking what passed for a cocktail. In one corner a tired pianist played, and a waiter in a toupee crooned into a microphone:

> "AAAAAAAAAAAonce-pon-a-time-dere-was
> LITTLE WHITE BOOOL
> AAAAAAAAAAAvery-sad-because-e-was
> LITTLE WHITE BOOL . . ."

A man threw himself through the window, a knife between his teeth, a Kalashnikov automatic rifle in one hand, a grenade in the other.

"I glaim gis oteg id der gaing og der—" he paused. He took the knife out of his mouth and began again. "I claim this hotel in the name of the pro-Turkish Liberation Faction!"

The last two holidaymakers remaining on the island* climbed underneath their table. Red unconcernedly withdrew the maraschino cherry from her drink, put it to her scarlet lips, and sucked it slowly off its stick in a way that made several men in the room break into a cold sweat.

The pianist stood up, reached into his piano, and pulled out a vintage sub-machine gun. "This hotel has already been claimed by the pro-Greek Territorial Brigade!" he screamed. "Make one false move, and I shoot out your living daylight!"

There was a motion at the door. A huge, black-bearded individual with a golden smile and a genuine antique Gatling gun stood there, with a cohort of equally huge although less impressively armed men behind him.

"This strategically important hotel, for years a symbol of the fascist imperialist Turko-Greek running dog tourist trade, is now the property of the Italo-Maltese Freedom Fighters!" he boomed affably. "Now we kill everybody!"

"Rubbish!" said the pianist. "Is not strategically important. Just has extremely well-stocked wine cellar!"

* Mr. and Mrs. Thomas Threlfall, of 9, The Elms, Paignton. They always maintained that one of the nice things about going on holiday was not having to read the newspapers or listen to the news, just getting away from it all really. And due to a tummy bug contracted by Mr. Threlfall, and Mrs. Threlfall rather overdoing it in the sun their first day, this was their first time out of their hotel room for a week and a half.

"He's right, Pedro," said the man with the Kalashnikov, "That's why my lot wanted it. Il General Ernesto de Montoya said to me, he said, Fernando, the war'll be over by Saturday, and the lads'll be wanting a good time. Pop down to the Hotel de Palomar del Sol and claim it as booty, will you?"

The bearded man turned red. "Is bloddy important strategically, Fernando Chianti! I drew big map of the island and is right in the middle, which makes it pretty bloddy strategically important, I can tell you."

"Ha!" said Fernando. "You might as well say that just because Little Diego's house has a view of the decadent capitalist topless private beach, that it's strategically important!"

The pianist blushed a deep red. "Our lot got that this morning," he admitted.

There was silence.

In the silence was a faint, silken rasping. Red had uncrossed her legs.

The pianist's Adam's apple bobbed up and down. "Well, it's pretty strategically important," he managed, trying to ignore the woman on the bar stool. "I mean, if someone landed a submarine on it, you'd want to be somewhere you could see it all."

Silence.

"Well, it's a lot more strategically important than this hotel anyway," he finished.

Pedro coughed, ominously. "The next person who says *anything*. Anything *at all*. Is dead." He grinned. Hefted his gun. "Right. Now—everyone against far wall."

Nobody moved. They weren't listening to him

any more. They were listening to a low, indistinct murmuring from the hallway behind him, quiet and monotonous.

There was some shuffling among the cohort in the doorway. They seemed to be doing their best to stand firm, but they were being inexorably edged out of the way by the muttering, which had begun to resolve itself into audible phrases. "Don't mind me, gents, what a night, eh? Three times round the island, nearly didn't find the place, someone doesn't believe in signposts, eh? Still, found it in the end, had to stop and ask four times, finally asked at the post office, they always know at the post office, had to draw me a map though, got it here somewhere . . ."

Sliding serenely past the men with guns, like a pike through a trout pond, came a small, bespectacled man in a blue uniform, carrying a long, thin, brown paper-wrapped parcel, tied with string. His sole concession to the climate were his open-toed brown plastic sandals, although the green woolen socks he wore underneath them showed his deep and natural distrust of foreign weather.

He had a peaked cap on, with *International Express* written on it in large white letters.

He was unarmed, but no one touched him. No one even pointed a gun at him. They just stared.

The little man looked around the room, scanning the faces, and then looking back down at his clipboard; then he walked straight over to Red, still sitting on her bar stool. "Package for you, miss," he said.

Red took it, and began to untie the string.

The International Express man coughed discreetly and presented the journalist with a well-thumbed receipt pad and a yellow plastic ballpoint pen attached to the clipboard by a piece of string. "You have to sign for it, miss. Just there. Print your full name over here, signature down there."

"Of course." Red signed the receipt pad, illegibly, then printed her name. The name she wrote was not Carmine Zuigiber. It was a much shorter name.

The man thanked her kindly, and made his way out, muttering lovely place you've got here, gents, always meant to come out here on holiday, sorry to trouble you, excuse me, sir . . . And he passed out of their lives as serenely as he had come.

Red finished opening the parcel. People began to edge around to get a better look. Inside the package was a large sword.

She examined it. It was a very straightforward sword, long and sharp; it looked both old and unused; and it had nothing ornamental or impressive about it. This was no magical sword, no mystic weapon of power and might. It was very obviously a sword created to slice, chop, cut, preferably kill, but, failing that, irreparably maim, a very large number of people indeed. It had an indefinable aura of hatred and menace.

Red clasped the hilt in her exquisitely manicured right hand, and held it up to eye level. The blade glinted.

"Awww*right*!" she said, stepping down from the stool. "*Fi*nally."

She finished the drink, hefted the sword over one shoulder, and looked around at the puzzled factions, who now encircled her completely. "Sorry to run out on you, chaps," she said. "Would love to stay and get to know you better."

The men in the room suddenly realized that they didn't want to know her better. She was beautiful, but she was beautiful in the way a forest fire was beautiful: something to be admired from a distance, not up close.

And she held her sword, and she smiled like a knife.

There were a number of guns in that room, and slowly, tremblingly, they were focused on her chest, and her back, and head.

They encircled her completely.

"Don't move!" croaked Pedro.

Everybody else nodded.

Red shrugged. She began to walk forward.

Every finger on every trigger tightened, almost of its own accord. Lead and the smell of cordite filled the air. Red's cocktail glass smashed in her hand. The room's remaining mirrors exploded in lethal shards. Part of the ceiling fell down.

And then it was over.

Carmine Zuigiber turned and stared at the bodies surrounding her as if she hadn't the faintest idea of how they came to be there.

She licked a spatter of blood—someone else's—from the back of her hand with a scarlet, cat-like tongue. Then she smiled.

And she walked out of the bar, her heels clicking on the tiles like the tapping of distant hammers.

The two holidaymakers climbed out from under the table and surveyed the carnage.

"This wouldn't of happened if we'd of gone to Torremolinos like we usually do," said one of them, plaintively.

"Foreigners," sighed the other. "They're just not like us, Patricia."

"That settles it, then. Next year we go to Brighton," said Mrs. Threlfall, completely missing the significance of what had just happened.

It meant there wouldn't be any next year.

It rather lowered the odds on there being any next week to speak of.

THURSDAY

THERE WAS A NEWCOMER IN THE VILLAGE.

New people were always a source of interest and speculation among the Them,* but this time Pepper had impressive news.

"She's moved into Jasmine Cottage and she's a witch," she said. "I know, because Mrs. Henderson does the cleaning and she told my mother she gets a witches' newspaper. She gets loads of ordinary newspapers, too, but she gets this special witches' one."

"My father says there's no such thing as witches," said Wensleydale, who had fair, wavy hair, and

* It didn't matter what the four had called their gang over the years, the frequent name changes usually being prompted by whatever Adam had happened to have read or viewed the previous day (the Adam Young Squad; Adam and Co.; The Hole-in-the-Chalk Gang; The Really Well-Known Four; The Legion of Really Super-Heroes; The Quarry Gang; The Secret Four; The Justice Society of Tadfield; The Galaxatrons; The Four Just Persons; The Rebels). Everyone else always referred to them darkly as Them, and eventually they did too.

peered seriously out at life through thick black-rimmed spectacles. It was widely believed that he had once been christened Jeremy, but no one ever used the name, not even his parents, who called him Youngster. They did this in the subconscious hope that he might take the hint; Wensleydale gave the impression of having been born with a mental age of forty-seven.

"Don't see why not," said Brian, who had a wide, cheerful face, under an apparently permanent layer of grime. "I don't see why witches shouldn't have their own newspaper. With stories about all the latest spells and that. My father gets *Angler's Mail*, and I bet there's more witches than anglers."

"It's called *Psychic News*," volunteered Pepper.

"That's not witches," said Wensleydale. "My aunt has that. That's just spoon-bending and fortune-telling and people thinking they were Queen Elizabeth the First in another life. There's no witches any more, actually. People invented medicines and that and told 'em they didn't need 'em any more and started burning 'em."

"It could have pictures of frogs and things," said Brian, who was reluctant to let a good idea go to waste. "An'—an' road tests of broomsticks. And a cats' column."

"Anyway, your aunt could be a witch," said Pepper. "In secret. She could be your aunt all day and go witching at night."

"Not *my* aunt," said Wensleydale darkly.

"An' recipes," said Brian. "New uses for leftover toad."

"Oh, shut up," said Pepper.

Brian snorted. If it had been Wensley who had said that, there'd have been a half-hearted scuffle, as between friends. But the other Them had long ago learned that Pepper did not consider herself bound by the informal conventions of brotherly scuffles. She could kick and bite with astonishing physiological accuracy for a girl of eleven. Besides, at eleven years old the Them were beginning to be bothered by the dim conception that laying hands on good ole Pep moved things into blood-thumping categories they weren't entirely at home with yet, besides earning you a snake-fast blow that would have floored the Karate Kid.

But she was good to have in your gang. They remembered with pride the time when Greasy Johnson and *his* gang had taunted them for playing with a girl. Pepper had erupted with a fury that had caused Greasy's mother to come round that evening and complain.*

* Greasy Johnson was a sad and oversized child. There's one in every school; not exactly *fat,* but simply huge and wearing almost the same size clothes as his father. Paper tore under his tremendous fingers, pens shattered in his grip. Children whom he tried to play with in quiet, friendly games ended up getting under his huge feet, and Greasy Johnson had become a bully almost in self-defense. After all, it was better to be called a bully, which at least implied some sort of control and desire, than to be called a big clumsy oaf. He was the despair of the sports master, because if Greasy Johnson had taken the slightest interest in sport, then the school could have been champions. But Greasy Johnson had never found

Pepper looked upon him, a giant male, as a natural enemy.

She herself had short red hair and a face which was not so much freckled as one big freckle with occasional areas of skin.

Pepper's given first names were Pippin Galadriel Moonchild. She had been given them in a naming ceremony in a muddy valley field that contained three sick sheep and a number of leaky polythene teepees. Her mother had chosen the Welsh valley of Pant-y-Gyrdl as the ideal site to Return to Nature. (Six months later, sick of the rain, the mosquitoes, the men, the tent-trampling sheep who ate first the whole commune's marijuana crop and then its antique minibus, and by now beginning to glimpse why almost the entire drive of human history has been an attempt to get as far away from Nature as possible, Pepper's mother returned to Pepper's surprised grandparents in Tadfield, bought a bra, and enrolled in a sociology course with a deep sigh of relief.)

There are only two ways a child can go with a name like Pippin Galadriel Moonchild, and Pepper had chosen the other one: the three male Them had learned this on their first day of school, in the playground, at the age of four.

---

a sport that suited him. He was instead secretly devoted to his collection of tropical fish, which won him prizes. Greasy Johnson was the same age as Adam Young, to within a few hours, and his parents had never told him he was adopted. See? You were *right* about the babies.

They had asked her her name, and, all innocent, she had told them.

Subsequently a bucket of water had been needed to separate Pippin Galadriel Moonchild's teeth from Adam's shoe. Wensleydale's first pair of spectacles had been broken, and Brian's sweater needed five stitches.

The Them were together from then on, and Pepper was Pepper forever, except to her mother, and (when they were feeling especially courageous, and the Them were almost out of earshot) Greasy Johnson and the Johnsonites, the village's only other gang.

Adam drummed his heels on the edge of the milk crate that was doing the office of a seat, listening to this bickering with the relaxed air of a king listening to the idle chatter of his courtiers.

He chewed lazily on a straw. It was a Thursday morning. The holidays stretched ahead, endless and unsullied. They needed filling up.

He let the conversation float around him like the buzzing of grasshoppers or, more precisely, like a prospector watching the churning gravel for a glint of useful gold.

"In our Sunday paper it said there was thousands of witches in the country," said Brian. "Worshiping Nature and eating health food an' that. So I don't see why we shouldn't have one round here. They were floodin' the country with a Wave of Mindless Evil, it said."

"What, by worshipin' Nature and eatin' health food?" said Wensleydale.

"That's what it said."

The Them gave this due consideration. They had once—at Adam's instigation—tried a health food diet for a whole afternoon. Their verdict was that you could live very well on healthy food provided you had a big cooked lunch beforehand.

Brian leaned forward conspiratorially.

"*And* it said they dance round with no clothes on," he added. "They go up on hills and Stonehenge and stuff, and dance with no clothes on."

This time the consideration was more thoughtful. The Them had reached that position where, as it were, the roller coaster of Life had almost completed the long haul to the top of the first big humpback of puberty so that they could just look down into the precipitous ride ahead, full of mystery, terror, and exciting curves.

"Huh," said Pepper.

"Not my aunt," said Wensleydale, breaking the spell. "Definitely not my aunt. She just keeps trying to talk to my uncle."

"Your uncle's dead," said Pepper.

"She says he still moves a glass about," said Wensleydale defensively. "My father says it was moving glasses about the whole time that made him dead in the first place. Don't know why she wants to talk to him," he added, "they never talked much when he was alive."

"That's necromancy, that is," said Brian. "It's in the Bible. She ought to stop it. God's dead against necromancy. And witches. You can go to Hell for it."

There was a lazy shifting of position on the milk crate throne. Adam was going to speak.

The Them fell silent. Adam was always worth listening to. Deep in their hearts, the Them knew that they weren't a gang of four. They were a gang of three, which belonged to Adam. But if you wanted excitement, and interest, and crowded days, then every Them would prize a lowly position in Adam's gang above leadership of any other gang anywhere.

"Don't see why everyone's so down on witches," Adam said.

The Them glanced at one another. This sounded promising.

"Well, they blight crops," said Pepper. "And sink ships. And tell you if you're going to be king and stuff. And brew up stuff with herbs."

"My mother uses herbs," said Adam. "So does yours."

"Oh, *those* are all right," said Brian, determined not to lose his position as occult expert. "I expect God said it was all right to use mint and sage and so on. Stands to reason there's nothing wrong with mint and sage."

"And they can make you be ill just by looking at you," said Pepper. "It's called the Evil Eye. They give you a look, and then you get ill and no one knows why. And they make a model of you and stick it full of pins and you get ill where all the pins are," she added cheerfully.

"That sort of thing doesn't happen any more," reiterated Wensleydale, the rational thinking person. " 'Cos we invented Science and all the vicars set fire to the witches for their own good. It was called the Spanish Inquisition."

"Then I reckon we should find out if her at Jasmine Cottage is a witch and if she is we should tell

Mr. Pickersgill," said Brian. Mr. Pickersgill was the vicar. Currently he was in dispute with the Them over subjects ranging from climbing the yew tree in the churchyard to ringing the bells and running away.

"I don't reckon it's allowed, going round setting fire to people," said Adam. "Otherwise people'd be doin' it all the time."

"It's all right if you're religious," said Brian reassuringly. "And it stops the witches from goin' to Hell, so I expect they'd be quite grateful if they understood it properly."

"Can't see Picky setting fire to anyone," said Pepper.

"Oh, I dunno," said Brian, meaningfully.

"Not actually setting them on actual fire," sniffed Pepper. "He's more likely to tell their parents, and leave it up to them if anyone's goin' to be set on fire or not."

The Them shook their heads in disgust at the current low standards of ecclesiastical responsibility. Then the other three looked expectantly at Adam.

They always looked expectantly at Adam. He was the one that had the ideas.

"P'raps we ought to do it ourselves," he said. "Someone ought to be doing *something* if there's all these witches about. It's—it's like that Neighborhood Watch scheme."

"Neighborhood Witch," said Pepper.

"No," said Adam coldly.

"But we can't be the Spanish Inquisition," said Wensleydale. "We're not Spanish."

"I bet you don't have to be Spanish to be the Spanish Inquisition," said Adam. "I bet it's like Scottish eggs or American hamburgers. It just has to look Spanish. We've just got to make it *look* Spanish. Then everyone would know it's the Spanish Inquisition."

There was silence.

It was broken by the crackling of one of the empty crisp packets that accumulated wherever Brian was sitting. They looked at him.

"I've got a bullfight poster with my name on it," said Brian, slowly.

LUNCHTIME CAME AND WENT. The new Spanish Inquisition reconvened.

The Head Inquisitor inspected it critically.

"What're those?" he demanded.

"You click them together when you dance," said Wensleydale, a shade defensively. "My aunt brought them back from Spain years ago. They're called maracas, I think. They've got a picture of a Spanish dancer on them, look."

"What's she dancing with a bull for?" said Adam.

"That's to show it's Spanish," said Wensleydale. Adam let it pass.

The bullfight poster was everything Brian had promised.

Pepper had something rather like a gravy boat made out of raffia.

"It's for putting wine in," she said defiantly. "My mother brought it back from Spain."

"It hasn't got a bull on it," said Adam severely.

"It doesn't have to," Pepper countered, moving just ever so slightly into a fighting stance.

Adam hesitated. His sister Sarah and her boyfriend had also been to Spain. Sarah had returned with a very large purple toy donkey which, while definitely Spanish, did not come up to what Adam instinctively felt should be the tone of the Spanish Inquisition. The boyfriend, on the other hand, had brought back a very ornate sword which, despite its tendency to bend when picked up and go blunt when asked to cut paper, proclaimed itself to be made of Toledo steel. Adam had spent an instructive half-hour with the encyclopedia and felt that this was just what the Inquisition needed. Subtle hints had not worked, however.

In the end Adam had taken a bunch of onions from the kitchen. They might well have been Spanish. But even Adam had to concede that, as decor for the Inquisitorial premises, they lacked that certain something. He was in no position to argue too vehemently about raffia wine holders.

"Very good," he said.

"You certain they're *Spanish* onions?" said Pepper, relaxing.

" 'Course," said Adam. "Spanish onions. Everyone knows that."

"They could be French," said Pepper doggedly. "France is famous for onions."

"It doesn't matter," said Adam, who was getting fed up with onions. "France is *nearly* Spanish, an' I don't expect witches know the difference, what with spendin' all their time flyin' around at night. It all looks like the Continong to witches. Anyway, if you don't like it you can jolly well go and start your own Inquisition, anyway."

For once, Pepper didn't push it. She'd been promised the post of Head Torturer. No one doubted who was going to be Chief Inquisitor. Wensleydale and Brian were less enthralled with their roles of Inquisitorial Guards.

"Well, you don't know any Spanish," said Adam, whose lunch hour had included ten minutes with a phrase book Sarah had bought in a haze of romanticism in Alicanté.

"That doesn't matter, because *actually* you have to talk in Latin," said Wensleydale, who had also been doing some slightly more accurate lunchtime reading.

"*And* Spanish," said Adam firmly. "That's why it's the Spanish Inquisition."

"I don't see why it shouldn't be a British Inquisition," said Brian. "Don't see why we should of fought the Armada and everything, just to have their smelly Inquisition."

This had been slightly bothering Adam's patriotic sensibilities as well.

"I reckon," he said, "that we should sort of start Spanish, and then make it the British Inquisition when we've got the hang of it. And now," he added, "the Inquisitorial Guard will go and fetch the first witch, *por favor*."

The new inhabitant of Jasmine Cottage would have to wait, they'd decided. What they needed to do was start small and work their way up.

"ART THOU A WITCH, *oh lay?*" said the Chief Inquisitor.

"Yes," said Pepper's little sister, who was six and built like a small golden-haired football.

"You mustn't say yes, you've got to say no," hissed the Head Torturer, nudging the suspect.

"And then what?" demanded the suspect.

"And then we torture you to make you say yes," said the Head Torturer. "I *told* you. It's good fun, the torturin'. It doesn't hurt. *Hastar lar visa,*" she added quickly.

The little suspect gave the decor of the Inquisitorial headquarters a disparaging look. There was a decided odor of onions.

"Huh," she said. "I *want* to be a witch, wiv a warty nose an' a green skin an' a lovely cat an' I'd call it Blackie, an' lots of potions an'—"

The Head Torturer nodded to the Chief Inquisitor.

"Look," said Pepper, desperately, "no one's saying you *can't* be a witch, you jus' have to *say* you're *not* a witch. No point in us taking all this trouble," she added severely, "if you're going to go round saying *yes* the minute we ask you."

The suspect considered this.

"But I *wants* to be a witch," she wailed. The male Them exchanged exhausted glances. This was out of their league.

"If you just say *no*," said Pepper, "you can have my Sindy stable set. I've never ever used it," she added, glaring at the other Them and daring them to make a comment.

"You *have* used it," snapped her sister, "I've *seen* it and it's all worn out and the bit where you put the hay is broke and—"

Adam gave a magisterial cough.

"Art thou a witch, *viva espana?*" he repeated.

The sister took a look at Pepper's face, and decided not to chance it.

"No," she decided.

IT WAS A VERY GOOD TORTURE, everyone agreed. The trouble was getting the putative witch off it.

It was a hot afternoon and the Inquisitorial guards felt that they were being put upon.

"Don't see why me and Brother Brian should have to do all the work," said Brother Wensleydale, wiping the sweat off his brow. "I reckon it's about time she got off and we had a go. *Benedictine ina decanter.*"

"Why have we stopped?" demanded the suspect, water pouring out of her shoes.

It had occurred to the Chief Inquisitor during his researches that the British Inquisition was probably not yet ready for the reintroduction of the Iron Maiden and the choke-pear. But an illustration of a medieval ducking stool suggested that it was tailor-made for the purpose. All you needed was a pond and some planks and a rope. It was the sort of combination that always attracted the Them, who never had much difficulty in finding all three.

The suspect was now green to the waist.

"It's just like a seesaw," she said. "Whee!"

"I'm going to go home unless I can have a go," muttered Brother Brian. "Don't see why evil witches should have all the fun."

"It's not allowed for inquisitors to be tortured too," said the Chief Inquisitor sternly, but without much real feeling. It was a hot afternoon, the Inquisitorial robes of old sacking were scratchy and smelled of stale barley, and the pond looked astonishingly inviting.

"All right, all right," he said, and turned to the suspect. "You're a witch, all right, don't do it again, and now you get off and let someone else have a turn. *Oh lay*," he added.

"What happens now?" said Pepper's sister.

Adam hesitated. Setting fire to her would probably cause no end of trouble, he reasoned. Besides, she was too soggy to burn.

He was also distantly aware that at some future point there would be questions asked about muddy shoes and duckweed-encrusted pink dresses. But that was the future, and it lay at the other end of a long warm afternoon that contained planks and ropes and ponds. The future could wait.

THE FUTURE CAME AND WENT in the mildly discouraging way that futures do, although Mr. Young had other things on his mind apart from muddy dresses and merely banned Adam from watching television, which meant he had to watch it on the old black and white set in his bedroom.

"I don't see why we should have a hosepipe ban," Adam heard Mr. Young telling Mrs. Young. "I pay my rates like everyone else. The garden looks like the Sahara desert. I'm surprised there was any water *left* in the pond. I blame it on the lack of nuclear testing, myself. You used to get proper summers when I was a boy. It used to rain all the time."

Now Adam slouched alone along the dusty lane. It was a good slouch. Adam had a way of slouching along that offended all right-thinking people. It wasn't that he just allowed his body to droop. He could slouch with *inflections*, and now the set of his shoulders reflected the hurt and bewilderment of those unjustly thwarted in their selfless desire to help their fellow men.

Dust hung heavy on the bushes.

"Serve everyone right if the witches took over the whole country and made everyone eat health food and not go to church and dance around with no clothes on," he said, kicking a stone. He had to admit that, except perhaps for the health food, the prospect wasn't too worrying.

"I bet if they'd jus' let us get started properly we could of found *hundreds* of witches," he told himself, kicking a stone. "I bet ole Torturemada dint have to give up jus' when he was getting started just because some stupid witch got her dress dirty."

Dog slouched along dutifully behind his Master. This wasn't, insofar as the hell-hound had any expectations, what he had imagined life would be like in the last days before Armageddon, but despite himself he was beginning to enjoy it.

He heard his Master say: "Bet even the *Victorians* didn't force people to have to watch black and white television."

Form shapes nature. There are certain ways of behavior appropriate to small scruffy dogs which are in fact welded into the genes. You can't just become small-dog-shaped and hope to stay the same person; a certain intrinsic small-dogness begins to permeate your very Being.

He'd already chased a rat. It had been the most enjoyable experience of his life.

"Serve 'em right if we're all overcome by Evil Forces," his Master grumbled.

And then there were cats, thought Dog. He'd surprised the huge ginger cat from next door and had attempted to reduce it to cowering jelly by means of the usual glowing stare and deep-throated growl, which had always worked on the damned in the past. This time they earned him a whack on the nose that had made his eyes water. Cats, Dog considered, were clearly a lot tougher than lost souls. He was looking forward to a further cat experiment, which he'd planned would consist of jumping around and yapping excitedly at it. It was a long shot, but it might just work.

"They just better not come running to me when ole Picky is turned into a frog, that's all," muttered Adam.

It was at this point that two facts dawned on him. One was that his disconsolate footsteps had led him past Jasmine Cottage. The other was that someone was crying.

Adam was a soft touch for tears. He hesitated a moment, and then cautiously peered over the hedge.

To Anathema, sitting in a deck chair and halfway through a packet of Kleenex, it looked like the rise of a small, disheveled sun.

Adam doubted that she was a witch. Adam had a very clear mental picture of a witch. The Youngs restricted themselves to the only possible choice amongst the better class of Sunday newspaper, and so a hundred years of enlightened occultism had passed Adam by. She didn't have a hooked nose or warts, and she was young . . . well, *quite* young. That was good enough for him.

"Hallo," he said, unslouching.

She blew her nose and stared at him.

What was looking over the hedge should be described at this point. What Anathema saw was, she said later, something like a prepubescent Greek god. Or maybe a Biblical illustration, one which showed muscular angels doing some righteous smiting. It was a face that didn't belong in the twentieth century. It was thatched with golden curls which glowed. Michelangelo should have sculpted it.

He probably would not have included the battered sneakers, frayed jeans, or grubby T-shirt, though.

"Who're you?" she said.

"I'm Adam Young," said Adam. "I live just down the lane."

"Oh. Yes. I've heard of you," said Anathema, dabbing at her eyes. Adam preened.

"Mrs. Henderson said I was to be sure to keep an eye out for you," she went on.

"I'm well known around here," said Adam.

"She said you were born to hang," said Anathema.

Adam grinned. Notoriety wasn't as good as fame, but was heaps better than obscurity.

"She said you were the worst of the lot of Them," said Anathema, looking a little more cheerful. Adam nodded.

"She said: 'You watch out for Them, Miss, they're nothing but a pack of ringleaders. That young Adam's full of the Old Adam,' " she said.

"What've you been cryin' for?" said Adam bluntly.

"Oh? Oh, I've just lost something," said Anathema. "A book."

"I'll help you look for it, if you like," said Adam gallantly. "I know quite a lot about books, actually. *I* wrote a book once. It was a triffic book. It was nearly eight pages long. It was about this pirate who was a famous detective. *And* I drew the pictures." And then, in a flash of largess, he added, "If you like I'll let you read it. I bet it was a lot more excitin' than any book you've lost. 'Specially the bit in the spaceship where the dinosaur comes out and fights with the cowboys. I bet it'd cheer you up, my book. It cheered up Brian no end. He said he'd never been so cheered up."

"Thank you, I'm sure your book is a very good book," she said, endearing herself to Adam forever. "But I don't need you to help look for my book—I think it's too late now."

She looked thoughtfully at Adam. "I expect you know this area very well?" she said.

"For miles an' *miles*," said Adam.

"You haven't seen two men in a big black car?" said Anathema.

"Did they steal it?" said Adam, suddenly full of interest. Foiling a gang of international book thieves would make a rewarding end to the day.

"Not really. Sort of. I mean, they didn't mean to. They were looking for the Manor, but I went up there today and no one knows anything about them. There was some sort of accident or something, I believe."

She stared at Adam. There was something odd about him, but she couldn't put her finger on it. She just had an urgent feeling that he was important and shouldn't be allowed to drift away. Something about him . . .

"What's the book called?" said Adam.

"*The Nice and Accurate Prophecies of Agnes Nutter, Witch*," said Anathema.

"Which what?"

"No. Witch. Like in *Macbeth*," said Anathema.

"I saw that," said Adam. "It was really interesting, the way them kings carried on. Gosh. What's nice about 'em?"

"Nice used to mean, well, precise. Or exact." Definitely something strange. A sort of laid-back intensity. You started to feel that if he was around, then everyone else, even the landscape, was just background.

She'd been here a month. Except for Mrs. Henderson, who in theory looked after the cottage and probably went through her things given half a chance, she hadn't exchanged more than a dozen real words with anyone. She let them think she was an artist. This was the kind of countryside that artists liked.

Actually, it was bloody beautiful. Just around this village it was superb. If Turner and Landseer had met Samuel Palmer in a pub and worked it all out, and then got Stubbs to do the horses, it couldn't have been better.

And that was depressing, because this was where *it* was going to happen. According to Agnes, anyway. In a book which she, Anathema, had allowed to be lost. She had the file cards, of course, but they just weren't the same.

If Anathema had been in full control of her own mind at that moment—and no one around Adam was ever in full control of his or her own mind—she'd have noticed that whenever she tried to think about him beyond a superficial level her thoughts slipped away like a duck off water.

"Wicked!" said Adam, who had been turning over in his mind the implications of a book of nice and accurate prophecies. "It tells you who's going to win the Grand National, does it?"

"No," said Anathema.

"Any spaceships in it?"

"Not many," said Anathema.

"Robots?" said Adam hopefully.

"Sorry."

"Doesn't sound very nice to *me*, then," said Adam. "Don't see what the future's got in it if there's no robots and spaceships."

About three days, thought Anathema glumly. *That's what it's got in it.*

"Would you like a lemonade?" she said.

Adam hesitated. Then he decided to take the bull by the horns.

"Look, 'scuse me for askin', if it's not a personal question, but are you a witch?" he said.

Anathema narrowed her eyes. So much for Mrs. Henderson poking around.

"Some people might say so," she said. "Actually, I'm an occultist."

"Oh. Well. That's all right, then," said Adam, cheering up.

She looked him up and down.

"You know what an occultist is, do you?" she said.

"Oh, yes," said Adam confidently.

"Well, so long as you're happier now," said Anathema. "Come on in. I could do with a drink myself. And . . . Adam Young?"

"Yes?"

"You were thinking 'Nothin' wrong with my eyes, they don't need examining,' weren't you?"

"Who, me?" said Adam guiltily.

DOG WAS THE PROBLEM. He wouldn't go in the cottage. He crouched on the doorstep, growling.

"Come on, you silly dog," said Adam. "It's only old Jasmine Cottage." He gave Anathema an embarrassed look. "Normally he does everything I say, right off."

"You can leave him in the garden," said Anathema.

"No," said Adam. "He's got to do what he's tole. I read it in a book. Trainin' is very important. Any dog can be trained, it said. My father said I can only keep him if he's prop'ly trained. Now, *Dog*. Go inside."

Dog whined and gave him a pleading look. His stubby tail thumped on the floor once or twice.

His Master's voice.

With extreme reluctance, as if making progress in the teeth of a gale, he slunk over the doorstep.

"There," said Adam proudly. "Good boy."

And a little bit more of Hell burned away . . .

Anathema shut the door.

There had always been a horseshoe over the door of Jasmine Cottage, ever since its first tenant centuries before; the Black Death was all the rage at the time and he'd considered that he could use all the protection he could get.

It was corroded and half covered with the paint of centuries. So neither Adam nor Anathema gave it a thought, or noticed how it was now cooling from a white heat.

AZIRAPHALE'S COCOA WAS STONE COLD.

The only sound in the room was the occasional turning of a page.

Every now and again there was a rattling at the door when prospective customers of Intimate Books next door mistook the entrance. He ignored it.

Occasionally he would very nearly swear.

ANATHEMA HADN'T REALLY made herself at home in the cottage. Most of her implements were piled up on the table. It looked interesting. It looked, in fact, as though a voodoo priest had just had the run of a scientific equipment store.

"Brilliant!" said Adam, prodding at it. "What's the thing with the three legs?"

"It's a theodolite," said Anathema from the kitchen. "It's for tracking ley-lines."

"What are they, then?" said Adam.

She told him.

"Cor," he said. "Are they?"

"Yes."

"All over the place?"

"Yes."

"I've never seen 'em. Amazin', there bein' all these invisible lines of force around and me not seeing 'em."

Adam didn't often listen, but he spent the most enthralling twenty minutes of his life, or at least of his life that day. No one in the Young household so much as touched wood or threw salt over their shoulder. The only nod in the direction of the supernatural was a half-hearted pretense, when Adam had been younger, that Father Christmas came down the chimney.*

He'd been starved of anything more occult than a Harvest Festival. Her words poured into his mind like water into a quire of blotting paper.

Dog lay under the table and growled. He was beginning to have serious doubts about himself.

* If Adam had been in full possession of his powers in those days, the Youngs' Christmas would have been spoiled by the discovery of a dead fat man upside down in their central-heating duct.

Anathema didn't only believe in ley-lines, but in seals, whales, bicycles, rain forests, whole grain in loaves, recycled paper, white South Africans out of South Africa, and Americans out of practically everywhere down to and including Long Island. She didn't compartmentalize her beliefs. They were welded into one enormous, seamless belief, compared with which that held by Joan of Arc seemed a mere idle notion. On any scale of mountain moving it shifted at least point five of an alp.*

No one had even used the word *environment* in Adam's hearing before. The South American rain forests were a closed book to Adam, and it wasn't even made of recycled paper.

The only time he interrupted her was to agree with her views on nuclear power: "I've been to a nucular power station. It was *boring*. There was no green smoke and bubbling stuff in tubes. Shouldn't be allowed, not having proper bubbling stuff when people have come all the way to see it, and having just a lot of men standin' around not even wearin' space suits."

"They do all the bubbling after visitors have gone home," said Anathema grimly.

"Huh," said Adam.

"They should be done away with this minute."

"Serve them right for not bubblin'," said Adam.

Anathema nodded. She was still trying to put her

* It may be worth noting here that most human beings can rarely raise more than .3 of an alp (30 centi-alps). Adam believed things on a scale ranging from 2 through to 15,640 Everests.

finger on what was so odd about Adam, and then she realized what it was.

He had no aura.

She was quite an expert on auras. She could see them, if she stared hard enough. They were a little glow of light around people's heads, and according to a book she'd read the color told you things about their health and general well-being. Everyone had one. In mean-minded, closed-in people they were a faint, trembling outline, whereas expansive and creative people might have one extending several inches from the body.

She'd never heard of anyone without one, but she couldn't see one around Adam at all. Yet he seemed cheerful, enthusiastic, and as well-balanced as a gyroscope.

Maybe I'm just tired, she thought.

Anyway, she was pleased and gratified to find such a rewarding student, and even loaned him some copies of *New Aquarian Digest*, a small magazine edited by a friend of hers.

It changed his life. At least, it changed his life for that day.

To his parents' astonishment he went to bed early, and then lay under the blankets until after midnight with a torch, the magazines, and a bag of lemon drops. The occasional "Brilliant!" emerged from his ferocious-chewing mouth.

When the batteries ran out he emerged into the darkened room and lay back with his head pillowed in his hands, apparently watching the squadron of X-wing™ fighters that hung from the ceiling. They moved gently in the night breeze.

But Adam wasn't really watching them. He was staring instead into the brightly lit panorama of his own imagination, which was whirling like a fairground.

This wasn't Wensleydale's aunt and a wineglass. This sort of occulting was a lot more interesting.

Besides, he liked Anathema. Of course, she was very old, but when Adam liked someone he wanted to make them happy.

He wondered how he could make Anathema happy.

It used to be thought that the events that changed the world were things like big bombs, maniac politicians, huge earthquakes, or vast population movements, but it has now been realized that this is a very old-fashioned view held by people totally out of touch with modern thought. The things that *really* change the world, according to Chaos theory, are the tiny things. A butterfly flaps its wings in the Amazonian jungle, and subsequently a storm ravages half of Europe.

Somewhere in Adam's sleeping head, a butterfly had emerged.

It might, or might not, have helped Anathema get a clear view of things if she'd been allowed to spot the very obvious reason why she couldn't see Adam's aura.

It was for the same reason that people in Trafalgar Square can't see England.

ALARMS WENT OFF.

Of course, there's nothing special about alarms

going off in the control room of a nuclear power station. They do it all the time. It's because there are so many dials and meters and things that something important might not get noticed if it doesn't at least beep.

And the job of Shift Charge Engineer calls for a solid, capable, unflappable kind of man, the kind you can depend upon not to make a beeline for the car-park in an emergency. The kind of man, in fact, who gives the impression of smoking a pipe even when he's not.

It was 3:00 A.M. in the control room of Turning Point power station, normally a nice quiet time when there is nothing much to do but fill in the log and listen to the distant roar of the turbines.

Until now.

Horace Gander looked at the flashing red lights. Then he looked at some dials. Then he looked at the faces of his fellow workers. Then he raised his eyes to the big dial at the far end of the room. Four hundred and twenty practically dependable and very nearly cheap megawatts were leaving the station. According to the other dials, nothing was producing them.

He didn't say "That's weird." He wouldn't have said "That's weird" if a flock of sheep had cycled past playing violins. It wasn't the sort of thing a responsible engineer said.

What he *did* say was: "Alf, you'd better ring the station manager."

Three very crowded hours went past. They involved quite a lot of phone calls, telexes, and faxes. Twenty-seven people were got out of bed in quick succession and they got another fifty-three out of bed, because if there is one thing a man wants to know when he's woken up in a panic at 4:00 A.M., it's that he's not alone.

Anyway, you need all sorts of permissions before they let you unscrew the lid of a nuclear reactor and look inside.

They got them. They unscrewed it. They had a look inside.

Horace Gander said, "There's got to be a sensible reason for this. Five hundred tons of uranium don't just get up and walk away."

A meter in his hand should have been screaming. Instead, it let out the occasional halfhearted tick.

Where the reactor should have been was an empty space. You could have had quite a nice game of squash in it.

Right at the bottom, all alone in the center of the bright cold floor, was a lemon drop.

Outside in the cavernous turbine hall the machines roared on.

And, a hundred miles away, Adam Young turned over in his sleep.

FRIDAY

Raven Sable, slim and bearded and dressed all in black, sat in the back of his slimline black limousine, talking on his slimline black telephone to his West Coast base.

"How's it going?" he asked.

"Looking good, chief," said his marketing head. "I'm doing breakfast with the buyers from all the leading supermarket chains tomorrow. No problem. We'll have MEALS™ in all the stores this time next month."

"Good work, Nick."

"No problem. No problem. It's knowing you're behind us, Rave. You give great leadership, guy. Works for me every time."

"Thank you," said Sable, and he broke the connection.

He was particularly proud of MEALS™.

The Newtrition corporation had started small, eleven years ago. A small team of food scientists, a huge team of marketing and public relations personnel, and a neat logo.

Two years of Newtrition investment and research had produced CHOW™. CHOW™ contained spun, plaited, and woven protein molecules, capped and coded, carefully designed to be ignored by even the most ravenous digestive tract enzymes; no-cal sweeteners; mineral oils replacing vegetable oils; fibrous materials, colorings, and flavorings. The end result was a foodstuff almost indistinguishable from any other except for two things. Firstly, the price, which was slightly higher, and secondly the nutritional content, which was roughly equivalent to that of a Sony Walkman. It didn't matter how much you ate, you lost weight.*

Fat people had bought it. Thin people who didn't want to get fat had bought it. CHOW™ was the ultimate diet food—carefully spun, woven, textured, and pounded to imitate anything, from potatoes to venison, although the chicken sold best.

Sable sat back and watched the money roll in. He watched CHOW™ gradually fill the ecological niche that used to be filled by the old, untrademarked food.

He followed CHOW™ with SNACKS™—junk food made from real junk.

MEALS™ was Sable's latest brainwave.

MEALS™ was CHOW™ with added sugar and fat. The theory was that if you ate enough MEALS™ you would a) get very fat, and b) die of malnutrition.

The paradox delighted Sable.

MEALS™ were currently being tested all over America. Pizza MEALS, Fish MEALS, Szechuan MEALS, macrobiotic rice MEALS. Even Hamburger MEALS.

* And hair. And skin tone. And, if you ate enough of it long enough, vital signs.

Sable's limousine was parked in the lot of a Des Moines, Iowa, Burger Lord—a fast food franchise wholly owned by his organization. It was here they'd been piloting Hamburger MEALS for the last six months. He wanted to see what kind of results they'd been getting.

He leaned forward, tapped the chauffeur's glass partition. The chauffeur pressed a switch, and the glass slid open.

"Sir?"

"I'm going to take a look at our operation, Marlon. I'll be ten minutes. Then back to L.A."

"Sir."

Sable sauntered into the Burger Lord. It was exactly like every other Burger Lord in America.* McLordy the Clown danced in the Kiddie Korner. The serving staff had identical gleaming smiles that never reached their eyes. And behind the counter a chubby, middle-aged man in a Burger Lord uniform slapped burgers onto the griddle, whistling softly, happy in his work.

* But not like every other Burger Lord across the world. German Burger Lords, for example, sold lager instead of root beer, while English Burger Lords managed to take any American fast food virtues (the speed with which your food was delivered, for example) and carefully remove them; your food arrived after half an hour, at room temperature, and it was only because of the strip of warm lettuce between them that you could distinguish the burger from the bun. The Burger Lord pathfinder salesmen had been shot twenty-five minutes after setting foot in France.

Sable went up to the counter.

"Hello-my-name-is-Marie," said the girl behind the counter. "How-can-I-help-you?"

"A double blaster thunder biggun, extra fries, hold the mustard," he said.

"Anything-to-drink?"

"A special thick whippy chocobanana shake."

She pressed the little pictogram squares on her till. (Literacy was no longer a requirement for employment in these restaurants. Smiling was.) Then she turned to the chubby man behind the counter.

"DBTB, E F, hold mustard," she said. "Chocshake."

"Uhnnhuhn," crooned the cook. He sorted the food into little paper containers, pausing only to brush the graying cowlick from his eyes.

"Here y'are," he said.

She took them without looking at him, and he returned cheerfully to his griddle, singing quietly, "Loooove me tender, looooove me long, neeever let me go . . ."

The man's humming, Sable noted, clashed with the Burger Lord background music, a tinny tape loop of the Burger Lord commercial jingle, and he made a mental note to have him fired.

Hello-my-name-is-Marie gave Sable his MEAL™ and told him to have a nice day.

He found a small plastic table, sat down in the plastic seat, and examined his food.

Artificial bread roll. Artificial burger. Fries that had never even seen potatoes. Foodless sauces. Even (and Sable was especially pleased with this) an artificial slice of dill pickle. He didn't bother to examine his milkshake. It had no actual food content, but then again, neither did those sold by any of his rivals.

All around him people were eating their unfood with, if not actual evidence of enjoyment, then with no more actual disgust than was to be found in burger chains all over the planet.

He stood up, took his tray over to the PLEASE DISPOSE OF YOUR REFUSE WITH CARE receptacle, and dumped the whole thing. If you had told him that there were children starving in Africa he would have been flattered that you'd noticed.

There was a tug at his sleeve. "Party name of Sable?" asked a small, bespectacled man in an International Express cap, holding a brown paper parcel.

Sable nodded.

"Thought it was you. Looked around, thought, tall gent with a beard, nice suit, can't be that many of them here. Package for you, sir."

Sable signed for it, his real name—one word, six letters. Sounds like examine.

"Thank you kindly, sir," said the delivery man. He paused. "Here," he said. "That bloke behind the counter. Does he remind you of anyone?"

"No," said Sable. He gave the man a tip—five dollars—and opened the package.

In it was a small pair of brass scales.

Sable smiled. It was a slim smile, and was gone almost instantly.

"About time," he said. He thrust the scales into his pocket, unheeding of the damage being done to the sleek line of his black suit, and went back to the limo.

"Back to the office?" asked the chauffeur.

"The airport," said Sable. "And call ahead. I want a ticket to England."

"Yessir. Return ticket to England."

Sable fingered the scales in his pocket. "Make that a single," he said. "I'll be making my own way back. Oh, and call the office for me, cancel all appointments."

"How long for, sir?"

"The foreseeable future."

And in the Burger Lord, behind the counter, the stout man with the cowlick slid another half-dozen burgers onto the grill. He was the happiest man in the whole world and he was singing, very softly.

". . . y'ain't never caught a rabbit," he hummed to himself, "and y'ain't no friend of mine . . ."

THE THEM LISTENED with interest. There was a light drizzle which was barely kept at bay by the old iron sheets and frayed bits of lino that roofed their den in the quarry, and they always looked to Adam to think up things to do when it was raining. They weren't disappointed. Adam's eyes were agleam with the joy of knowledge.

It had been 3:00 A.M. before he'd gone to sleep under a pile of *New Aquarian*s.

"An' then there was this man called Charles Fort," he said. "He could make it rain fish and frogs and stuff."

"Huh," said Pepper. "I *bet.* Alive frogs?"

"Oh, yes," said Adam, warming to his subject. "Hopping around and croaking and everything.

People paid him money to go away in the end an', an' . . ." He racked his brains for something that would satisfy his audience; he'd done, for Adam, a lot of reading in one go. ". . . And he sailed off in the *Mary Celeste* and founded the Bermuda Triangle. It's in Bermuda," he added helpfully.

"No, he couldn't of done that," said Wensleydale sternly, "because I've read about the *Mary Celeste*, and there was no one on it. It's famous for having no one on it. They found it floating around all by itself with no one on it."

"I dint say he was on it when they *found* it, did I?" said Adam scathingly. "Course he wasn't on it. 'Cos of the UFOs landin' and takin' him off. I thought everyone *knew* about that."

The Them relaxed a bit. They were on firmer ground with UFOs. They weren't entirely certain about New Age UFOs, though; they'd listened politely to Adam on the subject, but somehow modern UFOs lacked punch.

"If *I* was an alien," said Pepper, voicing the opinion of them all, "I wouldn't go round telling people all about mystic cosmic harmony. I'd say," her voice became hoarse and nasal, like someone hampered by an evil black mask, " 'Thish ish a lasher blashter, sho you do what you're told, rebel swine.' "

They all nodded. A favorite game in quarry had been based on a highly successful film series with lasers, robots, and a princess who wore her hair like a pair of stereo headphones™. (It had been agreed without a word being said that if anyone was going to play the part of any stupid princesses, it wasn't going to be Pepper.) But the game normally ended in a fight to be the one who was allowed to wear the coal scuttle™ and blow up planets. Adam was best at it—when he was the villain, he really sounded as if he *could* blow up the world. The Them were, anyway, temperamentally on the side of planet destroyers, provided they could be allowed to rescue princesses *at the same time*.

"I s'pect that's what they *used* to do," said Adam. "But now it's different. They all have this bright blue light around 'em and go around doing good. Sort of g'lactic policemen, going round tellin' everyone to live in universal harmony and stuff."

There was a moment's silence while they pondered this waste of perfectly good UFOs.

"What I've always wondered," said Brian, "is why they call 'em UFOs when they know they're flying saucers. I mean, they're *Identified* Flying Objects then."

"It's 'cos the Goverment hushes it all up," said Adam. "Millions of flying saucers landin' all the time and the Goverment keeps hushing it up."

"Why?" said Wensleydale.

Adam hesitated. His reading hadn't provided a quick explanation for this; *New Aquarian* just took it as the foundation of belief, both of itself and its readers, that the Government hushed everything up.

"'Cos they're the *Goverment*," said Adam simply. "That's what goverments do. They've got this great big building in London full of books of all the things they've hushed up. When the Prime Minister gets in to work in the morning, the first thing he does is go through the big list of everything that's happened in the night and put this big red stamp on them."

"I bet he has a cup of tea first, and then reads the paper," said Wensleydale, who had on one memorable occasion during the holidays gone unexpectedly into his father's office, where he had formed certain impressions. "And talks about what was on TV last night."

"Well, orlright, but after *that* he gets out the book and the big stamp."

"Which says 'Hush It Up,'" said Pepper.

"It says Top Secret," said Adam, resenting this attempt at bipartisan creativity. "It's like nucular power stations. They keep blowin' up all the time but no one ever finds out 'cos the Goverment hushes it up."

"They don't keep blowing *all* the time," said Wensleydale severely. "My father says they're dead safe and mean we don't have to live in a greenhouse. Anyway, there's a big picture of one in my comic* and it doesn't say anything about it blowing up."

* Wensleydale's alleged comic was a 94-week part-work called *Wonders of Nature and Science.* He had every single one so far, and had asked for a set of binders for his birthday. Brian's weekly reading was anything with a lot of exclamation marks in the title, like "WhiZZ!!" or "Clang!!" So was Pepper's, although even under the most refined of tortures she still wouldn't admit to the fact that she also bought *Just Seventeen* under plain covers. Adam didn't read any comics at all. They never lived up to the kind of things he could do in his head.

"Yes," said Brian, "but you lent me that comic afterwards and I know what *type* of picture it was."

Wensleydale hesitated, and then said in a voice heavy with badly tried patience, "Brian, just because it says Exploded Diagram—"

There was the usual brief scuffle.

"Look," said Adam severely. "Do you want me to tell you about the Aquarium Age, or not?"

The fight, never very serious amongst the siblinghood of the Them, subsided.

"Right," said Adam. He scratched his head. "Now you've made me forget where I've got to," he complained.

"Flyin' saucers," said Brian.

"Right. Right. Well, if you *do* see a flying UFO, these Goverment men come and tell you off," said Adam, getting back into his stride. "In a big black car. It happens all the time in America."

The Them nodded sagely. Of this at least they had no doubt. America was, to them, the place that good people went to when they died. They were prepared to believe that just about anything could happen in America.

"Prob'ly causes traffic jams," said Adam, "all these men in black cars, going about telling people off for seeing UFOs. They tell you that if you go on seeing 'em, you'll have a Nasty Accident."

"Prob'ly get run over by a big black car," said Brian, picking at a scab on a dirty knee. He brightened up. "Do you know," he said, "my cousin said that in America there's shops that sell thirty-nine different flavors of ice cream?"

This even silenced Adam, briefly.

"There aren't thirty-nine flavors of ice cream," said Pepper. "There aren't thirty-nine flavors in the whole world."

"There could be, if you mixed them up," said Wensleydale, blinking owlishly. "You know. Strawberry *and* chocolate. Chocolate *and* vanilla." He sought for more English flavors. "Strawberry *and* vanilla *and* chocolate," he added, lamely.

"And then there's Atlantis," said Adam loudly.

He had their interest there. They enjoyed Atlantis. Cities that sank under the sea were right up the Them's street. They listened intently to a jumbled account of pyramids, weird priesthoods, and ancient secrets.

"Did it just happen sudden, or slowly?" said Brian.

"Sort of sudden *an'* slowly," said Adam, " 'cos a lot of 'em got away in boats to all the other countries and taught 'em how to do maths an' English an' history an' stuff."

"Don't see what's so great about that," said Pepper.

"Could of been good fun, when it was sinking," said Brian wistfully, recalling the one occasion when Lower Tadfield had been flooded. "People deliverin' the milk and newspapers by boat, no one having to go to school."

"If *I* was an Atlantisan, I'd of stayed," said Wensleydale. This was greeted with disdainful laughter, but he pressed on. "You'd just have to wear a diver's helmet, that's all. And nail all the windows shut and fill the houses with air. It would be great."

Adam greeted this with the chilly stare he reserved for any of the Them who came up with an idea he really wished he'd thought of first.

"They *could* of done," he conceded, somewhat weakly. "After they'd sent all the teachers off in the boats. Maybe everyone else stayed on when it went down."

"You wouldn't have to wash," said Brian, whose parents forced him to wash a great deal more than he thought could possibly be healthy. Not that it did any good. There was something basically *ground in* about Brian. "Because everything would stay clean. An', an' you could grow seaweed and stuff in the garden and shoot sharks. And have pet octopuses and stuff. And there wouldn't be any schools and stuff because they'd of got rid of all the teachers."

"They could still be down there now," said Pepper.

They thought about the Atlanteans, clad in flowing mystic robes and goldfish bowls, enjoying themselves deep under the choppy waters of the ocean.

"Huh," said Pepper, summing up their feelings.

"What shall we do now?" said Brian. "It's brightened up a bit."

In the end they played Charles Fort Discovering Things. This consisted of one of the Them walking around with the ancient remains of an umbrella, while the others treated him to a rain of frogs or, rather, frog. They could only find one in the pond. It was an elderly frog, who knew the Them of old, and tolerated their interest as the price it paid for a pond otherwise free of moorhens and pike. It put up with things good-naturedly for a while before hopping off to a secret and so-far-undiscovered hideout in an old drainpipe.

Then they went home for lunch.

Adam felt very pleased about the morning's work. He'd always *known* that the world was an interesting place, and his imagination had peopled it with pirates and bandits and spies and astronauts and similar. But he'd also had a nagging suspicion that, when you seriously got right down to it, they were all just things in books and didn't properly exist any more.

Whereas this Aquarium Age stuff was *really* real. Grown-up people wrote lots of books about it (*New Aquarian* was full of adverts for them) and Bigfoots and Mothmen and Yetis and sea monsters and Surrey pumas *really* existed. If Cortez, on his peak in Darien, had had slightly damp feet from efforts at catching frogs, he'd have felt just like Adam at that moment.

The world was bright and strange and he was in the middle of it.

He bolted his lunch and retired to his room. There were still quite a few *New Aquarian*s he hadn't read yet.

THE COCOA WAS A CONGEALED brown sludge half filling the cup.

Certain people had spent hundreds of years trying to make sense of the prophecies of Agnes Nutter. They had been very intelligent, in the main. Anathema Device, who was about as close to *being* Agnes as genetic drift would allow, was the best of the bunch. But none of them had been angels.

Many people, meeting Aziraphale for the first time, formed three impressions: that he was English, that he was intelligent, and that he was gayer than a tree full of monkeys on nitrous oxide. Two of these were wrong; Heaven is not in England, whatever certain poets may have thought, and angels are sexless unless they really want to make an effort. But he *was* intelligent. And it was an angelic intelligence which, while not being particularly higher than human intelligence, is much broader and has the advantage of having thousands of years of practice.

Aziraphale was the first angel ever to own a computer. It was a cheap, slow, plasticky one, much touted as ideal for the small businessman. Aziraphale used it religiously for doing his accounts, which were so scrupulously accurate that the tax authorities had inspected him five times in the deep belief that he was getting away with murder somewhere.

But these other calculations were of a kind no computer could ever do. Sometimes he would scribble something on a sheet of paper by his side. It was covered in symbols which only eight other people in the world would have been able to comprehend; two of them had won Nobel prizes, and one of the other six dribbled a lot and wasn't allowed anything sharp because of what he might do with it.

ANATHEMA LUNCHED on miso soup and pored over her maps. There was no doubt the area around Tadfield was rich in ley-lines; even the famous Alfred Watkins had identified some. But unless she was totally wrong, they were beginning to shift position.

She'd spent the week taking soundings with theodolite and pendulum, and the Ordnance Survey map of the Tadfield area was now covered with little dots and arrows.

She stared at them for some time. Then she picked up a felt-tip pen and, with occasional references to her notebook, began to join them up.

The radio was on. She wasn't really listening. So quite a lot of the main news item passed right by her unheeding ears, and it wasn't until a couple of key words filtered down into her consciousness that she began to take notice.

Someone called A Spokesman sounded close to hysteria.

". . . danger to employees or the public," he was saying.

"And precisely how much nuclear material has escaped?" said the interviewer.

There was a pause. "We wouldn't say escaped," said the spokesman. "Not escaped. Temporarily mislaid."

"You mean it is still on the premises?"

"We certainly cannot see how it could have been removed from them," said the spokesman.

"Surely you have considered terrorist activity?"

There was another pause. Then the spokesman said, in the quiet tones of someone who has had enough and is going to quit after this and raise chickens somewhere, "Yes, I suppose we must. All we need to do is find some terrorists who are capable of taking an entire nuclear reactor out of its can while it's running and without anyone noticing. It weighs about a thousand tons and is forty feet high.

So they'll be quite *strong* terrorists. Perhaps you'd like to ring them up, sir, and ask them questions in that supercilious, accusatory way of yours."

"But you said the power station is still producing electricity," gasped the interviewer.

"It is."

"How can it still be doing that if it hasn't got any reactors?"

You could see the spokesman's mad grin, even on the radio. You could see his pen, poised over the "Farms for Sale" column in *Poultry World*. "We don't know," he said. "We were hoping you clever buggers at the BBC would have an idea."

Anathema looked down at her map.

What she had been drawing looked like a galaxy, or the type of carving seen on the better class of Celtic monolith.

The ley-lines were shifting. They were forming a spiral.

It was centered—loosely, with some margin for error, but nevertheless centered—on Lower Tadfield.

SEVERAL THOUSAND miles away, at almost the same moment as Anathema was staring at her spirals, the pleasure cruiser *Morbilli* was aground in three hundred fathoms of water.

For Captain Vincent, this was just another problem. For example, he knew he should contact the owners, but he never knew from day to day—or from hour to hour, in this computerized world—actually who the current owners were.

Computers, that was the bloody trouble. The ship's papers were computerized and it could switch to the most currently advantageous flag of convenience in microseconds. Its navigation had been computerized as well, constantly updating its position by satellites. Captain Vincent had explained patiently to the owners, whoever they were, that several hundred square meters of steel plating and a barrel of rivets would be a better investment, and had been informed that his recommendation did not accord with current cost/benefit flow predictions.

Captain Vincent strongly suspected that despite all its electronics the ship was worth more sunk than afloat, and would probably go down as the most perfectly pinpointed wreck in nautical history.

By inference, this also meant that he was more valuable dead than alive.

He sat at his desk quietly leafing through *International Maritime Codes*, whose six hundred pages contained brief yet pregnant messages designed to transmit the news of every conceivable nautical eventuality across the world with the minimum of confusion and, above all, cost.

What he wanted to say was this: Was sailing SSW at position 33° N 47° 72'W. First Mate, who you may recall was appointed in New Guinea against my wishes and is probably a headhunter, indicated by signs that something was amiss. It appears that quite a vast expanse of seabed has risen up in the night. It contains a large number of buildings, many of which appeared pyramid-like in structure. We are aground in the courtyard of one of these. There are some rather unpleasant statues. Amiable old men in long robes and diving helmets have come aboard the ship and are mingling happily with the passengers, who think we organized this. Please advise.

His questing finger moved slowly down the page, and stopped. Good old *International Codes.* They'd been devised eighty years before, but the men in those days had really thought hard about the kind of perils that might possibly be encountered on the deep.

He picked up his pen and wrote down: "XXXV QVVX."

Translated, it meant: "Have found Lost Continent of Atlantis. High Priest has just won quoits contest."

"IT JOLLY WELL ISN'T!"

"It jolly well is!"

"It isn't, you know!"

"It jolly well is!"

"It isn't—all right, then, what about volcanoes?" Wensleydale sat back, a look of triumph on his face.

"What about 'em?" said Adam.

"All that lather comes up from the center of the Earth, where it's all hot," said Wensleydale. "I saw a program. It had David Attenborough, so it's true."

The other Them looked at Adam. It was like watching a tennis match.

The Hollow Earth Theory was not going over well in the quarry. A beguiling idea that had stood up to the probings of such remarkable thinkers as Cyrus Reed Teed, Bulwer-Lytton, and Adolf Hitler was bending dangerously in the wind of Wensleydale's searingly bespectacled logic.

"I dint say it was hollow all the way through," said Adam. "No one said it was hollow *all* the way through. It prob'ly goes down miles and miles to make room for all the lather and oil and coal and Tibetan tunnels and suchlike. But then it's hollow after that. That's what people think. And there's a hole at the North Pole to let the air in."

"Never seen it on an atlas," sniffed Wensleydale.

"The Goverment won't let them put it on a map in case people go and have a look in," said Adam. "The reason being, the people livin' inside don't want people lookin' down on 'em all the time."

"What do you mean, Tibetan tunnels?" said Pepper. "You said Tibetan tunnels."

"Ah. Dint I tell you about them?"

Three heads shook.

"It's amazing. You know Tibet?"

They nodded doubtfully. A series of images had risen in their minds: yaks, Mount Everest, people called Grasshopper, little old men sitting on mountains, other people learning kung fu in ancient temples, and snow.

"*Well*, you know all those teachers that left Atlantis when it sunk?"

They nodded again.

"*Well*, some of them went to Tibet and now they run the world. They're called the Secret Masters. On account of being teachers, I suppose. An' they've got this secret underground city called Shambala and tunnels that go all over the world so's they know everythin' that goes on and control everythin'. Some people reckon that they really live under the Gobby Desert," he added loftily, "but mos' competent authorities reckon it's Tibet all right. Better for the tunneling, anyway."

The Them instinctively looked down at the grubby, dirt-covered chalk beneath their feet.

"How come they know everything?" said Pepper.

"They just have to listen, right?" hazarded Adam. "They just have to sit in their tunnels and listen. You know what hearin' teachers have. They can hear a whisper right across the room."

"My granny used to put a glass against the wall," said Brian. "She said it was disgustin', the way she could hear everything that went on next door."

"And these tunnels go everywhere, do they?" said Pepper, still staring at the ground.

"All over the world," said Adam firmly.

"Must of took a long time," said Pepper doubtfully. "You remember when we tried digging that tunnel out in the field, we were at it all afternoon, and you had to scrunch up to get all in."

"Yes, but they've been doin' it for millions of years. You can do really good tunnels if you've got millions of years."

"*I* thought the Tibetans were conquered by the Chinese and the Daily Llama had to go to India," said Wensleydale, but without much conviction. Wensleydale read his father's newspaper every evening, but the prosaic everydayness of the world always seemed to melt under the powerhouse of Adam's explanations.

"I bet they're down there now," said Adam, ignoring this. "They'd be all over the place by now. Sitting underground and listenin'."

They looked at one another.

"If we dug down quickly—" said Brian. Pepper, who was a lot quicker on the uptake, groaned.

"What'd you have to go an' say that for?" said Adam. "Fat lot of good us trying to surprise them now, isn't it, with you shoutin' out something like that. I was just thinkin' we could dig down, an' you jus' have to go an' warn 'em!"

"I don't think they'd dig all those tunnels," said Wensleydale doggedly. "It doesn't make any *sense*. Tibet's hundreds of miles away."

"Oh, yes. Oh, yes. An' I s'pose you know more about it than Madame Blatvatatatsky?" sniffed Adam.

"Now, if *I* was a Tibetan," said Wensleydale, in a reasonable tone of voice, "I'd just dig straight down to the hollow bit in the middle and then run around the inside and dig straight up where I wanted to be."

They gave this due consideration.

"You've got to admit that's more sensible than tunnels," said Pepper.

"Yes, well, I expect that's what they do," said Adam. "They'd be bound to of thought of something as simple as that."

Brian stared dreamily at the sky, while his finger probed the contents of one ear.

"Funny, reely," he said. "You spend your whole life goin' to school and learnin' stuff, and they never tell you about stuff like the Bermuda Triangle and UFOs and all these Old Masters running around the inside of the Earth. Why do we have to learn boring stuff when there's all this brilliant stuff we could be learnin', that's what I want to know."

There was a chorus of agreement.

Then they went out and played Charles Fort and the Atlantisans versus the Ancient Masters of Tibet, but the Tibetters claimed that using mystic ancient lasers was cheating.

THERE WAS A TIME when witchfinders were respected, although it didn't last very long.

Matthew Hopkins, for example, the Witchfinder General, found witches all over the east of England in the middle of the seventeenth century, charging each town and village ninepence a witch for every one he discovered.

That was the trouble. Witchfinders didn't get paid by the hour. Any witchfinder who spent a week examining the local crones and then told the mayor, "Well done, not a pointy hat among the lot of them," would get fulsome thanks, a bowl of soup and a meaningful goodbye.

So in order to turn a profit Hopkins had to find a remarkable number of witches. This made him more than a little unpopular with the village councils, and he was himself hanged as a witch by an East Anglian village who had sensibly realized that they could cut their overheads by eliminating the middleman.

It is thought by many that Hopkins was the last Witchfinder General.

In this they would, strictly speaking, be correct. Possibly not in the way they imagine, however. The

Witchfinder Army marched on, just slightly more quietly.

There is no longer a real Witchfinder General.

Nor is there a Witchfinder Colonel, a Witchfinder Major, a Witchfinder Captain, or even a Witchfinder Lieutenant (the last one was killed falling out of a very tall tree in Caterham, in 1933, while attempting to get a better view of something he believed was a satanic orgy of the most degenerate persuasion, but was, in fact, the Caterham and Whyteleafe Market Traders' Association annual dinner and dance).

There is, however, a Witchfinder Sergeant.

There is also, now, a Witchfinder Private. His name is Newton Pulsifer.

It was the advertisement that got him, in the *Gazette*, between a fridge for sale and a litter of not-exactly dalmatians:

JOIN THE PROFESSIONALS.
PART TIME

ASSISTANT REQUIRED TO COMBAT THE FORCES OF DARKNESS. UNIFORM, BASIC TRAINING PROVIDED. FIELD PROMOTION CERTAIN. BE A MAN!

In his lunch hour he phoned the number at the bottom of the ad. A woman answered.

"Hello," he began, tentatively. "I saw your advert."

"Which one, love?"

"Er, the one in the paper."

"Right, love. Well, Madame Tracy Draws Aside the Veil every afternoon except Thursdays. Parties welcome. When would you be wanting to Explore the Mysteries, love?"

Newton hesitated. "The advert says 'Join the Professionals,'" he said. "It didn't mention Madame Tracy."

"That'll be Mister Shadwell you'll be wanting, then. Just a sec, I'll see if he's in."

Later, when he was on nodding terms with Madame Tracy, Newt learned that if he had mentioned the other ad, the one in the magazine, Madame Tracy would have been available for strict discipline and intimate massage every evening except Thursdays. There was yet another ad in a phone box somewhere. When, much later, Newt asked her what this one involved, she said "Thursdays." Eventually there was the sound of feet in uncarpeted hallways, a deep coughing, and a voice the color of an old raincoat rumbled:

"Aye?"

"I read your advert. 'Join the professionals.' I wanted to know a bit more about it."

"Aye. There's many as would like to know more about it, an' there's many . . ." the voice trailed off impressively, then crashed back to full volume, ". . . there's many as WOULDN'T."

"Oh," squeaked Newton.

"What's your name, lad?"

"Newton. Newton Pulsifer."

"*LUCIFER?* What's that you say? Are ye of the Spawn of Darkness, a tempting beguiling creature from the pit, wanton limbs steaming from the fleshpots of Hades, in tortured and lubricious thrall to your Stygian and hellish masters?"

"That's Pulsifer," explained Newton. "With a P. I don't know about the other stuff, but we come from Surrey."

The voice on the phone sounded vaguely disappointed.

"Oh. Aye. Well, then. Pulsifer. *Pulsifer.* I've seen that name afore, maybe?"

"I don't know," said Newton. "My uncle runs a toy shop in Hounslow," he added, in case this was any help.

"Is that sooo?" said Shadwell.

Mr. Shadwell's accent was unplaceable. It careered around Britain like a milk race. Here a mad Welsh drill sergeant, there a High Kirk elder who'd just seen someone doing something on a Sunday, somewhere between them a dour Daleland shepherd, or bitter Somerset miser. It didn't matter where the accent went; it didn't get any nicer.

"Have ye all your own teeth?"

"Oh, yes. Except for fillings."

"Are ye fit?"

"I suppose so," Newt stuttered. "I mean, that was why I wanted to join the territorials. Brian Potter in Accounting can bench-press almost a hundred since he joined. And he paraded in front of the Queen Mother."

"How many nipples?"

"Pardon?"

"Nipples, laddie, nipples," said the voice testily. "How many nipples hae ye got?"

"Er. Two?"

"Good. Have ye got your ane scissors?"

"What?"

"Scissors! *Scissors!* Are ye deaf?"

"No. Yes. I mean, I've got some scissors. I'm not deaf."

THE COCOA HAD NEARLY ALL SOLIDIFIED. Green fur was growing on the inside of the mug.

There was a thin layer of dust on Aziraphale, too.

The stack of notes was building up beside him. *The Nice and Accurate Prophecies* was a mass of improvised bookmarks made of torn strips of *Daily Telegraph.*

Aziraphale stirred, and pinched his nose.

He was nearly there.

He'd got the shape of it.

He'd never met Agnes. She was too bright, obviously. Normally Heaven or Hell spotted the prophetic types and broadcast enough noises on the same mental channel to prevent any undue accuracy. Actually that was rarely necessary; they normally found ways of generating their own static in self-defense against the images that echoed around their heads. Poor old St. John had his mushrooms, for example. Mother Shipton had her ale. Nostradamus had his collection of interesting oriental preparations. St. Malachi had his still.

Good old Malachi. He'd been a nice old boy, sitting there, dreaming about future popes. Complete piss artist, of course. Could have been a real thinker, if it hadn't been for the poteen.

A sad end. Sometimes you really had to hope that the ineffable plan had been properly thought out.

Thought. There was something he had to do. Oh, yes. Phone his contact, get things sorted out.

He stood up, stretched his limbs, and made a phone call.

Then he thought: why not? Worth a try.

He went back and shuffled through his sheaf of notes. Agnes really had been good. And clever. No one was interested in accurate prophecies.

Paper in hand, he phoned Directory Enquiries.

"Hallo? Good afternoon. So kind. Yes. This will be a Tadfield number, I think. Or Lower Tadfield . . . ah. Or possibly Norton, I'm not sure of the precise code. Yes. Young. Name of Young. Sorry, no initial. Oh. Well, can you give me all of them? Thank you."

Back on the table, a pencil picked itself up and scribbled furiously.

At the third name it broke its point.

"Ah," said Aziraphale, his mouth suddenly running on automatic while his mind exploded. "I think that's the one. Thank you. So kind. Good day to you."

He hung up almost reverentially, took a few deep breaths, and dialed again. The last three digits gave him some trouble, because his hand was shaking.

He listened to the ringing tone. Then a voice answered. It was a middle-aged voice, not unfriendly, but probably it had been having a nap and was not feeling at its best.

It said "Tadfield Six double-six."

Aziraphale's hand started to shake.

"Hallo?" said the receiver. "Hallo."

Aziraphale got a grip on himself.

"Sorry," he said, "right number."

He replaced the receiver.

NEWT WASN'T DEAF. And he did have his own scissors.

He also had a huge pile of newspapers.

If he had known that army life consisted chiefly of applying the one to the other, he used to muse, he would never have joined.

Witchfinder Sergeant Shadwell had made him a list, which was taped to the wall in Shadwell's tiny crowded flat situated over Rajit's Newsagents and Video Rental. The list read:

1. Witches.
2. Unexplainable Phenomenons. Phenomenatrices. Phenomenice. Things, *ye ken* well what I mean.

Newt was looking for either. He sighed and picked up another newspaper, scanned the front page, opened it, ignored page two (never anything on there) then blushed crimson as he performed the obligatory nipple count on page three. Shadwell had been insistent about this. "Ye can't trust them, the cunning buggers," he said. "It'd be just like them to come right out in the open, like, defyin' us."

A couple in black turtleneck sweaters glowered at the camera on page nine. They claimed to lead the largest coven in Saffron Walden, and to restore sexual potency by the use of small and very phallic dolls. The newspaper was offering ten of the dolls to readers who were prepared to write "My Most Embarrassing Moment of Impotency" stories. Newt cut the story out and stuck it into a scrapbook.

There was a muffled thumping on the door.

Newt opened it; a pile of newspapers stood there. "Shift yerself, Private Pulsifer," it barked, and it shuffled into the room. The newspapers fell to the floor, revealing Witchfinder Sergeant Shadwell, who coughed, painfully, and relit his cigarette, which had gone out.

"You want to watch him. He's one o' *them*," he said.

"Who, sir?"

"Tak yer ease, Private. Him. That little brown feller. Mister so-called Rajit. It's them terrible forn arts. The ruby squinty eye of the little yellow god. Women wi' too many arms. Witches, the lot o' them."

"He does give us the newspapers free, though, Sergeant," said Newt. "And they're not too old."

"And voodoo. I bet he does voodoo. Sacrificing chickens to that Baron Saturday. Ye know, tall darkie bugger in the top hat. Brings people back from the dead, aye, and makes them work on the Sabbath day. Voodoo." Shadwell sniffed speculatively.

Newt tried to picture Shadwell's landlord as an exponent of voodoo. Certainly Mr. Rajit worked on the Sabbath. In fact, with his plump quiet wife and plump cheerful children he worked around the clock, never mind the calendar, diligently filling the area's needs in the matter of soft drinks, white bread, tobacco, sweets, newspapers, magazines, and the type of top-shelf pornography that made Newt's eyes water just to think about. The worst you could imagine Mr. Rajit doing with a chicken was selling it after the "Sell-By" date.

"But Mister Rajit's from Bangladesh, or India, or somewhere," he said. "I thought voodoo came from the West Indies."

"Ah," said Witchfinder Sergeant Shadwell, and took another drag on his cigarette. Or appeared to. Newt had never actually quite seen one of his superior's cigarettes—it was something to do with the way he cupped his hands. He even made the ends disappear when he'd finished with them. "Ah."

"Well, doesn't it?"

"Hidden wisdom, lad. Inner mili'try secrets of the Witchfinder army. When you're all initiated proper ye'll know the secret truth. Some voodoo *may* come from the West Indies. I'll grant ye that. Oh yes, I'll grant ye that. But the *worst* kind. The darkest kind, that comes from, um . . ."

"Bangladesh?"

"Errrukh! Yes lad, that's it. Words right out of me mouth. Bangladesh. Exactly."

Shadwell made the end of his cigarette vanish, and managed furtively to roll another, never letting papers or tobacco be seen.

"So. Ye got anything, Witchfinder Private?"

"Well, there's this." Newton held out the clipping.

Shadwell squinted at it. "Oh *them*," he said. "Load o' rubbish. Call themselves bloody witches? I checked them out last year. Went down with me armory of righteousness and a packet of firelighters, jemmied the place open, they were clean as a whistle. Mail order bee jelly business they're trying to pep up. Load o' rubbish. Wouldn't know a familiar spirit if it chewed out the bottoms o' their trousers. Rubbish. It's not like it used to be, laddie."

He sat down and poured himself a cup of sweet tea from a filthy thermos.

"Did I ever tell you how I was recruited to the army?" he asked.

Newt took this as his cue to sit down. He shook his head. Shadwell lit his roll-up with a battered Ronson lighter, and coughed appreciatively.

"My cellmate, he was. Witchfinder Captain Ffolkes. Ten years for arson. Burning a coven in Wimbledon. Would have got them all too, if it wasn't the wrong day. Good fellow. Told me about the battle—the great war between Heaven and Hell . . . It was him that told me the Inner Secrets of the Witchfinder Army. Familiar spirits. Nipples. All that . . .

"Knew he was dying, you see. Got to have someone to carry on the tradition. Like you is, now . . ." He shook his head.

"That's what we'm reduced to, lad," he said. "A few hundred years ago, see, we was powerful. We stood between the world and the darkness. We was the thin red line. Thin red line o' fire, ye see."

"I thought the churches . . ." Newt began.

"Pah!" said Shadwell. Newt had seen the word in print, but this was the first time he'd ever heard anyone say it. "Churches? What good did they ever do? They'm just as bad. Same line o' business, nearly. You can't trust them to stamp out the Evil One, 'cos if they did, they'd be out o' that line o' business. If yer goin' up against a tiger, ye don't want fellow travelers whose idea of huntin' is tae throw meat at it. Nay, lad. It's up to us. Against the darkness."

Everything went quiet for a moment.

Newt always tried to see the best in everyone, but it had occurred to him shortly after joining the WA that his superior and only fellow soldier was as well balanced as an upturned pyramid. "Shortly," in this case, meant under five seconds. The WA's headquarters was a fetid room with walls the color of nicotine, which was almost certainly what they were coated with, and a floor the color of cigarette ash, which was almost certainly what it was. There was a small square of carpet. Newt avoided walking on it if possible, because it sucked at his shoes.

One of the walls had a yellowing map of the British Isles tacked to it, with homemade flags sticking in it here and there; most of them were within a Cheap Day Return fare of London.

But Newt had stuck with it the past few weeks because, well, horrified fascination had turned into horrified pity and then a sort of horrified affection. Shadwell had turned out to be about five feet high and wore clothes which, no matter what they actually *were*, always turned up even in your short-term memory as an old mackintosh. The old man may have had all his own teeth, but only because no one else could possibly have wanted them; just one of them, placed under the pillow, would have made the Tooth Fairy hand in its wand.

He appeared to live entirely on sweet tea, condensed milk, hand-rolled cigarettes, and a sort of sullen internal energy. Shadwell had a Cause, which he followed with the full resources of his soul and his Pensioner's Concessionary Travel Pass. He believed in it. It powered him like a turbine.

Newton Pulsifer had never had a cause in his life. Nor had he, as far as he knew, ever believed in anything. It had been embarrassing, because he quite *wanted* to believe in something, since he recognized that belief was the lifebelt that got most people through the choppy waters of Life. He'd have liked to believe in a supreme God, although he'd have preferred a half-hour's chat with Him before committing himself, to clear up one or two points. He'd sat in all sorts of churches, waiting for that single flash of blue light, and it hadn't come. And then he'd tried to become an official Atheist and hadn't got the rock-hard, self-satisfied strength of belief even for that. And every single political party had seemed to him equally dishonest. And he'd given up on ecology when the ecology magazine he'd been subscribing to had shown its readers a plan of a self-sufficient garden, and had drawn the ecological goat tethered within three feet of the ecological beehive. Newt had spent a lot of time at his grandmother's house in the country and thought he knew something about the habits of both goats and bees, and concluded therefore that the magazine was run by a bunch of bib-overalled maniacs. Besides, it used the word "community" too often; Newt had always suspected that people who regularly used the word "community" were using it in a very specific sense that excluded him and everyone he knew.

Then he'd tried believing in the Universe, which seemed sound enough until he'd innocently started reading new books with words like Chaos and Time and Quantum in the titles. He'd found that even the people whose job of work was, so to speak, the Universe, didn't really believe in it and were actually quite proud of not knowing what it really was or even if it could theoretically exist.

To Newt's straightforward mind this was intolerable.

Newt had not believed in the Cub Scouts and then, when he was old enough, not in the Scouts either.

He was prepared to believe, though, that the job of wages clerk at United Holdings [Holdings] PLC, was possibly the most boring in the world.

This is how Newton Pulsifer looked as a man: if he went into a phone booth and changed, he might manage to come out looking like Clark Kent.

But he found he rather liked Shadwell. People often did, much to Shadwell's annoyance. The Rajits liked him because he always eventually paid his rent and didn't cause any trouble, and was racist in such a glowering, undirected way that it was quite inoffensive; it was simply that Shadwell hated everyone in the world, regardless of caste, color, or creed, and wasn't going to make any exceptions for anyone.

Madame Tracy liked him. Newt had been amazed to find that the tenant of the other flat was a middle-aged, motherly soul, whose gentlemen callers called as much for a cup of tea and a nice chat as for what little discipline she was still able to exact. Sometimes, when he'd nursed a half pint of Guinness on a Saturday night, Shadwell would stand in the corridor between their rooms and shout things like "Hoor of Babylon!" but she told Newt privately that she'd always felt rather gratified about this even though the closest she'd been to Babylon was Torremolinos. It was like free advertising, she said.

She said she didn't mind him banging on the wall and swearing during her seance afternoons, either. Her knees had been giving her gyp and she wasn't always up to operating the table rapper, she said, so a bit of muffled thumping came in useful.

On Sundays she'd leave him a bit of dinner on his doorstep, with another plate over the top of it to keep it warm.

You couldn't help liking Shadwell, she said. For all the good it did, though, she might as well be flicking bread pellets into a black hole.

Newt remembered the other cuttings. He pushed them across the stained desk.

"What are these?" said Shadwell, suspiciously.

"Phenomena," said Newt. "You said to look for phenomena. There's more phenomena than witches these days, I'm afraid."

"Anyone bin shootin' hares wi' a silver bullet and next day an old crone in the village is walkin' wi' a limp?" Shadwell said hopefully.

"I'm afraid not."

"Any cows droppin' dead after some woman has looked at 'em?"

"No."

"What is it, then?" said Shadwell. He shuffled across to the sticky brown cupboard and pulled out a tin of condensed milk.

"Odd things happening," said Newt.

He'd spent weeks on this. Shadwell had really let the papers pile up. Some of them went back for years. Newt had quite a good memory, perhaps because in his twenty-three years very little had happened to fill it up, and he had become quite expert on some very esoteric subjects.

"Seems to be something new every day," said Newt, flicking through the rectangles of newsprint. "Something weird has been happening to nuclear power stations, and no one seems to know what it is. And some people are claiming that the Lost Continent of Atlantis has risen." He looked proud of his efforts.

Shadwell's penknife punctured the condensed milk tin. There was the distant sound of a telephone ringing. Both men instinctively ignored it. All the calls were for Madame Tracy anyway and some of them were not intended for the ear of man; Newt had conscientiously answered the phone on his first day, listened carefully to the question, said "Marks and Spencer's 100% Cotton Y-fronts, actually," and had been left with a dead receiver.

Shadwell sucked deeply. "Ach, that's no' proper phenomena," he said. "Can't see any witches doing that. They're more for the sinking o' things, ye ken."

Newt's mouth opened and shut a few times.

"If we're strong in the fight against witchery we can't afford to be sidetracked by this style o' thing," Shadwell went on. "Haven't ye got anything more witchcrafty?"

"But American troops have landed on it to protect it from things," moaned Newt. "A nonexistent continent . . ."

"Any witches on it?" said Shadwell, showing a spark of interest for the first time.

"It doesn't say," said Newt.

"Ach, then it's just politics and geography," said Shadwell dismissively.

Madame Tracy poked her head around the door. "Coo-ee, Mr. Shadwell," she said, giving Newt a friendly little wave. "A gentleman on the telephone for you. Hallo, Mr. Newton."

"Awa' wi' ye, harlot," said Shadwell, automatically.

"He sounds ever so refined," said Madame Tracy, taking no notice. "And I'll be getting us a nice bit of liver for Sunday."

"I'd sooner sup wi' the De'el, wumman."

"So if you'd let me have the plates back from last week it'd be a help, there's a love," said Madame Tracy, and tottered unsteadily back on three-inch heels to her flat and whatever it was that had been interrupted.

Newt looked despondently at his cuttings as Shadwell went out, grumbling, to the phone. There was one about the stones of Stonehenge moving out of position, as though they were iron filings in a magnetic field.

He was vaguely aware of one side of a telephone conversation.

"Who? Ah. Aye. Aye. Ye say? Wha' class o' thing wud that be? Aye. Just as you say, sor. And where is this place, then—?"

But mysteriously moving stones wasn't Shadwell's cup of tea or, rather, tin of milk.

"Fine, fine," Shadwell reassured the caller. "We'll get onto it right awa'. I'll put my best squad on it and report success to ye any minute, I ha' no doubt. Goodbye to you, sor. And bless you too, sor." There was the ting of a receiver going back on the hook, and then Shadwell's voice, no longer metaphorically crouched in deference, said, "'Dear boy'! Ye great Southern pansy."*

He shuffled back into the room, and then stared at Newt as if he had forgotten why he was there.

"What was it ye was goin' on about?" he said.

"All these things that are happening—" Newt began.

"Aye." Shadwell continued to look through him while thoughtfully tapping the empty tin against his teeth.

"Well, there's this little town which has been having some amazing weather for the last few years," Newt went on helplessly.

"What? Rainin' frogs and similar?" said Shadwell, brightening up a bit.

"No. It just has normal weather for the time of year."

"Call that a phenomena?" said Shadwell. "I've seen phenomenas that'd make your hair curl, laddie." He started tapping again.

"When do you remember normal weather for the time of year?" said Newt, slightly annoyed. "Normal weather for the time of year isn't normal, Sergeant. It has snow at Christmas. When did you last see snow at Christmas? And long hot Augusts? Every year? And crisp autumns? The kind of weather you used to dream of as a kid? It never rained on No-

* Shadwell hated all Southerners and, by inference, was standing at the North Pole.

vember the Fifth and always snowed on Christmas Eve?"

Shadwell's eyes looked unfocused. He paused with the condensed milk tin halfway to his lips.

"I never used to dream when I was a kid," he said quietly.

Newt was aware of skidding around the lip of some deep, unpleasant pit. He mentally backed away.

"It's just very odd," he said. "There's a weatherman here talking about averages and norms and microclimates and things like that."

"What's that mean?" said Shadwell.

"Means he doesn't know why," said Newt, who hadn't spent years on the littoral of business without picking up a thing or two. He looked sidelong at the Witchfinder Sergeant.

"Witches are well known for affecting the weather," he prompted. "I looked it up in the *Discouverie.*"

Oh God, he thought, or other suitable entity, don't let me spend another evening cutting newspapers to bits in this ashtray of a room. Let me get out in the fresh air. Let me do whatever is the WA's equivalent of going waterskiing in Germany.

"It's only forty miles away," he said tentatively. "I thought I could just sort of nip over there tomorrow. And have a look around, you know. I'll pay my own petrol," he added.

Shadwell wiped his upper lip thoughtfully.

"This place," he said, "it wouldna be called Tadfield, would it?"

"That's right, Mr. Shadwell," said Newt. "How did you know that?"

"Wonder what the Southerners is playing at noo?" said Shadwell under his breath.

"Weeell," he said, out loud. "And why not?"

"Who'll be playing, Sergeant?" said Newt.

Shadwell ignored him. "Aye. I suppose it can't do any harm. Ye'll pay yer ane petrol, ye say?"

Newt nodded.

"Then ye'll come here at nine o' the clock in the morning," he said, "afore ye go."

"What for?" said Newt.

"Yer armor o' righteousness."

JUST AFTER NEWT HAD LEFT the phone rang again. This time it was Crowley, who gave approximately the same instructions as Aziraphale. Shadwell took them down again for form's sake, while Madame Tracy hovered delightedly behind him.

"Two calls in one day, Mr. Shadwell," she said. "Your little army must be marching away like anything!"

"Ach, awa' wi' ye, ye murrain plashed berrizene," muttered Shadwell, and slammed the door. Tadfield, he thought. Och, weel. So long as they paid up on time . . .

Neither Aziraphale or Crowley ran the Witchfinder Army, but they both approved of it, or at least knew that it would be approved of by their superiors. So it appeared on the list of Aziraphale's agencies because it was, well, a *Witch*finder Army, and you had to support anyone calling themselves witchfinders in the same way that the U.S.A. had to support anyone calling themselves anti-communist. And it appeared on Crowley's list for the slightly more sophisticated reason that people like Shadwell did the cause of Hell no harm at all. Quite the reverse, it was felt.

Strictly speaking, Shadwell didn't run the WA either. According to Shadwell's pay ledgers it was run by Witchfinder General Smith. Under him were Witchfinder Colonels Green and Jones, and Witchfinder Majors Jackson, Robinson, and Smith (no relation). Then there were Witchfinder Majors Saucepan, Tin, Milk, and Cupboard, because Shadwell's limited imagination had been beginning to struggle at this point. And Witchfinder Captains Smith, Smith, Smith, and Smythe and Ditto. And five hundred Witchfinder Privates and Corporals and Sergeants. Many of them were called Smith, but this didn't matter because neither Crowley nor Aziraphale had ever bothered to read that far. They simply handed over the pay.

After all, both lots put together only came to around £60 a year.

Shadwell didn't consider this in any way criminal. The army was a sacred trust, and a man had to do something. The old ninepences weren't coming in like they used to.

SATURDAY

IT WAS VERY EARLY on Saturday morning, on the last day of the world, and the sky was redder than blood.

The International Express delivery man rounded the corner at a careful thirty-five miles an hour, shifted down to second, and pulled up on the grass verge.

He got out of the van, and immediately threw himself into a ditch to avoid an oncoming lorry that had barreled around the bend at something well in excess of eighty miles an hour.

He got up, picked up his glasses, put them back on, retrieved his parcel and clipboard, brushed the grass and mud from his uniform, and, as an afterthought, shook his fist at the rapidly diminishing lorry.

"Shouldn't be allowed, bloody lorries, no respect for other road users, what I always say, what I always say, is remember that without a car, son, you're just a pedestrian too . . ."

He climbed down the grassy verge, clambered over a low fence, and found himself beside the river Uck.

The International Express delivery man walked along the banks of the river, holding the parcel.

Farther down the riverbank sat a young man dressed all in white. He was the only person in sight. His hair was white, his skin chalk pale, and he sat and stared up and down the river, as if he were admiring the view. He looked like how Victorian Romantic poets looked just before the consumption and drug abuse really started to cut it.

The International Express man couldn't understand it. I mean, in the old days, and it wasn't that long ago really, there had been an angler every dozen yards along the bank; children had played there; courting couples had come to listen to the splish and gurgle of the river, and to hold hands, and to get all lovey-dovey in the Sussex sunset. He'd done that with Maud, his missus, before they were married. They'd come here to spoon and, on one memorable occasion, fork.

Times changed, reflected the delivery man.

Now white and brown sculptures of foam and sludge drifted serenely down the river, often covering it for yards at a stretch. And where the surface of the water was visible it was covered with a molecules-thin petrochemical sheen.

There was a loud whirring as a couple of geese, thankful to be back in England again after the long, exhausting flight across the Northern Atlantic, landed on the rainbow-slicked water, and sank without trace.

Funny old world, thought the delivery man. Here's the Uck, used to be the prettiest river in this part of the world, and now it's just a glorified industrial sewer. The swans sink to the bottom, and the fishes float on the top.

Well, that's progress for you. You can't stop progress.

He had reached the man in white.

"'Scuse me, sir. Party name of Chalky?"

The man in white nodded, said nothing. He continued to gaze out at the river, following an impressive sludge and foam sculpture with his eyes.

"So beautiful," he whispered. "It's all so damn beautiful."

The delivery man found himself temporarily devoid of words. Then his automatic systems cut in. "Funny old world isn't it and no mistake I mean you go all over the world delivering and then here you are practically in your own home so to speak, I mean I was born and bred 'round here, sir, and I've been to the Mediterranean, and to Des O' Moines, and that's in America, sir, and now here I am, and here's your parcel, sir."

Party name of Chalky took the parcel, and took the clipboard, and signed for the parcel. The pen developed a leak as he did so, and his signature obliterated itself as it was written. It was a long word, and it began with a P, and then there was a splodge, and then it ended in something that might have been—*ence* and might have been—*ution*.

"Much obliged, sir," said the delivery man.

He walked back along the river, back toward the busy road where he had left his van, trying not to look at the river as he went.

Behind him the man in white opened the parcel. In it was a crown—a circlet of white metal, set with diamonds. He gazed at it for some seconds, with satisfaction, then put it on. It glinted in the light of the rising sun. Then the tarnish, which had begun to suffuse its silver surface when his fingers touched it, spread to cover it completely; and the crown went black.

White stood up. There's one thing you can say for air pollution, you get utterly amazing sunrises. It looked like someone had set fire to the sky.

And a careless match would have set fire to the river, but, alas, there was no time for that now. In his mind he knew where the Four Of Them would be meeting, and when, and he was going to have to hurry to be there by this afternoon.

Perhaps we *will* set fire to the sky, he thought. And he left that place, almost imperceptibly.

It was nearly time.

The delivery man had left his van on the grass verge by the dual carriageway. He walked around to the driver's side (carefully, because other cars and lorries were still rocketing around the bend), reached in through the open window, and took the schedule from the dashboard.

Only one more delivery to make, then.

He read the instructions on the delivery voucher carefully.

He read them again, paying particular attention to the address, and the message. The address was one word: Everywhere.

Then, with his leaking pen, he wrote a brief note to Maud, his wife. It read simply, *I love you.*

Then he put the schedule back on the dashboard, looked left, looked right, looked left again and began to walk purposefully across the road. He was halfway across when a German juggernaut came around the corner, its driver crazed on caffeine, little white pills, and EEC transport regulations.

He watched its receding bulk.

Cor, he thought, that one nearly had me.

Then he looked down at the gutter.

Oh, he thought.

YES, agreed a voice from behind his left shoulder, or at least from behind the memory of his left shoulder.

The delivery man turned, and looked, and saw. At first he couldn't find the words, couldn't find anything, and then the habits of a working lifetime took over and he said, "Message for you, sir."

FOR ME?

"Yes, sir." He wished he still had a throat. He could have swallowed, if he still had a throat. "No package, I'm afraid, Mister . . . uh, sir. It's a message."

DELIVER IT, THEN.

"It's this, sir. Ahem. *Come and See.*"

FINALLY. There was a grin on its face, but then, given the face, there couldn't have been anything else.

THANK YOU, it continued. I MUST COMMEND YOUR DEVOTION TO DUTY.

"Sir?" The late delivery man was falling through a gray mist, and all he could see were two spots of blue, that might have been eyes, and might have been distant stars.

DON'T THINK OF IT AS DYING, said Death, JUST THINK OF IT AS LEAVING EARLY TO AVOID THE RUSH.

The delivery man had a brief moment to wonder whether his new companion was making a joke, and to decide that he wasn't; and then there was nothing.

RED SKY IN THE MORNING. IT WAS GOING TO RAIN.

Yes.

WITCHFINDER SERGEANT Shadwell stood back with his head on one side. "Right, then," he said. "Ye're all ready. Hae ye got it all?"

"Yes, sir."

"Pendulum o' discovery?"

"Pendulum of discovery, yes."

"Thumbscrew?"

Newt swallowed, and patted a pocket.

"Thumbscrew," he said.

"Firelighters?"

"I really think, Sergeant, that—"

"Firelighters?"

"Firelighters,"* said Newt sadly. "And matches."

* Note for Americans and other city-dwelling life-forms: the rural British, having eschewed central heating as being far too complicated and in any case weakening moral fiber, prefer a system of piling small pieces of wood and lumps of coal, topped by large, wet logs, possibly made of asbestos, into small, smoldering heaps,

"Bell, book, and candle?"

Newt patted another pocket. It contained a paper bag inside which was a small bell, of the sort that maddens budgerigars, a pink candle of the birthday cake persuasion, and a tiny book called *Prayers for Little Hands.* Shadwell had impressed upon him that, although witches were the primary target, a good Witchfinder should never pass up the chance to do a quick exorcism, and should have his field kit with him at all times.

"Bell, book, and candle," said Newt.

"Pin?"

"Pin."

"Good lad. Never forget yer pin. It's the bayonet in yer artillery o' light."

Shadwell stood back. Newt noticed with amazement that the old man's eyes had misted over.

"I wish I was goin' with ye," he said. "O' course, this won't be anything, but it'd be good to get out and about again. It's a tryin' life, ye ken, all this lyin' in the wet bracken spying on their devilish dancin'. It gets into yer bones somethin' cruel."

He straightened up, and saluted.

"Off ye go, then, Private Pulsifer. May the armies o' glorification march wi' ye."

After Newt had driven off Shadwell thought

---

known as "There's nothing like a roaring open fire is there?" Since none of these ingredients are naturally inclined to burn, underneath all this they apply a small, rectangular, waxy white lump, which burns cheerfully until the weight of the fire puts it out. These little white blocks are called firelighters. No one knows why.

of something, something that he'd never had the chance to do before. What he needed now was a pin. Not a military issue pin, witches, for the use of. Just an ordinary pin, such as you might stick in a map.

The map was on the wall. It was old. It didn't show Milton Keynes. It didn't show Harlow. It barely showed Manchester and Birmingham. It had been the army's HQ map for three hundred years. There were a few pins in it still, mainly in Yorkshire and Lancashire and a few in Essex, but they were almost rusted through. Elsewhere, mere brown stubs indicated the distant mission of a long-ago witchfinder.

Shadwell finally found a pin among the debris in an ashtray. He breathed on it, polished it to a shine, squinted at the map until he located Tadfield, and triumphantly rammed the pin home.

It gleamed.

Shadwell took a step backward, and saluted again. There were tears in his eyes.

Then he did a smart about turn and saluted the display cabinet. It was old and battered and the glass was broken but in a way it *was* the WA. It contained the Regimental silver (the Interbattalion Golf Trophy, not competed for, alas, in seventy years); it contained the patent muzzle-loading Thundergun of Witchfinder-Colonel Ye-Shall-Not-Eat-Any-Living-Thing-With-The-Blood-Neither-Shall-Ye-Use-Enchantment-Nor-Observe-Times Dalrymple; it contained a display of what were apparently walnuts but were in reality a collection of shrunken headhunter heads donated by Witchfinder CSM Horace

"Get them afore they Get You" Narker, who'd traveled widely in foreign parts; it contained memories.

Shadwell blew his nose, noisily, on his sleeve.

Then he opened a tin of condensed milk for breakfast.

IF THE ARMIES OF GLORIFICATION had tried to march with Newt, bits of them would have dropped off. This is because, apart from Newt and Shadwell, they had been dead for quite a long time.

It was a mistake to think of Shadwell (Newt never found out if he had a first name) as a lone nut.

It was just that all the others were dead, in most cases for several hundred years. Once the Army had been as big as it currently appeared in Shadwell's creatively edited bookkeeping. Newt had been surprised to find that the Witchfinder Army had antecedents as long and almost as bloody as its more mundane counterpart.

The rates of pay for witchfinders had last been set by Oliver Cromwell and never reviewed. Officers got a crown, and the General got a sovereign. It was just an honorarium, of course, because you got ninepence per witch found and first pick of their property.

You really got to rely on those ninepences. And so times had been a bit hard before Shadwell had gone on the payrolls of Heaven and Hell.

Newt's pay was one old shilling per year.*

In return for this, he was charged to keep "glim-

* NOTE FOR YOUNG PEOPLE AND AMERICANS: One shilling = Five Pee. It helps to understand the antique

mer, firelock, firebox, tinderbox or igniferous matches" about his person at all times, although Shadwell indicated that a Ronson gas lighter would do very well. Shadwell had accepted the invention of the patent cigarette lighter in the same way that conventional soldiers welcomed the repeating rifle.

The way Newt looked at it, it was like being in one of those organizations like the Sealed Knot or those people who kept on refighting the American Civil War. It got you out at weekends, and meant that you were keeping alive fine old traditions that had made Western civilization what it was today.

AN HOUR AFTER LEAVING the headquarters, Newt pulled into a layby and rummaged in the box on the passenger seat.

Then he opened the car window, using a pair of pliers for the purpose since the handle had long since fallen off.

The packet of firelighters was sent winging over

---

finances of the Witchfinder Army if you know the original British monetary system:

Two farthings = One Ha'penny. Two ha'pennies = One Penny. Three pennies = A Thruppenny Bit. Two Thruppences = A Sixpence. Two Sixpences = One Shilling, or Bob. Two Bob = A Florin. One Florin and One Sixpence = Half a Crown. Four Half Crowns = Ten Bob Note. Two Ten Bob Notes = One Pound (or 240 pennies). One Pound and One Shilling = One Guinea.

The British resisted decimalized currency for a long time because they thought it was too complicated.

the hedge. A moment later the thumbscrew followed it.

He debated about the rest of the stuff, and then put it back in the box. The pin was Witchfinder military issue, with a good ebony knob on the end like a ladies' hat pin.

He knew what it was for. He'd done quite a lot of reading. Shadwell had piled him up with pamphlets at their first meeting, but the Army had also accumulated various books and documents which, Newt suspected, would be worth a fortune if they ever hit the market.

The pin was to jab into suspects. If there was a spot on their body where they didn't feel anything, they were a witch. Simple. Some of the fraudulent Witchfinders had used special retracting pins, but this one was honest, solid steel. He wouldn't be able to look old Shadwell in the face if he threw away the pin. Besides, it was probably bad luck.

He started the engine and resumed his journey.

Newt's car was a Wasabi. He called it Dick Turpin, in the hope that one day someone would ask him why.

It would be a very accurate historian who could pinpoint the precise day when the Japanese changed from being fiendish automatons who copied everything from the West, to becoming skilled and cunning engineers who would leave the West standing. But the Wasabi had been designed on that one confused day, and combined the traditional bad points of most Western cars with a host of innovative disasters the avoidance of which had made firms like Honda and Toyota what they were today.

Newt had never actually seen another one on the road, despite his best efforts. For years, and without much conviction, he'd enthused to his friends about its economy and efficiency in the desperate hope that one of them might buy one, because misery loves company.

In vain did he point out its 823cc engine, its three-speed gearbox, its incredible safety devices like the balloons which inflated on dangerous occasions such as when you were doing 45 mph on a straight dry road but were about to crash because a huge safety balloon had just obscured the view. He'd also wax slightly lyrical about the Korean-made radio, which picked up Radio Pyongyang incredibly well, and the simulated electronic voice which warned you about not wearing a seatbelt even when you were; it had been programmed by someone who not only didn't understand English, but didn't understand Japanese either. It was state of the art, he said.

The art in this case was probably pottery.

His friends nodded and agreed and privately decided that if ever it came to buying a Wasabi or walking, they'd invest in a pair of shoes; it came to the same thing anyway, since one reason for the Wasabi's incredible m.p.g. was that fact that it spent a lot of time waiting in garages while crankshafts and things were in the post from the world's only surviving Wasabi agent in Nigirizushi, Japan.

In that vague, zen-like trance in which most people drive, Newt found himself wondering exactly how you used the pin. Did you say, "I've got a pin, and I'm not afraid to use it"? *Have Pin, Will*

Travel . . . The Pinslinger . . . The Man with the Golden Pin . . . The Pins of Navarone . . .

It might have interested Newt to know that, of the thirty-nine thousand women tested with the pin during the centuries of witch-hunting, twenty-nine thousand said "ouch," nine thousand, nine hundred and ninety-nine didn't feel anything because of the use of the aforesaid retractable pins, and one witch declared that it had miraculously cleared up the arthritis in her leg.

Her name was Agnes Nutter.

She was the Witchfinder Army's great failure.

ONE OF THE EARLY ENTRIES in *The Nice and Accurate Prophecies* concerned Agnes Nutter's own death.

The English, by and large, being a crass and indolent race, were not as keen on burning women as other countries in Europe. In Germany the bonfires were built and burned with regular Teutonic thoroughness. Even the pious Scots, locked throughout history in a long-drawn-out battle with their arch-enemies the Scots, managed a few burnings to while away the long winter evenings. But the English never seemed to have the heart for it.

One reason for this may have to do with the manner of Agnes Nutter's death, which more or less marked the end of the serious witch-hunting craze in England. A howling mob, reduced to utter fury by her habit of going around being intelligent and curing people, arrived at her house one April evening to find her sitting with her coat on, waiting for them.

"Ye're tardie," she said to them. **"I shoulde have beene aflame ten minutes since."**

Then she got up and hobbled slowly through the suddenly silent crowd, out of the cottage, and to the bonfire that had been hastily thrown together on the village green. Legend says that she climbed awkwardly onto the pyre and thrust her arms around the stake behind her.

"Tye yt well," she said to the astonished witchfinder. And then, as the villagers sidled toward the pyre, she raised her handsome head in the firelight and said, **"Gather ye ryte close, goode people. Come close untyl the fire near scorch ye, for I charge ye that alle must see how thee last true wytch in England dies. For wytch I am, for soe I am judgéd, yette I knoe not what my true Cryme may be. And therefore let myne deathe be a messuage to the worlde. Gather ye ryte close, I saye, and *marke well the fate of alle who meddle with suche as theye do notte understande.*"**

And, apparently, she smiled and looked up at the sky over the village and added, **"That goes for you as welle, yowe daft old foole."**

And after that strange blasphemy she said no more. She let them gag her, and stood imperiously as the torches were put to the dry wood.

The crowd grew nearer, one or two of its members a little uncertain as to whether they'd done the right thing, now they came to think about it.

Thirty seconds later an explosion took out the village green, scythed the valley clean of every living thing, and was seen as far away as Halifax.

There was much subsequent debate as to whether

this had been sent by God or by Satan, but a note later found in Agnes Nutter's cottage indicated that any divine or devilish intervention had been materially helped by the contents of Agnes's petticoats, wherein she had with some foresight concealed eighty pounds of gunpowder and forty pounds of roofing nails.

What Agnes also left behind, on the kitchen table beside a note canceling the milk, was a box and a book. There were specific instructions as to what should be done with the box, and equally specific instructions about what should be done with the book; it was to be sent to Agnes's son-in-law, John Device.

The people who found it—who were from the next village, and had been woken up by the explosion—considered ignoring the instructions and just burning the cottage, and then looked around at the twinkling fires and nail-studded wreckage and decided not to. Besides, Agnes's note included painfully precise predictions about what would happen to people who did not carry out her orders.

The man who put the torch to Agnes Nutter was a Witchfinder Major. They found his hat in a tree two miles away.

His name, stitched inside on a fairly large piece of tape, was Thou-Shalt-Not-Commit-Adultery Pulsifer, one of England's most assiduous witchfinders, and it might have afforded him some satisfaction to know that his last surviving descendant was now, even if unawares, heading toward Agnes Nutter's last surviving descendant. He might have felt that some ancient revenge was at last going to be dis-charged.

If he'd known what was actually going to happen when that descendant met her he would have turned in his grave, except that he had never got one.

FIRSTLY, HOWEVER, Newt had to do something about the flying saucer.

It landed in the road ahead of him just as he was trying to find the Lower Tadfield turning and had the map spread over the steering wheel. He had to brake hard.

It looked like every cartoon of a flying saucer Newt had ever seen.

As he stared over the top of his map, a door in the saucer slid aside with a satisfying whoosh, revealing a gleaming walkway which extended automatically down to the road. Brilliant blue light shone out, outlining three alien shapes. They walked down the ramp. At least, two of them walked. The one that looked like a pepper pot just skidded down it, and fell over at the bottom.

The other two ignored its frantic beeping and walked over to the car quite slowly, in the worldwide approved manner of policemen already compiling the charge sheet in their heads. The tallest one, a yellow toad dressed in kitchen foil, rapped on Newt's window. He wound it down. The thing was wearing the kind of mirror-finished sunglasses that Newt always thought of as Cool Hand Luke shades.

"Morning, sir or madam or neuter," the thing said. "This your planet, is it?"

The other alien, which was stubby and green, had wandered off into the woods by the side of the road. Out of the corner of his eye Newt saw it kick a tree, and then run a leaf through some complicated gadget on its belt. It didn't look very pleased.

"Well, yes. I suppose so," he said.

The toad stared thoughtfully at the skyline.

"Had it long, have we, sir?" it said.

"Er. Not personally. I mean, as a species, about half a million years. I think."

The alien exchanged glances with its colleague. "Been letting the old acid rain build up, haven't we, sir?" it said. "Been letting ourselves go a bit with the old hydrocarbons, perhaps?"

"I'm sorry?"

"Could you tell me your planet's albedo, sir?" said the toad, still staring levelly at the horizon as though it was doing something interesting.

"Er. No."

"Well, I'm sorry to have to tell you, sir, that your polar ice caps are below regulation size for a planet of this category, sir."

"Oh, dear," said Newt. He was wondering who he could tell about this, and realizing that there was absolutely no one who would believe him.

The toad bent closer. It seemed to be worried about something, insofar as Newt was any judge of the expressions of an alien race he'd never encountered before.

"We'll overlook it on this occasion, sir."

Newt gabbled. "Oh. Er. I'll see to it—well, when I say *I*, I mean, I think Antarctica or something belongs to every country, or something, and—"

"The fact is, sir, that we have been asked to give you a message."

"Oh?"

"Message runs 'We give you a message of universal peace and cosmic harmony an' suchlike.' Message ends," said the toad.

"Oh." Newt turned this over in his mind. "Oh. That's very kind."

"Have you got any idea why we have been asked to bring you this message, sir?" said the toad.

Newt brightened. "Well, er, I suppose," he flailed, "what with Mankind's, er, harnessing of the atom and—"

"Neither have we, sir." The toad stood up. "One of them phenomena, I expect. Well, we'd better be going." It shook its head vaguely, turned around and waddled back to the saucer without another word.

Newt stuck his head out of the window.

"Thank you!"

The small alien walked past the car.

"CO_2 level up point five percent," it rasped, giving him a meaningful look. "You do know you could find yourself charged with being a dominant species while under the influence of impulse-driven consumerism, don't you?"

The two of them righted the third alien, dragged it back up the ramp, and shut the door.

Newt waited for a while, in case there were any spectacular light displays, but it just stood there.

Eventually he drove up on the verge and around it. When he looked in his rearview mirror it had gone.

I must be overdoing something, he thought guiltily. But what?

And I can't even tell Shadwell, because he'd probably bawl me out for not counting their nipples.

"ANYWAY," SAID ADAM, "you've got it all wrong about witches."

The Them were sitting on a field gate, watching Dog rolling in cowpats. The little mongrel seemed to be enjoying himself immensely.

"I've been reading about them," he said, in a slightly louder voice. "Actually, they've been right all along and it's wrong to persecute 'em with British Inquisitions and stuff."

"My mother said they were just intelligent women protesting in the only way open to them against the stifling injustices of a male-dominated social hierarchy," said Pepper.

Pepper's mother lectured at Norton Polytechnic.*

"Yes, but your mother's always saying things like that," said Adam, after a while.

Pepper nodded amiably. "And she said, at worst they were just free-thinking worshipers of the progenerative principle."

"Who's the progenratty principle?" said Wensleydale.

* During the day. In the evenings she gave Power tarot readings to nervous executives, because old habits die hard.

"Dunno. Something to do with maypoles, I think," said Pepper vaguely.

"Well, *I* thought they worshipped the Devil," said Brian, but without automatic condemnation. The Them had an open mind on the whole subject of devil worship. The Them had an open mind about *everything*. "Anyway, the Devil'd be better than a stupid maypole."

"That's where you're wrong," said Adam. "It's not the Devil. It's another god, or something. With horns."

"The Devil," said Brian.

"No," said Adam patiently. "People just got 'em mixed up. He's just got horns similar. He's called Pan. He's half a goat."

"Which half?" said Wensleydale.

Adam thought about it.

"The bottom half," he said at length. "Fancy you not knowin' that. I should of thought everyone knew *that*."

"Goats haven't got a bottom half," said Wensleydale. "They've got a front half and a back half. Just like cows."

They watched Dog some more, drumming their heels on the gate. It was too hot to think.

Then Pepper said, "If he's got goat legs, he shouldn't have horns. They belong to the front half."

"I didn't make him up, did I?" said Adam, aggrieved. "I was just telling you. It's news to me I made him up. No need to go on at *me*."

"Anyway," said Pepper. "This stupid Pot can't go around complaining if people think he's the Devil.

Not with having horns on. People are *bound* to say, oh, here comes the Devil."

Dog started to dig up a rabbit hole.

Adam, who seemed to have a weight on his mind, took a deep breath.

"You don't have to be so *lit'ral* about everything," he said. "That's the trouble these days. Grass materialism. 'S people like you who go round choppin' down rain forests and makin' holes in the ozone layer. There's a great big hole in the ozone layer 'cos of grass materialism people like you."

"I can't do anythin' about it," said Brian automatically. "I'm still paying off on a stupid cucumber frame."

"It's in the magazine," said Adam. "It takes millions of acres of rain forest to make one beefburger. And all this ozone is leakin' away because of . . ." he hesitated, "people sprayin' the enviroment."

"And there's whales," said Wensleydale. "We've got to save 'em."

Adam looked blank. His plunder of *New Aquarian*'s back issues hadn't included anything about whales. Its editors had assumed that the readers were all for saving whales in the same way they assumed that those readers breathed and walked upright.

"There was this program about them," explained Wensleydale.

"What've we got to save 'em for?" said Adam. He had confused visions of saving up whales until you had enough for a badge.

Wensleydale paused and racked his memory. "Because they can sing. And they've got big brains. There's hardly any of them left. And we don't need to kill them anyway 'cos they only make pet food and stuff."

"If they're so clever," said Brian, slowly, "what are they doin' in the sea?"

"Oh, I dunno," said Adam, looking thoughtful. "Swimmin' around all day, just openin' their mouths and eating stuff . . . sounds pretty clever to me—"

A squeal of brakes and a long drawn-out crunch interrupted him. They scrambled off the gate and ran up the lane to the crossroads, where a small car lay on its roof at the end of a long skidmark.

A little further down the road was a hole. It looked as though the car had tried to avoid it. As they looked at it, a small Oriental-looking head darted out of sight.

The Them dragged the door open and pulled out the unconscious Newt. Visions of medals for heroic rescue thronged Adam's head. Practical considerations of first aid thronged around that of Wensleydale.

"We shouldn't move him," he said. "Because of broken bones. We ought to get someone."

Adam cast around. There was a rooftop just visible in the trees down the road. It was Jasmine Cottage.

And in Jasmine Cottage Anathema Device was sitting in front of a table on which some bandages, aspirins, and assorted first-aid items had been laid out for the past hour.

ANATHEMA HAD BEEN looking at the clock. He'll be coming around any moment now, she'd thought.

And then, when he got there, he wasn't what she'd been expecting. More precisely, he wasn't what she'd been hoping for.

She had been hoping, rather self-consciously, for someone tall, dark, and handsome.

Newt was tall, but with a rolled-out, thin look. And while his hair was undoubtedly dark, it wasn't any sort of fashion accessory; it was just a lot of thin, black strands all growing together out of the top of his head. This was not Newt's fault; in his younger days he would go every couple of months to the barber's shop on the corner, clutching a photograph he'd carefully torn from a magazine which showed someone with an impressively cool haircut grinning at the camera, and he would show the picture to the barber, and ask to be made to look like that, please. And the barber, who knew his job, would take one look and then give Newt the basic, all-purpose, short-back-and-sides. After a year of this, Newt realized that he obviously didn't have the face that went with haircuts. The best Newton Pulsifer could hope for after a haircut was shorter hair.

It was the same with suits. The clothing hadn't been invented that would make him look suave and sophisticated and comfortable. These days he had learned to be satisfied with anything that would keep the rain off and give him somewhere to keep his change.

And he wasn't handsome. Not even when he took

off his glasses.* And, she discovered when she took off his shoes to lay him on her bed, he wore odd socks: one blue one, with a hole in the heel, and one gray one, with holes around the toes.

I suppose I'm meant to feel a wave of warm, tender female something-or-other about this, she thought. I just wish he'd wash them.

So . . . tall, dark, but not handsome. She shrugged. Okay. Two out of three isn't bad.

The figure on the bed began to stir. And Anathema, who in the very nature of things always looked to the future, suppressed her disappointment and said:

"How are we feeling now?"

Newt opened his eyes.

He was lying in a bedroom, and it wasn't his. He knew this instantly because of the ceiling. His bedroom ceiling still had the model aircraft hanging from bits of cotton. He'd never got around to taking them down.

This ceiling just had cracked plaster. Newt had never been in a woman's bedroom before, but he sensed that this was one largely by a combination of soft smells. There was a hint of talcum and lily-of-the-valley, and no rank suggestion of old T-shirts that had forgotten what the inside of a tumble-dryer looked like.

He tried to lift his head up, groaned, and let it sink back onto the pillow. Pink, he couldn't help noticing.

* Actually, less so when he took off his glasses, because then he tripped over things and wore bandages a lot.

"You banged your head on the steering wheel," said the voice that had roused him. "Nothing broken, though. What happened?"

Newt opened his eyes again.

"Car all right?" he said.

"Apparently. A little voice inside it keeps repeating 'Prease to frasten sleat-bert.' "

"See?" said Newt, to an invisible audience. "They knew how to build them in those days. That plastic finish hardly takes a dent."

He blinked at Anathema.

"I swerved to avoid a Tibetan in the road," he said. "At least, I think I did. I think I've probably gone mad."

The figure walked around into his line of sight. It had dark hair, and red lips, and green eyes, and it was almost certainly female. Newt tried not to stare. It said, "If you have, no one's going to notice." Then she smiled. "Do you know, I've never met a witchfinder before?"

"Er—" Newt began. She held up his open wallet.

"I had to look inside," she said.

Newt felt extremely embarrassed, a not unusual state of affairs. Shadwell had given him an official witchfinder's warrant card, which among other things charged all beadles, magistrates, bishops, and bailiffs to give him free passage and as much dry kindling as he required. It was incredibly impressive, a masterpiece of calligraphy, and probably quite old. He'd forgotten about it.

"It's really just a hobby," he said wretchedly. "I'm really a . . . a . . ." he wasn't going to say wages clerk, not here, not now, not to a girl like this, "a computer engineer," he lied. *Want* to be, *want* to be; in my *heart* I'm a computer engineer, it's only the brain that's letting me down. "Excuse me, could I know—"

"Anathema Device," said Anathema. "I'm an occultist, but that's just a hobby. I'm really a witch. Well done. You're half an hour late," she added, handing him a small sheet of cardboard, "so you'd better read this. It'll save a lot of time."

NEWT DID IN FACT own a small home computer, despite his boyhood experiences. In fact, he'd owned several. You always *knew* which ones he owned. They were desktop equivalents of the Wasabi. They were the ones which, for example, dropped to half price just after he'd bought them. Or were launched in a blaze of publicity and disappeared into obscurity within a year. Or only worked at all if you stuck them in a fridge. Or, if by some fluke they were basically good machines, Newt always got the few that were sold with the early, bug-infested version of the operating system. But he persevered, because he *believed.*

Adam also had a small computer. He used it for playing games, but never for very long. He'd load a game, watch it intently for a few minutes, and then proceed to play it until the High Score counter ran out of zeroes.

When the other Them wondered about this strange skill, Adam professed mild amazement that everyone didn't play games like this.

"All you have to do is learn how to play it, and then it's just easy," he said.

QUITE A LOT OF THE FRONT parlor in Jasmine Cottage was taken up, Newt noticed with a sinking feeling, with piles of newspapers. Clippings were stuck around the walls. Some of them had bits circled in red ink. He was mildly gratified to spot several he had cut out for Shadwell.

Anathema owned very little in the way of furniture. The only thing she'd bothered to bring with her had been her clock, one of the family heirlooms. It wasn't a full-cased grandfather clock, but a wall clock with a free-swinging pendulum that E. A. Poe would cheerfully have strapped someone under.

Newt kept finding his eye drawn to it.

"It was built by an ancestor of mine," said Anathema, putting the coffee cups down on the table. "Sir Joshua Device. You may have heard of him? He invented the little rocking thing that made it possible to build accurate clocks cheaply? They named it after him."

"The Joshua?" said Newt guardedly.

"The device."

In the last half hour Newt had heard some pretty unbelievable stuff and was close to believing it, but you have to draw the line somewhere.

"The device is named after a real person?" he said.

"Oh, yes. Fine old Lancashire name. From the French, I believe. You'll be telling me next you've never heard of Sir Humphrey Gadget—"

"Oh, now come *on*—"

"—who devised a *gadget* that made it possible

to pump out flooded mineshafts. Or Pietr Gizmo? Or Cyrus T. Doodad, America's foremost black inventor? Thomas Edison said that the only other contemporary practical scientists he admired were Cyrus T. Doodad and Ella Reader Widget. And—"

She looked at Newt's blank expression.

"I did my Ph.D. on them," she said. "The people who invented things so simple and universally useful that everyone forgot that they'd ever actually needed to be invented. Sugar?"

"Er—"

"You normally have two," said Anathema sweetly.

Newt stared back at the card she'd handed him.

She'd seemed to think it would explain everything.

It didn't.

It had a ruled line down the middle. On the left-hand side was a short piece of what seemed to be poetry, in black ink. On the right-hand side, in red ink this time, were comments and annotations. The effect was as follows:

3819. When Orient's chariot inverted be, four wheles in the skye, a man with bruises be upon Youre Bedde, achinge his hedd for willow fine, a manne who testeth with a pyn yette his hart be clene, yette seed of myne own undoing, take the means of flame from himme for to mayk ryght certain, together ye sharle be, untyl the Ende that is to come.	*Japanese car? Upturned.* *Car smash . . . not serious injury??* *. . . take in . . .* *. . . willowfine = Aspirin (cf. 3757)* *Pin = witchfinder (cf. 102)* *Good witchfinder??* *Refers to Pulsifer (cf. 002)* *Search for matches, etc. In the1990s!* *Hmm.* *. . . less than a day (cf. 712, 3803, 4004)*

Newt's hand went automatically to his pocket. His cigarette lighter had gone.

"What's this mean?" he said hoarsely.

"Have you ever heard of Agnes Nutter?" said Anathema.

"No," said Newt, taking a desperate defense in sarcasm. "You're going to tell me she invented mad people, I suppose."

"Another fine old Lancashire name," said Anathema coldly. "If you don't believe, read up on the witch trials of the early seventeenth century. She was an ancestress of mine. As a matter of fact, one of your ancestors burned her alive. Or tried to."

Newt listened in fascinated horror to the story of Agnes Nutter's death.

"Thou-Shalt-Not-Commit-Adultery Pulsifer?" he said, when she'd finished.

"That sort of name was quite common in those days," said Anathema. "Apparently there were ten children and they were a very religious family. There was Covetousness Pulsifer, False-Witness Pulsifer—"

"I think I understand," said Newt. "Gosh. I *thought* Shadwell said he'd heard the name before. It must be in the Army records. I suppose if I'd gone around being called Adultery Pulsifer I'd want to hurt as many people as possible."

"I think he just didn't like women very much."

"Thanks for taking it so well," said Newt. "I mean, he must have been an ancestor. There aren't many Pulsifers. Maybe . . . that's why I sort of met up with the Witchfinder Army? Could be Fate," he said hopefully.

She shook her head. "No," she said. "No such thing."

"Anyway, witchfinding isn't like it was in those days. I don't even think old Shadwell's ever done more than kick over Doris Stokes's dustbins."

"Between you and me, Agnes was a bit of a difficult character," said Anathema, vaguely. "She had no middle gears."

Newt waved the bit of paper.

"But what's it got to do with this?" he said.

"She wrote it. Well, the original. It's No. 3819 of *The Nice and Accurate Prophecies of Agnes Nutter*, first published 1655."

Newt stared at the prophecy again. His mouth opened and shut.

"She knew I'd crash my car?" he said.

"Yes. No. Probably not. It's hard to say. You see, Agnes was the worst prophet that's ever existed. Because she was always right. That's why the book never sold."

MOST PSYCHIC ABILITIES are caused by a simple lack of temporal focus, and the mind of Agnes Nutter was so far adrift in Time that she was considered pretty mad even by the standards of seventeenth-century Lancashire, where mad prophetesses were a growth industry.

But she was a treat to listen to, everyone agreed.

She used to go on about curing illnesses by using a sort of mold, and the importance of washing your hands so that the tiny little animals who caused diseases would be washed away, when every sensible person knew that a good stink was the only defense against the demons of ill health. She advocated running at a sort of gentle bouncing trot as an aid to living longer, which was extremely suspicious and first put the Witchfinders onto her, and stressed the importance of fiber in diet, although here she was clearly ahead of her time since most people were less bothered about the fiber in their diet than the gravel. And she wouldn't cure warts.

"Itt is alle in youre Minde," she'd say. **"Fogett about Itte, ane it wille goe Away."**

It was obvious that Agnes had a line to the Future, but it was an unusually narrow and specific line. In other words, almost totally useless.

"HOW DO YOU MEAN?" SAID NEWT.

"She managed to come up with the kind of predictions that you can only understand after the thing has happened," said Anathema. "Like **'Do Notte Buye Betamacks.'** That was a prediction for 1972."

"You mean she *predicted* videotape recorders?"

"No! She just picked up one little fragment of information," said Anathema. "That's the point. Most of the time she comes up with such an oblique reference that you can't work it out until it's gone past, and then it all slots into place. And she didn't know what was going to be important or not, so it's all a bit hit and miss. Her prediction for November 22, 1963, was about a house falling down in King's Lynn."

"Oh?" Newt looked politely blank.

"President Kennedy was assassinated," said Anathema helpfully. "But Dallas didn't exist then, you see. Whereas King's Lynn was quite important."

"Oh."

"She was generally very good if her descendants were involved."

"Oh?"

"And she wouldn't know anything about the internal combustion engine. To her they were just funny chariots. Even my mother thought it referred to an Emperor's carriage overturning. You see, it's not enough to know what the future *is*. You have to know what it *means*. Agnes was like someone looking at a huge picture down a tiny little tube. She wrote down what seemed like good advice based on what she understood of the tiny little glimpses.

"Sometimes you can be lucky," Anathema went on. "My great-grandfather worked out about the stock market crash of 1929, for example, two days before it actually happened. Made a fortune. You could say we're professional descendants."

She looked sharply at Newt. "You see, what no one ever realized until about two hundred years ago is that *The Nice and Accurate Prophecies* was Agnes's idea of a family heirloom. Many of the prophecies relate to her descendants and their well-being. She was sort of trying to look after us after she'd gone. That's the reason for the King's Lynn prophecy, we think. My father was visiting there at the time, so from Agnes's point of view, while he was unlikely to be struck by stray rounds from Dallas, there was a good chance he might be hit by a brick."

"What a nice person," said Newt. "You could almost overlook her blowing up an entire village."

Anathema ignored this. "Anyway, that's about it," she said. "Ever since then we've made it our job to interpret them. After all, it averages out at about one prophecy a month—more now, in fact, as we get closer to the end of the world."

"And when is that going to be?" said Newt.

Anathema looked meaningfully at the clock.

He gave a horrible little laugh that he hoped sounded suave and worldly. After the events so far today, he wasn't feeling very sane. And he could smell Anathema's perfume, which made him uncomfortable.

"Think yourself lucky I don't need a stopwatch," said Anathema. "We've got, oh, about five or six hours."

Newt turned this over in his mind. Thus far in his life he'd never had the urge to drink alcohol, but something told him there had to be a first time.

"Do witches keep drink in the house?" he ventured.

"Oh, yes." She smiled the sort of smile Agnes Nutter probably smiled when unpacking the contents of her lingerie drawer. "Green bubbly stuff with strange Things squirming on the congealing surface. *You* should know that."

"Fine. Got any ice?"

It turned out to be gin. There was ice. Anathema, who had picked up witchcraft as she went along, disapproved of liquor in general but approved of it in her specific case.

"Did I tell you about the Tibetan coming out of a hole in the road?" Newt said, relaxing a bit.

"Oh, I know about them," she said, shuffling the papers on the table. "The two of them came out of the front lawn yesterday. The poor things were quite bewildered, so I gave them a cup of tea and then they borrowed a spade and went down again. I don't think they quite know what they're supposed to be doing."

Newt felt slightly aggrieved. "How did you know they were Tibetan?" he said.

"If it comes to that, how did *you* know? Did he go 'Ommm' when you hit him?"

"Well, he—he looked Tibetan," said Newt. "Saffron robes, bald head . . . you know . . . *Tibetan.*"

"One of mine spoke quite good English. It seems that one minute he was repairing radios in Lhasa, next minute he was in a tunnel. He doesn't know how he's going to get home."

"If you'd sent him up the road, he could probably have got a lift on a flying saucer," said Newt gloomily.

"Three aliens? One of them a little tin robot?"

"They landed on your lawn too, did they?"

"It's about the only place they didn't land, according to the radio. They keep coming down all over the world delivering a short trite message of cosmic peace, and when people say 'Yes, well?' they give them a blank look and take off again. Signs and portents, just like Agnes said."

"You're going to tell me she predicted all this too, I suppose?"

Agnes leafed through a battered card index in front of her.

"I kept meaning to put it all on computer," she said. "Word searches and so forth. You know? It'd make it a lot simpler. The prophecies are arranged in any old order but there are clues, handwriting and so."

"She did it all in a card index?" said Newt.

"No. A book. But I've, er, mislaid it. We've always had copies, of course."

"Lost it, eh?" said Newt, trying to inject some humor into the proceedings. "Bet she didn't foresee that!"

Anathema glowered at him. If looks could kill, Newt would have been on a slab.

Then she went on: "We've built up quite a concordance over the years, though, and my grandfather came up with a useful cross-referencing system . . . ah. Here we are."

She pushed a sheet of paper in front of Newt.

3988. Whene menne of crocus come frome the Earth and green manne frome thee Sky, yette ken not why, and Pluto's barres quitte the lightning castels, and sunken landes riseth, and Leviathan runneth free, and Brazil is vert, then Three cometh together and Four arise, upon iron horses ride; I tell you the ende draweth nigh.	*. . . Crocus = saffron (cf.2003)* *. . . Aliens . . . ??* *. . . paratroops?* *. . . nuclear power stations (see cuttings Nos. 798–806)* *Atlantis, cuttings 812–819* *. . . leviathan = whale (cf.1981)?* *South America is green?* *? 3 = 4? Railways? ('iron road,' cf.2675)*

"I didn't get all of this one in advance," Anathema admitted. "I filled it in after listening to the news."

"You must be incredibly good at crosswords in your family," said Newt.

"I think Agnes is getting a bit out of her depth here, anyway. The bits about leviathan and South America and threes and fours could mean anything." She sighed. "The problem is newspapers. You never know if Agnes is referring to some tiny little incident that you might miss. Do you know how long it takes to go through *every* daily paper *thoroughly* every morning?"

"Three hours and ten minutes," said Newt automatically.

"I EXPECT WE'LL GET a medal or something," said Adam optimistically. "Rescuing a man from a blazing wreck."

"It wasn't blazing," said Pepper. "It wasn't even very wrecked when we put it back rightside up."

"It *could* of been," Adam pointed out. "I don't see why we shouldn't have a medal just because some old car doesn't know when to catch fire."

They stood looking down at the hole. Anathema had called the police, who had put it down to subsidence and put some cones around it; it was dark, and went down a long way.

"Could be good fun, going to Tibet," said Brian. "We could learn marital arts and stuff. I saw this old film where there's this valley in Tibet and everyone there lives for hundreds of years. It's called Shangri-La."

"My aunt's bungalow's called Shangri-La," said Wensleydale.

Adam snorted.

"Not very clever, naming a valley after some ole bungalow," he said. "Might as well call it Dunroamin', or, or The Laurels."

" 'S lot better than Shambles, anyway," said Wensleydale mildly.

"Shambala," corrected Adam.

"I expect it's the same place. Prob'ly got both names," said Pepper, with unusual diplomacy. "Like our house. We changed the name from The Lodge to Norton View when we moved in, but we still get letters addressed to Theo C. Cupier, The Lodge. Perhaps they've named it Shambala now but people still call it The Laurels."

Adam flicked a pebble into the hole. He was becoming bored with Tibetans.

"What shall we do now?" said Pepper. "They're dipping sheep over at Norton Bottom Farm. We could go and help."

Adam threw a larger stone into the hole, and waited for the thump. It didn't come.

"Dunno," he said distantly. "I reckon we should do something about whales and forests and suchlike."

"Like what?" said Brian, who enjoyed the diversions available at a good sheep-dipping. He began to empty his pockets of crisp packets and drop them, one by one, into the hole.

"We could go into Tadfield this afternoon and not have a hamburger," said Pepper. "If all four of us don't have one, that's millions of acres of rainforest they won't have to cut down."

"They'll be cutting 'em down anyway," said Wensleydale.

"It's grass materialism again," said Adam. "Same with the whales. It's amazin', the stuff that's goin' on." He stared at Dog.

He was feeling very odd.

The little mongrel, noticing the attention, balanced expectantly on its hind legs.

" 'S people like you that's eating all the whales," said Adam severely. "I bet you've used up nearly a whole whale already."

Dog, one last tiny satanic spark of his soul hating himself for it, put his head on one side and whined.

" 'S gonna be a fine ole world to grow up in," Adam said. "No whales, no air, and everyone paddlin' around because of the seas risin'."

"Then the Atlantisans'd be the only ones well off," said Pepper cheerfully.

"Huh," said Adam, not really listening.

Something was happening inside his head. It was aching. Thoughts were arriving there without him having to think them. Something was saying, *You can do something, Adam Young. You can make it all better. You can do anything you want.* And what was saying this to him was . . . him. Part of him, deep down. Part of him that had been attached to him all these years and not really noticed, like a shadow. It was saying: yes, it's a rotten world. It could have been great. But now it's rotten, and it's time to do something about it. That's what you're here for. To make it all better.

"Because they'd be able to go everywhere," Pepper went on, giving him a worried look. "The Atlantisans, I mean. Because—"

"I'm fed up with the ole Atlantisans and Tibetans," snapped Adam.

They stared at him. They'd never seen him like this before.

"It's all very well for *them*," said Adam. "Everyone's goin' around usin' up all the whales and coal and oil and ozone and rainforests and that, and there'll be none left for us. We should be goin' to Mars and stuff, instead of sittin' around in the dark and wet with the air spillin' away."

This wasn't the old Adam the Them knew. The Them avoided one another's faces. With Adam in this mood, the world seemed a chillier place.

"Seems to me," said Brian, pragmatically, "seems to *me*, the best thing you could do about it is stop readin' about it."

"It's like you said the other day," said Adam. "You grow up readin' about pirates and cowboys and spacemen and stuff, and jus' when you think the world's all full of amazin' things, they tell you it's really all dead whales and chopped-down forests and nucular waste hangin' about for millions of years. 'Snot worth growin' up for, if you ask my opinion."

The Them exchanged glances.

There *was* a shadow over the whole world. Storm clouds were building up in the north, the sunlight glowing yellow off them as though the sky had been painted by an enthusiastic amateur.

"Seems to me it ought to be rolled up and started all over again," said Adam.

That hadn't sounded like Adam's voice.

A bitter wind blew through the summer woods.

Adam looked at Dog, who tried to stand on his head. There was a distant mutter of thunder. He reached down and patted the dog absentmindedly.

"Serve everyone right if all the nucular bombs went off and it all started again, only prop'ly organized," said Adam. "Sometimes I think that's what I'd like to happen. An' then we could sort everythin' out."

The thunder growled again. Pepper shivered. This wasn't the normal Them Möbius bickering, which passed many a slow hour. There was a look in Adam's eye that his friend couldn't quite fathom—not devilment, because that was more or less there all the time, but a sort of blank grayness that was far worse.

"Well, I dunno about *we*," Pepper tried. "Dunno about the *we*, because, if there's all these bombs goin' off, we all get blown up. Speaking as a mother of unborn generations, I'm against it."

They looked at her curiously. She shrugged.

"And then giant ants take over the world," said Wensleydale nervously. "I saw this film. Or you go around with sawn-off shotguns and everyone's got these cars with, you know, knives and guns stuck on—"

"I wouldn't allow any giant ants or anything like that," said Adam, brightening up horribly. "And you'd all be all right. I'd see to that. It'd be *wicked*, eh, to have all the world to ourselves. Wouldn't it? We could share it out. We could have amazing games. We could have War with real armies an' stuff."

"But there wouldn't be any *people*," said Pepper.

"Oh, I could make us some people," said Adam airily. "Good enough for armies, at any rate. We could all have a quarter of the world each. Like, *you*"—he pointed to Pepper, who recoiled as though Adam's finger were a white-hot poker—"could have Russia because it's red and you've got red hair, right? And Wensley can have America, and Brian can have, can have Africa and Europe, an', an'—"

Even in their state of mounting terror the Them gave this the consideration it deserved.

"H-huh," stuttered Pepper, as the rising wind whipped at her T-shirt, "I don't s-see why Wensley's got America an' all I've g-got is just Russia. Russia's *boring*."

"You can have China and Japan and India," said Adam.

"That means I've got jus' Africa and a lot of jus' borin' little countries," said Brian, negotiating even on the curl of the catastrophe curve. "I wouldn't mind Australia," he added.

Pepper nudged him and shook her head urgently.

"Dog's goin' to have Australia," said Adam, his eyes glowing with the fires of creation, "on account of him needin' a lot of space to run about. An' there's all those rabbits and kangaroos for him to chase, an'—"

The clouds spread forwards and sideways like ink poured into a bowl of clear water, moving across the sky faster than the wind.

"But there won't *be* any rab—" Wensleydale shrieked.

Adam wasn't listening, at least to any voices outside his own head. "It's all too much of a mess," he said. "We should start again. Just save the ones we want and start again. That's the best way. It'd be doing the Earth a favor, when you come to think about it. It makes me *angry*, seeing the way those old loonies are messing it up . . ."

"IT'S MEMORY, YOU SEE," said Anathema. "It works backwards as well as forwards. Racial memory, I mean."

Newt gave her a polite but blank look.

"What I'm trying to say," she said patiently, "is that Agnes didn't *see* the future. That's just a metaphor. She *remembered* it. Not very well, of course, and by the time it'd been filtered through her own understanding it's often a bit confused. We think she's best at remembering things that were going to happen to her descendants."

"But if you're going to places and doing things because of what she wrote, and what she wrote is her recollection of the places you went to and the things you did," said Newt, "then—"

"I know. But there's, er, some evidence that that's how it works," said Anathema.

They looked at the map spread out between them. Beside them the radio murmured. Newt was very aware that a woman was sitting next to him. Be professional, he told himself. You're a soldier, aren't you? Well, practically. Then act like a soldier. He thought hard for a fraction of a second. Well, act like a respectable soldier on his best behavior, then. He forced his attention back to the matter at hand.

"Why Lower Tadfield?" said Newt. "*I* just got interested because of the weather. Optimal microclimate, they call it. That means it's a small place with its own personal nice weather."

He glanced at her notebooks. There was definitely something odd about the place, even if you ignored Tibetans and UFOs, which seemed to be infesting the whole world these days. The Tadfield area didn't only have the kind of weather you could set your calendar by, it was also remarkably resistant to change. No one seemed to build new houses there. The population didn't seem to move much. There seemed to be more woods and hedges than you'd normally expect these days. The only battery farm to open in the area had failed after a year or two, and been replaced by an old-fashioned pig farmer who let his pigs run loose in his apple orchards and sold the pork at premium prices. The two local schools seemed to soldier on in blissful immunity from the changing fashions of education. A motorway which should have turned most of Lower Tadfield into little more than the Junction 18 Happy Porker Rest Area changed course five miles away, detoured in a great semicircle, and continued on its way oblivious to the little island of rural changelessness it had avoided. No one quite seemed to know why; one of the surveyors involved had a nervous breakdown, a second had become a monk, and a third had gone off to Bali to paint nude women.

It was as if a large part of the twentieth century had marked a few square miles Out of Bounds.

Anathema pulled another a card out of her index and flicked it across the table.

2315. Sum say It cometh in London Town, or New Yorke, butte they be Wronge, for the plase is Taddes Fild, Stronge inne hys powr, he cometh like a knight inne the fief, he divideth the Worlde into 4 partes, he bringeth the storme.

. . . 4 years early [New Amsterdam till 1664] . . .
. . . Taddville, Norfolk . . .
. . . Tardesfield, Devon . . .
. . . Tadfield, Oxon . . . <
. . ! . . See Revelation, C6, v10

"I had to go and look through a lot of county records," said Anathema.

"Why's this one 2315? It's earlier than the others."

"Agnes was a bit slapdash about timing. I don't think she always knew what went where. I told you, we've spent ages devising a sort of system for chaining them together."

Newt looked at a few cards. For example:

1111. An the Great Hound sharl coom, and the Two Powers sharl watch in Vane, for it Goeth where is its Master, Where they Wot Notte, and he sharl name it, True to Ittes Nature, and Hell sharl flee it.

? Is this something to do with Bismark? [A F Device, June 8, 1888]
. . . ?

. . . Schleswig-Holstein?

"She's being unusually obtuse for Agnes," said Anathema.

3017. I see Four Riding, bringing the Ende, and the Angells of Hell ride with them, And Three sharl Rise. And Four and Four Together be Four, an the Dark Angel sharl Own Defeat, Yette the Manne sharl claim his Own.

The Apocalyptic Horsemen
The Man = Pan, The Devil
(The Witch Trials of Lancashire, *Brewster, 1782).*
??
I feel good Agnes had drunk well this night, [Quincy Device, Octbr. 15, 1789]

I concur. We are all human, alas. [Miss O J Device, Janry. 5, 1854]

"Why *Nice* and Accurate?" said Newt.

"Nice as in exact, or precise," said Anathema, in the weary tones of one who'd explained this before. "That's what it used to mean."

"But *look*," said Newt—

—he'd nearly convinced himself about the non-existence of the UFO, which was clearly a figment of his imagination, and the Tibetan could have been a, well, he was working on it, but whatever it was it wasn't a Tibetan, but what he *was* more and more convinced of was that he was in a room with a very attractive woman, who appeared actually to like him, or at least not to dislike him, which was a definite first for Newt. And admittedly there seemed to be a lot of strange stuff going on, but if he really tried, poling the boat of common sense upstream against the raging current of the evidence, he could pretend it was all, well, weather balloons, or Venus, or mass hallucination.

In short, whatever Newt was now thinking with, it wasn't his brain.

"But look," he said, "the world isn't *really* going to end now, is it? I mean, just look around. It's not like there's any international tension . . . well, any more than there normally is. Why don't we leave this stuff for a while and just go and, oh, I don't know, maybe we could just go for a walk or something, I mean—"

"Don't you understand? There's something here! Something that affects the area!" she said. "It's twisted all the ley-lines. It's protecting the area against anything that might change it! It's . . . it's . . ." There it was again: the thought in her mind that she could not, was not allowed to grasp, like a dream upon waking.

The windows rattled. Outside, a sprig of jasmine, driven by the wind, started to bang insistently on the glass.

"But I can't get a fix on it," said Anathema, twisting her fingers together. "I've tried everything."

"Fix?" said Newt.

"I've tried the pendulum. I've tried the theodolite. I'm psychic, you see. But it seems to move around."

Newt was still in control of his own mind enough to do the proper translation. When most people said "I'm psychic, you see," they meant "I have an overactive but unoriginal imagination / wear black nail varnish / talk to my budgie"; when Anathema said it, it sounded as though she was admitting to a hereditary disease which she'd much prefer not to have.

"Armageddon moves around?" said Newt.

"Various prophecies say the Antichrist has to arise first," said Anathema. "Agnes says *he*. I can't spot him—"

"Or her," said Newt.

"What?"

"Could be a her," said Newt. "This is the twentieth century, after all. Equal opportunities."

"I don't think you're taking this entirely seriously," she said severely. "Anyway, there isn't any *evil* here. That's what I don't understand. There's just love."

"Sorry?" said Newt.

She gave him a helpless look. "It's hard to describe it," she said. "Something or someone loves this place. Loves every inch of it so powerfully that it shields and protects it. A deep-down, huge, fierce love. How can anything bad start here? How can the end of the world start in a place like this? This is the kind of town you'd want to raise your kids in. It's a kids' paradise." She smiled weakly. "You should *see* the local kids. They're unreal! Right out of the *Boy's Own Paper!* All scabby knees and 'brilliant!' and bulls-eyes—"

She nearly had it. She could feel the shape of the thought, she was gaining on it.

"What's this place?" said Newt.

"What?" Anathema screamed, as her train of thought was derailed.

Newt's finger tapped at the map.

"'Disused aerodrome,' it says. Just here, look, west of Tadfield itself—"

Anathema snorted. "Disused? Don't you believe it. Used to be a wartime fighter base. It's been

Upper Tadfield Airbase for about ten years or so. And before you say it, the answer's no. I hate everything about the bloody place, but the colonel's saner than you are by a long way. His wife does yoga, for God's sake."

Now. What was it she'd said before? The kids round here . . .

She felt her mental feet slipping away from under her, and she fell back into the more personal thought waiting there to catch her. Newt was okay, really. And the thing about spending the rest of your life with him was, he wouldn't be around long enough to get on your nerves.

The radio was talking about South American rainforests.

New ones.

It began to hail.

BULLETS OF ICE shredded the leaves around the Them as Adam led them down into the quarry.

Dog slunk along with his tail between his legs, whining.

This wasn't right, he was thinking. Just when I was getting the hang of rats. Just when I'd nearly sorted out that bloody German Shepherd across the road. Now He's going to end it all and I'll be back with the ole glowin' eyes and chasin' lost souls. What's the sense in that? They don't fight back, and there's no taste to 'em . . .

Wensleydale, Brian, and Pepper were not thinking quite so coherently. All that they were aware of was that they could no more not follow Adam than fly; to try to resist the force marching them forward would simply result in multiply broken legs, and they'd *still* have to march.

Adam wasn't thinking at all. Something had opened in his mind and was aflame.

He sat them down on the crate.

"We'll all be all right down here," he said.

"Er," said Wensleydale, "don't you think our mothers and fathers—"

"Don't you worry about them," said Adam loftily. "I can make some new ones. There won't be any of this being in bed by half past nine, either. You don't ever have to go to bed ever, if you don't want to. Or tidy your room or anything. You just leave it all to me and it will be great." He gave them a manic smile. "I've got some new friends comin'," he confided. "You'll like 'em."

"But—" Wensleydale began.

"You jus' think of all the amazin' stuff afterwards," said Adam enthusiastically. "You can fill up America with all new cowboys an' Indians an' policemen an' gangsters an' cartoons an' spacemen and stuff. Won't that be fantastic?"

Wensleydale looked miserably at the other two. They were sharing a thought that none of them would be able to articulate very satisfactorily even in normal times. Broadly, it was that there had once been real cowboys and gangsters, and that was great. And there would always be pretend cowboys and gangsters, and that was also great. But *real* pretend cowboys and gangsters, that were alive and not alive and could be put back in their box when you were tired of them—this did not seem great at all. The whole point about gangsters and cowboys and aliens and pirates was that you could stop being them and go home.

"But before all that," said Adam darkly, "we're really goin' to *show* 'em . . ."

THERE WAS A TREE in the plaza. It wasn't very big and the leaves were yellow and the light it got through the excitingly dramatic smoked glass was the wrong sort of light. And it was on more drugs than an Olympic athlete, and loudspeakers nested in the branches. But it was a tree, and if you half-closed your eyes and looked at it over the artificial waterfall, you could almost believe that you were looking at a sick tree through a fog of tears.

Jaime Hernez liked to have his lunch under it. The maintenance supervisor would shout at him if he found out, but Jaime had grown up on a farm and it had been quite a good farm and he had liked trees and he didn't want to have to come into the city, but what could you do? It wasn't a bad job and the money was the kind of money his father hadn't dreamed of. His grandfather hadn't dreamed of any money at all. He hadn't even known what money was until he was fifteen. But there were times when you needed trees, and the shame of it, Jaime thought, was that his children were growing up thinking of trees as firewood and his grandchildren would think of trees as history.

But what could you do? Where there were trees now there were big farms, where there were small farms now there were plazas, and where there were plazas there were still plazas, and that's how it went.

He hid his trolley behind the newspaper stand, sat down furtively, and opened his lunchbox.

It was then that he became aware of the rustling, and a movement of shadows across the floor. He looked around.

The tree was moving. He watched it with interest. Jaime had never seen a tree growing before.

The soil, which was nothing more than a scree of some sort of artificial chippings, was actually crawling as the roots moved around under the surface. Jaime saw a thin white shoot creep down the side of the raised garden area and prod blindly at the concrete of the floor.

Without knowing why, without ever knowing why, he nudged it gently with his foot until it was close to the crack between the slabs. It found it, and bored down.

The branches were twisting into different shapes.

Jaime heard the screech of traffic outside the building, but didn't pay it any attention. Someone was yelling something, but someone was always yelling in Jaime's vicinity, often at him.

The questing root must have found the buried soil. It changed color and thickened, like a fire hose when the water is turned on. The artificial waterfall stopped running; Jaime visualized fractured pipes blocked with sucking fibers.

Now he could see what was happening outside. The street surface was heaving like a sea. Saplings were pushing up between the cracks.

Of course, he reasoned; they had sunlight. His tree didn't. All it had was the muted gray light that came through the dome four stories up. Dead light.

But what could you do?

You could do this:

The elevators had stopped running because the power was off, but it was only four flights of stairs. Jaime carefully shut his lunchbox and padded back to his cart, where he selected his longest broom.

People were pouring out of the building, yelling. Jaime moved amiably against the flow like a salmon going upstream.

A white framework of girders, which the architect had presumably thought made a dynamic statement about something or other, held up the smoked glass dome. In fact it was some sort of plastic, and it took Jaime, perched on a convenient strip of girder, all his strength and the full leverage of the broom's length to crack it. A couple more swings brought it down in lethal shards.

The light poured in, lighting up the dust in the plaza so that the air looked as though it was full of fireflies.

Far below, the tree burst the walls of its brushed concrete prison and rose like an express train. Jaime had never realized that trees made a sound when they grew, and no one else had realized it either, because the sound is made over hundreds of years in waves twenty-four hours from peak to peak.

Speed it up, and the sound a tree makes is *vroooom.*

Jaime watched it come toward him like a green mushroom cloud. Steam was billowing out from around its roots.

The girders never stood a chance. The remnant of the dome went up like a ping-pong ball on a water spray.

It was the same over all the city, except that you couldn't see the city any more. All you could see was the canopy of green. It stretched from horizon to horizon.

Jaime sat on his branch, clung to a liana, and laughed and laughed and laughed.

Presently, it began to rain.

THE *KAPPAMAKI*, a whaling research ship, was currently researching the question: How many whales can you catch in one week?

Except that, today, there weren't any whales. The crew stared at the screens, which by the application of ingenious technology could spot anything larger than a sardine and calculate its net value on the international oil market, and found them blank. The occasional fish that did show up was barreling through the water as if in a great hurry to get elsewhere.

The captain drummed his fingers on the console. He was afraid that he might soon be conducting his own research project to find out what happened to a statistically small sample of whaler captains who came back without a factory ship full of research material. He wondered what they did to you. Maybe they locked you in a room with a harpoon gun and expected you to do the honorable thing.

This was unreal. There ought to be *something*.

The navigator punched up a chart and stared at it.

"Honorable sir?" he said.

"What is it?" said the captain testily.

"We seem to have a miserable instrument failure. Seabed in this area should be two hundred meters."

"What of it?"

"I'm reading fifteen thousand meters, honorable sir. And still falling."

"That is foolish. There is no such depth."

The captain glared at several million yens worth of cutting-edge technology, and thumped it.

The navigator gave a nervous smile.

"Ah, sir," he said, "it is shallower already."

Beneath the thunders of the upper deep, as Aziraphale and Tennyson both knew, *Far, far beneath in the abyssal sea/The kraken sleepeth*.

And now it was waking up.

Millions of tons of deep ocean ooze cascade off its flanks as it rises.

"See," said the navigator. "Three thousand meters already."

The kraken doesn't have eyes. There has never been anything for it to look at. But as it billows up through the icy waters it picks up the microwave noise of the sea, the sorrowing beeps and whistles of the whalesong.

"Er," said the navigator, "one thousand meters?"

The kraken is not amused.

"Five hundred meters?"

The factory ship rocks on the sudden swell.

"A hundred meters?"

There is a tiny metal thing above it. The kraken stirs.

And ten billion sushi dinners cry out for vengeance.

THE COTTAGE WINDOWS burst inward. This wasn't a storm, it was war. Fragments of jasmine whirled across the room, mingled with the rain of file cards.

Newt and Anathema clung to one another in the space between the overturned table and the wall.

"Go on," muttered Newt. "Tell me Agnes predicted this."

"She did say he bringeth the storm," said Anathema.

"This is a bloody hurricane. Did she say what's supposed to happen next?"

"2315 is cross-referenced to 3477," said Anathema.

"You can remember details like that at a time like this?"

"Since you mention it, yes," she said. She held out a card.

3477. Lette the wheel of Fate turne, let harts enjoin, there are othere fyres than mine; when the wynd blowethe the blossoms, reach oute one to anothere, for the calm cometh when Redde and Whyte and Blacke and Pale approche to Peas is Our Professioune.

? Some mysticism here, one fears. [A F Device, Octbr 17, 1889]

Peas / blossoms? [OFD, 1929, Sept 4

Revelations Ch 6 again, I presume. [Dr Thos. Device, 1835]

Newt read it again. There was a sound outside like a sheet of corrugated iron pinwheeling across the garden, which was exactly what it was.

"Is this supposed to mean," he said slowly, "that we're supposed to become an, an *item*? That Agnes, what a joker."

Courting is always difficult when the one being courted has an elderly female relative in the house; they tend to mutter or cackle or bum cigarettes or, in the worst cases, get out the family photograph album, an act of aggression in the sex war which ought to be banned by a Geneva Convention. It's much worse when the relative has been dead for three hundred years. Newt had indeed been harboring certain thoughts about Anathema; not just harboring them, in fact, but dry-docking them, refitting them, giving them a good coat of paint and scraping the barnacles off their bottom. But the idea of Agnes's second sight boring into the back of his neck sloshed over his libido like a bucketful of cold water.

He had even been entertaining the idea of inviting her out for a meal, but he hated the idea of some Cromwellian witch sitting in her cottage three centuries earlier and watching him eat.

He was in the mood in which people burned witches. His life was quite complicated enough without it being manipulated across the centuries by some crazed old woman.

A thump in the grate sounded like part of the chimney stack coming down.

And then he thought: my life isn't complicated at all. I can see it as clearly as Agnes might. It stretches all the way to early retirement, a whip-round from the people in the office, a bright little neat flat somewhere, a neat little empty death. Except now

I'm going to die under the ruins of a cottage during what might just possibly be the end of the world.

The Recording Angel won't have any trouble with me, my life must have been dittoes on every page for years. I mean, what have I ever really done? I've never robbed a bank. I've never had a parking ticket. I've never eaten Thai food—

Somewhere another window caved in, with a merry tinkle of breaking glass. Anathema put her arms around him, with a sigh which really didn't sound disappointed at all.

I've never been to America. Or France, because Calais doesn't really count. I've never learned to play a musical instrument.

The radio died as the power lines finally gave up.

He buried his face in her hair.

I've never—

THERE WAS A *PINGING* SOUND.

Shadwell, who had been bringing the Army pay books up to date, looked up in the middle of signing for Witchfinder Lance-Corporal Smith.

It took him a while to notice that the gleam of Newt's pin was no longer on the map.

He got down from his stool, muttering under his breath, and searched around on the floor until he found it. He gave it another polish and put it back in Tadfield.

He was just signing for Witchfinder Private Table, who got an extra tuppence a year hay allowance, when there was another *ping*.

He retrieved the pin, glared at it suspiciously, and

pushed it so hard into the map that the plaster behind it gave way. Then he went back to the ledgers.

There was a *ping*.

This time the pin was several feet from the wall. Shadwell picked it up, examined its point, pushed it into the map, and watched it.

After about five seconds it shot past his ear.

He scrabbled for it on the floor, replaced it on the map, and held it there.

It moved under his hand. He leaned his weight on it.

A tiny thread of smoke curled out of the map. Shadwell gave a whimper and sucked his fingers as the red-hot pin ricocheted off the opposite wall and smashed a window. It didn't want to be in Tadfield.

Ten seconds later Shadwell was rummaging through the WA's cash box, which yielded a handful of copper, a ten-shilling note, and a small counterfeit coin from the reign of James I. Regardless of personal safety, he rummaged in his own pockets. The results of the trawl, even with his pensioner's concessionary travel pass taken into consideration, were barely enough to get him out of the house, let alone to Tadfield.

The only other people he knew who had money were Mr. Rajit and Madame Tracy. As far as the Rajits were concerned, the question of seven weeks' rent would probably crop up in any financial discussion he instigated at this point, and as for Madame Tracy, who'd only be too willing to lend him a handful of used tenners . . .

"I'll be swaggit if I'll tak the Wages o' Sin frae the painted jezebel," he said.

Which left no one else.

Save one.

The southern pansy.

They'd each been here, just once, spending as little time as possible in the room and, in Aziraphale's case, trying not to touch any flat surface. The other one, the flash Southern bastard in the sunglasses, was—Shadwell suspected—not someone he ought to offend. In Shadwell's simple world, anyone in sunglasses who wasn't actually on a beach was probably a criminal. He suspected that Crowley was from the Mafia, or the underworld, although he would have been surprised how right he nearly was. But the soft one in the camelhair coat was a different matter, and he'd risked trailing him back to his base once, and he could remember the way. He thought Aziraphale was a Russian spy. He could ask him for money. Threaten him a bit.

It was terribly risky.

Shadwell pulled himself together. Even now young Newt might be suffering unimaginable tortures at the hands of the daughters o' night and he, Shadwell, had sent him.

"We canna leave our people in there," he said, and put on his thin overcoat and shapeless hat and went out into the street.

The weather seemed to be blowing up a bit.

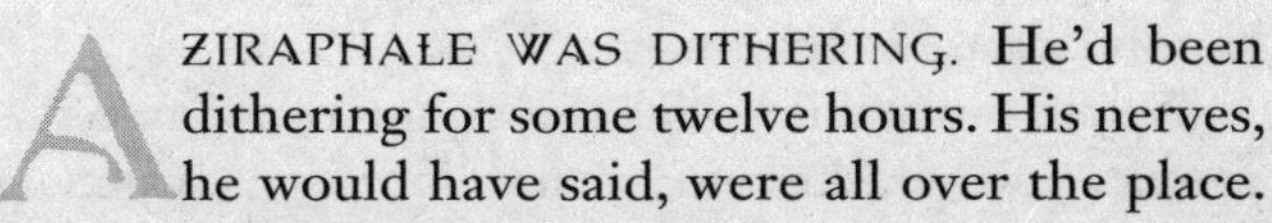

AZIRAPHALE WAS DITHERING. He'd been dithering for some twelve hours. His nerves, he would have said, were all over the place.

He walked around the shop, picking up bits of paper and dropping them again, fiddling with pens.

He ought to tell Crowley.

No, he didn't. He *wanted* to tell Crowley. He *ought* to tell Heaven.

He was an angel, after all. You had to do the right thing. It was built in. You see a wile, you thwart. Crowley had put his finger on it, right enough. He ought to have told Heaven right from the start.

But he'd known him for thousands of years. They got along. They nearly understood one another. He sometimes suspected they had far more in common with one another than with their respective superiors. They both liked the world, for one thing, rather than viewing it simply as the board on which the cosmic game of chess was being played.

Well, of course, that was it. That was the answer, staring him in the face. It'd be true to the *spirit* of his pact with Crowley if he tipped Heaven the wink, and then they could quietly do something about the child, although nothing too bad of course because we were all God's creatures when you got down to it, even people like Crowley and the Antichrist, and the world would be saved and there wouldn't have to be all that Armageddon business, which would do nobody any good anyway, because everyone *knew* Heaven would win in the end, and Crowley would be bound to understand.

Yes. And then everything would be all right.

There was a knock at the shop door, despite the CLOSED sign. He ignored it.

Getting in touch with Heaven for two-way communications was far more difficult for Aziraphale than it is for humans, who don't expect an answer and in nearly all cases would be rather surprised to get one.

He pushed aside the paper-laden desk and rolled up the threadbare bookshop carpet. There was a small circle chalked on the floorboards underneath, surrounded by suitable passages from the Cabala. The angel lit seven candles, which he placed ritually at certain points around the circle. Then he lit some incense, which was not necessary but did make the place smell nice.

And then he stood in the circle and said the Words.

Nothing happened.

He said the Words again.

Eventually a bright blue shaft of light shot down from the ceiling and filled the circle.

A well-educated voice said, "Well?"

"It's me, Aziraphale."

"We know," said the voice.

"I've got great news! I've located the Antichrist! I can give you his address and everything!"

There was a pause. The blue light flickered.

"Well?" it said again.

"But, d'you see, you can ki—can stop it all happening! In the nick of time! You've only got a few hours! You can stop it all and there needn't be the war and everyone will be saved!"

He beamed madly into the light.

"Yes?" said the voice.

"Yes, he's in a place called Lower Tadfield, and the address—"

"Well done," said the voice, in flat, dead tones.

"There doesn't have to be any of that business

with one third of the seas turning to blood or anything," said Aziraphale happily.

When it came, the voice sounded slightly annoyed.

"Why not?" it said.

Aziraphale felt an icy pit opening under his enthusiasm, and tried to pretend it wasn't happening.

He plunged on: "Well, you can simply make sure that—"

"We will *win*, Aziraphale."

"Yes, but—"

"The forces of darkness must be *beaten*. You seem to be under a misapprehension. The point is not to *avoid* the war, it is to *win* it. We have been waiting a long time, Aziraphale."

Aziraphale felt the coldness envelop his mind. He opened his mouth to say, "Do you think perhaps it would be a good idea not to hold the war on Earth?" and changed his mind.

"I see," he said grimly. There was a scraping near the door, and if Aziraphale had been looking in that direction he would have seen a battered felt hat trying to peer over the fanlight.

"This is not to say you have not performed well," said the voice. "You will receive a commendation. Well done."

"Thank you," said Aziraphale. The bitterness in his voice would have soured milk. "I'd forgotten about ineffability, obviously."

"We thought you had."

"May I ask," said the angel, "to whom have I been speaking?"

The voice said, "We are the Metatron."*

"Oh, yes. Of course. Oh. Well. Thank you very much. Thank you."

Behind him the letterbox tilted open, revealing a pair of eyes.

"One other thing," said the voice. "You will of course be joining us, won't you?"

"Well, er, of course it has been simply ages since I've held a flaming sword—" Aziraphale began.

"Yes, we recall," said the voice. "You will have a lot of opportunity to relearn."

"Ah. Hmm. What sort of initiating event will precipitate the war?" said Aziraphale.

"We thought a multination nuclear exchange would be a nice start."

"Oh. Yes. Very imaginative." Aziraphale's voice was flat and hopeless.

"Good. We will expect you directly, then," said the voice.

"Ah. Well. I'll just clear up a few business matters, shall I?" said Aziraphale desperately.

"There hardly seems to be any necessity," said the Metatron.

Aziraphale drew himself up. "I really feel that probity, not to say morality, demands that as a reputable businessman I should—"

"Yes, yes," said the Metatron, a shade testily. "Point taken. We shall await you, then."

The light faded, but did not quite vanish. They're

* The Voice of God. But not the *voice* of God. An entity in its own right. Rather like a presidential spokesman.

leaving the line open, Aziraphale thought. I'm not getting out of this one.

"Hallo?" he said softly, "Anyone still there?"

There was silence.

Very carefully, he stepped over the circle and crept to the telephone. He opened his notebook and dialed another number.

After four rings it gave a little cough, followed by a pause, and then a voice which sounded so laid back you could put a carpet on it said, "Hi. This is Anthony Crowley. Uh. I—"

"Crowley!" Aziraphale tried to hiss and shout at the same time, "Listen! I haven't got much time! The—"

"—probably not in right now, or asleep, and busy, or something, but—"

"Shutup! Listen! It was in Tadfield! It's all in that book! You've got to stop—"

"—after the tone and I'll get right back to you. *Ciao.*"

"I want to talk to you *now*—"

BeeeEEeeeEEeee

"Stop making noises! It's in Tadfield! That was what I was sensing! You must go there and—"

He took the phone away from his mouth.

"Bugger!" he said. It was the first time he'd sworn in more than six thousand years.

Hold on. The demon had another line, didn't he? He was that kind of person. Aziraphale fumbled in the book, nearly dropping it on the floor. They would be getting impatient soon.

He found the other number. He dialed it. It was

answered almost immediately, at the same time as the shop's bell tingled gently.

Crowley's voice, getting louder as it neared the mouthpiece, said, "—really mean it. Hallo?"

"Crowley, it's me!"

"Ngh." The voice was horribly noncommittal. Even in his present state, Aziraphale sensed trouble.

"Are you alone?" he said cautiously.

"Nuh. Got an old friend here."

"Listen—!"

"Awa' we ye, ye spawn o' Hell!"

Very slowly, Aziraphale turned around.

SHADWELL WAS TREMBLING with excitement. He'd seen it all. He'd heard it all. He hadn't understood any of it, but he knew what people did with circles and candlesticks and incense. He knew that all right. He'd seen *The Devil Rides Out* fifteen times, sixteen times if you included the time he'd been thrown out of the cinema for shouting his unflattering opinions of amateur witchfinder Christopher Lee.

The buggers were using him. They'd been making fools out o' the glorious traditions o' the Army.

"I'll have ye, ye evil bastard!" he shouted, advancing like a moth-eaten avenging angel. "I ken what ye be about, comin' up here and seducin' wimmen to do yer evil will!"

"I think perhaps you've got the wrong shop," said Aziraphale. "I'll call back later," he told the receiver, and hung up.

"I could see what yer were aboot," snarled Shadwell. There were flecks of foam around his mouth. He was more angry than he could ever remember.

"Er, things are not what they seem—" Aziraphale began, aware even as he said it that as conversational gambits went it lacked a certain polish.

"I bet they ain't!" said Shadwell triumphantly.

"No, I mean—"

Without taking his eyes off the angel, Shadwell shuffled backwards and grabbed the shop door, slamming it hard so that the bell jangled.

"*Bell,*" he said.

He grabbed *The Nice and Accurate Prophecies* and thumped it down heavily on the table.

"*Book,*" he snarled.

He fumbled in his pocket and produced his trusty Ronson.

"*Practically candle!*" he shouted, and began to advance.

In his path, the circle glowed with a faint blue light.

"Er," said Aziraphale, "I think it might not be a very good idea to—"

Shadwell wasn't listening. "By the powers invested in me by virtue o' my office o' Witchfinder," he intoned, "I charge ye to quit from this place—"

"You see, the circle—"

"—and return henceforth to the place from which ye came, pausin' not to—"

"—it would really be unwise for a human to set foot in it without—"

"—and deliver us frae evil—"

"Keep out of the circle, you stupid man!"

"—never to come again to vex—"

"Yes, yes, but *please* keep out of—"

Aziraphale ran toward Shadwell, waving his hands urgently.

"—returning NAE MORE!" Shadwell finished. He pointed a vengeful, black-nailed finger.

Aziraphale looked down at his feet, and swore for the second time in five minutes. He'd stepped into the circle.

"Oh, *fuck*," he said.

There was a melodious twang, and the blue glow vanished. So did Aziraphale.

Thirty seconds went by. Shadwell didn't move. Then, with a trembling left hand, he reached up and carefully lowered his right hand.

"Hallo?" he said. "Hallo?"

No one answered.

Shadwell shivered. Then, with his hand held out in front of him like a gun that he didn't dare fire and didn't know how to unload, he stepped out into the street, letting the door slam behind him.

It shook the floor. One of Aziraphale's candles fell over, spilling burning wax across the old, dry wood.

CROWLEY'S LONDON FLAT was the epitome of style. It was everything that a flat should be: spacious, white, elegantly furnished, and with that designer unlived-in look that only comes from not being lived in.

This is because Crowley did not live there.

It was simply the place he went back to, at the end

of the day, when he was in London. The beds were always made; the fridge was always stocked with gourmet food that never went off (that was why Crowley had a fridge, after all), and for that matter the fridge never needed to be defrosted, or even plugged in.

The lounge contained a huge television, a white leather sofa, a video and a laserdisc player, an ansaphone, two telephones—the ansaphone line, and the private line (a number so far undiscovered by the legions of telephone salesmen who persisted in trying to sell Crowley double glazing, which he already had, or life insurance, which he didn't need)—and a square matte black sound system, the kind so exquisitely engineered that it just has the on-off switch and the volume control. The only sound equipment Crowley had overlooked was speakers; he'd forgotten about them. Not that it made any difference. The sound reproduction was quite perfect anyway.

There was an unconnected fax machine with the intelligence of a computer and a computer with the intelligence of a retarded ant. Nevertheless, Crowley upgraded it every few months, because a sleek computer was the sort of thing Crowley felt that the sort of human he tried to be would have. This one was like a Porsche with a screen. The manuals were still in their transparent wrapping.*

* Along with the standard computer warranty agreement which said that if the machine 1) didn't work, 2) didn't do what the expensive advertisements said, 3) electrocuted the immediate neighborhood, 4) and in fact failed entirely to be inside the expensive box when you opened it, this was expressly, absolutely, implicitly and in no

In fact the only things in the flat Crowley devoted any personal attention to were the houseplants. They were huge and green and glorious, with shiny, healthy, lustrous leaves.

This was because, once a week, Crowley went around the flat with a green plastic plant mister, spraying the leaves, and talking to the plants.

He had heard about talking to plants in the early seventies, on Radio Four, and thought it an excellent idea. Although *talking* is perhaps the wrong word for what Crowley did.

What he did was put the fear of God into them.

More precisely, the fear of Crowley.

In addition to which, every couple of months Crowley would pick out a plant that was growing too slowly, or succumbing to leaf-wilt or browning, or just didn't look quite as good as the others, and he would carry it around to all the other plants. "Say goodbye to your friend," he'd say to them. "He just couldn't cut it . . ."

Then he would leave the flat with the offending

---

event the fault or responsibility of the manufacturer, that the purchaser should consider himself lucky to be allowed to give his money to the manufacturer, and that any attempt to treat what had just been paid for as the purchaser's own property would result in the attentions of serious men with menacing briefcases and very thin watches. Crowley had been extremely impressed with the warranties offered by the computer industry, and had in fact sent a bundle Below to the department that drew up the Immortal Soul agreements, with a yellow memo form attached just saying: "Learn, guys."

plant, and return an hour or so later with a large, empty flower pot, which he would leave somewhere conspicuously around the flat.

The plants were the most luxurious, verdant, and beautiful in London. Also the most terrified.

The lounge was lit by spotlights and white neon tubes, of the kind one casually props against a chair or a corner.

The only wall decoration was a framed drawing—the cartoon for the *Mona Lisa*, Leonardo da Vinci's original sketch. Crowley had bought it from the artist one hot afternoon in Florence, and felt it was superior to the final painting.*

Crowley had a bedroom, and a kitchen, and an office, and a lounge, and a toilet: each room forever clean and perfect.

He had spent an uncomfortable time in each of these rooms, during the long wait for the End of the world.

He had phoned his operatives in the Witchfinder Army again, to try to get news, but his contact, Sergeant Shadwell, had just gone out, and the dimwitted receptionist seemed unable to grasp that he was willing to talk to any of the others.

* Leonardo had felt so too. "I got her bloody smile right in the roughs," he told Crowley, sipping cold wine in the lunchtime sun, "but it went all over the place when I painted it. Her husband had a few things to say about it when I delivered it, but, like I tell him, Signor del Giocondo, apart from you, who's going to see it? Anyway . . . explain this helicopter thing again, will you?"

"Mr. Pulsifer is out too, love," she told him. "He went down to Tadfield this morning. On a mission."

"I'll speak to anyone," Crowley had explained.

"I'll tell Mr. Shadwell that," she had said, "when he gets back. Now if you don't mind, it's one of my mornings, and I can't leave my gentleman like that for long or he'll catch his death. And at two I've got Mrs. Ormerod and Mr. Scroggie and young Julia coming over for a sitting, and there's the place to clean and all beforehand. But I'll give Mr. Shadwell your message."

Crowley gave up. He tried to read a novel, but couldn't concentrate. He tried to sort his CDs into alphabetical order, but gave up when he discovered they already were in alphabetical order, as was his bookcase, and his collection of Soul Music.*

Eventually he settled down on the white leather sofa and gestured on the television.

"Reports are coming in," said a worried newscaster, "uh, reports are, well, nobody seems to know what's going on, but reports available to us would seem to, uh, indicate an increase in international tensions that would have undoubtedly been viewed as impossible this time last week when, er, everyone seemed to be getting on so nicely. Er.

"This would seem at least partly due to the spate of unusual events which have occurred over the last few days.

* He was very proud of his collection. It had taken him ages to put together. This was *real* Soul Music. James Brown wasn't in it.

"Off the coast of Japan—"

CROWLEY?

"Yes," admitted Crowley.

WHAT THE HELL IS GOING ON, CROWLEY? WHAT EXACTLY HAVE YOU BEEN DOING?

"How do you mean?" Crowley asked, although he already knew.

THE BOY CALLED WARLOCK. WE HAVE BROUGHT HIM TO THE FIELDS OF MEGGIDO. THE DOG IS NOT WITH HIM. THE CHILD KNOWS NOTHING OF THE GREAT WAR. HE IS NOT OUR MASTER'S SON.

"Ah," said Crowley.

IS THAT ALL YOU CAN SAY, CROWLEY? OUR TROOPS ARE ASSEMBLED, THE FOUR BEASTS HAVE BEGUN TO RIDE—BUT WHERE ARE THEY RIDING TO? SOMETHING HAS GONE WRONG, CROWLEY. AND IT IS YOUR RESPONSIBILITY. AND, IN ALL PROBABILITY, YOUR FAULT. WE TRUST YOU HAVE A PERFECTLY REASONABLE EXPLANATION FOR ALL THIS . . .

"Oh, yes," agreed Crowley, readily. "Perfectly reasonable."

. . . BECAUSE YOU ARE GOING TO HAVE YOUR CHANCE TO EXPLAIN IT ALL TO US. YOU ARE GOING TO HAVE ALL THE TIME THERE IS TO EXPLAIN. AND WE WILL LISTEN WITH GREAT INTEREST TO EVERYTHING YOU HAVE TO SAY. AND YOUR CONVERSATION, AND THE CIRCUMSTANCES THAT WILL ACCOMPANY IT, WILL PROVIDE A SOURCE OF ENTERTAINMENT

AND PLEASURE FOR ALL THE DAMNED OF HELL, CROWLEY. BECAUSE NO MATTER HOW RACKED WITH TORMENT, NO MATTER WHAT AGONIES THE LOWEST OF THE DAMNED ARE SUFFERING, CROWLEY, YOU WILL HAVE IT WORSE—

With a gesture, Crowley turned the set off.

The dull gray-green screen continued enunciating; the silence formed itself into words.

DO NOT EVEN THINK ABOUT TRYING TO ESCAPE US, CROWLEY. THERE IS NO ESCAPE. STAY WHERE YOU ARE. YOU WILL BE . . . COLLECTED . . .

Crowley went to the window and looked out. Something black and car-shaped was moving slowly down the street toward him. It was car-shaped enough to fool the casual observer. Crowley, who was observing very carefully, noticed that not only were the wheels not going round, but they weren't even attached to the car. It was slowing down as it passed each house; Crowley assumed that the car's passengers (neither of them would be driving; neither of them knew how) were peering out at the house numbers.

He had a little time. Crowley went into the kitchen, and got a plastic bucket from under the sink. Then he went back into the lounge.

The Infernal Authorities had ceased communicating. Crowley turned the television to the wall, just in case.

He walked over to the *Mona Lisa*.

Crowley lifted the picture down from the wall, revealing a safe. It was not a wall safe; it had been bought from a company that specialized in servicing the nuclear industry.

He unlocked it, revealing an inner door with a dial combination lock. He spun the dial (4-0-0-4 was the code, easy to remember, the year he had slithered onto this stupid, marvelous planet, back when it was gleaming and new).

Inside the safe were a thermos flask, two heavy PVC gloves, of the kind that covered one's entire arms, and some tongs.

Crowley paused. He eyed the flask nervously.

(There was a crash from downstairs. That had been the front door . . .)

He pulled on the gloves and gingerly took the flask, and the tongs, and the bucket—and, as an afterthought, he grabbed the plant mister from beside a luxuriant rubber plant—and headed for his office, walking like a man carrying a thermos flask full of something that might cause, if he dropped it or even thought about dropping it, the sort of explosion that impels graybeards to make statements like "And where this crater is now, once stood the City of Wah-Shing-Ton," in SF B-movies.

He reached his office, nudged open the door with his shoulder. Then he bent his legs, and slowly put things down on the floor. Bucket . . . tongs . . . plant mister . . . and finally, deliberately, the flask.

A bead of sweat began to form on Crowley's forehead, and trickled down into one eye. He flicked it away.

Then, with care and deliberation, he used the tongs to unscrew the top of the flask . . . carefully . . . carefully . . . that was it . . .

(A pounding on the stairs below him, and a muffled scream. That would have been the little old lady on the floor below.)

He could not afford to rush.

He gripped the flask with the tongs, and taking care not to spill the tiniest drop, he poured the contents into the plastic bucket. One false move was all it would take.

There.

Then he opened the office door about six inches, and placed the bucket on top.

He used the tongs to replace the top of the flask, then (—a crash from his outer hallway—) pulled off the PVC gloves, picked up the plant mister, and settled himself behind his desk.

"Crawlee . . . ?" called a guttural voice. Hastur.

"He's through there," hissed another voice. "I can feel the slimy little creep." Ligur.

Hastur and Ligur.

Now, as Crowley would be the first to protest, most demons weren't *deep down* evil. In the great cosmic game they felt they occupied the same position as tax inspectors—doing an unpopular job, maybe, but essential to the overall operation of the whole thing. If it came to that, some angels weren't paragons of virtue; Crowley had met one or two who, when it came to righteously smiting the ungodly, smote a good deal harder than was strictly necessary. On the whole, everyone had a job to do, and just did it.

And on the other hand you got people like Ligur and Hastur, who took such a dark delight in unpleasantness you might even have mistaken them for human.

Crowley leaned back in his executive chair. He forced himself to relax and failed appallingly.

"In here, people," he called.

"We want a word with you," said Ligur (in a tone of voice intended to imply that "word" was synonymous with "horrifically painful eternity"), and the squat demon pushed open the office door.

The bucket teetered, then fell neatly on Ligur's head.

Drop a lump of sodium in water. Watch it flame and burn and spin around crazily, flaring and sputtering. This was like that; just nastier.

The demon peeled and flared and flickered. Oily brown smoke oozed from it, and it screamed and it screamed and it screamed. Then it crumpled, folded in on itself, and what was left lay glistening on the burnt and blackened circle of carpet, looking like a handful of mashed slugs.

"Hi," said Crowley to Hastur, who had been walking behind Ligur, and had unfortunately not been so much as splashed.

There are some things that are unthinkable: there are some depths that not even demons would believe other demons would stoop to.

". . . Holy water. You bastard," said Hastur. "You complete *bastard*. He hadn't never done nothing to *you*."

"Yet," corrected Crowley, who felt a little more comfortable, now the odds were closer to even. Closer, but not yet even, not by a long shot. Hastur was a Duke of Hell. Crowley wasn't even a local counselor.

"Your fate will be whispered by mothers in dark

places to frighten their young," said Hastur, and then felt that the language of Hell wasn't up to the job. "You're going to get taken to the bloody *cleaners*, pal," he added.

Crowley raised the green plastic plant mister, and sloshed it around threateningly. "Go away," he said. He heard the phone downstairs ringing. Four times, and then the ansaphone caught it. He wondered vaguely who it was.

"You don't frighten me," said Hastur. He watched a drip of water leak from the nozzle and slide slowly down the side of the plastic container, toward Crowley's hand.

"Do you know what this is?" asked Crowley. "This is a Sainsbury's plant mister, cheapest and most efficient plant mister in the world. It can squirt a fine spray of water into the air. Do I need to tell you what's in it? It can turn *you* into *that*." He pointed to the mess on the carpet. "Now, go away."

Then the drip on the side of the plant mister reached Crowley's curled fingers, and stopped. "You're bluffing," said Hastur.

"Maybe I am," said Crowley, in a tone of voice which he hoped made it quite clear that bluffing was the last thing on his mind. "And maybe I'm not. Do you feel lucky?"

Hastur gestured, and the plastic bulb dissolved like rice paper, spilling water all over Crowley's desk, and all over Crowley's suit.

"Yes," said Hastur. And then he smiled. His teeth were too sharp, and his tongue flickered between them. "Do you?"

Crowley said nothing. Plan A had worked. Plan

B had failed. Everything depended on Plan C, and there was one drawback to this: he had only ever planned as far as B.

"So," hissed Hastur, "time to go, Crowley."

"I think there's something you ought to know," said Crowley, stalling for time.

"And that is?" smiled Hastur.

Then the phone on Crowley's desk rang.

He picked it up, and warned Hastur, "Don't move. There's something very important you should know, and I really mean it. Hallo?

"Ngh," said Crowley. Then he said, "Nuh. Got an old friend here."

Aziraphale hung up on him. Crowley wondered what he had wanted.

And suddenly Plan C was there, in his head. He didn't replace the handset on the receiver. Instead he said, "Okay, Hastur. You've passed the test. You're ready to start playing with the big boys."

"Have you gone mad?"

"Nope. Don't you understand? This was a test. The Lords of Hell had to know that you were trustworthy before we gave you command of the Legions of the Damned, in the War ahead."

"Crowley, you are lying, or you are insane, or possibly you are both," said Hastur, but his certainty was shaken.

Just for a moment he had entertained the possibility; that was where Crowley had got him. It *was* just possible that Hell was testing him. That Crowley *was* more than he seemed. Hastur was paranoid, which was simply a sensible and well-adjusted reaction to living in Hell, where they really were all out to get you.

Crowley began to dial a number. "'S' okay, Duke Hastur. I wouldn't expect you to believe it from *me*," he admitted. "But why don't we talk to the Dark Council—I am sure that they can convince you."

The number he had dialed clicked and started to ring.

"So long, sucker," he said.

And vanished.

In a tiny fraction of a second, Hastur was gone as well.

OVER THE YEARS a huge number of theological man-hours have been spent debating the famous question:

How Many Angels Can Dance on the Head of a Pin?

In order to arrive at an answer, the following facts must be taken into consideration:

Firstly, angels simply don't dance. It's one of the distinguishing characteristics that mark an angel. They may listen appreciatively to the Music of the Spheres, but they don't feel the urge to get down and boogie to it. So, *none.*

At least, nearly none. Aziraphale had learned to gavotte in a discreet gentlemen's club in Portland Place, in the late 1880s, and while he had initially taken to it like a duck to merchant banking, after a while he had become quite good at it, and was quite put out when, some decades later, the gavotte went out of style for good.

So providing the dance was a gavotte, and providing that he had a suitable partner (also able, for the sake of argument, both to gavotte, and to dance it on the head of a pin), the answer is a straightforward *one*.

Then again, you might just as well ask how many demons can dance on the head of a pin. They're of the same original stock, after all. And at least they dance.*

And if you put it that way, the answer is, quite a lot actually, providing they abandon their physical bodies, which is a picnic for a demon. Demons aren't bound by physics. If you take the long view, the universe is just something small and round, like those water-filled balls which produce a miniature snowstorm when you shake them.** But if you look from really close up, the only problem about dancing on the head of a pin is all those big gaps between electrons.

For those of angel stock or demon breed, size, and shape, and composition, are simply options.

Crowley is currently traveling incredibly fast down a telephone line.

RING.

Crowley went through two telephone exchanges at a very respectable fraction of lightspeed. Hastur

* Although it's not what you and I would call *dancing*. Not good dancing anyway. A demon moves like a white band on "Soul Train."

** Although, unless the ineffable plan is a lot more ineffable than it's given credit for, it does not have a giant plastic snowman at the bottom.

was a little way behind him: four or five inches, but at that size it gave Crowley a very comfortable lead. One that would vanish, of course, when he came out the other end.

They were too small for sound, but demons don't necessarily need sound to communicate. He could hear Hastur screaming behind him, "You bastard! I'll get you. You can't escape me!"

RING.

"Wherever you come out, I'll come out too! You won't get away!"

Crowley had traveled through over twenty miles of cable in less than a second.

Hastur was close behind him. Crowley was going to have to time this whole thing very, very carefully.

RING.

That was the third ring. Well, thought Crowley, here goes nothing.

He stopped, suddenly, and watched Hastur shoot past him. Hastur turned and—

RING.

Crowley shot out through the phone line, zapped through the plastic sheathing, and materialized, full-size and out of breath, in his lounge.

CLICK.

The outgoing message tape began to turn on his ansaphone. Then there was a beep, and, as the incoming message tape turned, a voice from the speaker screamed, after the beep, "Right! What? . . . *You bloody snake!*"

The little red message light began to flash.

On and off and on and off, like a tiny, red, angry eye.

Crowley really wished he had some more holy

water and the time to hold the cassette in it until it dissolved. But getting hold of Ligur's terminal bath had been dangerous enough, he'd had it for years just in case, and even its presence in the room made him uneasy. Or . . . or maybe . . . yes, what *would* happen if he put the cassette in the car? He could play Hastur over and over again, until he turned into Freddie Mercury. No. He might be a bastard, but you could only go so far.

There was a rumble of distant thunder.

He had no time to spare.

He had nowhere to go.

He went anyway. He ran down to his Bentley and drove toward the West End as if all the demons of Hell were after him. Which was more or less the case.

MADAME TRACY HEARD Mr. Shadwell's slow tread come up the stairs. It was slower than usual, and paused every few steps. Normally he came up the stairs as if he hated every one of them.

She opened her door. He was leaning against the landing wall.

"Why, Mr. Shadwell," she said, "whatever have you done to your hand?"

"Get away frae me, wumman," Shadwell groaned. "I dinna know my ane powers!"

"Why are you holding it out like that?"

Shadwell tried to back into the wall.

"Stand back, I tell ye! I canna be responsible!"

"What on earth has happened to you, Mr. Shadwell?" said Madame Tracy, trying to take his hand.

"Nothing on earth! Nothing on earth!"

She managed to grab his arm. He, Shadwell, scourge of evil, was powerless to resist being drawn into her flat.

He'd never been in it before, at least in his waking moments. His dreams had furnished it in silks, rich hangings, and what he thought of as scented ungulants. Admittedly, it did have a bead curtain in the entrance to the kitchenette and a lamp made rather inexpertly from a Chianti bottle, because Madame Tracy's apprehension of what was chic, like Aziraphale's, had grounded around 1953. And there was a table in the middle of the room with a velvet cloth on it and, on the cloth, the crystal ball which increasingly was Madame Tracy's means of earning a living.

"I think you could do with a good lie-down, Mr. Shadwell," she said, in a voice that brooked no argument, and led him on into the bedroom. He was too bewildered to protest.

"But young Newt is out there," Shadwell muttered, "in thrall to heathen passions and occult wiles."

"Then I'm sure he'll know what to do about them," said Madame Tracy briskly, whose mental picture of what Newt was going through was probably much closer to reality than was Shadwell's. "And I'm sure he wouldn't like to think of you getting yourself worked up into a state here. Just you lie down, and I'll make us both a nice cup of tea."

She disappeared in a clacking of bead curtains.

Suddenly Shadwell was alone on what he was just capable of recalling, through the wreckage of his shattered nerves, was a bed of sin, and right at this moment was incapable of deciding whether that was in fact better or worse than *not* being alone on a bed of sin. He turned his head to take in his surroundings.

Madame Tracy's concepts of what was erotic stemmed from the days when young men grew up thinking that women had beach balls affixed firmly in front of their anatomy, Brigitte Bardot could be called a sex kitten without anyone bursting out laughing, and there really were magazines with names like *Girls, Giggles and Garters.* Somewhere in this cauldron of permissiveness she had picked up the idea that soft toys in the bedroom created an intimate, coquettish air.

Shadwell stared for some time at a large, threadbare teddy bear, which had one eye missing and a torn ear. It probably had a name like Mr. Buggins.

He turned his head the other way. His gaze was blocked by a pajama case shaped like an animal that may have been a dog but, there again, might have been a skunk. It had a cheery grin.

"Urg," he said.

But recollection kept storming back. He really had done it. No one else in the Army had ever exorcised a demon, as far as he knew. Not Hopkins, not Siftings, not Diceman. Probably not even Witchfinder Company Sergeant Major Narker,* who held

* The WA enjoyed a renaissance during the great days of Empire expansionism. The British army's endless

the all-time record for most witches found. Sooner or later every Army runs across its ultimate weapon and now it existed, Shadwell reflected, on the end of his arm.

Well, screw No First Use. He'd have a bit of a rest, seeing as he was here, and then the Powers of Darkness had met their match at last . . .

When Madame Tracy brought the tea in he was snoring. She tactfully closed the door, and rather thankfully as well, because she had a seance due in twenty minutes and it was no good turning down money these days.

Although Madame Tracy was by many yardsticks quite stupid, she had an instinct in certain matters, and when it came to dabbling in the occult her reasoning was faultless. Dabbling, she'd realized, was exactly what her customers wanted. They didn't want to be shoved in it up to their necks. They didn't want the multi-planular mysteries of Time

---

skirmishes frequently brought it up against witch doctors, bone-pointers, shamans, and other occult adversaries. This was the cue for the deployment of the likes of WA CSM Narker, whose striding, bellowing, six-foot-six, eighteen-stone figure, clutching an armor-plated Book, eight-pound Bell, and specially reinforced Candle, could clear the veldt of adversaries faster than a Gatling gun. Cecil Rhodes wrote of him: "Some remote tribes consider him to be a kind of god, and it is an extremely brave or foolhardy witch doctor who will stand his ground with CSM Narker bearing down on him. I would rather have this man on my side than two battalions of Gurkhas."

and Space, they just wanted to be reassured that Mother was getting along fine now she was dead. They wanted just enough Occult to season the simple fare of their lives, and preferably in portions no longer than forty-five minutes, followed by tea and biscuits.

They certainly didn't want odd candles, scents, chants, or mystic runes. Madame Tracy had even removed most of the Major Arcana from her Tarot card pack, because their appearance tended to upset people.

And she made sure that she had always put sprouts on to boil just before a seance. Nothing is more reassuring, nothing is more true to the comfortable spirit of English occultism, than the smell of Brussels sprouts cooking in the next room.

IT WAS EARLY AFTERNOON, and the heavy storm clouds had turned the sky the color of old lead. It would rain soon, heavily, blindingly. The firemen hoped the rain would come soon. The sooner the better.

They had arrived fairly promptly, and the younger firemen were dashing around excitedly, unrolling their hosepipe and flexing their axes; the older firemen knew at a glance that the building was a dead loss, and weren't even sure that the rain would stop it spreading to neighboring buildings, when a black Bentley skidded around the corner and drove up onto the pavement at a speed somewhere in excess of sixty miles per hour, and stopped with a screech of brakes half an inch away from the wall of the bookshop. An extremely agitated young man in dark glasses got out and ran toward the door of the blazing bookshop.

He was intercepted by a fireman.

"Are you the owner of this establishment?" asked the fireman.

"Don't be stupid! Do I *look* like I run a bookshop?"

"I really wouldn't know about that, sir. Appearances can be very deceptive. For example, I am a fireman. However, upon meeting me socially, people unaware of my occupation often suppose that I am, in fact, a chartered accountant or company director. Imagine me out of uniform, sir, and what kind of man would you see before you? Honestly?"

"A prat," said Crowley, and he ran into the bookshop.

This sounds easier than it actually was, since in order to manage it Crowley needed to avoid half a dozen firemen, two policemen, and a number of interesting Soho night people,* out early, and arguing heatedly amongst themselves about which particular section of society had brightened up the afternoon, and why.

Crowley pushed straight through them. They scarcely spared him a glance.

Then he pushed open the door, and stepped into an inferno.

* In any other place than Soho it is quite possible that spectators at a fire might have been interested.

The whole bookshop was ablaze. "Aziraphale!" he called. "Aziraphale, you—you *stupid—Aziraphale?* Are you here?"

No answer. Just the crackle of burning paper, the splintering of glass as the fire reached the upstairs rooms, the crash of collapsing timbers.

He scanned the shop urgently, desperately, looking for the angel, looking for *help*.

In the far corner a bookshelf toppled over, cascading flaming books across the floor. The fire was all around him, and Crowley ignored it. His left trouser leg began to smolder; he stopped it with a glance.

"Hello? Aziraphale! For Go—, for Sa—, for *somebody's* sake! Aziraphale!"

The shop window was smashed from outside. Crowley turned, startled, and an unexpected jet of water struck him full in the chest, knocking him to the ground.

His shades flew to a far corner of the room, and became a puddle of burning plastic. Yellow eyes with slitted vertical pupils were revealed. Wet and steaming, face ash-blackened, as far from cool as it was possible for him to be, on all fours in the blazing bookshop, Crowley cursed Aziraphale, and the ineffable plan, and Above, and Below.

Then he looked down, and saw it. The book. The book that the girl had left in the car in Tadfield, on Wednesday night. It was slightly scorched around the cover, but miraculously unharmed. He picked it up, stuffed it into his jacket pocket, stood up, unsteadily, and brushed himself off.

The floor above him collapsed. With a roar and

gargantuan shrug the building fell in on itself, in a rain of brick and timber and flaming debris.

Outside, the passersby were being herded back by the police, and a fireman was explaining to anyone who would listen, "I couldn't stop him. He must have been mad. Or drunk. Just ran in. I couldn't stop him. Mad. Ran straight in. Horrible way to die. Horrible, horrible. Just ran straight in . . ."

Then Crowley came out of the flames.

The police and the firemen looked at him, saw the expression on his face, and stayed exactly where they were.

He climbed into the Bentley and reversed back into the road, swung around a fire truck, into Wardour Street, and into the darkened afternoon.

They stared at the car as it sped away. Finally one policeman spoke. "Weather like this, he ought to of put his lights on," he said, numbly.

"Especially driving like that. Could be dangerous," agreed another, in flat, dead tones, and they all stood there in the light and the heat of the burning bookshop, wondering what was happening to a world they had thought they understood.

There was a flash of lightning, blue-white, strobing across the cloud-black sky, a crack of thunder so loud it hurt, and a hard rain began to fall.

SHE RODE A RED MOTORBIKE. Not a friendly Honda red; a deep, bloody red, rich and dark and hateful. The bike was apparently, in every other respect, ordinary except for the sword, resting in its scabbard, set onto the side of the bike.

Her helmet was crimson, and her leather jacket was the color of old wine. In ruby studs on the back were picked out the words HELL'S ANGELS.

It was ten past one in the afternoon and it was dark and humid and wet. The motorway was almost deserted, and the woman in red roared down the road on her red motorbike, smiling lazily.

It had been a good day so far. There was something about the sight of a beautiful woman on a powerful motorbike with a sword stuck on the back that had a powerful effect on a certain type of man. So far four traveling salesmen had tried to race her, and bits of Ford Sierra now decorated the crash barriers and bridge supports along forty miles of motorway.

She pulled up at a service area, and went into the Happy Porker Café. It was almost empty. A bored waitress was darning a sock behind the counter, and a knot of black-leathered bikers, hard, hairy, filthy, and huge, were clustered around an even taller individual in a black coat. He was resolutely playing something that in bygone years would have been a fruit machine, but now had a video screen, and advertised itself as TRIVIA SCRABBLE.

The audience were saying things like:

"It's D! Press D!—*The Godfather must*'ve got more Oscars than *Gone with the Wind!*"

"Puppet on a String! Sandie Shaw! Honest. I'm bleeding positive!"

"1666!"

"No, you great pillock! That was the fire! The Plague was 1665!"

"It's B—the Great Wall of China *wasn't* one of the Seven Wonders of the world!"

There were four options: Pop Music, Sport, Current Events, and General Knowledge. The tall biker, who had kept his helmet on, was pressing the buttons, to all intents and purposes oblivious of his supporters. At any rate, he was consistently winning.

The red rider went over to the counter.

"A cup of tea, please. And a cheese sandwich," she said.

"You on your own, then, dear?" asked the waitress, passing the tea, and something white and dry and hard, across the counter.

"Waiting for friends."

"Ah," she said, biting through some wool. "Well, you're better off waiting in here. It's hell out there."

"No," she told her. "Not yet."

She picked a window table, with a good view of the parking lot, and she waited.

She could hear the Trivia Scrabblers in the background.

"Thass a new one, 'How many times has England been officially at war with France since 1066?' "

"Twenty? Nah, s' never twenty . . . Oh. It was. Well, I never."

"American war with Mexico? I know that. It's June 1845. D—see! I tol' you!"

The second-shortest biker, Pigbog (6' 3"), whispered to the shortest, Greaser (6' 2"):

"What happened to Sport, then?" He had LOVE tattooed on one set of knuckles, HATE on the other.

"It's random wossit, selection, innit. I mean they do it with microchips. It's probably got, like, millions of different subjects in there, in its RAM." He had FISH across his right-hand knuckle, and CHIP on the left.

"Pop Music, Current Events, General Knowledge, and War. It's just I've never seen War before. That's why I mentioned it." Pigbog cracked his knuckles, loudly, and pulled the ring tab on a can of beer. He swigged back half a can, belched carelessly, then sighed. "I just wish they'd do more bleeding Bible questions."

"Why?" Greaser had never thought of Pigbog as being a Bible trivia freak.

"'Cos, well, you remember that bit of bother in Brighton?"

"Oh, yeah. You was on *Crimewatch*," said Greaser, with a trace of envy.

"Well, I had to hang out in that hotel where me mam worked, dinni? Free months. And nothin' to read, only this bugger Gideon had left his Bible behind. It kind of sticks in your mind."

Another motorbike, jet black and gleaming, drew up in the car-park outside.

The door to the café opened. A blast of cold wind blew through the room; a man dressed all in black leather, with a short black beard, walked over to the table, sat next to the woman in red, and the bikers around the video scrabble machine suddenly noticed how hungry they all were, and deputed Skuzz to go and get them something to eat. All of them except the player, who said nothing, just pressed the buttons for the right answers and let his winnings accumulate in the tray at the bottom of the machine.

"I haven't seen you since Mafeking," said Red. "How's it been going?"

"I've been keeping pretty busy," said Black. "Spent a lot of time in America. Brief world tours. Just killing time, really."

("What do you mean, you've got no steak and kidney pies?" asked Skuzz, affronted.

"I thought we had some, but we don't," said the woman.)

"Feels funny, all of us finally getting together like this," said Red.

"Funny?"

"Well, you know. When you've spent all these thousands of years waiting for the big day, and it finally comes. Like waiting for Christmas. Or birthdays."

"We don't have birthdays."

"I didn't say we do. I just said that was what it was like."

("Actually," admitted the woman,"it doesn't look like we've got anything left at all. Except that slice of pizza."

"Has it got anchovies on it?" asked Skuzz gloomily. None of the chapter liked anchovies. Or olives.

"Yes, dear. It's anchovy and olives. Would you like it?"

Skuzz shook his head sadly. Stomach rumbling, he made his way back to the game. Big Ted got irritable when he got hungry, and when Big Ted got irritable everyone got a slice.)

A new category had come up on the video screen. You could now answer questions about Pop Music, Current Events, Famine, or War. The bikers seemed marginally less informed about the Irish Potato Famine of 1846, the English everything famine of 1315, and the 1969 dope famine in San Francisco than they had been about War, but the player was still racking up a perfect score, punctuated occasionally by a whir, ratchet, and chink as the machine disgorged pound coins into its tray.

"Weather looks a bit tricky down south," said Red.

Black squinted at the darkening clouds. "No. Looks fine to me. We'll have a thunderstorm along any minute."

Red looked at her nails. "That's good. It wouldn't be the same if we didn't have a good thunderstorm. Any idea how far we've got to ride?"

Black shrugged. "A few hundred miles."

"I thought it'd be longer, somehow. All that waiting, just for a few hundred miles."

"It's not the traveling," said Black. "It's the arriving that matters."

There was a roar outside. It was the roar of a motorbike with a defective exhaust, untuned engine, leaky carburetor. You didn't have to see the bike to imagine the clouds of black smoke it traveled in, the oil slicks it left in its wake, the trail of small motorbike parts and fittings that littered the roads behind it.

Black went up to the counter.

"Four teas, please," he said. "One black."

The café door opened. A young man in dusty

white leathers entered, and the wind blew empty crisp packets and newspapers and ice cream wrappers in with him. They danced around his feet like excited children, then fell exhausted to the floor.

"Four of you, are there, dear?" asked the woman. She was trying to find some clean cups and teaspoons—the entire rack seemed suddenly to have been coated in a light film of motor oil and dried egg.

"There will be," said the man in black, and he took the teas and went back to the table, where his two comrades waited.

"Any sign of him?" said the boy in white.

They shook their heads.

An argument had broken out around the video screen (current categories showing on the screen were War, Famine, Pollution, and Pop Trivia 1962–1979).

"Elvis Presley? 'Sgotta be C—it was 1977 he snuffed it, wasn't it?"

"Nah. D. 1976. I'm positive."

"Yeah. Same year as Bing Crosby."

"And Marc Bolan. He was dead good. Press D, then. Go on."

The tall figure made no motion to press any of the buttons.

"Woss the matter with you?" asked Big Ted, irritably. "Go on. Press D. Elvis Presley died in 1976."

I DON'T CARE WHAT IT SAYS, said the tall biker in the helmet, I NEVER LAID A FINGER ON HIM.

The three people at the table turned as one. Red spoke. "When did you get here?" she asked.

The tall man walked over to the table, leaving the

astonished bikers, and his winnings, behind him. I NEVER WENT AWAY, he said, and his voice was a dark echo from the night places, a cold slab of sound, gray, and dead. If that voice was a stone it would have had words chiseled on it a long time ago: a name, and two dates.

"Your tea's getting cold, lord," said Famine.

"It's been a long time," said War.

There was a flash of lightning, almost immediately followed by a low rumble of thunder.

"Lovely weather for it," said Pollution.

YES.

The bikers around the game were getting progressively baffled by this exchange. Led by Big Ted, they shambled over to the table and stared at the four strangers.

It did not escape their notice that *all* four strangers had HELL'S ANGELS on their jackets. And they looked dead dodgy as far as the Angels were concerned: too clean for a start; and none of the four looked like they'd ever broken anyone's arm just because it was Sunday afternoon and there wasn't anything good on the telly. And one was a woman, too, only not ridin' around on the back of someone's bike but actually allowed one of her own, like she had any right to it.

"You're Hell's Angels, then?" asked Big Ted, sarcastically. If there's one thing real Hell's Angels can't abide, it's weekend bikers.*

* There are a number of other things real Hell's Angels can't abide. These include the police, soap, Ford Cortinas, and, in Big Ted's case, anchovies and olives.

The four strangers nodded.

"What chapter are you from, then?"

The Tall Stranger looked at Big Ted. Then he stood up. It was a complicated motion; if the shores of the seas of night had deck chairs, they'd open up something like that.

He seemed to be unfolding himself forever.

He wore a dark helmet, completely hiding his features. And it was made of that weird plastic, Big Ted noted. Like, you looked in it, and all you could see was your own face.

REVELATIONS, he said. CHAPTER SIX.

"Verses two to eight," added the boy in white, helpfully.

Big Ted glared at the four of them. His lower jaw began to protrude, and a little blue vein in his temple started to throb. "Wossat mean then?" he demanded.

There was a tug at his sleeve. It was Pigbog. He had gone a peculiar shade of gray, under the dirt.

"It means we're in trouble," said Pigbog.

And then the tall stranger reached up a pale motorbike gauntlet, and raised the visor of his helmet, and Big Ted found himself wishing, for the first time in his existence, that he'd lived a better life.

"Jesus Christ!" he moaned.

"I think He may be along in a minute," said Pigbog urgently. "He's probably looking for somewhere to park his bike. Let's go and, and join a youf club or somethin' . . ."

But Big Ted's invincible ignorance was his shield and armor. He didn't move.

"Cor," he said. "Hell's Angels."

War flipped him a lazy salute.

"That's us, Big Ted," she said. "The real McCoy."

Famine nodded. "The Old Firm," he said.

Pollution removed his helmet and shook out his long white hair. He had taken over when Pestilence, muttering about penicillin, had retired in 1936. If only the old boy had known what opportunities the future had held . . .

"Others promise," he said, "we deliver."

Big Ted looked at the fourth Horseman. " 'Ere, I seen you before," he said. "You was on the cover of that Blue Oyster Cult album. An' I got a ring wif your . . . your . . . your head on it."

I GET EVERYWHERE.

"Cor." Big Ted's big face screwed up with the effort of thought.

"Wot kind of bike you ridin'?" he said.

THE STORM RAGED around the quarry. The rope with the old car tire on it danced in the gale. Sometimes a sheet of iron, relic of an attempt at a tree house, would shake loose from its insubstantial moorings and sail away.

The Them huddled together, staring at Adam. He seemed bigger, somehow. Dog sat and growled. He was thinking of all the smells he would lose. There were no smells in Hell, apart from the sulphur. While some of them here, were, were . . . well, the fact was, there were no bitches in Hell either.

Adam was marching about excitedly, waving his hands in the air.

"There'll be no end to the fun we can have," he said. "There'll be exploring and everything. I 'spect I can soon get the ole jungles to grow again."

"But—but who—who'll do the, you know, all the cooking and washing and suchlike?" quavered Brian.

"No one'll have to do any of that stuff," said Adam. "You can have all the food you like, loads of chips, fried onion rings, anything you like. An' never have to wear any new clothes or have a bath if you don't want to or anything. Or go to school or anything. Or do anything you don't want to do, ever again. It'll be *wicked*!"

THE MOON CAME UP over the Kookamundi Hills. It was very bright tonight.

Johnny Two Bones sat in the red basin of the desert. It was a sacred place, where two ancestral rocks, formed in the Dreamtime, lay as they had since the beginning. Johnny Two Bones' walkabout was coming to an end. His cheeks and chest were smeared with red ochre, and he was singing an old song, a sort of singing map of the hills, and he was drawing patterns in the dust with his spear.

He had not eaten for two days; he had not slept. He was approaching a trance state, making him one with the Bush, putting him into communion with his ancestors.

He was nearly there.

Nearly . . .

He blinked. Looked around wonderingly.

"*Excuse me, dear boy,*" he said to himself, out loud, in precise, enunciated tones. "*But have you any idea where I am?*"

"Who said that?" said Johnny Two Bones.

His mouth opened. "*I did.*"

Johnny scratched, thoughtfully. "I take it you're one of me ancestors, then, mate?"

"*Oh. Indubitably, dear boy. Quite indubitably. In a manner of speaking. Now, to get back to my original question. Where am I?*"

"Only if you're one of my ancestors," continued Johnny Two Bones, "why are you talking like a poofter?"

"*Ah. Australia,*" said Johnny Two Bones' mouth, pronouncing the word as though it would have to be properly disinfected before he said it again. "*Oh dear. Well, thank you anyway.*"

"Hello? Hello?" said Johnny Two Bones.

He sat in the sand, and he waited, and he waited, but he didn't reply.

Aziraphale had moved on.

CITRON DEUX-CHEVAUX was *tonton macoute*, a traveling *houngan:** he had a satchel over his shoulder, containing magical plants, medicinal plants, bits of wild cat, black candles, a powder derived chiefly from the skin of a certain dried fish, a dead centi-

* Magician, or priest. Voodoun is a very interesting religion for the whole family, even those members of it who are dead.

pede, a half-bottle of Chivas Regal, ten Rothmans, and a copy of *What's On In Haiti.*

He hefted the knife, and, with an experienced slicing motion, cut the head from a black cockerel. Blood washed over his right hand.

"*Loa* ride me," he intoned. "*Gros Bon Ange* come to me."

"*Where am I?*" he said.

"Is that my *Gros Bon Ange?*" he asked himself.

"*I think that's a rather personal question,*" he replied. "*I mean, as these things go. But one tries, as it were. One does one's best.*"

Citron found one of his hands reaching for the cockerel.

"*Rather unsanitary place to do your cooking, don't you think? Out here in the jungle. Having a barbecue, are we? What kind of place is this?*"

"Haitian," he answered.

"*Damn! Nowhere near. Still, could be worse. Ah, I must be on my way. Be good.*"

And Citron Deux-Chevaux was alone in his head.

"*Loas* be buggered," he muttered to himself. He stared into nothing for a while, and then reached for the satchel and its bottle of Chivas Regal. There are at least two ways to turn someone into a zombie. He was going to take the easiest.

The surf was loud on the beaches. The palms shook.

A storm was coming.

THE LIGHTS WENT UP. The Power Cable (Nebraska) Evangelical Choir launched into "Jesus Is the Telephone Repairman on the Switchboard of My Life," and almost drowned out the sound of the rising wind.

Marvin O. Bagman adjusted his tie, checked his grin in the mirror, patted the bottom of his personal assistant (Miss Cindi Kellerhals, *Penthouse* Pet of the Month three years ago last July; but she had put that all behind her when she got Career), and he walked out onto the studio floor.

Jesus won't cut you off before you're through
With him you won't never get a crossed line,
And when your bill comes it'll all be properly itemized
He's the telephone repairman on the switchboard of
my life,

the choir sang. Marvin was fond of that song. He had written it himself.

Other songs he had written included: "Happy Mister Jesus," "Jesus, Can I Come and Stay at Your Place?" "That Ol' Fiery Cross," "Jesus Is the Sticker on the Bumper of My Soul," and "When I'm Swept Up by the Rapture Grab the Wheel of My Pick-Up." They were available on *Jesus Is My Buddy* (LP, cassette, and CD), and were advertised every four minutes on Bagman's evangelical network.*

Despite the fact that the lyrics didn't rhyme, or, as a rule, make any sense, and that Marvin, who was not particularly musical, had stolen all the tunes

* $12.95 per LP or cassette, $24.95 per CD, although you got a free copy of the LP with every $500 you donated to Marvin Bagman's mission.

from old country songs, *Jesus Is My Buddy* had sold over four million copies.

Marvin had started off as a country singer, singing old Conway Twitty and Johnny Cash songs.

He had done regular live concerts from San Quentin jail until the civil rights people got him under the Cruel and Unusual Punishment clause.

It was then that Marvin got religion. Not the quiet, personal kind, that involves doing good deeds and living a better life; not even the kind that involves putting on a suit and ringing people's doorbells; but the kind that involves having your own TV network and getting people to send you money.

He had found the perfect TV mix, on *Marvin's Hour of Power* ("The show that put the FUN back into Fundamentalist!"). Four three-minute songs from the LP, twenty minutes of Hellfire, and five minutes of healing people. (The remaining twenty-three minutes were spent alternately cajoling, pleading, threatening, begging, and occasionally simply asking for money.) In the early days he had actually brought people into the studio to heal, but had found that too complicated, so these days he simply proclaimed visions vouchsafed to him of viewers all across America getting magically cured as they watched. This was much simpler—he no longer needed to hire actors, and there was no way anyone could check on his success rate.*

The world is a lot more complicated than most

* It might have surprised Marvin to know there actually was a success rate. Some people would get better from *anything*.

people believe. Many people believed, for example, that Marvin was not a true Believer because he made so much money out of it. They were wrong. He believed with all his heart. He believed utterly, and spent a lot of the money that flooded in on what he really thought was the Lord's work.

The phone line to the savior's always free of
interference
He's in at any hour, day or night
And when you call J-E-S-U-S you always call toll
free
He's the telephone repairman on the switchboard of
my life.

The first song concluded, and Marvin walked in front of the cameras and raised his arms modestly for silence. In the control booth, the engineer turned down the Applause track.

"Brothers and sisters, thank you, thank you, wasn't that beautiful? And remember, you can hear that song and others just as edifyin' on *Jesus Is My Buddy*, just phone 1-800-CASH and pledge your donation now."

He became more serious.

"Brothers and sisters, I've got a message for you all, an urgent message from our Lord, for you all, man and woman and little babes, friends, let me tell you about the Apocalypse. It's all there in your Bible, in the Revelation our Lord gave Saint John on Patmos, and in the Book of Daniel. The Lord always gives it to you straight, friends—your future. So what's goin' to happen?

"War. Plague. Famine. Death. Rivers urv blurd. Great earthquakes. Nukyeler missiles. Horrible times are comin', brothers and sisters. And there's only one way to avoid 'em.

"Before the Destruction comes—before the four horsemen of the apocalypse ride out—before the nukerler missles rain down on the unbelievers—there will come The Rapture.

"What's the Rapture? I hear you cry.

"When the Rapture comes, brothers and sisters, all the True Believers will be swept up in the air—it don't mind what you're doin', you could be in the bath, you could be at work, you could be drivin' your car, or just sittin' at home readin' your Bible. Suddenly you'll be up there in the air, in perfect and incorruptible bodies. And you'll be up in the air, lookin' down at the world as the years of destruction arrive. Only the faithful will be saved, only those of you who have been born again will avoid the pain and the death and the horror and the burnin'. Then will come the great war between Heaven and Hell, and Heaven will destroy the forces of Hell, and God shall wipe away the tears of the sufferin', and there shall be no more death, or sorrow, or cryin', or pain, and he shall rayon in glory for ever and ever—"

He stopped, suddenly.

"*Well, nice try,*" he said, in a completely different voice, "*only it won't be like that at all. Not really.*

"*I mean, you're right about the fire and war, all that. But that Rapture stuff—well, if you could see them all in Heaven—serried ranks of them as far as the mind can follow and beyond, league after league of us, flaming swords, all that, well, what I'm trying to say is who has time to go round picking people out and popping them up in the air to sneer at the people dying of radiation sickness on the parched and burning earth below them? If that's your idea of a morally acceptable time, I might add.*

"And as for that stuff about Heaven inevitably winning . . . Well, to be honest, if it were that cut and dried, there wouldn't be a Celestial War in the first place, would there? It's propaganda. Pure and simple. We've got no more than a fifty percent chance of coming out on top. You might just as well send money to a Satanist hotline to cover your bets, although to be frank when the fire falls and the seas of blood rise you lot are all going to be civilian casualties either way. Between our war and your war, they're going to kill everyone and let God sort it out—right?

"Anyway, sorry to stand here wittering, I've just a quick question—where am I?"

Marvin O. Bagman was gradually going purple.

"It's the devil! Lord protect me! The devil is speakin' through me!" he erupted, and interrupted himself, *"Oh no, quite the opposite in fact. I'm an angel. Ah. This has to be America, doesn't it? So sorry, can't stay . . ."*

There was a pause. Marvin tried to open his mouth, but nothing happened. Whatever was in his head looked around. He looked at the studio crew, those who weren't phoning the police, or sobbing in corners. He looked at the gray-faced cameramen.

"Gosh," he said, *"am I on television?"*

CROWLEY WAS DOING a hundred and twenty miles an hour down Oxford Street.

He reached into the glove compartment for his spare pair of sunglasses, and found only cassettes. Irritably he grabbed one at random and pushed it into the slot.

He wanted Bach, but he would settle for The Traveling Wilburys.

. . . All we hear is, Radio Ga Ga, sang Freddie Mercury.

All I need is, out, thought Crowley.

He swung around the Marble Arch Roundabout the wrong way, doing ninety. Lightning made the London skies flicker like a malfunctioning fluorescent tube.

A livid sky on London, Crowley thought, *And I knew the end was near.* Who had written that? Chesterton, wasn't it? The only poet in the twentieth century to even come close to the Truth.

The Bentley headed out of London while Crowley sat back in the driver's seat and thumbed through the singed copy of *The Nice and Accurate Prophecies of Agnes Nutter.*

Near the end of the book he found a folded sheet of paper covered in Aziraphale's neat copperplate handwriting. He unfolded it (while the Bentley's gearstick shifted itself down to third and the car accelerated around a fruit lorry, which had unexpectedly backed out of a side street), and then he read it again.

Then he read it one more time, with a slow sinking feeling at the base of his stomach.

The car changed direction suddenly. It was now heading for the village of Tadfield, in Oxfordshire. He could be there in an hour if he hurried.

Anyway, there wasn't really anywhere else to go.

The cassette finished, activating the car radio.

". . . Gardeners' Question Time coming to you from Tadfield Gardening Club. We were last here in 1953, a very nice summer, and as the team will remember it's a rich Oxfordshire loam in the east of the parish, rising to chalk in the west, the kind of place oi say, don't matter what you plant here, it'll come up beautiful. Isn't that right, Fred?"

"Yep," *said Professor Fred Windbright, Royal Botanical Gardens,* "couldn't of put it better meself."

"Right—First question for the team, and this comes from Mr. R. P. Tyler, chairman of the local Residents Association, I do believe."

" 'hem. That's right. Well, I'm a keen rose grower, but my prize-winning Molly McGuire lost a couple of blossoms yesterday in a rain of what were apparently fish. What does the team recommend for this, other than place netting over the garden? I mean, I've written to the council . . ."

"Not a common problem, I'd say. Harry?"

"Mr. Tyler, let me ask you a question—were these fresh fish, or preserved?"

"Fresh, I believe."

"Well, you've got no problems, my friend. I hear you've also been having rains of blood in these parts—and I wish we had these up in the Dales, where my garden is. Save me a fortune in fertilizers. Now, what you do is, you dig them in to your . . ."

CROWLEY?

Crowley said nothing.

CROWLEY. THE WAR HAS BEGUN, CROWLEY. WE NOTE WITH INTEREST THAT YOU

AVOIDED THE FORCES WE EMPOWERED TO COLLECT YOU.

"Mm," Crowley agreed.

CROWLEY . . . WE WILL WIN THIS WAR. BUT EVEN IF WE LOSE, AT LEAST AS FAR AS YOU ARE CONCERNED, IT WILL MAKE NO DIFFERENCE AT ALL. FOR AS LONG AS THERE IS ONE DEMON LEFT IN HELL, CROWLEY, YOU WILL WISH YOU HAD BEEN CREATED MORTAL.

Crowley was silent.

MORTALS CAN HOPE FOR DEATH, OR FOR REDEMPTION. YOU CAN HOPE FOR NOTHING.

ALL YOU CAN HOPE FOR IS THE MERCY OF HELL.

"Yeah?"

JUST OUR LITTLE JOKE.

"Ngk," said Crowley.

". . . now as keen gardeners know, it goes without sayin' that he's a cunnin' little devil, your Tibetan. Tunnelin' straight through your begonias like it was nobody's business. A cup of tea'll shift him, with rancid yak butter for preference—you should be able to get some at any good gard—"

Wheee. Whizz. Pop. Static drowned out the rest of the program.

Crowley turned off the radio and bit his lower lip. Beneath the ash and soot that flaked his face, he looked very tired, and very pale, and very scared.

And, suddenly, very angry. It was the way they talked to you. As if you were a houseplant who had started shedding leaves on the carpet.

And then he turned a corner, which was meant to take him onto the slip road to the M25, from which he'd swing off onto the M40 up to Oxfordshire.

But something had happened to the M25. Something that hurt your eyes, if you looked directly at it.

From what had been the M25 London Orbital Motorway came a low chanting, a noise formed of many strands: car horns, and engines, and sirens, and the bleep of cellular telephones, and the screaming of small children trapped by back-seat seat belts for ever. "Hail the Great Beast, Devourer of Worlds," came the chanting, over and over again, in the secret tongue of the Black priesthood of ancient Mu.

The dreaded sigil Odegra, thought Crowley, as he swung the car around, heading for the North Circular. *I did that—that's my fault. It could have been just another motorway. A good job, I'll grant you, but was it really worthwhile? It's all out of control. Heaven and Hell aren't running things any more, it's like the whole planet is a Third World country that's finally got the Bomb . . .*

Then he began to smile. He snapped his fingers. A pair of dark glasses materialized out of his eyes. The ash vanished from his suit and his skin.

What the hell. If you had to go, why not go with style?

Whistling softly, he drove.

THEY CAME DOWN the outside lane of the motorway like destroying angels, which was fair enough.

They weren't going that fast, all things considered. The four of them were holding a steady 105 mph, as if they were confident that the show could not start before they got there. It couldn't. They had all the time in the world, such as it was.

Just behind them came four other riders: Big Ted, Greaser, Pigbog, and Skuzz.

They were elated. They were *real* Hell's Angels now, and they rode the silence.

Around them, they knew, was the roar of the thunderstorm, the thunder of traffic, the whipping of the wind and the rain. But in the wake of the Horsemen there was silence, pure and dead. Almost pure, anyway. Certainly dead.

It was broken by Pigbog, shouting to Big Ted.

"What you going to be, then?" he asked, hoarsely.

"What?"

"I said, what you—"

"I heard what you said. It's not what you *said.* Everyone heard what you *said.* What did you *mean*, tha's what I wanter know?"

Pigbog wished he'd paid more attention to the Book of Revelation. If he'd known he was going to be in it, he'd have read it more carefully. "What I mean is, *they're* the Four Horsemen of the Apocalypse, right?"

"Bikers," said Greaser.

"Right. Four Bikers of the Apocalypse. War, Famine, Death, and—and the other one. P'lution."

"Yeah? So?"

"So they said it was all right if we came with them, right?"

"So?"

"So we're the *other* Four Horse—, um, Bikers of the Apocalypse. So which ones *are* we?"

There was a pause. The lights of passing cars shot past them in the opposite lane, lightning after-imaged the clouds, and the silence was close to absolute.

"Can I be War as well?" asked Big Ted.

"Course you can't be War. How can you be War? *She's* War. You've got to be something else."

Big Ted screwed up his face with the effort of thought. "G.B.H.," he said, eventually. "I'm Grievous Bodily Harm. That's me. There. Wott're you going to be?"

"Can I be Rubbish?" asked Skuzz. "Or Embarrassing Personal Problems?"

"Can't be Rubbish," said Grievous Bodily Harm. "He's got that one sewn up, Pollution. You can be the other, though."

They rode on in the silence and the dark, the rear red lights of the Four a few hundred yards in front of them.

Grievous Bodily Harm, Embarrassing Personal Problems, Pigbog, and Greaser.

"I wonter be Cruelty to Animals," said Greaser. Pigbog wondered if he was for or against it. Not that it really mattered.

And then it was Pigbog's turn.

"I, uh . . . I think I'll be them answer phones. They're pretty bad," he said.

"You can't be ansaphones. What kind of a Biker of the Repocalypse is ansaphones? That's stupid, that is."

"S'not!" said Pigbog, nettled. "It's like War, and

Famine, and that. It's a problem of life, isn't it? Answer phones. I hate bloody answer phones."

"I hate ansaphones, too," said Cruelty to Animals.

"You can shut up," said G.B.H.

"Can I change mine?" asked Embarrassing Personal Problems, who had been thinking intently since he last spoke. "I want to be Things Not Working Properly Even After You've Given Them A Good Thumping."

"All right, you can change. But *you* can't be ansaphones, Pigbog. Pick something else."

Pigbog pondered. He wished he'd never broached the subject. It was like the careers interviews he had had as a schoolboy. He deliberated.

"Really cool people," he said at last. "I hate them."

"Really cool people?" said Things Not Working Properly Even After You've Given Them A Good Thumping.

"Yeah. You know. The kind you see on telly, with stupid haircuts, only on them it dunt look stupid 'cos it's them. They wear baggy suits, an' you're not allowed to say they're a bunch of wankers. I mean, speaking for me, what I always want to do when I see one of them is push their faces very slowly through a barbed-wire fence. An' what I think is this." He took a deep breath. He was sure this was the longest speech he had ever made in his life.* "What *I* think is *this*. If they get up my nose like that, they pro'lly get up everyone else's."

"Yeah," said Cruelty to Animals. "An' they all wear sunglasses even when they dunt need 'em."

* Except for one about ten years earlier, throwing himself on the mercy of the court.

"Eatin' runny cheese, and that stupid bloody No Alcohol Lager," said Things Not Working Properly Even After You've Given Them A Good Thumping. "I hate that stuff. What's the point of drinking the stuff if it dunt leave you puking? Here, I just thought. Can I change again, so I'm No Alcohol Lager?"

"No you bloody can't," said Grievous Bodily Harm. "You've changed once already."

"Anyway," said Pigbog. "That's why I wonter be Really Cool People."

"All right," said his leader.

"Don't see why I can't be No bloody Alcohol Lager if I want."

"Shut your face."

Death and Famine and War and Pollution continued biking toward Tadfield.

And Grievous Bodily Harm, Cruelty to Animals, Things Not Working Properly Even After You've Given Them A Good Thumping But Secretly No Alcohol Lager, and Really Cool People traveled with them.

IT WAS A WET AND BLUSTERY Saturday afternoon, and Madame Tracy was feeling very occult.

She had her flowing dress on, and a saucepan full of sprouts on the stove. The room was lit by candlelight, each candle carefully placed in a wax-encrusted wine bottle at the four corners of her sitting room.

There were three other people at her sitting.

Mrs. Ormerod from Belsize Park, in a dark green hat that might have been a flowerpot in a previous life; Mr. Scroggie, thin and pallid, with bulging colorless eyes; and Julia Petley from *Hair Today,** the hairdressers' on the High Street, fresh out of school and convinced that she herself had unplumbed occult depths. In order to enhance the occult aspects of herself, Julia had begun to wear far too much handbeaten silver jewelry and green eyeshadow. She felt she looked haunted and gaunt and romantic, and she would have, if she had lost another thirty pounds. She was convinced that she was anorexic, because every time she looked in the mirror she did indeed see a fat person.

"Can you link hands?" asked Madame Tracy. "And we must have complete silence. The spirit world is very sensitive to vibration."

"Ask if my Ron is there," said Mrs. Ormerod. She had a jaw like a brick.

"I will, love, but you've got to be quiet while I make contact."

There was silence, broken only by Mr. Scroggie's stomach rumbling. "Pardon, ladies," he mumbled.

Madame Tracy had found, through years of Drawing Aside the Veil and Exploring the Mysteries, that two minutes was the right length of time to sit in silence, waiting for the Spirit World to make

* Formerly *A Cut Above the Rest,* formerly *Mane Attraction,* formerly *Curl Up And Dye,* formerly *A Snip At the Price,* formerly *Mister Brian's Art-de-Coiffeur,* formerly *Robinson the Barber's,* formerly *Fone-a-Car Taxis.*

contact. More than that and they got restive, less than that and they felt they weren't getting their money's worth.

She did her shopping list in her head.

Eggs. Lettuce. Ounce of cooking cheese. Four tomatoes. Butter. Roll of toilet paper. Mustn't forget that, we're nearly out. And a really nice piece of liver for Mr. Shadwell, poor old soul, it's a shame . . .

Time.

Madame Tracy threw back her head, let it loll on one shoulder, then slowly lifted it again. Her eyes were almost shut.

"She's going under now, dear," she heard Mrs. Ormerod whisper to Julia Petley. "Nothing to be alarmed about. She's just making herself a Bridge to the Other Side. Her spirit guide will be along soon."

Madame Tracy found herself rather irritated at being upstaged, and she let out a low moan. "Oooooooooh."

Then, in a high-pitched, quavery voice, "Are you there, my Spirit Guide?"

She waited a little, to build up the suspense. Washing-up liquid. Two cans of baked beans. Oh, and potatoes.

"How?" she said, in a dark brown voice.

"Is that you, Geronimo?" she asked herself.

"Is um me, how," she replied.

"We have a new member of the circle with us this afternoon," she said.

"How, Miss Petley?" she said, as Geronimo. She had always understood that Red Indian spirit guides were an essential prop, and she rather liked the name. She had explained this to Newt. She didn't know anything about Geronimo, he realized, and he didn't have the heart to tell her.

"Oh," squeaked Julia. "Charmed to make your acquaintance."

"Is my Ron there, Geronimo?" asked Mrs. Ormerod.

"How, squaw Beryl," said Madame Tracy. "Oh there are so many um of the poor lost souls um lined up against um door to my teepee. Perhaps your Ron is amongst them. How."

Madame Tracy had learned her lesson years earlier, and now never brought Ron through until near the end. If she didn't, Beryl Ormerod would occupy the rest of the seance telling the late Ron Ormerod everything that had happened to her since their last little chat. (". . . now Ron, you remember, our Eric's littlest, Sybilla, well you wouldn't recognize her now, she's taken up macramé, and our Letitia, you know, our Karen's oldest, she's become a lesbian but that's all right these days and is doing a dissertation on the films of Sergio Leone as seen from a feminist perspective, and our Stan, you know, our Sandra's twin, I told you about him last time, well, he won the darts tournament, which is nice because we all thought he was a bit of a mother's boy, while the guttering over the shed's come loose, but I spoke to our Cindi's latest, who's a jobbing builder, and he'll be over to see to it on Sunday, and ohh, that reminds me . . .")

No, Beryl Ormerod could wait. There was a flash of lightning, followed almost immediately by a rumble of distant thunder. Madame Tracy felt rather proud, as if she had done it herself. It was even better than the candles at creating *ambulance*. *Ambulance* was what mediuming was all about.

"Now," said Madame Tracy in her own voice. "Mr. Geronimo would like to know, is there anyone named Mr. Scroggie here?"

Scroggie's watery eyes gleamed. "Erm, actually that's *my* name," he said, hopefully.

"Right, well there's somebody here for you." Mr. Scroggie had been coming for a month now, and she hadn't been able to think of a message for him. His time had come. "Do you know anyone named, um, John?"

"No," said Mr. Scroggie.

"Well, there's some celestial interference here. The name could be Tom. Or Jim. Or, um, Dave."

"I knew a Dave when I was in Hemel Hempstead," said Mr. Scroggie, a trifle doubtfully.

"Yes, he's saying, Hemel Hempstead, that's what he's saying," said Madame Tracy.

"But I ran into him last week, walking his dog, and he looked perfectly healthy," said Mr. Scroggie, slightly puzzled.

"He says not to worry, and he's happier beyond the veil," soldiered on Madame Tracy, who felt it was always better to give her clients good news.

"Tell my Ron I've got to tell him about our Krystal's wedding," said Mrs. Ormerod.

"I will, love. Now, hold on a mo', there's something coming through . . ."

And then something came through. It sat in Madame Tracy's head and peered out.

"*Sprechen sie Deutsch?*" it said, using Madame

Tracy's mouth. *"Parlez-vous Français? Wo bu hui jiang zhongwhen."*

"Is that you, Ron?" asked Mrs. Ormerod. The reply, when it came, was rather testy.

"No. Definitely not. However, a question so manifestly dim can only have been put in one country on this benighted planet—most of which, incidentally, I have seen during the last few hours. Dear lady, this is not Ron."

"Well, I want to speak to Ron Ormerod," said Mrs. Ormerod, a little testily. "He's rather short, balding on top. Can you put him on, please?"

There was a pause. *"Actually there does appear to be a spirit of that description hovering over here. Very well. I'll hand you over, but you must make it quick. I am attempting to avert the apocalypse."*

Mrs. Ormerod and Mr. Scroggie gave each other looks. Nothing like this had happened at Madame Tracy's previous sittings. Julia Petley was rapt. This was more like it. She hoped Madame Tracy was going to start manifesting ectoplasm next.

"H-hello?" said Madame Tracy in another voice. Mrs. Ormerod started. It sounded exactly like Ron. On previous occasions Ron had sounded like Madame Tracy.

"Ron, is that you?"

"Yes, Buh-Beryl."

"Right. Now I've quite a bit to tell you. For a start I went to our Krystal's wedding, last Saturday, our Marilyn's eldest . . ."

"Buh-Beryl. You-you nuh-never let me guh-get a wuh-word in edgewise wuh-while I was alive. Nuh-now I'm duh-dead, there's juh-just one thing to suh-say . . ."

Beryl Ormerod was a little disgruntled by all this. Previously when Ron had manifested, he had told her that he was happier beyond the veil, and living somewhere that sounded more than a little like a celestial bungalow. Now he sounded like Ron, and she wasn't sure that was what she wanted. And she said what she had always said to her husband when he began to speak to her in that tone of voice.

"Ron, remember your heart condition."

"I duh-don't have a huh-heart any longer. Remuhmember? Anyway, Buh-Beryl . . . ?"

"Yes, Ron."

"Shut up," and the spirit was gone. *"Wasn't that touching? Right, now, thank you very much, ladies and gentleman, I'm afraid I shall have to be getting on."*

Madame Tracy stood up, went over to the door, and turned on the lights.

"Out!" she said.

Her sitters stood up, more than a little puzzled, and, in Mrs. Ormerod's case, outraged, and they walked out into the hall.

"You haven't heard the last of this, Marjorie Potts," hissed Mrs. Ormerod, clutching her handbag to her breast, and she slammed the door.

Then her muffled voice echoed from the hallway, "And you can tell our Ron that *he* hasn't heard the last of this either!"

Madame Tracy (and the name on her scooters-only driving license was indeed Marjorie Potts) went into the kitchen and turned off the sprouts.

She put on the kettle. She made herself a pot of tea. She sat down at the kitchen table, got out two cups, filled both of them. She added two sugars to one of them. Then she paused.

"*No sugar for me, please*," said Madame Tracy.

She lined up the cups on the table in front of her, and took a long sip from the tea-with-sugar.

"Now," she said, in a voice that anyone who knew her would have recognized as her own, although they might not have recognized her tone of voice, which was cold with rage. "Suppose you tell me what this is about. And it had better be good."

A LORRY HAD SHED its load all over the M6. According to its manifest the lorry had been filled with sheets of corrugated iron, although the two police patrolmen were having difficulty in accepting this.

"So what I want to know is, where did all the fish come from?" asked the sergeant.

"I told you. They fell from the sky. One minute I'm driving along at sixty, next second, whap! a twelve-pound salmon smashes through the windscreen. So I pulls the wheel over, and I skidded on *that*," he pointed to the remains of a hammerhead shark under the lorry, "and ran into *that*." *That* was a thirty-foot-high heap of fish, of different shapes and sizes.

"Have you been drinking, sir?" asked the sergeant, less than hopefully.

"Course I haven't been drinking, you great wazzock. You can see the fish, can't you?"

On the top of the pile a rather large octopus

waved a languid tentacle at them. The sergeant resisted the temptation to wave back.

The police constable was leaning into the police car, talking on the radio. ". . . corrugated iron and fish, blocking off the southbound M6 about half a mile north of junction ten. We're going to have to close off the whole southbound carriageway. Yeah."

The rain redoubled. A small trout, which had miraculously survived the fall, gamely began to swim toward Birmingham.

"THAT WAS WONDERFUL," SAID NEWT.

"Good," said Anathema. "The earth moved for everybody." She got up off the floor, leaving her clothes scattered across the carpet, and went into the bathroom.

Newt raised his voice. "I mean, it was really wonderful. Really *really* wonderful. I always hoped it was going to be, and it was."

There was the sound of running water.

"What are you doing?" he asked.

"Taking a shower."

"Ah." He wondered vaguely if everyone had to shower afterwards, or if it was just women. And he had a suspicion that bidets came into it somewhere.

"Tell you what," said Newt, as Anathema came out of the bathroom swathed in a fluffy pink towel. "We could do it again."

"Nope," she said, "not now." She finished drying herself, and started picking up clothes from the floor, and, unself-consciously, pulling them on. Newt, a man who was prepared to wait half an hour for a free changing cubicle at the swimming baths, rather than face the possibility of having to disrobe in front of another human being, found himself vaguely shocked, and deeply thrilled.

Bits of her kept appearing and disappearing, like a conjurer's hands; Newt kept trying to count her nipples and failing, although he didn't mind.

"Why not?" said Newt. He was about to point out that it might not take long, but an inner voice counseled him against it. He was growing up quite quickly in a short time.

Anathema shrugged, not an easy move when you're pulling on a sensible black skirt. "She said we only did it this once."

Newt opened his mouth two or three times, then said, "She didn't. She bloody didn't. She couldn't predict *that*. I don't believe it."

Anathema, fully dressed, walked over to her card index, pulled one out, and passed it to him.

Newt read it and blushed and gave it back, tight-lipped.

It wasn't simply the fact that Agnes had known, and had expressed herself in the most transparent of codes. It was that, down the ages, various Devices had scrawled encouraging little comments in the margin.

She passed him the damp towel. "Here," she said. "Hurry up. I've got to make the sandwiches, and we've got to get ready."

He looked at the towel. "What's this for?"

"Your shower."

Ah. So it was something men and women both did. He was pleased he'd got that sorted out.

"But you'll have to make it quick," she said.

"Why? Have we got to get out of here in the next ten minutes before the building explodes?"

"Oh no. We've got a couple of hours. It's just that I've used up most of the hot water. You've got a lot of plaster in your hair."

The storm blew a dying gust around Jasmine Cottage, and holding the damp pink towel, no longer fluffy, in front of him, strategically, Newt edged off to take a cold shower.

IN SHADWELL'S DREAM, *he is floating high above a village green. In the center of the green is a huge pile of kindling wood and dry branches. In the center of the pile is a wooden stake. Men and women and children stand around on the grass, eyes bright, cheeks pink, expectant, excited.*

A sudden commotion: ten men walk across the green, leading a handsome, middle-aged woman; she must have been quite striking in her youth, and the word "vivacious" creeps into Shadwell's dreaming mind. In front of her walks Witchfinder Private Newton Pulsifer. No, it isn't Newt. The man is older, and dressed in black leather. Shadwell recognizes approvingly the ancient uniform of a Witchfinder Major.

The woman climbs onto the pyre, thrusts her hands behind her, and is tied to the stake. The pyre is lit. She speaks to the crowd, says something, but Shadwell is too high to hear what it is. The crowd gathers around her.

A witch, thinks Shadwell. They're burning a witch. It gives him a warm feeling. That was the right and proper way of things. That's how things were meant to be.

Only . . .

She looks directly up at him now, and says "That goes for yowe as welle, yowe daft old foole."

Only she is going to die. She is going to burn to death. And, Shadwell realizes in his dream, it is a horrible way to die.

The flames lick higher.

And the woman looks up. She is staring straight at him, invisible though he is. And she is smiling.

And then it all goes boom.

A crash of thunder.

That was thunder, thought Shadwell, as he woke up, with the unshakable feeling that someone was still staring at him.

He opened his eyes, and thirteen glass eyes watched from the various shelves of Madame Tracy's boudoir, staring out from a variety of fuzzy faces.

He looked away, and into the eyes of someone staring intently at him. It was him.

Och, he thought in terror, I'm havin' one o' them out-o'-yer-body experiences, I can see mah ane self, I'm a goner this time right enough . . .

He made frantic swimming motions in an effort to reach his own body and then, as these things do, the perspectives clicked into place.

Shadwell relaxed, and wondered why anyone would want to put a mirror on his bedroom ceiling. He shook his head, baffled.

He climbed out of the bed, pulled on his boots, and stood up, warily. Something was missing. A cigarette. He thrust his hands deep into his pockets, pulled out a tin, and began to roll a cigarette.

He'd been dreaming, he knew. Shadwell didn't

remember the dream, but it made him feel uncomfortable, whatever it was.

He lit the cigarette. And he saw his right hand: the ultimate weapon. The doomsday device. He pointed one finger at the one-eyed teddy bear on the mantelpiece.

"Bang," he said, and chuckled, dustily. He wasn't used to chuckling, and he began to cough, which meant he was back on familiar territory. He wanted something to drink. A sweet can of condensed milk.

Madame Tracy would have some.

He stomped out of her boudoir, heading toward the kitchen.

Outside the little kitchen he paused. She was talking to someone. A man.

"So what exactly do you want me to do about this?" she was asking.

"Ach, ye beldame," muttered Shadwell. She had one of her gentlemen callers in there, obviously.

"To be frank, dear lady, my plans at this point are perforce somewhat fluid."

Shadwell's blood ran cold. He marched through the bead curtain, shouting, "The sins of Sodom an' Gomorrah! Takin' advantage of a defenseless hoor! Over my dead body!"

Madame Tracy looked up, and smiled at him. There wasn't anyone else in the room.

"Whurrizee?" asked Shadwell.

"Whom?" asked Madame Tracy.

"Some Southern pansy," he said, "I heard him. He was in here, suggestin' things to yer. I heard him."

Madame Tracy's mouth opened, and a voice said, *"Not just A Southern Pansy, Sergeant Shadwell. THE Southern Pansy."*

Shadwell dropped his cigarette. He stretched out his arm, shaking slightly, and pointed his hand at Madame Tracy.

"Demon," he croaked.

"No," said Madame Tracy, in the voice of the demon. *"Now, I know what you're thinking, Sergeant Shadwell. You're thinking that any second now this head is going to go round and round, and I'm going to start vomiting pea soup. Well, I'm not. I'm not a demon. And I'd like you to listen to what I have to say."*

"Daemonspawn, be silent," ordered Shadwell. "I'll no listen to yer wicked lies. Do yer know what *this* is? It's a hand. Four fingers. One thumb. It's already exorcised one of yer number this morning. Now get ye out of this gud wimmin's head, or I'll blast ye to kingdom come."

"That's the problem, Mr. Shadwell," said Madame Tracy in her own voice. "Kingdom come. It's going to. That's the problem. Mr. Aziraphale has been telling me all about it. Now stop being an old silly, Mr. Shadwell, sit down, and have some tea, and he'll explain it to you as well."

"I'll ne'r listen tae his hellish blandishments, woman," said Shadwell.

Madame Tracy smiled at him. "You old *silly*," she said.

He could have handled anything else.

He sat down.

But he didn't lower his hand.

THE SWINGING OVERHEAD SIGNS proclaimed that the southbound carriageway was closed, and a small forest of orange cones had sprung up, redirecting motorists onto a co-opted lane of the northbound carriageway. Other signs directed motorists to slow down to thirty miles per hour. Police cars herded the drivers around like red-striped sheepdogs.

The four bikers ignored all the signs, and cones, and police cars, and continued down the empty southbound carriageway of the M6. The other four bikers, just behind them, slowed a little.

"Shouldn't we, uh, stop or something?" asked Really Cool People.

"Yeah. Could be a pileup," said Treading in Dogshit (formerly All Foreigners Especially The French, formerly Things Not Working Properly Even After You've Given Them A Good Thumping, never actually No Alcohol Lager, briefly Embarrassing Personal Problems, formerly known as Skuzz).

"We're the *other* Four Horsemen of the Apocalypse," said G.B.H. "We do what they do. We follow them."

They rode south.

"IT'LL BE A WORLD JUST FOR US," said Adam. "Everything's always been messed up by other people but we can get rid of it all an' start again. Won't that be *great*?"

"YOU ARE, I TRUST, *familiar with the Book of Revelation?*" said Madame Tracy with Aziraphale's voice.

"Aye," said Shadwell, who wasn't. His biblical expertise began and ended with Exodus, chapter twenty-two, verse eighteen, which concerned Witches, the suffering to live of, and why you shouldn't. He had once glanced at verse nineteen, which was about putting to death people who lay down with beasts, but he had felt that this was rather outside his jurisdiction.

"Then you have heard of the Antichrist?"

"Aye," said Shadwell, who had seen a film once which explained it all. Something about sheets of glass falling off lorries and slicing people's heads off, as he recalled. No proper witches to speak of. He'd gone to sleep halfway through.

"The Antichrist is alive on earth at this moment, Sergeant. He is bringing about Armageddon, the Day of Judgment, even if he himself does not know it. Heaven and Hell are both preparing for war, and it's all going to be very messy."

Shadwell merely grunted.

"I am not actually permitted to act directly in this matter, Sergeant. But I am sure that you can see that the imminent destruction of the world is not something any reasonable man would permit. Am I correct?"

"Aye. S'pose," said Shadwell, sipping condensed milk from a rusting can Madame Tracy had discovered under the sink.

"Then there is only one thing to be done. And you are

the only man I can rely on. The Antichrist must be killed, Sergeant Shadwell. And you must do it."

Shadwell frowned. "I wouldna know about that," he said. "The witchfinder army only kills witches. 'Tis one of the rules. And demons and imps, o' course."

"*But, but the Antichrist is more than just a witch. He—he's THE witch. He's just about as witchy as you can get.*"

"Wud he be harder to get rid of than, say, a demon?" asked Shadwell, who had begun to brighten.

"*Not much more*," said Aziraphale, who had never done other to get rid of demons than to hint to them very strongly that he, Aziraphale, had some work to be getting on with, and wasn't it getting late? And Crowley had always got the hint.

Shadwell looked down at his right hand, and smiled. Then he hesitated.

"This Antichrist—how many nipples has he?"

The end justifies the means, thought Aziraphale. And the road to Hell is paved with good intentions.* And he lied cheerfully and convincingly: "*Oodles. Pots of them. His chest is covered with them—he makes Diana of the Ephesians look positively nippleless.*"

"I wouldna know about this Diana of yours," said Shadwell, "but if he's a witch, and it sounds tae me like he is, then, speaking as a sergeant in the WA, I'm yer man."

* This is not actually true. The road to Hell is paved with frozen door-to-door salesmen. On weekends many of the younger demons go ice skating down it.

"*Good*," said Aziraphale through Madame Tracy.

"I'm not sure about this killing business," said Madame Tracy herself. "But if it's this man, this Antichrist, or everybody else, then I suppose we don't really have any choice."

"*Exactly, dear lady*," she replied. "*Now, Sergeant Shadwell. Have you a weapon?*"

Shadwell rubbed his right hand with his left, clenching and unclenching the fist. "Aye," he said. "I have that." And he raised two fingers to his lips and blew on them gently.

There was a pause. "*Your hand?*" asked Aziraphale.

"Aye. 'Tis a turrible weapon. It did for ye, daemonspawn, did it not?"

"*Have you anything more, uh, substantial? How about the Golden Dagger of Meggido? Or the Shiv of Kali?*"

Shadwell shook his head. "I've got some pins," he suggested. "And the Thundergun of Witchfinder-Colonel Ye-Shall-Not-Eat-Any-Living-Thing-With-The-Blood-Neither-Shall-Ye-Use-Enchantment-Nor-Observe-Times Dalrymple . . . I could load it with silver bullets."

"*That's werewolves, I believe*," said Aziraphale.

"Garlic?"

"*Vampires*."

Shadwell shrugged. "Aye, weel, I dinna have any fancy bullets anyway. But the Thundergun will fire anything. I'll go and fetch it."

He shuffled out, thinking, why do I need another weapon? I'm a man with a hand.

"*Now, dear lady*," said Aziraphale. "*I trust you have a reliable mode of transportation at your disposal.*"

"Oh, yes," said Madame Tracy. She went over to

the corner of the kitchen and picked up a pink motorbike helmet, with a yellow sunflower painted on it, and put it on, strapping it under her chin. Then she rummaged in a cupboard, pulled out three or four hundred plastic shopping bags and a heap of yellowing local newspapers, then a dusty day-glo green helmet with EASY RIDER written across the top, a present from her niece Petula twenty years before.

Shadwell, returning with the Thundergun over his shoulder, stared at her unbelieving.

"I don't know what you're staring at, Mr. Shadwell," she told him. "It's parked in the road downstairs." She passed him the helmet. "You've got to put it on. It's the law. I don't think you're really allowed to have three people on a scooter, even if two of them are, er, sharing. But it's an emergency. And I'm sure you'll be quite safe, if you hold on to me nice and tight." And she smiled. "Won't that be fun?"

Shadwell paled, muttered something inaudible, and put on the green helmet.

"What was that, Mr. Shadwell?" Madame Tracy looked at him sharply.

"I said, De'il ding a divot aff yer wame wi' a flaughter spade," said Shadwell.

"That'll be quite enough of that kind of language, Mr. Shadwell," said Madame Tracy, and she marched him out of the hall and down the stairs to Crouch End High Street, where an elderly scooter waited to take the two, well, call it three of them away.

THE LORRY BLOCKED THE ROAD. And the corrugated iron blocked the road. And a thirty-foot-high pile of fish blocked the road. It was one of the most effectively blocked roads the sergeant had ever seen.

The rain wasn't helping.

"Any idea when the bulldozers are likely to get here?" he shouted into his radio.

"We're *crrrrk* doing the best we *crrrrk*," came the reply.

He felt something tugging at his trouser cuff, and looked down.

"Lobsters?" He gave a little skip, and a jump, and wound up on the top of the police car. "Lobsters," he repeated. There were about thirty of them—some over two feet long. Most of them were on their way up the motorway; half a dozen had stopped to check out the police car.

"Something wrong, Sarge?" asked the police constable, who was taking down the lorry driver's details on the hard shoulder.

"I just don't like lobsters," said the sergeant, grimly, shutting his eyes. "Bring me out in a rash. Too many legs. I'll just sit up here a bit, and you can tell me when they've all gone."

He sat on the top of the car, in the rain, and felt the water seeping into the bottom of his trousers.

There was a low roar. Thunder? No. It was continuous, and getting closer. Motorbikes. The sergeant opened one eye.

Jesus Christ!

There were four of them, and they had to be doing over a hundred. He was about to climb down, to wave at them, to shout, but they were past him, heading straight for the upturned lorry.

There was nothing the sergeant could do. He closed his eyes again, and listened for the collision. He could hear them coming closer. Then:

Whoosh.

Whoosh.

Whoosh.

And a voice in his head that said, I'LL CATCH UP WITH THE REST OF YOU.

("Did you see *that*?" asked Really Cool People. "They flew right over it!"

" 'kin'ell!" said G.B.H. "If they can do it, we can too!")

The sergeant opened his eyes. He turned to the police constable and opened his mouth.

The police constable said, "They. They actually. They flew righ . . ."

Thud. Thud. Thud.

Splat.

There was another rain of fish, although of shorter duration, and more easily explicable. A leather-jacketed arm waved feebly from the large pile of fish. A motorbike wheel spun hopelessly.

That was Skuzz, semi-conscious, deciding that if there was one thing he hated even more than the French it was being up to his neck in fish with what felt like a broken leg. He truly hated that.

He wanted to tell G.B.H. about his new role; but he couldn't move. Something wet and slippery slithered up one sleeve.

Later, when they'd dragged him out of the fish pile, and he'd seen the other three bikers, with the blankets over their heads, he realized it was too late to tell them anything.

That was why they hadn't been in that Book of Revelations Pigbog had been going on about. They'd never made it that far down the motorway.

Skuzz muttered something. The police sergeant leaned over. "Don't try to speak, son," he said. "The ambulance'll be here soon."

"Listen," croaked Skuzz. "Got something important to tell you. The Four Horsemen of the Apocalypse . . . they're right bastards, all four of them."

"He's delirious," announced the sergeant.

"I'm sodding not. I'm People Covered In Fish," croaked Skuzz, and passed out.

THE LONDON TRAFFIC SYSTEM is many hundreds of times more complex than anyone imagines.

This has nothing to do with influences, demonic or angelic. It's more to do with geography, and history, and architecture.

Mostly this works to people's advantage, although they'd never believe it.

London was not designed for cars. Come to that, it wasn't designed for people. It just sort of happened. This created problems, and the solutions that were implemented became the next problems, five or ten or a hundred years down the line.

The latest solution had been the M25: a motorway that formed a rough circle around the city. Up until now the problems had been fairly basic—things like it being obsolete before they had finished building it, Einsteinian tailbacks that eventually became tailforwards, that kind of thing.

The current problem was that it didn't exist; not in normal human spatial terms, anyway. The tailback of cars unaware of this, or trying to find alternate routes out of London, stretched into the city center, from every direction. For the first time ever, London was completely gridlocked. The city was one huge traffic jam.

Cars, in theory, give you a terrifically fast method of traveling from place to place. Traffic jams, on the other hand, give you a terrific opportunity to stay still. In the rain, and the gloom, while around you the cacophonous symphony of horns grew ever louder and more exasperated.

Crowley was getting sick of it.

He'd taken the opportunity to reread Aziraphale's notes, and to thumb through Agnes Nutter's prophecies, and to do some serious thinking.

His conclusions could be summarized as follows:

1. Armageddon was under way.
2. There was nothing Crowley could do about this.
3. It was going to happen in Tadfield. Or to begin there, at any rate. After that it was going to happen *everywhere*.
4. Crowley was in Hell's bad books.*
5. Aziraphale was—as far as could be estimated—out of the equation.

* Not that Hell has any other kind.

6. All was black, gloomy and awful. There was no light at the end of the tunnel—or if there was, it was an oncoming train.
7. He might just as well find a nice little restaurant and get completely and utterly pissed out of his mind while he waited for the world to end.
8. And yet . . .

And that was where it all fell apart.

Because, underneath it all, Crowley was an optimist. If there was one rock-hard certainty that had sustained him through the bad times—he thought briefly of the fourteenth century—then it was utter surety that he would come out on top; that the universe would look after him.

Okay, so Hell was down on him. So the world was ending. So the Cold War was over and the Great War was starting for real. So the odds against him were higher than a vanload of hippies on a blotterful of Owlsley's Old Original. There was still a chance.

It was all a matter of being in the right place at the right time.

The right place was Tadfield. He was certain of that; partly from the book, partly from some other sense: in Crowley's mental map of the world, Tadfield was throbbing like a migraine.

The right time was getting there before the end of the world. He checked his watch. He had two hours to get to Tadfield, although probably even the normal passage of Time was pretty shaky by now.

Crowley tossed the book into the passenger seat.

Desperate times, desperate measures: he had maintained the Bentley without a scratch for sixty years.

What the hell.

He reversed suddenly, causing severe damage to the front of the red Renault 5 behind him, and drove up onto the pavement.

He turned on his lights, and sounded his horn.

That should give any pedestrians sufficient warning that he was coming. And if they couldn't get out of the way . . . well, it'd all be the same in a couple of hours. Maybe. Probably.

"Heigh ho," said Anthony Crowley, and just drove anyway.

THERE WERE SIX WOMEN and four men, and each of them had a telephone and a thick wodge of computer printout, covered with names and telephone numbers. By each of the numbers was a penned notation saying whether the person dialed was in or out, whether the number was currently connected, and, most importantly, whether or not anybody who answered the phone was avid for cavity-wall insulation to enter their lives.

Most of them weren't.

The ten people sat there, hour after hour, cajoling, pleading, promising through plastic smiles. Between calls they made notations, sipped coffee, and marveled at the rain flooding down the windows. They were staying at their posts like the band on the *Titanic.* If you couldn't sell double glazing in weather like this, you couldn't sell it at all.

Lisa Morrow was saying, ". . . Now, if you'll only

let me finish, sir, and yes, I understand that, sir, but if you'll only . . . ," and then, seeing that he'd just hung up on her, she said, "Well, up yours, snot-face."

She put down the phone.

"I got another bath," she announced to her fellow telephone salespersons. She was well in the lead in the office daily Getting People Out of the Bath stakes, and only needed two more points to win the weekly Coitus Interruptus award.

She dialed the next number on the list.

Lisa had never intended to be a telephone salesperson. What she really wanted to be was an internationally glamorous jet-setter, but she didn't have the O-levels.

Had she been studious enough to be accepted as an internationally glamorous jet-setter, or a dental assistant (her second choice of profession), or indeed, anything other than a telephone salesperson in that particular office, she would have had a longer, and probably more fulfilled, life.

Perhaps not a very much longer life, all things considered, it being the Day of Armageddon, but several hours anyway.

For that matter, all she really needed to do for a longer life was not ring the number she had just dialed, listed on her sheet as the Mayfair home of, in the best traditions of tenth-hand mail-order lists, Mr. A. J. Cowlley.

But she had dialed. And she had waited while it rang four times. And she had said, "Oh, poot, another ansaphone," and started to put down the handset.

But then something climbed out of the earpiece. Something very big, and very angry.

It looked a little like a maggot. A huge, angry maggot made out of thousands and thousands of tiny little maggots, all writhing and screaming, millions of little maggot mouths opening and shutting in fury, and every one of them was screaming "Crowley."

It stopped screaming. Swayed blindly, seemed to be taking stock of where it was.

Then it went to pieces.

The thing split into thousands of thousands of writhing gray maggots. They flowed over the carpet, up over the desks, over Lisa Morrow and her nine colleagues; they flowed into their mouths, up their nostrils, into their lungs; they burrowed into flesh and eyes and brains and lights, reproducing wildly as they went, filling the room with a towering mess of writhing flesh and gunk. The whole began to flow together, to coagulate into one huge entity that filled the room from floor to ceiling, pulsing gently.

A mouth opened in the mass of flesh, strands of something wet and sticky adhering to each of the not-exactly lips, and Hastur said:

"I needed that."

Spending half an hour trapped on an ansaphone with only Aziraphale's message for company had not improved his temper.

Neither did the prospect of having to report back to Hell, and having to explain why he hadn't returned half an hour earlier, and, more importantly, why he was not accompanied by Crowley.

Hell did not go a bundle on failures.

On the plus side, however, he at least knew what

Aziraphale's message *was.* The knowledge could probably buy him his continued existence.

And anyway, he reflected, if he were going to have to face the possible wrath of the Dark Council, at least it wouldn't be on an empty stomach.

The room filled with thick, sulphurous smoke. When it cleared, Hastur was gone. There was nothing left in the room but ten skeletons, picked quite clean of meat, and some puddles of melted plastic with, here and there, a gleaming fragment of metal that might once have been part of a telephone. Much better to have been a dental assistant.

But, to look on the bright side, all this only went to prove that evil contains the seeds of its own destruction. Right now, across the country, people who would otherwise have been made just that little bit more tense and angry by being summoned from a nice bath, or having their names mispronounced at them, were instead feeling quite untroubled and at peace with the world. As a result of Hastur's action a wave of low-grade goodness started to spread exponentially through the population, and millions of people who ultimately would have suffered minor bruises of the soul did not in fact do so. So that was all right.

YOU WOULDN'T HAVE KNOWN it as the same car. There was scarcely an inch of it undented. Both front lights were smashed. The hubcaps were long gone. It looked like the veteran of a hundred demolition derbies.

The pavements had been bad. The pedestrian

underpass had been worse. The worst bit had been crossing the River Thames. At least he'd had the foresight to roll up all the windows.

Still, he was here, now.

In a few hundred yards he'd be on the M40; a fairly clear run up to Oxfordshire. There was only one snag: once more between Crowley and the open road was the M25. A screaming, glowing ribbon of pain and dark light.* *Odegra.* Nothing could cross it and survive.

Nothing mortal, anyway. And he wasn't sure what it would do to a demon. It couldn't kill him, but it wouldn't be pleasant.

There was a police roadblock in front of the flyover before him. Burnt-out wrecks—some still burning—testified to the fate of previous cars that had to drive across the flyover above the dark road.

The police did not look happy.

Crowley shifted down into second gear, and gunned the accelerator.

He went through the roadblock at sixty. That was the easy bit.

Cases of spontaneous human combustion are on record all over the world. One minute someone's quite happily chugging along with their life; the

* Not actually an oxymoron. It's the color past ultraviolet. The technical term for it is infra-black. It can be seen quite easily under experimental conditions. To perform the experiment simply select a healthy brick wall with a good run-up, and, lowering your head, charge.

The color that flashes in bursts behind your eyes, behind the pain, just before you die, is infra-black.

next there's a sad photograph of a pile of ashes and a lonely and mysteriously uncharred foot or hand. Cases of spontaneous vehicular combustion are less well documented.

Whatever the statistics were, they had just gone up by one.

The leather seatcovers began to smoke. Staring ahead of him, Crowley fumbled left-handedly on the passenger seat for Agnes Nutter's *Nice and Accurate Prophecies*, moved it to the safety of his lap. He wished she'd prophecied *this*.*

Then the flames engulfed the car.

He had to keep driving.

On the other side of the flyover was a further police roadblock, to prevent the passage of cars trying to come into London. They were laughing about a story that had just come over the radio, that a motorbike cop on the M6 had flagged down a stolen police car, only to discover the driver to be a large octopus.

Some police forces would believe anything. Not the Metropolitan police, though. The Met was the hardest, most cynically pragmatic, most stubbornly down-to-earth police force in Britain.

* She had. It read:

A street of light will screem, the black chariot of the Serpente will flayme, and a Queene wille sing quickfilveres songes no moar.

Most of the family had gone along with Gelatly Device, who wrote a brief monograph in the 1830s explaining it as a metaphor for the banishment of Weishaupt's Illuminati from Bavaria in 1785.

It would take a lot to faze a copper from the Met.

It would take, for example, a huge, battered car that was nothing more nor less than a fireball, a blazing, roaring, twisted metal lemon from Hell, driven by a grinning lunatic in sunglasses, sitting amid the flames, trailing thick black smoke, coming straight at them through the lashing rain and the wind at eighty miles per hour.

That would do it every time.

THE QUARRY WAS THE CALM center of a stormy world.

Thunder didn't just rumble overhead, it tore the air in half.

"I've got some more friends coming," Adam repeated. "They'll be here soon, and then we can really get started."

Dog started to howl. It was no longer the siren howl of a lone wolf, but the weird oscillations of a small dog in deep trouble.

Pepper had been sitting staring at her knees.

There seemed to be something on her mind.

Finally she looked up and stared Adam in the blank gray eyes.

"What bit 're you going to have, Adam?" she said.

The storm was replaced by a sudden, ringing silence.

"What?" said Adam.

"Well, you divided up the world, right, and we've all of us got to have a bit—what bit're you going to have?"

The silence sang like a harp, high and thin.

"Yeah," said Brian. "You never told us what bit *you're* having."

"Pepper's right," said Wensleydale. "Don't seem to *me* there's much left, if we've got to have all these countries."

Adam's mouth opened and shut.

"What?" he said.

"What bit's yours, Adam?" said Pepper.

Adam stared at her. Dog had stopped howling and had fixed his master with an intent, thoughtful mongrel stare.

"M-me?" he said.

The silence went on and on, one note that could drown out the noises of the world.

"But I'll have Tadfield," said Adam.

They stared at him.

"An', an' Lower Tadfield, and Norton, and Norton Woods—"

They still stared.

Adam's gaze dragged itself across their faces.

"They're all I've ever wanted," he said.

They shook their heads.

"I can have 'em if I want," said Adam, his voice tinged with sullen defiance and his defiance edged with sudden doubt. "I can make them better, too. Better trees to climb, better ponds, better . . ."

His voice trailed off.

"You can't," said Wensleydale flatly. "They're not like America and those places. They're really *real*. Anyway, they belong to all of us. They're ours."

"And you couldn't make 'em better," said Brian.

"Anyway, even if you did we'd all know," said Pepper.

"Oh, if that's all that's worryin' you, don't you worry," said Adam airily, " 'cos I could make you all just do whatever I wanted—"

He stopped, his ears listening in horror to the words his mouth was speaking. The Them were backing away.

Dog put his paws over his head.

Adam's face looked like an impersonation of the collapse of empire.

"No," he said hoarsely. "No. Come back! *I command you!*"

They froze in mid-dash.

Adam stared.

"No, I dint mean it—" he began. "You're my friends—"

His body jerked. His head was thrown back. He raised his arms and pounded the sky with his fists.

His face twisted. The chalk floor cracked under his sneakers.

Adam opened his mouth and screamed. It was a sound that a merely mortal throat should not have been able to utter; it wound out of the quarry, mingled with the storm, caused the clouds to curdle into new and unpleasant shapes.

It went on and on.

It resounded around the universe, which is a good deal smaller than physicists would believe. It rattled the celestial spheres.

It spoke of loss, and it did not stop for a very long time.

And then it did.

Something drained away.

Adam's head tilted down again. His eyes opened.

Whatever had been standing in the old quarry before, Adam Young was standing there now. A more knowledgeable Adam Young, but Adam Young nevertheless. Possibly more of Adam Young than there had ever been before.

The ghastly silence in the quarry was replaced by a more familiar, comfortable silence, the mere and simple absence of noise.

The freed Them cowered against the chalk cliff, their eyes fixed on him.

"It's all right," said Adam quietly. "Pepper? Wensley? Brian? Come back here. It's all right. It's all right. I know everything now. And you've got to help me. Otherwise it's all goin' to happen. It's really all goin' to happen. It's all goin' to happen, if we don't do somethin'."

THE PLUMBING IN Jasmine Cottage heaved and rattled and showered Newt with water that was slightly khaki in color. But it was cold. It was probably the coldest cold shower Newt had ever had in his life.

It didn't do any good.

"There's a red sky," he said, when he came back. He was feeling slightly manic. "At half past four in the afternoon. In *August*. What does that mean? In terms of delighted nautical operatives, would you say? I mean, if it takes a red sky at night to delight a sailor, what does it take to amuse the man who operates the computers on a supertanker? Or is it shepherds who are delighted at night? I can never remember."

Anathema eyed the plaster in his hair. The shower hadn't got rid of it; it had merely dampened it down and spread it out, so that Newt looked as though he was wearing a white hat with hair in it.

"You must have got quite a bump," she said.

"No, that was when I hit my head on the wall. You know, when you—"

"Yes." Anathema looked quizzically out of the broken window. "Would you say it's blood-colored?" she said. "It's very important."

"I wouldn't say that," said Newt, his train of thought temporarily derailed. "Not actual blood. More pinkish. Probably the storm put a lot of dust in the air."

Anathema was rummaging through *The Nice and Accurate Prophecies.*

"What are you doing?" he said.

"Trying to cross-reference. I still can't be—"

"I don't think you need to bother," said Newt. "I know what the rest of 3477 means. It came to me when I—"

"What do you mean, you know what it means?"

"I saw it on my way down here. And don't snap like that. My head aches. I mean I saw it. They've got it written down outside that air base of yours. It's got nothing to do with peas. It's 'Peace Is Our Profession.' It's the kind of thing they put up on boards outside air bases. You know: SAC 8657745th Wing, The Screaming Blue Demons, Peace Is Our Profession. That sort of thing." Newt clutched his head. The euphoria was definitely fading. "If Agnes is right, then there's probably some madman in there right now winding up all the missiles and cranking open the launch windows. Or whatever they are."

"No, there isn't," said Anathema firmly.

"Oh, yes? I've seen films! Name me one good reason why you can be so sure."

"There aren't any bombs there. Or missiles. Everyone round here knows that."

"But it's an air base! It's got runways!"

"That's just for transport planes and things. All they've got up there is communications gear. Radios and stuff. Nothing explosive at all."

Newt stared at her.

LOOK AT CROWLEY, doing 110 mph on the M40 heading toward Oxfordshire. Even the most resolutely casual observer would notice a number of strange things about him. The clenched teeth, for example, or the dull red glow coming from behind his sunglasses. And the car. The car was a definite hint.

Crowley had started the journey in his Bentley, and he was damned if he wasn't going to finish it in the Bentley as well. Not that even the kind of car buff who owns his own pair of motoring goggles would have been able to tell it was a vintage Bentley. Not any more. They wouldn't have been able to tell that it was a Bentley. They would only offer fifty-fifty that it had ever even been a car.

There was no paint left on it, for a start. It might still have been black, where it wasn't a rusty, smudged reddish-brown, but this was a dull charcoal black. It traveled in its own ball of flame, like a space capsule making a particularly difficult re-entry.

There was a thin skin of crusted, melted rubber left around the metal wheel rims, but seeing that the wheel rims were still somehow riding an inch above the road surface this didn't seem to make an awful lot of difference to the suspension.

It should have fallen apart miles back.

It was the effort of holding it together that was causing Crowley to grit his teeth, and the biospatial feedback that was causing the bright red eyes. That and the effort of having to remember not to start breathing.

He hadn't felt like this since the fourteenth century.

THE ATMOSPHERE in the quarry was friendlier now, but still intense.

"You've got to help me sort it out," said Adam. "People've been tryin' to sort it out for thousands of years, but we've got to sort it out now."

They nodded helpfully.

"You see, the thing is," said Adam, "this thing is, it's like—well, you know Greasy Johnson."

The Them nodded. They all knew Greasy Johnson and the members of the other gang in Lower Tadfield. They were older and not very pleasant. Hardly a week went by without a skirmish.

"*Well*," said Adam, "we always win, right?"

"Nearly always," said Wensleydale.

"Nearly always," said Adam, "an'—"

"More than half, anyway," said Pepper. "'Cos, you remember, when there was all that fuss over the ole folks' party in the village hall when we—"

"That doesn't count," said Adam. "They got told off just as much as us. Anyway, old folks are s'pposed to *like* listenin' to the sound of children playin', I read that somewhere, I don't see why we should get told off 'cos we've got the wrong kind of old folks—" He paused. "Anyway . . . we're better'n them."

"Oh, we're better'n them," said Pepper. "You're right about that. We're *better'n* them all right. We jus' don't always win."

"Just suppose," said Adam, slowly, "that we could beat 'em properly. Get—get them sent away or somethin'. Jus' make sure there's no more ole gangs in Lower Tadfield apart from us. What do you think about that?"

"What, you mean he'd be . . . dead?" said Brian.

"No. Jus'—jus' gone away."

The Them thought about this. Greasy Johnson had been a fact of life ever since they'd been old enough to hit one another with a toy railway engine. They tried to get their minds around the concept of a world with a Johnson-shaped hole in it.

Brian scratched his nose. "I reckon it'd be brilliant without Greasy Johnson," he said. "Remember what he did at my birthday party? *And* I got into trouble about it."

"I dunno," said Pepper. "I mean, it wouldn't be so interesting without ole Greasy Johnson and his gang. When you think about it. We've had a lot of fun with ole Greasy Johnson and the Johnsonites. We'd probably have to find some other gang or something."

"Seems to *me*," said Wensleydale, "that if you asked people in Lower Tadfield, they'd say they'd be better off without the Johnsonites *or* the Them."

Even Adam looked shocked at this. Wensleydale went on stoically: "The old folks' club would. An' Picky. An'—"

"But we're the good ones . . ." Brian began. He hesitated. "Well, all right," he said, "but I bet they'd think it'd be a jolly sight less interestin' if we all weren't here."

"Yes," said Wensleydale. "That's what I mean.

"People round here don't want us *or* the Johnsonites," he went on morosely, "the way they're always goin' on about us just riding our bikes or skateboarding on their pavements and making too much noise and stuff. It's like the man said in the history books. A plaque on both your houses."

This met with silence.

"One of those blue ones," said Brian, eventually, "saying 'Adam Young Lived Here,' or somethin'?"

Normally an opening like this could lead to five minutes' rambling discussion when the Them were in the mood, but Adam felt that this was not the time.

"What you're all sayin'," he summed up, in his best chairman tones, "is that it wouldn't be any good at all if the Greasy Johnsonites beat the Them or the other way round?"

"That's right," said Pepper. "Because," she added, "if we beat them, we'd have to be our own deadly enemies. It'd be me an' Adam against Brian an' Wensley." She sat back. "Everyone needs a Greasy Johnson," she said.

"Yeah," said Adam. "That's what I thought. It's no good anyone winning. That's what I thought." He stared at Dog, or through Dog.

"Seems simple enough to me," said Wensleydale, sitting back. "I don't see why it's taken thousands of years to sort out."

"That's because the people trying to sort it out were men," said Pepper, meaningfully.

"Don't see why you have to take sides," said Wensleydale.

"Of course I have to take sides," said Pepper. "Everyone has to take sides in *something*."

Adam appeared to reach a decision.

"Yes. But I reckon you can make your own side. I think you'd better go and get your bikes," he said quietly. "I think we'd better sort of go and talk to some people."

PUTPUTPUTPUTPUTPUT, went Madame Tracy's motor scooter down Crouch End High street. It was the only vehicle moving on a suburban London street jammed with immobile cars and taxis and red London buses.

"I've never seen a traffic jam like it," said Madame Tracy. "I wonder if there's been an accident."

"*Quite possibly*," said Aziraphale. And then, "Mr. Shadwell, unless you put your arms round me you're going to fall off. This thing wasn't built for two people, you know."

"Three," muttered Shadwell, gripping the seat with one white-knuckled hand, and his Thundergun with the other.

"Mr. Shadwell, I won't tell you again."

"Ye'll have ter stop, then, so as I can adjust me weapon," sighed Shadwell.

Madame Tracy giggled dutifully, but she pulled over to the curb, and stopped the motor scooter.

Shadwell sorted himself out, and put two grudging arms around Madame Tracy, while the Thundergun stuck up between them like a chaperon.

They rode through the rain without talking for another ten minutes, *putputputputput*, as Madame Tracy carefully negotiated her way around the cars and the buses.

Madame Tracy found her eyes being moved down to the speedometer—rather foolishly, she thought, since it hadn't worked since 1974, and it hadn't worked very well before that.

"*Dear lady, how fast would you say we were going?*" asked Aziraphale.

"Why?"

"*Because it seems to me that we would go slightly faster walking.*"

"Well, with just me on, the top speed is about fifteen miles an hour, but with Mr. Shadwell as well, it must be, ooh, about . . ."

"*Four or five miles per hour,*" she interrupted.

"I suppose so," she agreed.

There was a cough from behind her. "Can ye no slow down this hellish machine, wumman?" asked an ashen voice. In the infernal pantheon, which it goes without saying Shadwell hated uniformly and correctly, Shadwell reserved a special loathing for speed demons.

"In which case," said Aziraphale, *"we will get to Tadfield in something less than ten hours."*

There was a pause from Madame Tracy, then, "How far away *is* this Tadfield, anyway?"

"About forty miles."

"Um," said Madame Tracy, who had once driven the scooter the few miles to nearby Finchley to visit her niece, but had taken the bus since, because of the funny noises the scooter had started making on the way back.

". . . we should really be going at about seventy, if we're going to get there in time," said Aziraphale. *"Hmm. Sergeant Shadwell? Hold on very tightly now."*

Putputputputput and a blue nimbus began to outline the scooter and its occupants with a gentle sort of a glow, like an afterimage, all around them.

Putputputputputput and the scooter lifted awkwardly off the ground with no visible means of support, jerking slightly, until it reached a height of five feet, more or less.

"Don't look down, Sergeant Shadwell," advised Aziraphale.

". . ." said Shadwell, eyes screwed tightly shut, gray forehead beaded with sweat, not looking down, not looking anywhere.

"And off we go, then."

In every big-budget science fiction movie there's the moment when a spaceship as large as New York suddenly goes to light speed. A twanging noise like a wooden ruler being plucked over the edge of a desk, a dazzling refraction of light, and suddenly the stars have all been stretched out thin and it's gone. This was exactly like that, except that instead of a gleaming twelve-mile-long spaceship, it was an off-white twenty-year-old motor scooter. And you didn't have the special rainbow effects. And it probably wasn't going at more than two hundred miles an hour. And instead of a pulsing whine sliding up the octaves, it just went *putputputputput* . . .

VROOOOSH.

But it was exactly like that anyway.

WHERE THE M25, NOW a screaming frozen circle, intersects with the M40 to Oxfordshire, police were clustered around in ever-increasing quantities. Since Crowley crossed the divide, half an hour earlier, their number had doubled. On the M40 side, anyway. No one in London was getting out.

In addition to the police there were also approximately two hundred others standing around, and inspecting the M25 through binoculars. They included representatives from Her Majesty's Army, the Bomb Disposal Squad, MI5, MI6, the Special Branch, and the CIA. There was also a man selling hot dogs.

Everybody was cold and wet, and puzzled, and irritable, with the exception of one police officer, who was cold, wet, puzzled, irritable, and exasperated.

"Look. I don't care if you believe me or not," he sighed, "all I'm telling you is what I saw. It was an old car, a Rolls, or a Bentley, one of those flash vintage jobs, and it made it over the bridge."

One of the senior army technicians interrupted.

"It can't have done. According to our instruments the temperature above the M25 is somewhere in excess of seven hundred degrees centigrade."

"Or a hundred and forty degrees below," added his assistant.

". . . or a hundred and forty degrees below zero," agreed the senior technician. "There does appear to be some confusion on that score, although I think we can safely attribute it to mechanical error of some kind,* but the fact remains that we can't even get a helicopter directly over the M25 without winding up with Helicopter McNuggets. How on earth can you tell me that a vintage car drove over it unharmed?"

"I didn't say it drove over it unharmed," corrected the policeman, who was thinking seriously about leaving the Metropolitan Police and going into business with his brother, who was resigning his job with the Electricity Board, and was going to start breeding chickens. "It burst into flames. It just kept on going."

"Do you seriously expect any of us to believe . . ." began somebody.

A high-pitched keening noise, haunting and strange. Like a thousand glass harmonicas being played in unison, all slightly off-key; like the sound of the molecules of the air itself wailing in pain.

And VROOOOSH.

* This was true. There wasn't a thermometer on earth that could have been persuaded to register both 700°C and -140°C at the same time, which was the correct temperature.

Over their heads it sailed, forty feet in the air, engulfed in a deep blue nimbus which faded to red at the edges: a little white motor scooter, and riding it, a middle-aged woman in a pink helmet, and holding tightly to her, a short man in a mackintosh and a day-glo green crash helmet (the motor scooter was too far up for anyone to see that his eyes were tightly shut, but they were).

The woman was screaming. What she was screaming was this:

"Gerrrronnnimooooo!"

ONE OF THE ADVANTAGES of the Wasabi, as Newt was always keen to point out, was that when it was badly damaged it was very hard to tell. Newt had to keep driving Dick Turpin onto the shoulder to avoid fallen branches.

"You've made me drop all the cards on the floor!"

The car thumped back onto the road; a small voice from somewhere under the glove compartment said, "Oil plessure arert."

"I'll never be able to sort them out now," she moaned.

"You don't have to," said Newt manically. "Just pick one. Any one. It won't matter."

"What do you mean?"

"Well, if Agnes is right, and we're doing all this because she's predicted it, then any card *picked right now* has got to be relevant. That's logic."

"It's nonsense."

"Yeah? Look, you're even *here* because she predicted it. And have you thought what we're going to say to the colonel? If we get to see him, which of course we won't."

"If we're reasonable—"

"Listen, I know these kinds of places. They have huge guards there to guard the gates, Anathema, and they have white helmets and real guns, you understand, which fire real bullets made of real lead which can go right into you and bounce around and come out of the same hole before you can even say 'Excuse me, we have reason to believe that World War Three is due any moment and they're going to do the show right here,' and then they have serious men in suits with bulging jackets who take you into a little room without windows and ask you questions like are you now, or have you ever been, a member of a pinko subversive organization such as any British political party? And—"

"We're nearly there."

"Look, it's got gates and wire fences and everything! And probably the kind of dogs that eat people!"

"I think you're getting rather overexcited," said Anathema quietly, picking the last of the file cards up from the floor of the car.

"Overexcited? No! I'm getting very calmly worried that someone might shoot me!"

"I'm sure Agnes would have mentioned it if we were going to be shot. She's very good at that sort of thing." She began absentmindedly to shuffle the file cards.

"You know," she said, carefully cutting the cards and riffling the two piles together, "I read somewhere that there's a sect that believes that computers are the tools of the Devil. They say that Armageddon will come about because of the Antichrist being good with computers. Apparently it's mentioned somewhere in Revelations. I think I must have read about it in a newspaper recently . . ."

"*Daily Mail.* 'Letter From America.' Um, August the third," said Newt. "Just after the story about the woman in Worms, Nebraska, who taught her duck to play the accordion."

"Mm," said Anathema, spreading the cards facedown on her lap.

So computers are tools of the Devil? thought Newt. He had no problem believing it. Computers had to be the tools of *somebody*, and all he knew for certain was that it definitely wasn't him.

The car jerked to a halt.

The air base looked battered. Several large trees had fallen down near the entrance, and some men with a digger were trying to shift them. The guard on duty was watching them disinterestedly, but he half turned and looked coldly at the car.

"All right," said Newt. "Pick a card."

3001. BEHINDE THE EAGLE'S NESTE A GRATE ASH HATH FELLEN.

"Is that all?"

"Yes. We always thought it was something to do with the Russian Revolution. Keep going along this road and turn left."

The turning led to a narrow lane, with the base's perimeter fence on the left-hand side.

"And now pull in here. There's often cars here, and no one takes any notice," said Anathema.

"What is this place?"

"It's the local Lovers' Lane."

"Is that why it appears to be paved with rubber?"

They walked along the hedge-shaded lane for a hundred yards until they reached the ash tree. Agnes had been right. It was quite grate. It had fallen right across the fence.

A guard was sitting on it, smoking a cigarette. He was black. Newt always felt guilty in the presence of black Americans, in case they blamed him for two hundred years of slave trading.

The man stood up when they approached, and then sagged into an easier stance.

"Oh, hi, Anathema," he said.

"Hi, George. Terrible storm, wasn't it."

"Sure was."

They walked on. He watched them out of sight.

"You know him?" said Newt, with forced nonchalance.

"Oh, sure. Sometimes a few of them come down to the pub. Pleasant enough in a well-scrubbed way."

"Would he shoot us if we just walked in?" said Newt.

"He might well point a gun at us in a menacing way," Anathema conceded.

"That's good enough for me. What do you suggest we do, then?"

"Well, Agnes must have known something. So I suppose we just wait. It's not too bad now the wind's gone down."

"Oh." Newt looked at the clouds piling up on the horizon. "Good old Agnes," he said.

ADAM PEDALED STEADILY along the road, Dog running along behind and occasionally trying to bite his back tire out of sheer excitement.

There was a clacking noise and Pepper swung out of her drive. You could always tell Pepper's bike. She thought it was improved by a piece of cardboard cunningly held against the wheel by a clothes peg. Cats had learned to take evasive action when she was two streets away.

"I reckon we can cut along Drovers Lane and then up through Roundhead Woods," said Pepper.

" 'S all muddy," said Adam.

"That's right," said Pepper nervously. "It gets all muddy up there. We ort to go along by the chalk pit. 'S always dry because of the chalk. An' then up by the sewage farm."

Brian and Wensleydale pulled in behind them. Wensleydale's bicycle was black, and shiny, and sensible. Brian's might have been white, once, but its color was lost beneath a thick layer of mud.

"It's stupid calling it a milit'ry base," said Pepper. "I went up there when they had that open day and they had no guns or missiles or anythin'. Just knobs and dials and brass bands playin'."

"Yes," said Adam.

"Not much milit'ry about knobs and dials," said Pepper.

"I dunno, reely," said Adam. "It's amazin' what you can do with knobs and dials."

"I got a kit for Christmas," Wensleydale volunteered. "All electric bits. There were a few knobs and dials in it. You could make a radio or a thing that goes beep."

"I dunno," said Adam thoughtfully, "I'm thinkin' more of certain people patching into the worldwide milit'ry communications network and telling all the computers and stuff to start fightin'."

"Cor," said Brian. "That'd be *wicked.*"

"Sort of," said Adam.

IT IS A HIGH AND LONELY destiny to be Chairman of the Lower Tadfield Residents' Association.

R. P. Tyler, short, well-fed, satisfied, stomped down a country lane, accompanied by his wife's miniature poodle, Shutzi. R. P. Tyler knew the difference between right and wrong; there were no moral grays of any kind in his life. He was not, however, satisfied simply with being vouchsafed the difference between right and wrong. He felt it his bounden duty to tell the world.

Not for R. P. Tyler the soapbox, the polemic verse, the broadsheet. R. P. Tyler's chosen forum was the letter column of the *Tadfield Advertiser.* If a neighbor's tree was inconsiderate enough to shed leaves into R. P. Tyler's garden, R. P. Tyler would first carefully sweep them all up, place them in boxes, and leave the boxes outside his neighbor's front door, with a stern note. Then he would write a letter to the *Tadfield Advertiser.* If he sighted teenagers sitting on the village green, their portable cassette players playing, and they were enjoying themselves, he would take it upon himself to point out to them the error of their ways. And after he had fled their jeering, he would write to the *Tadfield Advertiser* on the Decline of Morality and the Youth of Today.

Since his retirement last year the letters had increased to the point where not even the *Tadfield Advertiser* was able to print all of them. Indeed, the letter R. P. Tyler had completed before setting out on his evening walk had begun:

> *Sirs,*
>
> *I note with distress that the newspapers of today no longer feel obligated to their public, we, the people who pay your wages . . .*

He surveyed the fallen branches that littered the narrow country road. I don't suppose, he pondered, they think of the cleaning up bill when they send us these storms. Parish Council has to foot the bill to clean it all up. And *we*, the taxpayers, pay their wages . . .

The *they* in this thought were the weather forecasters on Radio Four,* whom R. P. Tyler blamed for the weather.

* He did not have a television. Or as his wife put it, "Ronald wouldn't have one of those things in the house, would you Ronald?" and he always agreed, although secretly he would have liked to have seen some of the smut and filth and violence that the National Viewers and Listeners Association complained of. Not because he wanted to see it, of course. Just because he wanted to know what other people should be protected from.

Shutzi stopped by a roadside beech tree to cock its leg.

R. P. Tyler looked away, embarrassed. It might be that the sole purpose of his evening constitutional was to allow the dog to relieve itself, but he was dashed if he'd admit that to himself. He stared up at the storm clouds. They were banked up high, in towering piles of smudged gray and black. It wasn't just the flickering tongues of lightning that forked through them like the opening sequence of a Frankenstein movie; it was the way they stopped when they reached the borders of Lower Tadfield. And in their center was a circular patch of daylight; but the light had a stretched, yellow quality to it, like a forced smile.

It was so quiet.

There was a low roaring.

Down the narrow lane came four motorbikes. They shot past him, and turned the corner, disturbing a cock pheasant who whirred across the lane in a nervous arc of russet and green.

"Vandals!" called R. P. Tyler after them.

The countryside wasn't made for people like them. It was made for people like him.

He jerked Shutzi's lead, and they marched along the road.

Five minutes later he turned the corner, to find three of the motorcyclists standing around a fallen signpost, a victim of the storm. The fourth, a tall man with a mirrored visor, remained on his bike.

R. P. Tyler observed the situation, and leaped effortlessly to a conclusion. These vandals—he had, of course, been right—had come to the countryside in order to desecrate the War Memorial and to overturn signposts.

He was about to advance on them sternly, when it came to him that he was outnumbered, four to one, and that they were taller than he was, and that they were undoubtedly violent psychopaths. No one but a violent psychopath rode motorbikes in R. P. Tyler's world.

So he raised his chin and began to strut past them, without apparently noticing they were there,* all the while composing in his head a letter (Sirs, this evening I noted with distress a large number of hooligans on motorbicycles infesting Our Fair Village. Why, oh Why, does the government do nothing about this plague of . . .).

"Hi," said one of the motorcyclists, raising his visor to reveal a thin face and a trim black beard. "We're kinda lost."

"Ah," said R. P. Tyler disapprovingly.

"The signpost musta blew down," said the motorcyclist.

"Yes, I suppose it must," agreed R. P. Tyler. He noticed with surprise that he was getting hungry.

"Yeah. Well, we're heading for Lower Tadfield."

An officious eyebrow raised. "You're Americans. With the air force base, I suppose." (Sirs, when I did national service I was a credit to my country. I notice with horror and dismay that airmen from the Tadfield Air Base are driving around our noble

* Although as a member (read, founder) of his local Neighborhood Watch scheme he did attempt to memorize the motorbikes' number plates.

countryside dressed no better than common thugs. While I appreciate their importance in defending the freedom of the western world . . .)

Then his love of giving instructions took over. "You go back down that road for half a mile, then first left, it's in a deplorable state of disrepair I'm afraid, I've written numerous letters to the council about it, are you civil *servants* or civil *masters*, that's what I asked them, after all, who pays your wages? then second right, only it's not exactly right, it's on the left but you'll find it bends round toward the right eventually, it's signposted Porrit's Lane, but of course it isn't Porrit's Lane, you look at the Ordnance Survey map, you'll see, it's simply the eastern end of Forest Hill Lane, you'll come out in the village, now you go past the Bull and Fiddle—that's a public house—then when you get to the church (I have pointed out to the people who compile the Ordnance Survey map that it's a church with a *spire*, not a church with a *tower*, indeed I have written to the *Tadfield Advertiser*, suggesting they mount a local campaign to get the map corrected, and I have every hope that once these people realize with whom they are dealing you'll see a hasty U-turn from them) then you'll get to a crossroads, now, you go straight across that crossroads and you'll immediately come to a second crossroads, now, you can take either the left-hand fork or go straight on, either way you'll arrive at the air base (although the left-hand fork is almost a tenth of a mile shorter) and you can't miss it."

Famine stared at him blankly. "I, uh, I'm not sure I got that . . ." he began.

I DID. LET US GO.

Shutzi gave a little yelp and darted behind R. P. Tyler, where it remained, shivering.

The strangers climbed back onto their bikes. The one in white (a hippie, by the look of him, thought R. P. Tyler) dropped an empty crisp packet onto the grass shoulder.

"Excuse *me*," barked Tyler. "Is that your crisp packet?"

"Oh, it's not just mine," said the boy. "It's *everybody's*."

R. P. Tyler drew himself up to his full height.* "Young man," he said, "how would you feel if I came over to your house and dropped litter everywhere?"

Pollution smiled, wistfully. "Very, very pleased," he breathed. "Oh, that would be *wonderful*."

Beneath his bike an oil slick puddled a rainbow on the wet road.

Engines revved.

"I missed something," said War. "Now, why are we meant to make a U-turn by the church?"

JUST FOLLOW ME, said the tall one in front, and the four rode off together.

R. P. Tyler stared after them, until his attention was distracted by the sound of something going *clackclackclack*. He turned. Four figures on bicycles shot past him, closely followed by the scampering figure of a small dog.

"You! Stop!" shouted R. P. Tyler.

The Them braked to a halt and looked at him.

"I knew it was you, Adam Young, and your little,

* Five foot six.

hmph, cabal. What, might I enquire, are you children doing out at this time of night? Do your fathers know you're out?"

The leader of the cyclists turned. "I can't see how you can say it's *late*," he said, "seems to me, seems to *me*, that if the sun's still out then it's not *late*."

"It's past your bedtime, anyway," R. P. Tyler informed them, "and don't stick out your tongue at me, young lady," this was to Pepper, "or I will be writing a letter to your mother informing her of the lamentable and unladylike state of her offspring's manners."

"Well 'scuse *us*," said Adam, aggrieved. "Pepper was just looking at you. I didn't know there was any lor against *looking*."

There was a commotion on the grass. Shutzi, who was a particularly refined toy French poodle, of the kind only possessed by people who were never able to fit children into their household budgets, was being menaced by Dog.

"Master Young," ordered R. P. Tyler, "please get your—your *mutt* away from my Shutzi." Tyler did not trust Dog. When he had first met the dog, three days ago, it had snarled at him, and glowed its eyes red. This had impelled Tyler to begin a letter pointing out that Dog was undoubtedly rabid, certainly a danger to the community, and should be put down for the General Good, until his wife had reminded him that glowing red eyes weren't a symptom of rabies, or, for that matter, anything seen outside of the kind of film that neither of the Tylers would be caught dead at but knew all they needed to know about, thank you very much.

Adam looked astounded. "Dog's not a *mutt.* Dog's a remarkable dog. He's clever. *Dog,* you get off Mr. Tyler's horrible ol' poodle."

Dog ignored him. He'd got a lot of dog catching-up still to do.

"*Dog,*" said Adam, ominously. His dog slunk back to his master's bicycle.

"I don't believe you have answered my question. Where are you four off to?"

"To the air base," said Brian.

"*If* that's all right with you," said Adam, with what he hoped was bitter and scathing sarcasm. "I mean, we wun't want to go there if it wasn't all right with you."

"You cheeky little monkey," said R. P. Tyler. "When I see your father, Adam Young, I will inform him in no uncertain terms that . . ."

But the Them were already pedaling off down the road, in the direction of Lower Tadfield Air Base—traveling by the Them's route, which was shorter and simpler and more scenic than the route suggested by Mr. Tyler.

R. P. TYLER HAD COMPOSED a lengthy mental letter on the failings of the youth of today. It covered falling educational standards, the lack of respect given to their elders and betters, the way they always seemed to slouch these days instead of walking with a proper upright bearing, juvenile delinquency, the return of compulsory National Service, birching, flogging, and dog licenses.

He was very satisfied with it. He had a sneaking

suspicion that it would be too good for the *Tadfield Advertiser*, and had decided to send it to the *Times.*

Putputputputputput

"Excuse me, love," said a warm female voice. "I think we're lost."

It was an aging motor scooter, and it was being ridden by a middle-aged woman. Clutching her tightly, his eyes screwed shut, was a raincoated little man with a bright green crash helmet on. Sticking up between them was what appeared to be an antique gun with a funnel-shaped muzzle.

"Oh. Where are you going?"

"Lower Tadfield. I'm not sure of the exact address, but we're looking for someone," said the woman, then, in a totally different voice she said, *"His name is Adam Young."*

R. P. Tyler boggled. "You *want* that boy?" he asked. "What's he done now—no, no, don't tell me. I don't want to know."

"Boy?" said the woman. "You didn't tell me he was a boy. How old is he?" Then she said, *"He's eleven.* Well, I do wish you'd mentioned this before. It puts a completely different complexion on things."

R. P. Tyler just stared. Then he realized what was going on. The woman was a ventriloquist. What he had taken for a man in a green crash helmet, he now saw, was a ventriloquist's dummy. He wondered how he could ever have assumed it was human. He felt the whole thing was in vaguely bad taste.

"I saw Adam Young not five minutes ago," he told the woman. "He and his little cronies were on their way to the American air base."

"Oh dear," said the woman, paling slightly. "I've

never really liked the Yanks. *They're really very nice people, you know.* Yes, but you can't trust people who pick up the ball all the time when they play football."

"Ahh, excuse me," said R. P. Tyler, "I think it's very good. Very impressive. I'm deputy chairman of the local Rotary club, and I was wondering, do you do private functions?"

"Only on Thursdays," said Madame Tracy, disapprovingly. "And I charge extra. *And I wonder if you could direct us to—?*"

Mr. Tyler had been here before. He wordlessly extended a finger.

And the little scooter went *putputputputputput* down the narrow country lane.

As it did so, the gray dummy in the green helmet turned around and opened one eye. "Ye great southern pillock," it croaked.

R. P. Tyler was offended, but also disappointed. He'd hoped it would be more lifelike.

R. P. TYLER, ONLY TEN MINUTES away from the village, paused, while Shutzi attempted another of its wide range of eliminatory functions. He gazed over the fence.

His knowledge of country lore was a little hazy, but he felt fairly sure that if the cows lay down, it meant rain. If they were standing it would probably be fine. These cows were taking it in turns to execute slow and solemn somersaults; and Tyler wondered what it presaged for the weather.

He sniffed. Something was burning—there was

an unpleasant smell of scorched metal and rubber and leather.

"Excuse me," said a voice from behind him. R. P. Tyler turned around.

There was a large once-black car on fire in the lane and a man in sunglasses was leaning out of one window, saying through the smoke, "I'm sorry, I've managed to get a little lost. Can you direct me to Lower Tadfield Air Base? I know it's around here somewhere."

Your car is on fire.

No. Tyler just couldn't bring himself to say it. I mean, the man had to know that, didn't he? He was sitting in the middle of it. Possibly it was some kind of practical joke.

So instead he said, "I think you must have taken a wrong turn about a mile back. A signpost has blown down."

The stranger smiled, "That must be it," he said. The orange flames flickering below him gave him an almost infernal appearance.

The wind blew towards Tyler, across the car, and he felt his eyebrows frizzle.

Excuse me, young man, but your car is on fire and you're sitting in it without burning and incidentally it's red hot in places.

No.

Should he ask the man if he wanted him to phone the A.A.?

Instead he explained the route carefully, trying not to stare.

"That's terrific. Much obliged," said Crowley, as he began to wind up the window.

R. P. Tyler had to say something.

"Excuse me, young man," he said.

"Yes?"

I mean, it's not the kind of thing you don't notice, your car being on fire.

A tongue of flame licked across the charred dashboard.

"Funny weather we're having, isn't it?" he said, lamely.

"Is it?" said Crowley. "I honestly hadn't noticed." And he reversed back down the country lane in his burning car.

"That's probably because your car is on fire," said R. P. Tyler sharply. He jerked Shutzi's lead, dragged the little dog to heel.

To The Editor

Sir,

I would like to draw your attention to a recent tendency I have noticed for today's young people to ignore perfectly sensible safety precautions while driving. This evening I was asked for directions by a gentleman whose car was . . .

No.

Driving a car that . . .

No.

It was on fire . . .

His temper getting worse, R. P. Tyler stomped the final stretch back into the village.

"HOY!" SHOUTED R. P. TYLER. "YOUNG!"

Mr. Young was in his front garden, sitting on his deck chair, smoking his pipe.

This had more to do with Deirdre's recent discovery of the menace of passive smoking and banning of smoking in the house than he would care to admit to his neighbors. It did not improve his temper. Neither did being addressed as *Young* by Mr. Tyler.

"Yes?"

"Your son, Adam."

Mr. Young sighed. "What's he done now?"

"Do you know where he is?"

Mr. Young checked his watch. "Getting ready for bed, I would assume."

Tyler grinned, tightly, triumphantly. "I doubt it. I saw him and his little fiends, and that appalling mongrel, not half an hour ago, cycling towards the air base."

Mr. Young puffed on his pipe.

"You know how strict they are up there," said Mr. Tyler, in case Mr. Young hadn't got the message.

"You know what a one your son is for pressing buttons and things," he added.

Mr. Young took his pipe out of his mouth and examined the stem thoughtfully.

"Hmp," he said.

"I see," he said.

"Right," he said.

And he went inside.

AT EXACTLY THAT SAME MOMENT, four motorbikes swished to a halt a few hundred yards from the main gate. The riders switched off their engines and raised their helmet visors. Well, three of them did.

"I was rather hoping we could crash through the barriers," said War wistfully.

"That'd only cause trouble," said Famine.

"Good."

"Trouble for us, I mean. The power and phone lines must be down, but they're bound to have generators and they'll certainly have radio. If someone starts reporting that terrorists have invaded the base then people'll start acting logically and the whole Plan collapses."

"Huh."

WE GO IN, WE DO THE JOB, WE GO OUT, WE LET HUMAN NATURE TAKE ITS COURSE, said Death.

"This isn't how I imagined it, chaps," said War. "I haven't been waiting for thousands of years just to fiddle around with bits of wire. It's not what you'd call *dramatic*. Albrecht Dürer didn't waste his time doing woodcuts of the Four Button-Pressers of the Apocalypse, I do know that."

"I thought there'd be trumpets," said Pollution.

"Look at it like this," said Famine. "It's just groundwork. We get to do the riding forth afterwards. The proper riding forth. Wings of the storm and so on. You've got to be flexible."

"Weren't we supposed to meet . . . someone?" said War.

There was no sound but the metallic noises of cooling motorbike engines.

Then Pollution said, slowly, "You know, I can't say I imagined it'd be somewhere like this, either. I thought it'd be, well, a big city. Or a big country. New York, perhaps. Or Moscow. Or Armageddon itself."

There was another pause.

Then War said, "Where *is* Armageddon, anyway?"

"Funny you should ask," said Famine. "I've always meant to look it up."

"There's an Armageddon, Pennsylvania," said Pollution. "Or maybe it's Massachusetts, or one of them places. Lots of guys in heavy beards and seriously black hats."

"Nah," said Famine. "It's somewhere in Israel, I think."

MOUNT CARMEL.

"I thought that was where they grow avocados."

AND THE END OF THE WORLD.

"Is that right? That's one big avocado."

"I think I went there once," said Pollution. "The old city of Megiddo. Just before it fell down. Nice place. Interesting royal gateway."

War looked at the greenness around them.

"Boy," she said, "did *we* take a wrong turning."

THE GEOGRAPHY IS IMMATERIAL.

"Sorry, lord?"

IF ARMAGEDDON IS ANYWHERE, IT IS EVERYWHERE.

"That's right," said Famine, "we're not talking about a few square miles of scrub and goats any more."

There was another pause.

LET US GO.

War coughed. "It's just that I thought that . . . *he*'d be coming with us . . . ?"

Death adjusted his gauntlets.

THIS, he said firmly, IS A JOB FOR THE PROFESSIONALS.

AFTERWARDS, Sgt. Thomas A. Deisenburger recalled events at the gate as having happened like this:

A large staff car drew up by the gate. It was sleek and official-looking although, afterwards, he wasn't entirely sure why he had thought this, or why it sounded momentarily as though it were powered by motorbike engines.

Four generals got out. Again, the sergeant was a little uncertain of why he had thought this. They had proper identification. What kind of identification, admittedly, he couldn't quite recall, but it was proper. He saluted.

And one of them said, "Surprise inspection, soldier."

To which Sgt. Thomas A. Deisenburger replied, "Sir, I have not been informated as to the incidence of a surprise inspection at this time, sir."

"Of course not," said one of the generals. "That's because it's a surprise."

The sergeant saluted again.

"Sir, permission to confirmate this intelligence with base command, sir," he said, uneasily.

The tallest and thinnest of the generals strolled a little way from the group, turned his back, and folded his arms.

One of the others put a friendly arm around the sergeant's shoulders and leaned forward in a conspiratorial way.

"Now see here—" he squinted at the sergeant's name tag "—Deisenburger, maybe I'll give you a break. It's a surprise inspection, got that? Surprise. That means no getting on the horn the moment we've gone through, understand? And no leaving your post. Career soldier like you'll understand, am I right?" he added. He winked. "Otherwise you'll find yourself busted so low you'll have to say 'sir' to an imp."

Sgt. Thomas A. Deisenburger stared at him.

"Private," hissed one of the other generals. According to her tag, her name was Waugh. Sgt. Deisenburger had never seen a female general like her before, but she was certainly an improvement.

"What?"

"Private. Not imp."

"Yeah. That's what I meant. Yeah. Private. Okay, soldier?"

The sergeant considered the very limited number of options at his disposal.

"Sir, surprise inspection, sir?" he said.

"Provisionatedly classificisioned at this time," said Famine, who had spent years learning how to sell to the federal government and could feel the language coming back to him.

"Sir, affirmative, sir," said the sergeant.

"Good man," said Famine, as the barrier was

raised. "You'll go a long way." He glanced at his watch. "Very shortly."

SOMETIMES HUMAN BEINGS are very much like bees. Bees are fiercely protective of their hive, provided you are outside it. Once you're in, the workers sort of assume that it must have been cleared by management and take no notice; various freeloading insects have evolved a mellifluous existence because of this very fact. Humans act the same way.

No one stopped the four as they purposefully made their way into one of the long, low buildings under the forest of radio masts. No one paid any attention to them. Perhaps they saw nothing at all. Perhaps they saw what their minds were instructed to see, because the human brain is not equipped to see War, Famine, Pollution, and Death when they don't want to be seen, and has got so good at not seeing that it often manages not to see them even when they abound on every side.

The alarms were totally brainless and thought they saw four people where people shouldn't be, and went off like *anything*.

NEWT DID NOT SMOKE, because he did not allow nicotine or (until today) alcohol entry to the temple of his body or, more accurately, the small Welsh Methodist tin tabernacle of his body. If he did, he would have choked on the cigarette that he would have been smoking at this time in order to steady his nerves.

Anathema stood up purposefully and smoothed the creases in her skirt.

"Don't worry," she said. "They don't apply to us. Something's probably happening inside."

She smiled at his pale face. "Come on," she said, "It's not the O.K. Corral."

"No. They've got better guns, for one thing," said Newt.

She helped him up. "Never mind," she said. "I'm sure you'll think of a way."

IT WAS INEVITABLE that all four of them couldn't contribute equally, War thought. She'd been surprised at her natural affinity for modern weapons systems, which were so much more efficient than bits of sharp metal, and of course Pollution laughed at absolutely foolproof, fail-safe devices. Even Famine at least knew what computers were. Whereas . . . well, *he* didn't do anything much except hang around, although he did it with a certain style. It had occurred to War that there might one day be an end to War, an end to Famine, possibly even an end to Pollution, and perhaps this was why the fourth and greatest horseman was never exactly what you might call one of the lads. It was like having a tax inspector in your football team. Great to have him on your side, of course, but not the kind of person you wanted to have a drink and a chat with in the bar afterwards. You couldn't be one hundred per cent at your ease.

A couple of soldiers ran through him as he looked over Pollution's skinny shoulder.

WHAT ARE THOSE GLITTERY THINGS? he said, in the tones of one who knows he won't be able to understand the answer but wants to be seen to be taking an interest.

"Seven-segment LED displays," said the boy. He laid loving hands on a bank of relays, which fused under his touch, and then introduced a swath of self-replicating viruses that whirred away on the electronic ether.

"I could really do without those bloody alarms," muttered Famine.

Death absentmindedly snapped his fingers. A dozen klaxons gurgled and died.

"I don't know, I rather liked them," said Pollution.

War reached inside another metal cabinet. This wasn't the way she'd expected things to be, she had to admit, but when she ran her fingers over and sometimes through the electronics there was a familiar feel. It was an echo of what you got when you held a sword, and she felt a thrill of anticipation at the thought that this sword enclosed the whole world and a certain amount of the sky above it, as well. It *loved* her.

A flaming sword.

Mankind had not been very good at learning that swords are dangerous if left lying around, although it *had* done its limited best to make sure that the chances of one this size being wielded accidentally were high. A cheering thought, that. It was nice to think that mankind made a distinction between blowing their planet to bits by accident and doing it by design.

Pollution plunged his hands into another rack of expensive electronics.

THE GUARD ON THE HOLE in the fence looked puzzled. He was aware of excitement back in the base, and his radio seemed to be picking up nothing but static, and his eyes were being drawn again and again to the card in front of him.

He'd seen many identity cards in his time—military, CIA, FBI, KGB even—and, being a young soldier, had yet to grasp that the more insignificant an organization is, the more impressive are its identity cards.

This one was *hellishly* impressive. His lips moved as he read it again, all the way from "The Lord Protector of the Common Wealth of Britain charges and demands," through the bit about commandeering all kindling, rope, and igniferous oils, right down to the signature of the WA's first Lord Adjutant, Praise-Him-All-Ye-Works-Of-The-Lord-And-Flye-Fornication Smith. Newt kept his thumb over the bit about Nine Pence Per Witch and tried to look like James Bond.

Finally the guard's probing intellect found a word he thought he recognized.

"What's this here," he said suspiciously, "about us got to give you faggots?"

"Oh, we have to have them," said Newt. "We burn them."

"Say what?"

"We burn them."

The guard's face broadened into a grin. And

they'd told him England was soft. "Right on!" he said.

Something pressed into the small of his back.

"Drop your gun," said Anathema, behind him, "or I shall regret what I shall have to do next."

Well, it's true, she thought as she saw the man stiffen in terror. If he doesn't drop the gun he'll find out this is a stick, and I shall really regret having to be shot.

AT THE MAIN GATE, Sgt. Thomas A. Deisenburger was also having problems. A little man in a dirty mack kept pointing a finger at him and muttering, while a lady who looked slightly like his mother talked to him in urgent tones and kept interrupting herself in a different voice.

"It really is vitally important that we are allowed to speak to whoever is in charge," said Aziraphale. *"I really must ask that* he's right, you know, I'd be able to tell if he was lying *yes, thank you, I think we'd really achieve something if you kindly allowed me to carry on* all right *thank you* I was only trying to put in a good word *Yes! Er.* You were asking him to *yes, all right . . . now—"*

"D'yer see my finger?" shouted Shadwell, whose sanity was still attached to him but only on the end of a long and rather frayed string. "D'yer see it? This finger, laddie, could send ye to meet yer Maker!"

Sgt. Deisenburger stared at the black and purple nail a few inches from his face. As an offensive weapon it rated quite highly, especially if it was ever used in the preparation of food.

The telephone gave him nothing but static. He'd been told not to leave his post. His wound from Nam was starting to play up.* He wondered how much trouble he could get into for shooting non-American civilians.

THE FOUR BICYCLES pulled up a little way from the base. Tire marks in the dust, and a patch of oil, indicated that other travelers had briefly rested there.

"What're we stopping for?" said Pepper.

"I'm thinking," said Adam.

It was hard. The bit of his mind that he knew as *himself* was still there, but it was trying to stay afloat on a fountain of tumultuous darkness. What he was aware of, though, was that his three companions were one hundred percent human. He'd got them into trouble before, in the way of torn clothes, docked pocket money, and so on, but this one was almost certainly going to involve a lot more than being confined to the house and made to tidy up your room.

On the other hand, there wasn't anyone else.

"All right," he said. "We need some stuff, I think. We need a sword, a crown, and some scales."

They stared at him.

"What, just here?" said Brian. "There's nothin' like that here."

* He'd slipped and fallen in a hotel shower when he took a holiday there in 1983. Now the mere sight of a bar of yellow soap could send him into near-fatal flashbacks.

"I dunno," said Adam. "When you think about the games and that, you know, we've played . . ."

JUST TO MAKE SGT. DEISENBURGER'S day, a car pulled up and it was floating several inches off the ground because it had no tires. Or paintwork. What it did have was a trail of blue smoke, and when it stopped it made the *pinging* noises made by metal cooling down from a very high temperature.

It looked as if it had smoked glass windows, although this was just an effect caused by it having ordinary glass windows but a smoke-filled interior.

The driver's door opened, and a cloud of choking fumes got out. Then Crowley followed it.

He waved the smoke away from his face, blinked, and then turned the gesture into a friendly wave.

"Hi," he said. "How's it going? Has the world ended yet?"

"*He won't let us in, Crowley,*" said Madame Tracy.

"Aziraphale? Is that you? Nice dress," said Crowley vaguely. He wasn't feeling very well. For the last thirty miles he had been imagining that a ton of burning metal, rubber, and leather was a fully functioning automobile, and the Bentley had been resisting him fiercely. The hard part had been to keep the whole thing rolling after the all-weather radials had burned away. Beside him the remains of the Bentley dropped suddenly onto its distorted wheel rims as he stopped imagining that it had tires.

He patted a metal surface hot enough to fry eggs on.

"You wouldn't get that sort of performance out of one of these modern cars," he said lovingly.

They stared at him.

There was a little electronic click.

The gate was rising. The housing that contained the electric motor gave a mechanical groan, and then gave up in the face of the unstoppable force acting on the barrier.

"Hey!" said Sgt. Deisenburger, "Which one of you yo-yos did that?"

Zip. Zip. Zip. Zip. And a small dog, its legs a blur.

They stared at the four ferociously pedaling figures that ducked under the barrier and disappeared into the camp.

The sergeant pulled himself together.

"Hey," he said, but much more weakly this time, "did any of them kids have some space alien with a face like a friendly turd in a bike basket?"

"Don't think so," said Crowley.

"Then," said Sgt. Deisenburger, "they're in real trouble." He raised his gun. Enough of this pussyfooting around; he kept thinking of soap. "And so," he said, "are you."

"I warns ye—" Shadwell began.

"This has gone on too long," said Aziraphale. *"Sort it out, Crowley, there's a dear chap."*

"Hmm?" said Crowley.

"I'm the nice one," said Aziraphale. *"You can't expect me to—oh, blast it. You try to do the decent thing, and where does it get you?"* He snapped his fingers.

There was a pop like an old-fashioned flashbulb, and Sgt. Thomas A. Deisenburger disappeared.

"*Er*," said Aziraphale.

"See?" said Shadwell, who hadn't quite got the hang of Madame Tracy's split personality. "Nothing to it. Ye stick by me, ye'll be all right."

"Well done," said Crowley. "Never thought you had it in you."

"*No*," said Aziraphale. "*Nor did I, in fact. I do hope I haven't sent him somewhere dreadful.*"

"You'd better get used to it right now," said Crowley. "You just send 'em. Best not to worry about where they go." He looked fascinated. "Aren't you going to introduce me to your new body?"

"*Oh? Yes. Yes, of course. Madame Tracy, this is Crowley. Crowley, Madame Tracy.* Charmed, I'm sure."

"Let's get on in," said Crowley. He looked sadly at the wreckage of the Bentley, and then brightened. A jeep was heading purposefully towards the gate, and it looked as though it was crowded with people who were about to shout questions and fire guns and not worry about which order they did this in.

He brightened up. This was more what you might call his area of competence.

He took his hands out of his pockets and he raised them like Bruce Lee and then he smiled like Lee van Cleef. "Ah," he said, "here comes transport."

THEY PARKED THEIR BIKES outside one of the low buildings. Wensleydale carefully locked his. He was that kind of boy.

"So what will these people look like?" said Pepper.

"They could look like all sorts," said Adam doubtfully.

"They're grownups, are they?" said Pepper.

"Yes," said Adam. "More grown-up than you've ever seen before, I reckon."

"Fightin' grownups is never any use," said Wensleydale gloomily. "You always get into trouble."

"You don't have to fight 'em," said Adam. "You just do what I told you."

The Them looked at the things they were carrying. As far as tools to mend the world were concerned, they did not look incredibly efficient.

"How'll we find 'em, then?" said Brian, doubtfully. "I remember when we came to the Open Day, it's all rooms and stuff. Lots of rooms and flashing lights."

Adam stared thoughtfully at the buildings. The alarms were still yodeling.

"Well," he said, "it seems to *me*—"

"Hey, what are you kids doing here?"

It wasn't a one hundred percent threatening voice, but it was near the end of its tether and it belonged to an officer who'd spent ten minutes trying to make sense of a senseless world where alarms went off and doors didn't open. Two equally harassed soldiers stood behind him, slightly at a loss as to how to deal with four short and clearly Caucasian juveniles, one of them marginally female.

"Don't you worry about us," said Adam airily. "We're jus' lookin' around."

"Now you just—" the lieutenant began.

"Go to sleep," said Adam. "You just go to sleep. All you soldiers here go to sleep. Then you won't get hurt. You all just go to sleep *now*."

The lieutenant stared at him, his eyes trying to focus. Then he pitched forward.

"Coo," said Pepper, as the others collapsed, "how did you do that?"

"Well," said Adam cautiously, "you know that bit about hypnotism in the *Boy's Own Book of 101 Things To Do* that we could never make work?"

"Yes?"

"Well, it's sort of like that, only now I've found how to do it." He turned back to the communications building.

He pulled himself together, his body unfolding from its habitual comfortable slouch into an upright bearing Mr. Tyler would have been proud of.

"Right," he said.

He thought for a while.

Then he said, "Come and see."

IF YOU TOOK THE WORLD away and just left the electricity, it would look like the most exquisite filigree ever made—a ball of twinkling silver lines with the occasional coruscating spike of a satellite beam. Even the dark areas would glow with radar and commercial radio waves. It could be the nervous system of a great beast.

Here and there cities make knots in the web but most of the electricity is, as it were, mere musculature, concerned only with crude work. But for fifty years or so people had been giving electricity brains.

And now it was alive, in the same way that fire is alive. Switches were welding shut. Relays fused. In the heart of silicon chips whose microscopic architecture looked like a street plan of Los Angeles fresh pathways opened up, and hundreds of miles away bells rang in underground rooms and men stared in horror at what certain screens were telling them. Heavy steel doors shut firmly in secret hollow mountains, leaving people on the other side to pound on them and wrestle with fuse boxes which had melted. Bits of desert and tundra slid aside, letting fresh air into air-conditioned tombs, and blunt shapes ground ponderously into position.

And while it flowed where it should not, it ebbed from its normal beds. In cities the traffic lights went, then the street lights, then all the lights. Cooling fans slowed, flickered, and stopped. Heaters faded into darkness. Lifts stuck. Radio stations choked off, their soothing music silenced.

It has been said that civilization is twenty-four hours and two meals away from barbarism.

Night was spreading slowly around the spinning Earth. It should have been full of pinpricks of light. It was not.

There were five billion people down there. What was going to happen soon would make barbarism look like a picnic—hot, nasty, and eventually given over to the ants.

DEATH STRAIGHTENED UP. He appeared to be listening intently. It was anyone's guess what he listened with.

HE IS HERE, he said.

The other three looked up. There was a barely perceptible change in the way they stood there. A moment before Death had spoken *they*, the part of them that did not walk and talk like human beings, had been wrapped around the world. Now they were back.

More or less.

There was a strangeness about them. It was as if, instead of ill-fitting suits, they now had ill-fitting bodies. Famine looked as though he had been tuned slightly off-station, so that the hitherto dominant signal—of a pleasant, thrusting, successful businessman—was beginning to be drowned out by the ancient, horrible static of his basic personality. War's skin glistened with sweat. Pollution's skin just glistened.

"It's all . . . taken care of," said War, speaking with some effort. "It'll . . . take its course."

"It's not just the nuclear," Pollution said. "It's the chemical. Thousands of gallons of stuff in . . . little tanks all over the world. Beautiful liquids . . . with eighteen syllables in their names. And the . . . old standbys. Say what you like. Plutonium may give you grief for thousands of years, but arsenic is forever."

"And then . . . winter," said Famine. "I *like* winter. There's something . . . *clean* about winter."

"Chickens coming . . . home to roost," said War.

"No more chickens," said Famine, flatly.

Only Death hadn't changed. Some things don't.

The Four left the building. It was noticeable that Pollution, while still walking, nevertheless gave the impression of oozing.

And this was noticed by Anathema and Newton Pulsifer.

It had been the first building they'd come to. It

had seemed much safer inside than out, where there seemed to be a lot of excitement. Anathema had pushed open a door covered in signs that suggested that this would be a terminally dangerous thing to do. It had swung open at her touch. When they'd gone inside, it had shut and locked itself.

There hadn't been a lot of time to discuss this after the Four had walked in.

"What were they?" said Newt. "Some kind of terrorists?"

"In a very nice and accurate sense," said Anathema, "I think you're right."

"What was all that weird talk about?"

"I think possibly the end of the world," said Anathema. "Did you see their auras?"

"I don't think so," said Newt.

"Not nice at all."

"Oh."

"Negative auras, in fact."

"Oh?"

"Like black holes."

"That's bad, is it?"

"Yes."

Anathema glared at the rows of metal cabinets. For once, just now, because it wasn't just for play but was for real, the machinery that was going to bring about the end of the world, or at least that part of it that occupied the layers between about two meters down and all the way to the ozone layer, wasn't operating according to the usual script. There were no big red canisters with flashing lights. There were no coiled wires with a "cut me" look about them. No suspiciously large numeric displays were counting down toward a zero that could be averted with seconds to spare. Instead, the metal cabinets looked solid and heavy and very resistant to last-minute heroism.

"What takes its course?" said Anathema. "They've done something, haven't they?"

"Perhaps there's an off switch?" said Newt helplessly. "I'm sure if we looked around—"

"These sort of things are wired in. Don't be silly. I thought you knew about this sort of thing."

Newt nodded desperately. This was a long way from the pages of *Easy Electronics*. For the look of the thing, he peered into the back of one of the cabinets.

"Worldwide communications," he said indistinctly. "You could do practically anything. Modulate the mains power, tap into satellites. Absolutely anything. You could"—*zhip*—"argh, you could"—*zhap*—"ouch, make things do"—*zipt*—"uh, just about"—*zzap*—"ooh."

"How are you getting on in there?"

Newt sucked his fingers. So far he hadn't found anything that resembled a transistor. He wrapped his hand in his handkerchief and pulled a couple of boards out of their sockets.

Once, one of the electronics magazines to which he subscribed had published a joke circuit which was guaranteed not to work. At last, they'd said in an amusing way, here's something all you ham-fisted hams out there can build in the certain knowledge that if it does nothing, it's working. It had diodes the wrong way round, transistors upside down, and a flat battery. Newt had built it, and it picked up

Radio Moscow. He'd written them a letter of complaint, but they never replied.

"I really don't know if I'm doing any good," he said.

"James Bond just unscrews things," said Anathema.

"Not just unscrews," said Newt, his temper fraying. "And I'm not"—*zhip*—"James Bond. If I was"—*whizzle*—"the bad guys would have shown me all the megadeath levers and told me how they bloody well worked, wouldn't they?"—*Fwizzpt*—"Only it doesn't happen like that in real life! I don't *know* what's happening and I *can't* stop it."

CLOUDS CHURNED around the horizon. Overhead the sky was still clear, the air torn by nothing more than a light breeze. But it wasn't normal air. It had a crystallized look to it, so that you might feel that if you turned your head you might see new facets. It sparkled. If you had to find a word to describe it, the word *thronged* might slip insidiously into your mind. Thronged with insubstantial beings awaiting only the right moment to become very substantial.

Adam glanced up. In one sense there was just clear air overhead. In another, stretching off to infinity, were the hosts of Heaven and Hell, wingtip to wingtip. If you looked really closely, and had been specially trained, you could tell the difference.

Silence held the bubble of the world in its grip.

The door of the building swung open and the Four stepped out. There was no more than a hint of human about three of them now—they seemed to be humanoid shapes made up of all the things they were or represented. They made Death seem positively homely. His leather greatcoat and dark-visored helmet had become a cowled robe, but these were mere details. A skeleton, even a walking one, is at least human; Death of a sort lurks inside every living creature.

"The thing is," said Adam urgently, "they're not really real. They're just like nightmares, really."

"B-but we're not asleep," said Pepper.

Dog whined and tried to hide behind Adam.

"That one looks as if he's meltin'," said Brian, pointing at the advancing figure, if such it could still be called, of Pollution.

"There you are, then," said Adam, encouragingly. "It can't be real, can it? It's common sense. Something like that can't be *reelly* real."

The Four halted a few meters away.

IT HAS BEEN DONE, said Death. He leaned forward a little and stared eyelessly at Adam. It was hard to tell if he was surprised.

"Yes, well," said Adam. "The thing *is*, I don't want it done. I never *asked* for it to be done."

Death looked at the other three, and then back to Adam.

Behind them a jeep skewed to a halt. They ignored it.

I DO NOT UNDERSTAND, he said. SURELY YOUR VERY EXISTENCE REQUIRES THE ENDING OF THE WORLD. IT IS WRITTEN.

"I dunt see why anyone has to go an' write things like that," said Adam calmly. "The world is full of all sorts of brilliant stuff and I haven't found out all about it yet, so I don't want anyone messing it about or endin' it before I've had a chance to find out about it. So you can all just go away."

(*"That's the one, Mr. Shadwell,"* said Aziraphale, his words trailing into uncertainty even as he uttered them, *"the one with . . . the . . . T-shirt . . ."*)

Death stared at Adam.

"You . . . are part . . . of us," said War, between teeth like beautiful bullets.

"It is done. We make . . . the . . . world . . . anew," said Pollution, his voice as insidious as something leaking out of a corroded drum into a water table.

"You . . . lead . . . us," said Famine.

And Adam hesitated. Voices inside him still cried out that this was true, and that the world was his as well, and all he had to do was turn and lead them out across a bewildered planet. They were his kind of people.

In tiers above, the hosts of the sky waited for the Word.

("Ye canna want me to shoot him! He's but a bairn!"

"Er," said Aziraphale. *"Er. Yes. Perhaps we'd just better wait a bit, what do you think?"*

"Until he grows up, do you mean?" said Crowley.)

Dog began to growl.

Adam looked at the Them. *They* were his kind of people, too.

You just had to decide who your friends really were.

He turned back to the Four.

"Get them," said Adam, quietly.

The slouch and slur was gone from his voice. It

had strange harmonics. No one human could disobey a voice like that.

War laughed, and looked expectantly at the Them.

"Little boys," she said, "playing with your toys. Think of all the toys I can offer you . . . think of all the *games.* I can make you fall in love with me, little boys. Little boys with your little guns."

She laughed again, but the machine-gun stutter died away as Pepper stepped forward and raised a trembling arm.

It wasn't much of a sword, but it was about the best you could do with two bits of wood and a piece of string. War stared at it.

"*I see,*" she said. "Mano e mano, eh?" She drew her own blade and brought it up so that it made a noise like a finger being dragged around a wineglass.

There was a flash as they connected.

Death stared into Adam's eyes.

There was a pathetic jingling noise.

"Don't touch it!" snapped Adam, without moving his head.

The Them stared at the sword rocking to a standstill on the concrete path.

"'Little boys,'" muttered Pepper, disgustedly. Sooner or later everyone has to decide which gang they belong to.

"But, but," said Brian, "she sort of got sucked up the sword—"

The air between Adam and Death began to vibrate, as in a heatwave.

Wensleydale raised his head and looked Famine in the sunken eye. He held up something that, with a bit of imagination, could be considered to be a pair of scales made of more string and twigs. Then he whirled it around his head.

Famine stuck out a protective arm.

There was another flash, and then the jingle of a pair of silver scales bouncing on the ground.

"Don't . . . touch . . . them," said Adam.

Pollution had already started to run, or at least to flow quickly, but Brian snatched the circle of grass stalks from his own head and flung it. It shouldn't have handled like one, but a force took it out of his hands and it whirred like a discus.

This time the explosion was a red flame inside a billow of black smoke, and it smelled of oil.

With a rolling, tinny little sound a blackened silver crown bowled out of the smoke and then spun round with a noise like a settling penny.

At least they needed no warning about touching it. It glistened in a way that metal should not.

"Where'd they go?" said Wensley.

WHERE THEY BELONG, said Death, still holding Adam's gaze. WHERE THEY HAVE ALWAYS BEEN. BACK IN THE MINDS OF MAN.

He grinned at Adam.

There was a tearing sound. Death's robe split and his wings unfolded. Angel's wings. But not of feathers. They were wings of night, wings that were shapes cut through the matter of creation into the darkness underneath, in which a few distant lights glimmered, lights that may have been stars or may have been something entirely else.

BUT I, he said, AM NOT LIKE THEM. I AM AZRAEL, CREATED TO BE CREATION'S

SHADOW. YOU CANNOT DESTROY ME. THAT WOULD DESTROY THE WORLD.

The heat of their stare faded. Adam scratched his nose.

"Oh, I don't know," he said. "There might be a way." He grinned back.

"Anyway, it's going to stop now," he said. "All this stuff with the machines. You've got to do what I say just for now, and I say it's got to stop."

Death shrugged. IT IS STOPPING ALREADY, he said. WITHOUT THEM, he indicated the pathetic remnants of the other three Horsepersons, IT CANNOT PROCEED. NORMAL ENTROPY TRIUMPHS. Death raised a bony hand in what might have been a salute.

THEY'LL BE BACK, he said. THEY'RE NEVER FAR AWAY.

The wings flapped, just once, like a thunderclap, and the angel of Death vanished.

"Right, then," said Adam, to the empty air. "All right. It's not going to happen. All the stuff they started—it must stop *now*."

NEWT STARED desperately at the equipment racks.

"You'd think there'd be a manual or something," he said.

"We could see if Agnes has anything to say," volunteered Anathema.

"Oh, yes," said Newt bitterly. "That makes sense, does it? Sabotaging twentieth-century electronics with the aid of a seventeenth-century workshop manual? What did Agnes Nutter know of the transistor?"

"Well, my grandfather interpreted prediction 3328 rather neatly in 1948 and made some very shrewd investments," said Anathema. "She didn't know what it was going to be called, of course, and she wasn't very sound about electricity in general, but—"

"I was speaking rhetorically."

"You don't have to make it work, anyway. You have to stop it working. You don't need knowledge for that, you need ignorance."

Newt groaned.

"All right," he said wearily. "Let's try it. Give me a prediction."

Anathema pulled out a card at random.

"'He is Not that Which He Says he Is,'" she read. "It's number 1002. Very simple. Any ideas?"

"Well, look," said Newt, wretchedly, "this isn't really the time to say it but,"—he swallowed—"actually I'm not very good with electronics. Not very good at all."

"You said you were a computer engineer, I seem to remember."

"That was an exaggeration. I mean, just about as much of an exaggeration as you can possibly get, in fact, really, I suppose it was more what you might call an overstatement. I might go so far as to say that what it really was," Newt closed his eyes, "was a prevarication."

"A lie, you mean?" said Anathema sweetly.

"Oh, I wouldn't go *that* far," said Newt. "Although," he added, "I'm not actually a computer engineer. At all. Quite the opposite."

"What's the opposite?"

"If you must know, every time I try and make anything electronic work, it stops."

Anathema gave him a bright little smile, and posed theatrically, like that moment in every conjurer's stage act when the lady in the sequins steps back to reveal the trick.

"Tra-la," she said.

"Repair it," she said.

"What?"

"Make it work better," she said.

"I don't know," said Newt. "I'm not sure I can." He laid a hand on top of the nearest cabinet.

There was the noise of something he hadn't realized he'd been hearing suddenly stopping, and the descending whine of a distant generator. The lights on the panels flickered, and most of them went out.

All over the world, people who had been wrestling with switches found that they switched. Circuit breakers opened. Computers stopped planning World War III and went back to idly scanning the stratosphere. In bunkers under Novaya Zemlya, men found that the fuses they were frantically trying to pull out came away in their hands at last; in bunkers under Wyoming and Nebraska, men in fatigues stopped screaming and waving guns at one another, and would have had a beer if alcohol had been allowed in missile bases. It wasn't, but they had one anyway.

The lights came on. Civilization stopped its slide into chaos, and started writing letters to the newspapers about how people got overexcited about the least little thing these days.

In Tadfield, the machines ceased radiating menace. Something that had been in them was gone, quite apart from the electricity.

"Gosh," said Newt.

"There you are," said Anathema. "You fixed it *good.* You can trust old Agnes, take it from me. Now let's get out of here."

"HE DIDN'T WANT TO DO IT!" said Aziraphale. *"Haven't I always told you, Crowley? If you take the trouble to look, deep down inside anyone, you'll find that at bottom they're really quite—"*

"It's not over," said Crowley flatly.

Adam turned and appeared to notice them for the first time. Crowley was not used to people identifying him so readily, but Adam stared at him as though Crowley's entire life history was pasted inside the back of his skull and he, Adam, was reading it. For an instant he knew real terror. He'd always thought the sort he'd felt before was the genuine article, but that was mere abject fear beside this new sensation. Those Below could make you cease to exist by, well, hurting you in unbearable amounts, but this boy could not only make you cease to exist merely by thinking about it, but probably could arrange matters so that you never had existed at all.

Adam's gaze swept to Aziraphale.

" 'Scuse me, why're you two people?" said Adam.

"Well," said Aziraphale, *"it's a long—"*

"It's not right, being two people," said Adam. "I

reckon you'd better go back to being two sep'rate people."

There were no showy special effects. There was just Aziraphale, sitting next to Madame Tracy.

"Ooh, that felt tingly," she said. She looked Aziraphale up and down. "Oh," she said, in a slightly disappointed voice. "Somehow, I thought you'd be younger."

Shadwell glowered jealously at the angel and thumbed the Thundergun's hammer in a pointed sort of way.

Aziraphale looked down at his new body which was, unfortunately, very much like his old body, although the overcoat was cleaner.

"Well, that's over," he said.

"No," said Crowley. "No. It isn't, you see. Not at all."

Now there *were* clouds overhead, curling like a pot of tagliatelle on full boil.

"You see," said Crowley, his voice leaden with fatalistic gloom, "it doesn't really work that simply. You think wars get started because some old duke gets shot, or someone cuts off someone's ear, or someone's sited their missiles in the wrong place. It's not like that. That's just, well, just *reasons*, which haven't got anything to do with it. What really causes wars is two sides that can't stand the sight of one another and the pressure builds up and up and then anything will cause it. Anything at all. What's your name . . . er . . . boy?"

"That's Adam Young," said Anathema, as she strode up with Newt trailing after her.

"That's right. Adam Young," said Adam.

"Good effort. You've saved the world. Have a half-holiday," said Crowley. "But it won't really make any difference."

"I think you're right," said Aziraphale. "I'm sure my people *want* Armageddon. It's very sad."

"Would anyone mind telling us what's going on?" said Anathema sternly, folding her arms.

Aziraphale shrugged. "It's a very long story," he began.

Anathema stuck out her chin. "Go on, then," she said.

"Well. In the Beginning—"

The lightning flashed, struck the ground a few meters from Adam, and stayed there, a sizzling column that broadened at the base, as though the wild electricity was filling an invisible mold. The humans pressed back against the jeep.

The lightning vanished, and a young man made out of golden fire stood there.

"Oh dear," said Aziraphale. "It's him."

"Him who?" said Crowley.

"The Voice of God," said the angel. "The Metatron."

The Them stared.

Then Pepper said, "No, it isn't. The Metatron's made of plastic and it's got laser cannon and it can turn into a helicopter."

"That's the Cosmic Megatron," said Wensleydale weakly. "I had one, but the head fell off. I think this one is different."

The beautiful blank gaze fell on Adam Young, and then turned sharply to look at the concrete beside it, which was boiling.

A figure rose from the churning ground in the manner of the demon king in a pantomime, but if this one was ever in a pantomime, it was one where no one walked out alive and they had to get a priest to burn the place down afterwards. It was not greatly different to the other figure, except that its flames were blood-red.

"Er," said Crowley, trying to shrink into his seat. "Hi . . . er."

The red thing gave him the briefest of glances, as though marking him for future consumption, and then stared at Adam. When it spoke, its voice was like a million flies taking off in a hurry.

It buzzed a word that felt, to those humans who heard it, like a file dragged down the spine.

It was talking to Adam, who said, "Huh? No. I said already. My name's Adam Young." He looked the figure up and down. "What's yours?"

"Beelzebub," Crowley supplied. "He's the Lord of—"

"Thank you, Crowzley," said Beelzebub. "Later we muzzed have a seriouzz talk. I am sure thou hazzt muzzch to tell me."

"Er," said Crowley, "well, you see, what happened was—"

"Silenzz!"

"Right. Right," said Crowley hurriedly.

"Now then, Adam Young," said the Metatron, "while we can of course appreciate your assistance at this point, we must add that Armageddon should take place *now*. There may be some temporary inconvenience, but that should hardly stand in the way of the ultimate good."

"Ah," whispered Crowley to Aziraphale, "what he means is, we have to destroy the world in order to save it."

"Azz to what it standz in the way of, that hazz yet to be decided," buzzed Beelzebub. "But it muzzt be decided *now*, boy. That izz thy deztiny. It is written."

Adam took a deep breath. The human watchers held theirs. Crowley and Aziraphale had forgotten to breathe some time ago.

"I just don't see why everyone and everything has to be burned up and everything," Adam said. "Millions of fish an' whales an' trees an', an' sheep and stuff. An' not even for anything important. Jus' to see who's got the best gang. It's like us an' the Johnsonites. But even if you win, you can't really beat the other side, because you don't really want to. I mean, not for good. You'll just start all over again. You'll just keep on sending people like these two," he pointed to Crowley and Aziraphale, "to mess people around. It's hard enough bein' people as it is, without other people coming and messin' you around."

Crowley turned to Aziraphale.

"Johnsonites?" he whispered.

The angel shrugged. "Early breakaway sect, I think," he said. "Sort of Gnostics. Like the Ophites." His forehead wrinkled. "Or were they the Sethites? No, I'm thinking of the Collyridians. Oh dear. I'm sorry, there were hundreds of them, it's so hard to keep track."

"People bein' messed around," murmured Crowley.

"It doesn't matter!" snapped the Metatron. "The

whole point of the creation of the Earth and Good and Evil—"

"I don't see what's so triffic about creating people as people and then gettin' upset 'cos they act like people," said Adam severely. "Anyway, if you stopped tellin' people it's all sorted out after they're dead, they might try sorting it all out while they're alive. If *I* was in charge, I'd try makin' people live a lot longer, like ole Methuselah. It'd be a lot more interestin' and they might start thinkin' about the sort of things they're doing to all the enviro*m*ent and ecology, because they'll still be around in a hundred years' time."

"Ah," said Beelzebub, and he actually began to smile. "You wizzsh to rule the world. That'z more like thy Fath—"

"I thought about all that an' I don't want to," said Adam, half turning and nodding encouragingly at the Them. "I mean, there's some stuff could do with alt'rin', but then I expect people'd keep comin' up to me and gettin' me to sort out everythin' the whole time and get rid of all the rubbish and make more trees for 'em, and where's the good in all that? It's like havin' to tidy up people's bedrooms for them."

"You never tidy up even *your* bedroom," said Pepper, behind him.

"I never said anythin' about *my* bedroom," said Adam, referring to a room whose carpet had been lost to view for several years. "It's general bedrooms I mean. I dint mean my personal bedroom. It's an analoggy. That's jus' what I'm sayin'."

Beelzebub and the Metatron looked at one another.

"Anyway," said Adam, "it's bad enough having to think of things for Pepper and Wensley and Brian to do all the time so they don't get bored, so I don't want any more world than I've got. Thank you all the same."

The Metatron's face began to take on the look familiar to all those subjected to Adam's idiosyncratic line of reasoning.

"You *can't* refuse to be who you are," it said eventually. "Listen. Your birth and destiny are part of the Great Plan. Things *have* to happen like this. All the choices have been made."

"Rebellion izz a fine thing," said Beelzebub, "but some thingz are beyond rebellion. You muzzt understand!"

"I'm not rebelling against anything," said Adam in a reasonable tone of voice. "I'm pointin' out things. Seems to me you can't blame people for pointin' out things. Seems to me it'd be a lot better not to start fightin' and jus' see what people do. If you stop messin' them about they might start thinkin' properly an' they might stop messin' the world around. I'm not sayin' they *would*," he added conscientiously, "but they might."

"This makes no sense," said the Metatron. "You can't run counter to the Great Plan. You must *think*. It's in your genes. *Think*."

Adam hesitated.

The dark undercurrent was always ready to flow back, its reedy whisper saying yes, that was it, that was what it was all about, you have to follow the Plan because you were part of it—

It had been a long day. He was tired. Saving the world took it out of an eleven-year-old body.

Crowley stuck his head in his hands. "For a moment there, just for a moment, I thought we had a chance," he said. "He had them worried. Oh, well, it was nice while—"

He was aware that Aziraphale had stood up.

"Excuse me," said the angel.

The trio looked at him.

"This Great Plan," he said, "this would be the *ineffable* Plan, would it?"

There was a moment's silence.

"It's the Great Plan," said the Metatron flatly. "You are well aware. There shall be a world lasting six thousand years and it will conclude with—"

"Yes, yes, that's the Great Plan all right," said Aziraphale. He spoke politely and respectfully, but with the air of one who has just asked an unwelcome question at a political meeting and won't go away until he gets an answer. "I was just asking if it's ineffable as well. I just want to be clear on this point."

"It doesn't matter!" snapped the Metatron. "It's the same thing, surely!"

Surely? thought Crowley. They don't actually *know*. He started to grin like an idiot.

"So you're not one hundred percent clear on this?" said Aziraphale.

"It's not given to us to understand the *ineffable* Plan," said the Metatron, "but of course the Great Plan—"

"But the Great Plan can only be a tiny part of the overall ineffability," said Crowley. "You can't be certain that what's happening right now isn't exactly right, from an ineffable point of view."

"It izz written!" bellowed Beelzebub.

"But it might be written differently somewhere else," said Crowley. "Where you can't read it."

"In bigger letters," said Aziraphale.

"Underlined," Crowley added.

"Twice," suggested Aziraphale.

"Perhaps this isn't just a test of the world," said Crowley. "It might be a test of you people, too. Hmm?"

"God does not play games with His loyal servants," said the Metatron, but in a worried tone of voice.

"Whooo-eee," said Crowley. "Where have you *been*?"

Everyone found their eyes turning toward Adam. He seemed to be thinking very carefully.

Then he said: "I don't see why it matters what is written. Not when it's about people. It can always be crossed out."

A breeze swept across the airfield. Overhead, the assembled hosts rippled, like a mirage.

There was the kind of silence there might have been on the day before Creation.

Adam stood smiling at the two of them, a small figure perfectly poised exactly between Heaven and Hell.

Crowley grabbed Aziraphale's arm. "You know what happened?" he hissed excitedly. "He was left alone! He grew up human! He's not Evil Incarnate or Good Incarnate, he's just . . . a *human* incarnate—"

Then:

"I think," said the Metatron, "that I shall need to seek further instructions."

"I alzzo," said Beelzebub. His raging face turned to Crowley. "And I shall report of your part in thizz, thou hast better believe it." He glared at Adam. "And I do not know what *thy Father* will say . . ."

There was a thundering explosion. Shadwell, who had been fidgeting with horrified excitement for some minutes, had finally got enough control of his trembling fingers to pull the trigger.

The pellets passed through the space where Beelzebub had been. Shadwell never knew how lucky he had been that he'd missed.

The sky wavered, and then became just sky. Around the horizon, the clouds began to unravel.

MADAME TRACY BROKE THE SILENCE.

"Weren't they odd," she said.

She didn't mean "weren't they odd"; what she did mean she probably could never hope to express, except by screaming, but the human brain has amazing recuperative powers and saying "weren't they odd" was part of the rapid healing process. Within half an hour, she'd be thinking she'd just had too much to drink.

"Is it over, do you think?" said Aziraphale.

Crowley shrugged. "Not for us, I'm afraid."

"I don't think you need to go worryin'," said

Adam gnomically. "I know all about you two. Don't you worry."

He looked at the rest of the Them, who tried not to back away. He seemed to think for a while, and then he said, "There's been too much messin' around anyway. But it seems to me everyone's goin' to be a lot happier if they forget about this. Not actually *forget*, just not remember exactly. An' then we can go home."

"But you can't just leave it at that!" said Anathema, pushing forward. "Think of all the things you could do! *Good* things."

"Like what?" said Adam suspiciously.

"Well . . . you could bring all the whales back, to start with."

He put his head on one side. "An' that'd stop people killing them, would it?"

She hesitated. It would have been nice to say yes.

"An' if people *do* start killing 'em, what would you ask me to do about 'em?" said Adam. "No. I reckon I'm getting the hang of this now. Once I start messing around like that, there'd be no stoppin' it. Seems to me, the only sensible thing is for people to know if they kill a whale, they've got a dead whale."

"That shows a very responsible attitude," said Newt.

Adam raised an eyebrow.

"It's just sense," he said.

Aziraphale patted Crowley on the back. "We seem to have survived," he said. "Just imagine how terrible it might have been if we'd been at all competent."

"Um," said Crowley.

"Is your car operational?"

"I think it might need a bit of work," Crowley admitted.

"I was thinking that we might take these good people into town," said Aziraphale. "I owe Madame Tracy a meal, I'm sure. And her young man, of course."

Shadwell looked over his shoulder, and then up at Madame Tracy.

"Who's he talking aboot?" he asked her triumphant expression.

Adam rejoined the Them.

"I reckon we'll just be gettin' home," he said.

"But what actually *happened*?" said Pepper. "I mean, there was all this—"

"It doesn't matter any more," said Adam.

"But you could help so much—" Anathema began, as they wandered back to their bikes. Newt took her gently by the arm.

"That's not a good idea," he said. "Tomorrow is the first day of the rest of our lives."

"Do you know," she said, "of all the trite sayings I've ever really hated, that comes top?"

"Amazing, isn't it," said Newt happily.

"Why've you got 'Dick Turpin' painted on the door of your car?"

"It's a joke, really," said Newt.

"Hmm?"

"Because everywhere I go, I hold up traffic," he mumbled wretchedly.

Crowley looked glumly at the controls of the jeep.

"I'm sorry about the car," Aziraphale was saying.

"I know how much you liked it. Perhaps if you concentrated really hard—"

"It wouldn't be the same," said Crowley.

"I suppose not."

"I had it from new, you know. It wasn't a car, it was more a sort of whole body glove."

He sniffed.

"What's burning?" he said.

A breeze swept up the dust and dropped it again. The air became hot and heavy, imprisoning those within it like flies in syrup.

He turned his head, and looked into Aziraphale's horrified expression.

"But it's *over,*" he said. "It *can't* happen now! The—the thing, the correct moment or whatever—it's gone past! It's *over*!"

The ground began to shake. The noise was like a subway train, but not one passing under. It was more like the sound of one coming up.

Crowley fumbled madly with the gear shift.

"That's not Beelzebub!" he shouted, above the noise of the wind. "That's *Him.* His Father! This isn't Armageddon, this is *personal.* Start, you bloody thing!"

The ground moved under Anathema and Newt, flinging them onto the dancing concrete. Yellow smoke gushed from between the cracks.

"It feels like a volcano!" shouted Newt. "What is it?"

"Whatever it is, it's pretty angry," said Anathema.

In the jeep, Crowley was cursing. Aziraphale laid a hand on his shoulder.

"There are humans here," he said.

"Yes," said Crowley. "*And* me."

"I mean we shouldn't let this happen to them."

"Well, what—" Crowley began, and stopped.

"I mean, when you think about it, we've got them into enough trouble as it is. You and me. Over the years. What with one thing and another."

"We were only doing our jobs," muttered Crowley.

"Yes. So what? Lots of people in history have only done their jobs and look at the trouble *they* caused."

"You don't mean we should actually try to stop *Him*?"

"What have you got to lose?"

Crowley started to argue, and realized that he couldn't. There *was* nothing he could lose that he hadn't lost already. They couldn't do anything worse to him than he had coming to him already. He felt free at last.

He also felt under the seat and found a tire iron. It wouldn't be any good, but then, nothing would. In fact it'd be much more terrible facing the Adversary with anything like a decent weapon. That way you might have a bit of hope, which would make it worse.

Aziraphale picked up the sword lately dropped by War, and hefted its weight thoughtfully.

"Gosh, it's been years since I used this," he murmured.

"About six thousand," said Crowley.

"My word, yes," said the angel. "What a day that was, and no mistake. Good old days."

"Not really," said Crowley. The noise was growing.

"People knew the difference between right and wrong in those days," said Aziraphale dreamily.

"Well, *yes*. Think about it."

"Ah. Yes. Too much messin' about?"

"*Yes.*"

Aziraphale held up the sword. There was a *whoomph* as it suddenly flamed like a bar of magnesium.

"Once you've learned how to do it, you never forget," he said.

He smiled at Crowley.

"I'd just like to say," he said, "if we don't get out of this, that . . . I'll have known, deep down inside, that there was a spark of goodness in you."

"That's right," said Crowley bitterly. "Make my day."

Aziraphale held out his hand.

"Nice knowing you," he said.

Crowley took it.

"Here's to the next time," he said. "And . . . Aziraphale?"

"Yes."

"Just remember I'll have known that, deep down inside, you were just enough of a bastard to be worth liking."

There was a scuffling noise, and they were pushed aside by the small but dynamic shape of Shadwell, waving the Thundergun purposefully.

"I wouldna' trust you two Southern nancy boys to kill a lame rat in a barrel," he said. "Who're we fightin' noo?"

"The Devil," said Aziraphale, simply.

Shadwell nodded, as if this hadn't come as a

surprise, threw the gun down, and took off his hat to expose a forehead known and feared wherever street-fighting men were gathered together.

"Ah reckoned so," he said. "In that case, I'm gonna use mah *haid.*"

Newt and Anathema watched the three of them walk unsteadily away from the jeep. With Shadwell in the middle, they looked like a stylized W.

"What on earth are they going to do?" said Newt. "And what's happening—*what's happening to them?*"

The coats of Aziraphale and Crowley split along the seams. If you were going to go, you might as well go in your own true shape. Feathers unfolded towards the sky.

Contrary to popular belief, the wings of demons are the same as the wings of angels, although they're often better groomed.

"Shadwell shouldn't be going with them!" said Newt, staggering to his feet.

"What's a Shadwell?"

"He's my serg—he's this amazing old man, you'd never believe it . . . I've got to help him!"

"*Help* him?" said Anathema.

"I took an oath and everything." Newt hesitated. "Well, sort of an oath. And he gave me a month's wages in advance!"

"Who're those other two, then? Friends of yours—" Anathema began, and stopped. Aziraphale had half turned, and the profile had finally clicked into place.

"I know where I've seen him before!" she shouted, pulling herself upright against Newt as the ground bounced up and down. "Come on!"

"But something dreadful's going to happen!"

"If he's damaged The Book, you're bloody well right!"

Newt fumbled in his lapel and found his official pin. He didn't know what they were going up against this time, but a pin was all he had.

They ran . . .

Adam looked around. He looked down.
His face took on an expression
of calculated innocence.

There was a moment of conflict.
But Adam was on his own ground.
Always, and ultimately, on his own ground.

He moved one hand around
in a blurred
half circle.

. . . Aziraphale and Crowley felt the world *change.*

There was no noise. There were no cracks. There was just that where there had been the beginnings of a volcano of Satanic power, there was just clearing smoke, and a car drawing slowly to a halt, its engine loud in the evening hush.

It was an elderly car, but well preserved. Not using Crowley's method, though, where dents were simply wished away; this car looked like it did, you knew instinctively, because its owner had spent every weekend for two decades doing all the things the manual said should be done every weekend. Before every journey he walked around it and checked the lights and counted the wheels. Serious-minded men who smoked pipes and wore mustaches had written serious instructions saying that this should be done, and so he did it, because he was a serious-minded man who smoked a pipe and wore a mustache and did not take such injunctions lightly, because if you did, where would you be? He had exactly the right amount of insurance. He drove three miles per hour below the speed limit, or forty miles per hour, whichever was the lower. He wore a tie, even on Saturdays.

Archimedes said that with a long enough lever and a solid enough place to stand, he could move the world.

He could have stood on Mr. Young.

The car door opened and Mr. Young emerged.

"What's going on here?" he said. "Adam? Adam!"

But the Them were streaking towards the gate.

Mr. Young looked at the shocked assembly. At least Crowley and Aziraphale had had enough self-control left to winch in their wings.

"What's he been getting up to now?" he sighed, not really expecting an answer.

"Where's that boy got to? Adam! Come back here this instant!"

Adam seldom did what his father wanted.

SGT. THOMAS A. DEISENBURGER opened his eyes. The only thing strange about his surroundings was how familiar they were. There was his high school photograph on the wall, and his little Stars and Stripes flag in the toothmug, next to his toothbrush, and even his little teddy bear, still in its little uniform. The early afternoon sun flooded through his bedroom window.

He could smell apple pie. That was one of the things he'd missed most about spending his Saturday nights a long way from home.

He walked downstairs.

His mother was at the stove, taking a huge apple pie out of the oven to cool.

"Hi, Tommy," she said. "I thought you was in England."

"Yes, Mom, I am normatively in England, Mom, protecting democratism, Mom, sir," said Sgt. Thomas A. Deisenburger.

"That's nice, hon," said his mother. "Your Poppa's down in the Big Field, with Chester and Ted. They'll be pleased to see you."

Sgt. Thomas A. Deisenburger nodded.

He took off his military-issue helmet and his military-issue jacket, and he rolled up his military-issue shirtsleeves. For a moment he looked more thoughtful than he had ever done in his life. Part of his thoughts were occupied with apple pie.

"Mom, if any throughput eventuates premising to interface with Sgt. Thomas A. Deisenburger telephonically, Mom, sir, this individual will be—"

"Sorry, Tommy?"

Tom Deisenburger hung his gun on the wall, above his father's battered old rifle.

"I said, if anyone calls, Mom, I'll be down in the Big Field, with Pop and Chester and Ted."

THE VAN DROVE SLOWLY up to the gates of the air base. It pulled over. The guard on the midnight shift looked in the window, checked the credentials of the driver, and waved him in.

The van meandered across the concrete.

It parked on the tarmac of the empty airstrip, near where two men sat, sharing a bottle of wine. One of the men wore dark glasses. Surprisingly, no one else seemed to be paying them the slightest attention.

"Are you saying," said Crowley, "that He planned it this way all along? From the very beginning?"

Aziraphale conscientiously wiped the top of the bottle and passed it back.

"Could have," he said. "Could have. One could always ask Him, I suppose."

"From what I remember," replied Crowley, thoughtfully, "—and we were never actually on what you might call speaking terms—He wasn't exactly one for a straight answer. In fact, in fact, He'd never answer at all. He'd just *smile*, as if He knew something that you didn't."

"And of course that's true," said the angel. "Otherwise, what'd be the point?"

There was a pause, and both beings stared reflectively off into the distance, as if they were remembering things that neither of them had thought of for a long time.

The van driver got out of the van, carrying a cardboard box and a pair of tongs.

Lying on the tarmac were a tarnished metal crown and a pair of scales. The man picked them up with the tongs and placed them in the box.

Then he approached the couple with the bottle.

"Excuse me, gents," he said, "but there's meant to be a sword around here somewhere as well, at least, that's what it says here at any rate, and I was wondering . . ."

Aziraphale seemed embarrassed. He looked around himself, vaguely puzzled, then stood up, to discover that he had been sitting on the sword for the last hour or so. He reached down and picked it up. "Sorry," he said, and put the sword into the box.

The van driver, who wore an International Express cap, said not to mention it, and really it was a godsend them both being there like this, since someone was going to have to sign to say that he'd duly collected what he'd been sent for, and this had certainly been a day to remember, eh?

Aziraphale and Crowley both agreed with him that it had, and Aziraphale signed the clipboard that the van driver gave him, witnessing that a crown, a pair of balances, and a sword had been received in good order and were to be delivered to a smudged address and charged to a blurred account number.

The man began to walk back to his van. Then he stopped, and turned.

"If I was to tell my wife what happened to me today," he told them, a little sadly, "she'd never believe me. And I wouldn't blame her, because I don't either." And he climbed into his van, and he drove away.

Crowley stood up, a little unsteadily. He reached a hand down to Aziraphale.

"Come on," he said. "I'll drive us back to London."

He took a Jeep. No one stopped them.

It had a cassette player. This isn't general issue, even for American military vehicles, but Crowley automatically assumed that all vehicles he drove would have cassette players and therefore this one did, within seconds of his getting in.

The cassette that he put on as he drove was marked Handel's *Water Music*, and it stayed Handel's *Water Music* all the way home.

SUNDAY

(The first day
of the rest of
their lives.)

AT AROUND HALF PAST TEN the paper boy brought the Sunday papers to the front door of Jasmine Cottage. He had to make three trips.

The series of thumps as they hit the mat woke up Newton Pulsifer.

He left Anathema asleep. She was pretty shattered, poor thing. She'd been almost incoherent when he'd put her to bed. She'd run her life according to the *Prophecies* and now there were no more prophecies. She must be feeling like a train which had reached the end of the line but still had to keep going, somehow.

From now on she'd be able to go through life with everything coming as a surprise, just like everyone else. What luck.

The telephone rang.

Newt dashed for the kitchen and picked up the receiver on the second ring.

"Hello?" he said.

A voice of forced friendliness tinted with desperation gabbled at him.

"No," he said, "I'm not. And it's not Devissey, it's Device. As in Nice. And she's asleep.

"Well," he said, "I'm pretty sure she doesn't want

any cavities insulated. Or double glazing. I mean, she doesn't own the cottage, you know. She's only renting it."

"No, I'm *not* going to wake her up and ask her," he said. "And tell me, Miss, uh . . . right, Miss Morrow, why don't you lot take Sundays off, like everybody else does?"

"*Sunday*," he said. "Of course it's not Saturday. Why would it be Saturday? Saturday was yesterday. It's honestly Sunday today, really. What do you mean, you've lost a day? *I* haven't got it. Seems to me you've got a bit carried away with selling . . . Hello?"

He growled, and replaced the receiver.

Telephone salespeople! Something dreadful ought to happen to them.

He was assailed by a moment of sudden doubt. Today *was* Sunday, wasn't it? A glance at the Sunday papers reassured him. If the Sunday *Times* said it was Sunday, you could be sure that they'd investigated the matter. And yesterday was Saturday. Of course. Yesterday was Saturday, and he'd never forget Saturday for as long as he lived, if only he could remember what it was he wasn't meant to forget.

Seeing that he was in the kitchen, Newt decided to make breakfast.

He moved around the kitchen as quietly as possible, to avoid waking the rest of the household, and found every sound magnified. The antique fridge had a door that shut like the crack of doom. The kitchen tap dribbled like an incontinent gerbil and made a noise like Old Faithful. And he couldn't find where anything was. In the end, as every human being who has ever breakfasted on their own in someone else's kitchen has done since nearly the dawn of time, he made do with unsweetened instant black coffee.*

On the kitchen table was a roughly rectangular, leather-bound cinder. He could just make out the words 'Ni e and Acc' on the charred cover. What a difference a day made, he thought. It turns you from the ultimate reference book to a mere barbecue briquette.

Now, then. How, exactly, had they got it? He recalled a man who smelled of smoke and wore sunglasses even in darkness. And there was other stuff, all running together . . . boys on bikes . . . an unpleasant buzzing . . . a small, grubby, staring face . . . It all hung around in his mind, not exactly forgotten but forever hanging on the cusp of recollection,

* Except for Giovanni Jacopo Casanova (1725–1798), famed amourist and literatéur, who revealed in volume 12 of his Memoirs that, as a matter of course, he carried around with him at all times a small valise containing "a loaf of bread, a pot of choice Seville marmalade, a knife, fork, and small spoon for stirring, 2 fresh eggs packed with care in unspun wool, a tomato or love-apple, a small frying pan, a small sauce pan, a spirit burner, a chafing dish, a tin box of salted butter of the Italian type, 2 bone china plates. Also a portion of honey comb, as a sweetener, for my breath and for my coffee. Let my readers understand me when I say to them all: A true gentleman should always be able to break his fast in the manner of a gentleman, wheresoever he may find himself."

a memory of things that hadn't happened.* How could you have that?

He sat staring at the wall until a knock at the door brought him back to earth.

There was a small dapper man in a black raincoat standing on the doorstep. He was holding a cardboard box and he gave Newt a bright smile.

"Mr."—he consulted a piece of paper in one hand—"Pulzifer?"

"Pulsifer," said Newt. "It's a hard *ess.*"

"I'm ever so sorry," said the man. "I've only ever seen it written down. Er. Well, then. It would appear that this is for you and Mrs. Pulsifer."

Newt gave him a blank look.

"There is no Mrs. Pulsifer," he said coldly.

The man removed his bowler hat.

"Oh, I'm terribly sorry," he said.

"I mean that . . . well, there's my mother," said

* And there was the matter of Dick Turpin. It looked like the same car, except that for ever afterwards it seemed able to do 250 miles on a gallon of petrol, ran so quietly that you practically had to put your mouth over the exhaust pipe to see if the engine was firing, and issued its voice-synthesized warnings in a series of exquisite and perfectly phrased haikus, each one original and apt . . .

Late frost burns the bloom
Would a fool not let the belt
Restrain the body?

. . . it would say. And,

The cherry blossom
Tumbles from the highest tree.
One needs more petrol.

Newt. "But she's not dead, she's just in Dorking. I'm not married."

"How odd. The letter is quite, er, specific."

"Who *are* you?" said Newt. He was wearing only his trousers, and it was chilly on the doorstep.

The man balanced the box awkwardly and fished out a card from an inner pocket. He handed it to Newt.

GILES BADDICOMBE

Robey, Robey, Redfearn and Bychance

Solicitors

13 Demdyke Chambers,

PRESTON

"Yes?" he said politely. "And what can I do for you, Mr. Baddicombe?"

"You could let me in," said Mr. Baddicombe.

"You're not serving a writ or anything, are you?" said Newt. The events of last night hung in his memory like a cloud, constantly changing whenever he thought he could make out a picture, but he was vaguely aware of damaging things and had been expecting retribution in some form.

"No," said Mr. Baddicombe, looking slightly hurt. "We have people for that sort of thing."

He wandered past Newt and put the box down on the table.

"To be honest," he said, "we're all very interested in this. Mr. Bychance nearly came down himself, but he doesn't travel well these days."

"Look," said Newt, "I really haven't the faintest idea what you're talking about."

"This," said Mr. Baddicombe, proffering the box and beaming like Aziraphale about to attempt a conjuring trick, "is yours. Someone wanted you to have it. They were very specific."

"A present?" said Newt. He eyed the taped cardboard cautiously, and then rummaged in the kitchen drawer for a sharp knife.

"I think more a bequest," said Mr. Baddicombe. "You see, we've had it for three hundred years. Sorry. Was it something I said? Hold it under the tap, I should."

"What the hell is this all about?" said Newt, but a certain icy suspicion was creeping over him. He sucked at the cut.

"It's a funny story—do you mind if I sit down?—and of course I don't know the full details because I joined the firm only fifteen years ago, but . . ."

. . . It had been a very small legal firm when the box had been cautiously delivered; Redfearn, Bychance and both the Robeys, let alone Mr. Baddicombe, were a long way in the future. The struggling legal clerk who had accepted delivery had been surprised to find, tied to the top of the box with twine, a letter addressed to himself.

It had contained certain instructions and five interesting facts about the history of the next ten years which, if put to good use by a keen young man, would ensure enough finance to pursue a very successful legal career.

All he had to do was see that the box was carefully looked after for rather more than three hundred years, and then delivered to a certain address . . .

"... although of course the firm had changed hands many times over the centuries," said Mr. Baddicombe. "But the box has always been part of the chattels, as it were."

"I didn't even know they *made* Heinz Baby Foods in the seventeenth century," said Newt.

"That was just to keep it undamaged in the car," said Mr. Baddicombe.

"And no one's opened it all these years?" said Newt.

"Twice, I believe," said Mr. Baddicombe. "In 1757, by Mr. George Cranby, and in 1928 by Mr. Arthur Bychance, father of the present Mr. Bychance." He coughed. "Apparently Mr. Cranby found a letter—"

"—addressed to himself," said Newt.

Mr. Baddicombe sat back hurriedly. "My word. How did you guess that?"

"I think I recognize the style," said Newt grimly. "What happened to them?"

"Have you heard this before?" said Mr. Baddicombe suspiciously.

"Not in so many words. They weren't blown up, were they?"

"Well ... Mr. Cranby had a heart attack, it is believed. And Mr. Bychance went very pale and put his letter back in its envelope, I understand, and gave very strict instructions that the box wasn't to be opened again in his lifetime. He said anyone who opened the box would be sacked without references."

"A dire threat," said Newt, sarcastically.

"It was, in 1928. Anyway, their letters are in the box."

Newt pulled the cardboard aside.

There was a small ironbound chest inside. It had no lock.

"Go on, lift it out," said Mr. Baddicombe excitedly. "I must say I'd very much like to know what's in there. We've had bets on it, in the office . . ."

"I'll tell you what," said Newt, generously, "I'll make us some coffee, and *you* can open the box."

"Me? Would that be proper?"

"I don't see why not." Newt eyed the saucepans hanging over the stove. One of them was big enough for what he had in mind.

"Go on," he said. "Be a devil. I don't mind. You—you could have power of attorney, or something."

Mr. Baddicombe took off his overcoat. "Well," he said, rubbing his hands together, "since you put it like that . . . it'd be something to tell my grandchildren."

Newt picked up the saucepan and laid his hand gently on the door handle. "I hope so," he said.

"Here goes."

Newt heard a faint creak.

"What can you see?" he said.

"There's the two opened letters . . . oh, and a third one . . . addressed to . . ."

Newt heard the snap of a wax seal and the clink of something on the table. Then there was a gasp, the clatter of a chair, the sound of running feet in the hallway, the slam of a door, and the sound of a car engine being jerked into life and then redlined down the lane.

Newt took the saucepan off his head and came out from behind the door.

He picked up the letter and was not one hundred percent surprised to see that it was addressed to Mr. G. Baddicombe. He unfolded it.

It read: **"Here is A Florin, lawyer; nowe, runne faste, lest thee Worlde knoe the Truth about yowe and Mistrefs Spiddon the Type Writinge Machine slavey."**

Newt looked at the other letters. The crackling paper of the one addressed to George Cranby said: **"Remove thy thievinge Hande, Master Cranby. I minde well how yowe swindled the Widdowe Plashkin this Michelmas past, yowe skinnie owlde Snatch-pastry."**

Newt wondered what a snatch-pastry was. He would be prepared to bet that it didn't involve cookery.

The one that had awaited the inquisitive Mr. Bychance said: **"Yowe left them, yowe cowarde. Returne this letter to the bocks, lest the Worlde knoe the true Events of June 7th, Nineteen Hundred and Sixteene."**

Under the letters was a manuscript. Newt stared at it.

"What's that?" said Anathema.

He spun around. She was leaning against the doorframe, like an attractive yawn on legs.

Newt backed against the table. "Oh, nothing. Wrong address. Nothing. Just some old box. Junk mail. You know how—"

"On a Sunday?" she said, pushing him aside.

He shrugged as she put her hands around the yellowed manuscript and lifted it out.

"Further Nife and Accurate Prophecies of Agnes Nutter," she read slowly, **"Concerning the Worlde that Is To Com; Ye Saga Continuef!** Oh, my . . ."

She laid it reverentially on the table and prepared to turn the first page.

Newt's hand landed gently on hers.

"Think of it like this," he said quietly. "Do you want to be a descendant for the rest of your life?"

She looked up. Their eyes met.

IT WAS SUNDAY, the first day of the rest of the world, around eleven-thirty.

St. James' Park was comparatively quiet. The ducks, who were experts in *realpolitik* as seen from the bread end, put it down to a decrease in world tension. There really had been a decrease in world tension, in fact, but a lot of people were in offices trying to find out why, trying to find where Atlantis had disappeared to with three international fact-finding delegations on it, and trying to work out what had happened to all their computers yesterday.

The park was deserted except for a member of MI9 trying to recruit someone who, to their later mutual embarrassment, would turn out to be also a member of MI9, and a tall man feeding the ducks.

And there were also Crowley and Aziraphale.

They strolled side by side across the grass.

"Same here," said Aziraphale. "The shop's all there. Not so much as a soot mark."

"I mean, you can't just *make* an old Bentley," said Crowley. "You can't get the patina. But there it was, large as life. Right there in the street. You can't tell the difference."

"Well, *I* can tell the difference," said Aziraphale. "I'm sure I didn't stock books with titles like *Biggles Goes To Mars* and *Jack Cade, Frontier Hero* and *101 Things A Boy Can Do* and *Blood Dogs of the Skull Sea.*"

"Gosh, I'm sorry," said Crowley, who knew how much the angel had treasured his book collection.

"Don't be," said Aziraphale happily. "They're all mint first editions and I looked them up in *Skindle's Price Guide*. I think the phrase you use is *whoo-eee.*"

"I thought he was putting the world back just as it was," said Crowley.

"Yes," said Aziraphale. "More or less. As best he can. But he's got a sense of humor, too."

Crowley gave him a sideways look.

"Your people been in touch?" he said.

"No. Yours?"

"No."

"I think they're pretending it didn't happen."

"Mine too, I suppose. That's bureaucracy for you."

"And I think mine are waiting to see what happens next," said Aziraphale.

Crowley nodded. "A breathing space," he said. "A chance to morally re-arm. Get the defenses up. Ready for the big one."

They stood by the pond, watching the ducks scrabble for the bread.

"Sorry?" said Aziraphale. "I thought that *was* the big one."

"I'm not sure," said Crowley. "Think about it.

For my money, the really big one will be all of Us against all of Them."

"What? You mean Heaven and Hell against humanity?"

Crowley shrugged. "Of course, if he *did* change everything, then maybe he changed himself, too. Got rid of his powers, perhaps. Decided to stay human."

"Oh, I do hope so," said Aziraphale. "Anyway, I'm sure the alternative wouldn't be allowed. Er. Would it?"

"I don't know. You can never be certain about what's really intended. Plans within plans."

"Sorry?" said Aziraphale.

"Well," said Crowley, who'd been thinking about this until his head ached, "haven't you ever wondered about it all? You know—your people and my people, Heaven and Hell, good and evil, all that sort of thing? I mean, *why*?"

"As I recall," said the angel, stiffly, "there was the rebellion and—"

"Ah, yes. And why did it *happen*, eh? I mean, it didn't have to, did it?" said Crowley, a manic look in his eye. "Anyone who could build a universe in six days isn't going to let a little thing like that happen. Unless they want it to, of course."

"Oh, come on. Be sensible," said Aziraphale, doubtfully.

"That's not good advice," said Crowley. "That's not good advice at all. If you sit down and think about it *sensibly*, you come up with some very funny ideas. Like: why make people inquisitive, and then put some forbidden fruit where they can see it with a big neon finger flashing on and off saying THIS IS IT!?"

"I don't remember any neon."

"Metaphorically, I mean. I mean, why do that if you really don't *want* them to eat it, eh? I mean, maybe you just want to see how it all turns out. Maybe it's all part of a great big ineffable plan. All of it. You, me, him, everything. Some great big test to see if what you've built all works properly, eh? You start thinking: it *can't* be a great cosmic game of chess, it *has* to be just very complicated Solitaire. And don't bother to answer. If we could understand, we wouldn't be us. Because it's all—all—"

INEFFABLE, said the figure feeding the ducks.

"Yeah. Right. Thanks."

They watched the tall stranger carefully dispose of the empty bag in a litter bin, and stalk away across the grass. Then Crowley shook his head.

"What was I saying?" he said.

"Don't know," said Aziraphale. "Nothing very important, I think."

Crowley nodded gloomily. "Let me tempt you to some lunch," he hissed.

They went to the Ritz again, where a table was mysteriously vacant. And perhaps the recent exertions had had some fallout in the nature of reality because, while they were eating, for the first time ever, a nightingale sang in Berkeley Square.

No one heard it over the noise of the traffic, but it was there, right enough.

IT WAS ONE O'CLOCK ON SUNDAY.

For the last decade Sunday lunch in Witchfinder Sergeant Shadwell's world had followed an invariable routine. He would sit at the rickety, cigarette-burned table in his room, thumbing through an elderly copy of one of the Witchfinder Army library's* books on magic and Demonology—the *Necrotelecomnicon* or the *Liber Fulvarum Paginarum*, or his old favorite, the *Malleus Malleficarum*.**

Then there would be a knock on the door, and Madame Tracy would call out, "Lunch, Mr. Shadwell," and Shadwell would mutter, "Shameless hussy," and wait sixty seconds, to allow the shameless hussy time to get back into her room; then he'd open the door, and pick up the plate of liver, which was usually carefully covered by another plate to keep it warm. And he'd take it in, and he'd eat it, taking moderate care not to spill any gravy on the pages he was reading.***

That was what always happened.

Except on that Sunday, it didn't.

* Witchfinder Corporal Carpet, librarian, 11 pence per annum bonus.

** **"A relentlefs blockbufter of a boke: heartily recommended"—Pope Innocent VIII.**

*** To the right collector, the Witchfinder Army's library would have been worth millions. The right collector would have to have been very rich, and not have minded gravy stains, cigarette burns, marginal notations, or the late Witchfinder Lance Corporal Wotling's passion for drawing mustaches and spectacles on all woodcut illustrations of witches and demons.

For a start, he wasn't reading. He was just sitting.

And when the knock came on the door he got up immediately, and opened it. He needn't have hurried.

There was no plate. There was just Madame Tracy, wearing a cameo brooch, and an unfamiliar shade of lipstick. She was also standing in the center of a perfume zone.

"Aye, Jezebel?"

Madame Tracy's voice was bright and fast and brittle with uncertainty. "Hullo, Mister S, I was just thinking, after all we've been through in the last two days, seems silly for me to leave a plate out for you, so I've set a place for you. Come on . . ."

Mister S? Shadwell followed, warily.

He'd had another dream, last night. He didn't remember it properly, just one phrase, that still echoed in his head and disturbed him. The dream had vanished into a haze, like the events of the previous night.

It was this. *"Nothin' wrong with witchfinding. I'd like to be a witchfinder. It's just, well, you've got to take it in turns. Today we'll go out witchfinding, an' tomorrow we could hide, an' it'd be the witches' turn to find US . . ."*

For the second time in twenty-four hours—for the second time in his life—he entered Madame Tracy's rooms.

"Sit down there," she told him, pointing to an armchair. It had an antimacassar on the headrest, a plumped-up pillow on the seat, and a small footstool.

He sat down.

She placed a tray on his lap, and watched him eat,

and removed his plate when he had finished. Then she opened a bottle of Guinness, poured it into a glass and gave it to him, then sipped her tea while he slurped his stout. When she put her cup down, it tinkled nervously in the saucer.

"I've got a tidy bit put away," she said, apropos of nothing. "And you know, I sometimes think it would be a nice thing to get a little bungalow, in the country somewhere. Move out of London. I'd call it The Laurels, or Dunroamin, or, or . . ."

"Shangri-La," suggested Shadwell, and for the life of him could not think why.

"Exactly, Mister S. Exactly. Shangri-La." She smiled at him. "Are you comfy, love?"

Shadwell realized with dawning horror that he was comfortable. Horribly, terrifyingly comfortable. "Aye," he said, warily. He had never been so comfortable.

Madame Tracy opened another bottle of Guinness and placed it in front of him.

"Only trouble with having a little bungalow, called—what was your clever idea, Mister S?"

"Uh. Shangri-La."

"Shangri-La, exactly, is that it's not right for *one*, is it? I mean, two people, they say two can live as cheaply as one."

(Or five hundred and eighteen, thought Shadwell, remembering the massed ranks of the Witchfinder Army.)

She giggled. "I just wonder *where* I could find someone to settle down with . . ."

Shadwell realized that she was talking about him.

He wasn't sure about this. He had a distinct feeling that leaving Witchfinder Private Pulsifer with the young lady in Tadfield had been a bad move, as far as the Witchfinder Army ***Booke of Rules and Reggulations*** was concerned. And this seemed even more dangerous.

Still, at his age, when you're getting too old to go crawling about in the long grass, when the chill morning dew gets into your bones . . .

(An' tomorrow we could hide, an' it'd be the witches' turn to find us . . .)

Madame Tracy opened another bottle of Guinness, and giggled. "Oh Mister S," she said, "you'll be thinking I'm trying to get you tiddly."

He grunted. There was a formality that had to be observed in all this.

Witchfinder Sergeant Shadwell took a long, deep drink of Guinness, and he popped the question.

Madame Tracy giggled. "Honestly, you old silly," she said, and she blushed a deep red. "How many do you *think*?"

He popped it again.

"Two," said Madame Tracy.

"Ah, weel. That's all reet then," said Witchfinder Sergeant Shadwell (retired).

IT WAS SUNDAY AFTERNOON.

High over England a 747 droned westwards. In the first-class cabin a boy called Warlock put down his comic and stared out of the window.

It had been a very strange couple of days. He still wasn't certain why his father had been called to the Middle East. He was pretty sure that his father didn't know, either. It was probably something cultural. All that had happened was a lot of funny-looking guys with towels on their heads and very bad teeth had shown them around some old ruins. As ruins went, Warlock had seen better. And then one of the old guys had said to him, wasn't there anything he wanted to do? And Warlock had said he'd like to leave.

They'd looked very unhappy about that.

And now he was going back to the States. There had been some sort of problem with tickets or flights or airport destination-boards or something. It was weird; he was pretty sure his father had meant to go back to England. Warlock liked England. It was a nice country to be an American in.

The plane was at that point passing right above the Lower Tadfield bedroom of Greasy Johnson, who was aimlessly leafing through a photography magazine that he'd bought merely because it had a rather good picture of a tropical fish on the cover.

A few pages below Greasy's listless finger was a spread on American football, and how it was really catching on in Europe. Which was odd—because when the magazine had been printed, those pages had been about photography in desert conditions.

It was about to change his life.

And Warlock flew on to America. He deserved *something* (after all, you never forget the first friends you ever had, even if you were all a few hours old at the time) and the power that was controlling the fate of all mankind at that precise time was thinking: Well, he's going to *America*, isn't he? Don't see how you could have anythin' better than going to *America*.

They've got thirty-nine flavors of ice cream there. Maybe even more.

THERE WERE A MILLION exciting things a boy and his dog could be doing on a Sunday afternoon. Adam could think of four or five hundred of them without even trying. Thrilling things, stirring things, planets to be conquered, lions to be tamed, lost South American worlds teeming with dinosaurs to be discovered and befriended.

He sat in the garden, and scratched in the dirt with a pebble, looking despondent.

His father had found Adam asleep on his return from the air base—sleeping, to all intents and purposes, as if he had been in bed all evening. Even snoring once in a while, for verisimilitude.

At breakfast the next morning, however, it was made clear that this had not been enough. Mr. Young disliked gallivanting about of a Saturday evening on a wild goose chase. And if, by some unimaginable fluke, Adam was not responsible for the night's disturbances—whatever they had been, since nobody had seemed very clear on the details, only that there had been disturbances of some sort—then he was undoubtedly guilty of *something*. This was Mr. Young's attitude, and it had served him well for the last eleven years.

Adam sat dispiritedly in the garden. The August sun hung high in an August blue and cloudless sky, and behind the hedge a thrush sang, but it seemed to Adam that this was simply making it all much worse.

Dog sat at Adam's feet. He had tried to help, chiefly by exhuming a bone he had buried four days earlier and dragging it to Adam's feet, but all Adam had done was stare at it gloomily, and eventually Dog had taken it away and inhumed it once more. He had done all he could.

"Adam?"

Adam turned. Three faces stared over the garden fence.

"Hi," said Adam, disconsolately.

"There's a circus come to Norton," said Pepper. "Wensley was down there, and he saw them. They're just setting up."

"They've got tents, and elephants and jugglers and pratic'ly wild animals and stuff and—and everything!" said Wensleydale.

"We thought maybe we'd all go down there an' watch them setting up," said Brian.

For an instant Adam's mind swam with visions of circuses. Circuses were boring, once they were set up. You could see better stuff on television any day. But the *setting up* . . . Of course they'd all go down there, and they'd help them put up the tents, and wash the elephants, and the circus people would be so impressed with Adam's natural *rappore* with animals such that, that night, Adam (and Dog, the World's Most Famous Performing Mongrel) would lead the elephants into the circus ring and . . .

It was no good.

He shook his head sadly. "Can't go anywhere," he said. "*They* said so."

There was a pause.

"Adam," said Pepper, a trifle uneasily, "what *did* happen last night?"

Adam shrugged. "Just stuff. Doesn't matter," he said. " 'Salways the same. All you do is try to help, and people would think you'd *murdered* someone or something."

There was another pause, while the Them stared at their fallen leader.

"When d'you think they'll let you out, then?" asked Pepper.

"Not for years an' years. Years an' years an' *years*. I'll be an old man by the time they let me out," said Adam.

"How about tomorrow?" asked Wensleydale.

Adam brightened. "Oh, *tomorrow'll* be all right," he pronounced. "They'll have forgotten about it by then. You'll see. They always do." He looked up at them, a scruffy Napoleon with his laces trailing, exiled to a rose-trellissed Elba. "*You* all go," he told them, with a brief, hollow laugh. "Don't you worry about *me*. I'll be all right. I'll see you all tomorrow."

The Them hesitated. Loyalty was a great thing, but no lieutenants should be forced to choose between their leader and a circus with elephants. They left.

The sun continued to shine. The thrush continued to sing. Dog gave up on his master, and began to stalk a butterfly in the grass by the garden hedge. This was a serious, solid, impassible hedge, of thick and well-trimmed privet, and Adam knew it of old. Beyond it stretched open fields, and wonderful muddy ditches, and unripe fruit, and irate but slow-of-foot owners of fruit trees, and circuses, and streams to dam, and walls and trees just made for climbing . . .

But there was no way through the hedge.

Adam looked thoughtful.

"Dog," said Adam, sternly, "get away from that hedge, because if you went through it, then I'd have to chase you to catch you, and I'd have to go out of the garden, and I'm not allowed to do that. But I'd have to . . . if you went an' ran away."

Dog jumped up and down excitedly, and stayed where he was.

Adam looked around, carefully. Then, even more carefully, he looked Up, and Down. And then Inside.

Then . . .

And *now* there was a large hole in the hedge—large enough for a dog to run through, and for a boy to squeeze through after him. And it was a hole that had always been there.

Adam winked at Dog.

Dog ran through the hole in the hedge. And, shouting clearly, loudly and distinctly, "Dog, you bad dog! Stop! Come back here!" Adam squeezed through after him.

Something told him that something was coming to an end. Not the world, exactly. Just the summer. There would be other summers, but there would never be one like this. Ever again.

Better make the most of it, then.

He stopped halfway across the field. Someone

was burning something. He looked at the plume of white smoke above the chimney of Jasmine Cottage, and he paused. And he listened.

Adam could hear things that other people might miss.

He could hear laughter.

It wasn't a witch's cackle; it was the low and earthy guffaw of someone who knew a great deal more than could possibly be good for them.

The white smoke writhed and curled above the cottage chimney. For a fraction of an instant Adam saw, outlined in the smoke, a handsome, female face. A face that hadn't been seen on Earth for over three hundred years.

Agnes Nutter winked at him.

The light summer breeze dispersed the smoke; and the face and the laughter were gone.

Adam grinned, and began to run once more.

In a meadow a short distance away, across a stream, the boy caught up with the wet and muddy dog. "Bad Dog," said Adam, scratching Dog behind the ears. Dog yapped ecstatically.

Adam looked up. Above him hung an old apple tree, gnarled and heavy. It might have been there since the dawn of time. Its boughs were bent with the weight of apples, small and green and unripe.

With the speed of a striking cobra the boy was up the tree. He returned to the ground seconds later with his pockets bulging, munching noisily on a tart and perfect apple.

"Hey! You! Boy!" came a gruff voice from behind him. "You're that Adam Young! I can see you! I'll tell your father about you, you see if I don't!"

Parental retribution was now a certainty, thought Adam, as he bolted, his dog by his side, his pockets stuffed with stolen fruit.

It always was. But it wouldn't be till this evening.

And this evening was a long way off.

He threw the apple core back in the general direction of his pursuer, and he reached into a pocket for another.

He couldn't see why people made such a fuss about people eating their silly old fruit anyway, but life would be a lot less *fun* if they didn't. And there never was an apple, in Adam's opinion, that wasn't worth the trouble you got into for eating it.

IF YOU WANT TO IMAGINE the future, imagine a boy and his dog and his friends. And a summer that never ends.

And if you want to imagine the future, imagine a boot . . . no, imagine a sneaker, laces trailing, kicking a pebble; imagine a stick, to poke at interesting things, and throw for a dog that may or may not decide to retrieve it; imagine a tuneless whistle, pounding some luckless popular song into insensibility; imagine a figure, half angel, half devil, all human . . .

Slouching hopefully towards Tadfield. . . .

. . . forever.

GOOD OMENS, THE FACTS

(or, at least, lies that have been hallowed by time)

Once upon a time Neil Gaiman wrote half a short story. He didn't know how it ended. He sent it to Terry Pratchett, who didn't know, either. But it festered away in Terry's mind and he rang Neil about a year later and said: "I don't know how it ends, but I do know what happens next." The first draft took about two months, the second draft took about six months. Quite why, we don't know, but it did include explaining the jokes to the American publishers.

WHAT WAS IT LIKE WORKING WITH NEIL GAIMAN / TERRY PRATCHETT?

Ah. You have to remember, you see, that in those days Neil Gaiman was barely Neil Gaiman and Terry Pratchett was only just Terry Pratchett. They'd known one another for years, Neil having done an interview with Terry in 1985, after the first Discworld book came out. Look, it wasn't a big deal, okay? At no point in the whole thing did either of them say to the other, "Wow, I can't believe I'm working with you!"

HOW DID YOU WRITE IT?

Mostly by shouting excitedly at one another down the phone a couple of times a day for two months, and sending a disk off to the other guy several times a week. There were attempts toward the end of the writing process at machine-to-machine communication via 300/75 baud modems, but as a means of communication this turned out to be slightly less efficient than underwater yodeling.

Neil was mostly nocturnal back then, so he'd get up in the early afternoon and see the flashing red light on his ansaphone, which would mean there would be a message from Terry that would usually begin "Get up, get up, you bastard, I've just written a good bit!" And then the first phone call of the day would happen, when Terry would read Neil what he'd written that morning, and Neil would read Terry what he'd written much earlier that morning. Then they'd talk excitedly at each other, and it would be a race to get to the next good bit before the other guy.

IS THAT WHY THERE'S AN ANSAPHONE IN THE STORY?

Probably. It was a long time ago, you know.

WHO WROTE WHAT BIT?

Ah. Another tricky one. As the official Keeper of the One True Copy, Terry physically wrote more of Draft 1 than Neil. But if 2,000 words are written down after a lot of excited shouting, it's a moot point whose words they are. And, in any case, as a matter of honor both of them rewrote and footnoted the other guy's stuff, and both can write passably in the other one's style. The Agnes Nutter scenes and the kids mostly originated with Terry, the Four Horsemen and anything that involved maggots started with Neil. Neil had most influence on the opening, Terry on the ending. Apart from that, they just shouted excitedly a lot.

The point they both realized the text had wandered into its own world was in the basement of the old Gollancz books, where they'd got together to proofread the final copy, and Neil congratulated Terry on a line that Terry knew he hadn't written, and Neil was certain he hadn't written either. They both privately suspect that at some point the book had started to generate text on its own, but neither of them will actually admit this publicly for fear of being thought odd.

WHY DID YOU WRITE IT?

It seemed a shame not to. Besides, not writing it would mean that generations of readers would not have a book that could be dropped regularly in the bath.

WHY ISN'T THERE A SEQUEL?

We played around with ideas, but we could never work up the enthusiasm. Besides, we wanted to do other things (and some of those ideas probably ended up, bent to a different shape, in the works of both of us). Recently, though, we've both been wondering if "never again" is set in stone. So there might be a sequel one day. Maybe. Perhaps. Who knows? We don't.

DID YOU KNOW IT WOULD BE A "CULT CLASSIC" WHEN YOU WROTE IT?

If by "cult classic" you mean that all over the world there are people with their own copies of *Good Omens*, which they've read over and over and over, books they've dropped in baths and in puddles and in bowls of parsnip soup, books held together with duct tape and putty and string, books that are no longer lent out because no one in their right mind would actually borrow something like that without having it clinically sterilized first, then no, we didn't.

Whereas if by "cult classic" you mean a book that's sold millions and millions of copies around the world, many of them to the same people, because they buy them and then lend them out to their friends and never see them again so buy more copies, then no, we didn't.

Actually it doesn't really matter what definition of cult classic you use, we didn't think we were writing one. We were writing a book we thought was funny and we were trying to make each other laugh. We weren't even sure that anyone would actually want to publish it.

OH, COME ON, YOU'RE NEIL GAIMAN AND TERRY PRATCHETT.

Yes, but we weren't then (see *What was it like working with Neil Gaiman/Terry Pratchett?* above). We were these two blokes with an idea, who were telling each other a story.

WILL THERE BE A MOVIE, THEN?

Neil likes to think that one day maybe there will, and Terry is certain that it will never happen. In either case, neither of them will believe it until they're actually eating popcorn at the premiere. And even then, probably not.

NEIL GAIMAN ON TERRY PRATCHETT

Right.

So it's February of 1985, and it's a Chinese restaurant in London, and it's the author's first interview. His publicist had been pleasantly surprised that anyone would want to talk to him (the author has just written a funny fantasy book called *The Colour of Magic*), but she's set up this lunch with a young journalist anyway. The author, a former journalist, has a hat, but it's a small, black leathery cap, not a Proper Author Hat. Not yet. The journalist has a hat too. It's a grayish thing, sort of like the ones Humphrey Bogart wears in movies, only when the journalist wears it he doesn't look like Humphrey Bogart: he looks like someone wearing a grown-up's hat. The journalist is slowly discovering that, no matter how hard he tries, he cannot become a hat person: it's not just that it itches, or blows off at inconvenient moments, it's that he forgets, and leaves it in restaurants, and is now getting very used to knocking on the doors of restaurants about 11:00 A.M. and asking if they found a hat. One day, very soon now, the journalist will stop bothering with hats, and decide to buy a black leather jacket instead.

So they have lunch, and the interview gets printed in *Space Voyager* magazine, along with a photo of the author browsing the shelves in Forbidden Planet, and most important, they make each other laugh, and like the way the other one thinks.

And the author is Terry Pratchett, and the journalist is me, and it's been two decades since I left a hat in a restaurant, and one and a half decades since Terry discovered his inner Bestselling-Author-with-a-Proper-Author-Hat.

We don't see each other much these days, what with living on different continents, and, when we're on each other's continent, spending all our time signing books for other people. The last time we ate together was at a sushi counter in Minneapolis, after a signing. It was an all-you-can-eat night, where they put your sushi on little boats and floated it over to you. After a while, obviously feeling we were taking unfair advantage of the whole all-you-can-eat thing, the sushi chef gave up on the putting sushi on little boats, produced something that looked like the Leaning Tower of Yellowtail, handed it to us, and announced that he was going home.

Nothing much had changed, except everything.

These are the things I realized back in 1985:

Terry knew a lot. He had the kind of head that people get when they're interested in things, and go and ask questions and listen and read. He knew genre, enough to know the territory, and he knew enough outside genre to be interesting.

He was ferociously intelligent.

He was having fun. Then again, Terry is that rarity, the kind of author who likes Writing, not Having Written, or Being a Writer, but the actual sitting there and making things up in front of a screen. At the time we met, he was still working as a press officer for the South Western Electricity board. He wrote four hundred words a night, every night: it was the only way for him to keep a real job and still write books. One night, a year later, he finished a novel, with a hundred words still to go, so he put a piece of paper into his typewriter, and wrote a hundred words of the next novel.

(The day he retired to become a full-time writer, he phoned me up. "It's only been half an hour since I retired, and already I hate those bastards," he said cheerfully.)

There was something else that was obvious in 1985: Terry was a science fiction writer. It was the way his mind worked: the urge to take it all apart, and put it back together in different ways, to see how it all fit together. It was the engine that drove Discworld—it's not a "what if . . ." or an "if only . . ." or even an "if this goes on . . ."; it was the far more subtle and dangerous "If there was *really* a . . . , what would that mean? How would it work?"

In the Nicholls-Clute *Encyclopedia of Science Fiction*, there was an ancient woodcut of a man pushing his head through the back of the world, past the sky, and seeing the cogs and the wheels and the engines that drove the universe machine. That's what people do in Terry Pratchett books, even if the people doing it are sometimes rats and sometimes small girls. People learn things. They open their heads.

So we discovered we shared a similar sense of humor, and a similar set of cultural referents; we'd read the same obscure books, took pleasure in pointing each other to weird Victorian reference books.

A few years after we met, in 1988, Terry and I wrote a book together. It began as a parody of Richmal Crompton's *William* books, which we called *William the Antichrist*, but rapidly outgrew that conceit and became about a number of other things instead, and we called it *Good Omens*. It was a funny novel about the end of the world and how we're all going to die. Working with Terry, I felt like a journeyman alongside a master craftsman in some medieval guild. He constructs novels like a guildmaster might build a cathedral arch. There is art, of course, but that's the result of building it well. What there is more of is the pleasure taken in constructing something that does what it's meant to do—to make people read the story, and laugh, and possibly even think.

(This is how we wrote a novel together. I'd write late at night. Terry wrote early in the morning. In the afternoon we'd have very long phone conversations where we'd read each other the best bits we'd written, and talk about stuff that could happen next. The main objective was to make the other one laugh. We posted floppy disks back and forth, because this was before e-mail. There was one night when we tried using a modem to send some text across the country, at 300/75 speeds, directly from computer to computer because if e-mail had been invented back then nobody had told us about it. We managed it too. But the post was faster.)

Terry has been writing professionally for a very long time, honing his craft, getting quietly better and better. The biggest problem he faces is the problem of excellence: he makes it look easy. This can be a problem. The public doesn't know where the craft lies. It's wiser to make it look harder than it is, a lesson all jugglers learn.

In the early days the reviewers compared him to the late Douglas Adams, but then Terry went on to write books as enthusiastically as Douglas avoided writing them, and now, if there is any comparison to be made of anything from the formal rules of a Pratchett novel to the sheer prolific fecundity of the man, it might be to P. G. Wodehouse. But mostly newspapers, magazines, and critics do not compare him to anyone. He exists in a blind spot, with two strikes against him: he writes funny books, in a world in which funny is synonymous with trivial, and they are fantasies—or more precisely, they are set on the Discworld, a flat world, which rests on the back of four elephants, who in turn stand on the back of a turtle, heading off through space. It's a location in which Terry Pratchett can write anything, from hard-bitten crime dramas to vampiric political parodies, to children's books. And those children's books have changed things. Terry won the prestigious Carnegie Medal for his pied piper tale *The Amazing Maurice and His Educated Rodents*, awarded by the librarians of the U.K., and the Carnegie is an award that even newspapers have to respect. (Even so, the newspapers had their revenge, cheerfully misunderstanding Terry's acceptance speech and accusing him of bashing J. K. Rowling and J. R. R. Tolkien and fantasy, in a speech about the real magic of fantastic fiction.)

The most recent books have shown Terry in a new mode—books like *Night Watch* and *Monstrous Regiment* are darker, deeper, more outraged at what people can do to people, while prouder of what people can do for each other. And yes, the books are still funny, but they no longer follow the jokes: now the books follow the story and the people. *Satire* is a word that is often used to mean that there aren't any people in the fiction, and for that reason I'm uncomfortable calling Terry a satirist. What he is, is A Writer, and there are few enough of those around. There are lots of people who call themselves writers, mind you. But it's not the same thing at all.

In person, Terry is genial, driven, funny. Practical. He likes writing, and he likes writing fiction. That he became a bestselling author is a good thing: it allows him to write as much as he wishes. He wasn't joking about the Banana Daiquiris, although the last time I saw him we drank ice wine together in his hotel room, while we set the world to rights.

TERRY PRATCHETT ON NEIL GAIMAN

What can I say about Neil Gaiman that has not already been said in *The Morbid Imagination: Five Case Studies*?

Well, he's no genius. He's better than that.

He's not a wizard, in other words, but a conjurer.

Wizards don't have to work. They wave their hands, and the magic happens. But conjurers, now . . . conjurers work very hard. They spend a lot of time in their youth watching, very carefully, the best conjurers of their day. They seek out old books of trickery and, being natural conjurers, read everything else as well, because history itself is just a magic show. They observe the way people think, and the many ways in which they don't. They learn the subtle use of springs, and how to open mighty temple doors at a touch, and how to make the trumpets sound.

And they take center stage and amaze you with flags of all nations and smoke and mirrors, and you cry: "Amazing! How does he do it? What happened to the elephant? Where's the rabbit? Did he really smash my watch?"

And in the back row we, the other conjurers, say quietly: "Well *done*. Isn't that a variant of the Prague Levitating Sock? Wasn't that Pasqual's Spirit Mirror, where the girl isn't really there? But where the *hell* did that flaming sword come from?"

And we wonder if there may be such a thing as wizardry, after all. . . .

I met Neil in 1985, when *The Colour of Magic* had just come out. It was my first ever interview as an author. Neil was making a living as a freelance journalist and had the pale features of someone who had sat through the review showings of altogether too many bad movies in order to live off the freebie cold chicken legs they served at the receptions afterwards (and to build up his contacts book, which is now the size of the Bible and contains rather more interesting people). He was doing journalism in order to eat, which is a very good way of learning journalism. Probably the only real way, come to think of it.

He also had a very bad hat. It was a gray homburg. He was not a hat person. There was no natural unity between hat and man. That was the first and last time I saw the hat. As if subconsciously aware of the bad hatitude, he used to forget it and leave it behind in restaurants. One day, he never went back for it. I put this in for the serious fans out there: If you search really, really hard, you may find a small restaurant somewhere in London with a dusty gray homburg at the back of a shelf. Who knows what will happen if you try it on?

Anyway, we got on fine. Hard to say why, but at bottom was a shared delight and amazement at the sheer strangeness of the universe, in stories, in obscure details, in strange old books in unregarded bookshops. We stayed in contact.

[SFX: pages being ripped off a calendar. You know, you just don't get that in movies any more. . . .]

And one thing led to another, and he became big in graphic novels, and Discworld took off, and one day he sent me about six pages of a short story and said he didn't know how it continued, and I didn't either, and about a year later I took it out of the drawer and *did* see what happened next, even if I couldn't see how it all ended yet, and we wrote it together and that was *Good Omens*. It was done by two guys who didn't have anything to lose by having fun. We didn't do it for the money. But, as it turned out, we got a lot of money.

. . . Hey, let me tell you about the weirdness, like when he was staying with us for the editing and we heard a noise and went into his room and two of our white doves had got in and couldn't get out; they were panicking around the room and Neil was waking up in a storm of snowy white feathers saying "Wstfgl?," which is his normal ante-meridian vocabulary. Or the time when we were in a bar and he met the Spider Women. Or the time on tour when we checked into our hotel and in the morning it turned out that *his* TV had been showing him strange late-night seminaked bondage bisexual chat shows, and mine had picked up nothing but reruns of "Mr. Ed." And the moment, live on air, when we realized that an underinformed New York radio interviewer with ten minutes of chat still to go *thought* Good Omens *was not a work of fiction. . . .*

[cut to a train, pounding along the tracks. That's another scene they never show in movies these days. . . .]

And there we were, ten years on, traveling across Sweden and talking about the plot of *American Gods* (him) and *The Amazing Maurice* (me). Probably both of us at the same time. It was just like the old days. One of us says, "I don't know how to deal with this tricky bit of plot"; the other one listens and says, "The solution, Grasshopper, is in the way you state the problem. Fancy a coffee?"

A lot had happened in those ten years. He'd left the comics world shaken, and it'll never be quite the same. The effect was akin to that of Tolkien on the fantasy novel—everything afterwards is in some way influenced. I remember on one U.S. *Good Omens* tour walking round a comics shop. We'd been signing for a lot of comics fans, some of whom were clearly puzzled at the concept of "dis story wid no pitchers in it," and I wandered around the shelves looking at the opposition. That's when I realized he was *good.* There's a delicacy of touch, a subtle scalpel, which is the hallmark of his work.

And when I heard the premise of *American Gods* I wanted to write it so much I could taste it. . . .

When I read *Coraline*, I saw it as an exquisitely drawn animation; if I close my eyes I can see how the house looks, or the special dolls' picnic. No wonder he writes scripts now. When I read the book I remembered that children's stories are, indeed, where true horror lives. My childhood nightmares would have been quite featureless without the imaginings of Walt Disney, and there's a few little details concerning black button eyes in that book that make a small part of the adult brain want to go and hide behind the sofa. But the purpose of the book is not the horror, it is horror's defeat.

It might come as a surprise to many to learn that Neil is either a very nice, approachable guy or an incredible actor. He sometimes takes those shades off. The leather jacket I'm not sure about; I think I once saw him in a tux, or it may have been someone else.

He takes the view that mornings happen to other people. I think I once saw him at breakfast, although possibly it was just someone who looked a bit like him who was lying with his head in the plate of baked beans. He likes good sushi and quite likes people, too, although not raw; he is kind to fans who are not total jerks, and enjoys talking to people who know how to talk. He doesn't look as though he's in his forties; that may have happened to someone else, too. Or perhaps there's a special picture locked in his attic.

Have fun. We did. We never thought about the money until it went for auction and the big numbers started to get phoned in. Guess which one of us was amazingly cool about that. Hint: It wasn't me.

P.S.: He really, really likes it if you ask him to sign your battered, treasured copy of *Good Omens* that has been dropped in the tub at least once and is now held together with very old, yellowing transparent tape. You know the one.

ALSO BY NEIL GAIMAN

THE OCEAN AT THE END OF THE LANE
"A novel about truths—some wonderful, some terrible—that children know and adults do not."
—*Time Magazine*

STARDUST
"A twisting, wondrous tale full of magic."
—*Chicago Tribune*

CORALINE
"Inventive, scary, thrilling, and finally affirmative. Readers young and old will find something to startle them."
—*Washington Post Book World*

THE GRAVEYARD BOOK
"Like a bite of dark Halloween chocolate, this novel proves rich, bittersweet, and very satisfying."
—*Washington Post Book World*

AMERICAN GODS
"*American Gods* manages to reinvent . . . the enduring importance of fantastic literature . . . . Dark fun, and nourishing to the soul."
—Michael Chabon

ANANSI BOYS
"Delightful, funny, and affecting . . . . The literary equivalent of a hole-in-one."
—*Washington Post Book World*

NEVERWHERE
"Thrilling. . . . The chimerical stuff of nightmare and daydream."
—*USA Today*

GOOD OMENS (WITH TERRY PRATCHETT)
The classic collaboration from the internationally bestselling authors Neil Gaiman and Terry Pratchett

---

THE VIEW FROM THE CHEAP SEATS — SELECTED NONFICTION
"[Gaiman's] nonfiction is as compelling as his fiction, comics and screenplays."
—*Los Angeles Times*

TRIGGER WARNING — SHORT FICTIONS AND DISTURBANCES
"Everything that endears Gaiman to his legions of fans is on display."
—*Kirkus Reviews*

FRAGILE THINGS — SHORT FICTIONS AND WONDERS
"A prodigiously imaginative collection."
—*New York Times Book Review*

SMOKE AND MIRRORS — SHORT FICTIONS AND ILLUSIONS
"Readers will find echoes of H. P. Lovecraft, Harlan Ellison, Ray Bradbury, and Stephen King, but the voice is all Gaiman."
—*Dallas Morning News*

ART MATTERS — NEW IN HARDCOVER
A stunning and timely creative call-to-arms with the deft, striking illustrations of Chris Riddell

MAKE GOOD ART
A beautifully designed book containing the text of the graduation speech Gaiman delivered to The University of the Arts.